PRAISE FOR *THE WRITING ON THE WALL*

"As starkly elegant as the Chinese calligraphy Renata practices—and superior to the 9/11 fictions of both Ian McEwan and Jonathan Safran Foer in its melding of psychological and geopolitical dream worlds."   —John Leonard for *New York Magazine*

"A passionate, sensitive love letter to the wounded city of New York."   *—Chicago Sun Times*

"Schwartz is a connoisseur of anguish, especially survivor's guilt, yet she is also an adept choreographer of romance. Incisive, unafraid to flirt with melodrama in pursuit of a compelling story, acutely descriptive yet to the point."   *—Booklist*

"In this poignant and powerful novel, Lynne Sharon Schwartz imagines a complex private life brought into focus through a public tragedy."   *—Boston Globe*

"*The Writing on the Wall* dares to set an intimate story of many kinds of love—both uncomfortable and comforting—in the emotionally unsettled days just after September 11th. New York City in all its variety is a character in Lynne Sharon Schwartz's novel, and so is *language*, which, it turns out, is more capable of expressing our subtlest thoughts and feelings than we might have guessed. This is an absorbing story whose momentum draws us through surprising twists and turns—and reminds us of the fierce resolve it took to hang on when human connection seemed most fragile and most urgent."

—Rosellen Brown, author of *Before and After* and *Half a Heart*

"A powerful and sensitive novel about a real, catastrophic event. Lynne Sharon Schwartz goes beyond the headlines to the heart of the matter—how we cope with loss and go on."

—Hilma Wolitzer

"*The Writing on the Wall* is an authentic masterpiece. Reading it was a unique and overwhelming experience." —Hayden Carruth

"Lynne Sharon Schwartz's *The Writing on the Wall* is the first fiction to weave the shock of 9/11 into ordinary, credible lives. Her words are worth a thousand pictures."

—Dan Wakefield, author of *New York in the Fifties*

"An intellectually evocative and emotionally trenchant exploration of troubled intimacy and the constitutive effects of language. . . . Schwartz continues to show herself a rigorous novelist." —*Publishers Weekly*

"Schwartz well uses her powerful gift for description . . . a compelling New York story." —*Library Journal*

"Schwartz describes the emotional flavor of the days after 9/11 with great clarity." —*Kirkus*

THE WRITING ON THE WALL

Also by Lynne Sharon Schwartz

Fiction
Referred Pain
In the Family Way
The Fatigue Artist
Leaving Brooklyn
Disturbances in the Field
The Melting Pot and Other Subversive Stories
Acquainted with the Night
Balancing Acts
Rough Strife

Non-Fiction
Ruined by Reading
Face to Face
We Are Talking About Homes
A Lynne Sharon Schwartz Reader

Poems
In Solitary

Children's Books
The Four Questions

Translations
Smoke over Birkenau, by Liana Millù
A Place to Live: Selected Essays of Natalia Ginzburg
Aldabra, by Silvana Gandolfi

The Writing on the Wall

A NOVEL

LYNNE SHARON SCHWARTZ

COUNTERPOINT
A MEMBER OF THE PERSEUS BOOKS GROUP
NEW YORK

Hardcover edition first published in 2005 by Counterpoint
A Member of the Perseus Books Group
Paperback edition first published in 2006 by Counterpoint

Counterpoint books are available at special discounts for bulk
purchases in the United States by corporations, institutions, and
other organizations. For more information, please contact the
Special Markets Department at the Perseus Books Group, 11
Cambridge Center, Cambridge MA 02142, or call (617) 252-5298
or (800) 255-1514, or e-mail special.markets@perseusbooks.com.

Designed by Trish Wilkinson

The Library of Congress has catalogued this title as follows:
Schwartz, Lynne Sharon.
    The writing on the wall : a novel / Lynne Sharon Schwartz.
        p.   cm.
    ISBN-13: 978-1-58243-299-1
    ISBN-10: 1-58243-299-6 (alk. paper)
    I. Title.
PS3569.C567W75 2005
813'.54—dc22   2004024877

Paperback: ISBN-13: 978-1-58243-300-4; ISBN-13: 1-58243-300-3

06 07 08 / 10 9 8 7 6 5 4 3 2 1

The public reports about the shock and grief suffered after the attacks on September 11, 2001, implied that those feelings were uniform and generic in everyone. And probably extremes of shock and grief, like extremes of hunger and desire, do feel the same in everyone. Yet the people who endured the transforming effects of that day were not blank slates ready to be imprinted with the same images. They brought to that moment all the events of their lives until then, and the new events, by their very force, called forth earlier shocks and reconfigured them in a new context. So the collapse of the buildings made a different sound for everyone who heard it, and for each the noise echoed in a different key.

CELIA STRENG

The fire fed on wrecked office furniture, computers, carpets, and aircraft cargo, but primarily it fed on ordinary paper—an ample supply of the white sheets that were so much a part of the larger battlefield scene. Without that paper, the experts believed, the fire might not have achieved the intensity necessary to weaken the steel beyond its critical threshold. It would be simplifying things, but not by much, to conclude that it was paperwork that brought the South Tower down.

WILLIAM LANGEWIESCHE
American Ground, 2002

Prologue

On bright mornings, the sun sliding along her bedroom window stamps the wood floor with a dappled pattern that resembles large scattered petals. Or a magnified fragment of Chinese calligraphy. If she had the extraordinary powers of Ts'ang Chieh, an ancient Chinese sage credited with inventing written characters, she might be able to read something in the sun's design. Legend tells us that Ts'ang Chieh modeled his characters after patterns in nature: the constellations of the night sky, the designs on tortoise shells, animal tracks, tree branches silhouetted against the sky. But though Renata is a pretty good linguist herself, her talents don't go that far. Anyway, this morning the pattern hadn't appeared yet—it was too early.

She lay on her stomach and Jack held on to her as he always did, a leg and arm flung over her, his head buried near her shoulder. She liked being weighed down. He was gripping tight, fast asleep, then his body suddenly stiffened and shook in spasms. Christ, she thought, he's going to come in his sleep like a teenaged boy. And all over her. The nerve, a grown man, and dragging her along out of habit. If it really was her he was pumping in his sleep, who knows?

She was mistaken. This was no kind of pleasure. Jack's leg stiffened again, as if he were pressing down on the brake of a car, and he gave a few low moans, no, more like whimpers of fright. Near her head on the pillow, the fingers of his right hand made jerking movements, like plucking staccato notes on the strings of a bass fiddle. He gripped her tighter. She thought of waking him from his nightmare to save him from whatever was threatening, a collision maybe, but decided not to. People have a right to their dreams, even the bad ones. Maybe the dream was important, maybe it was delivering a shred of crucial information. Then again, Jack never analyzed his dreams. Once in a great while he would report one. So what do you think it means? he'd say. What do *you* think, she'd answer, as the therapists do. He didn't mind that, just shrugged. Renata, on the contrary, liked tinkering with puzzles; she saw all sorts of dire meanings in his dreams but never suggested them. People have a right to their ignorance, too.

She left him to his fate. When she next opened her eyes he was watching her. There were mornings when she woke feeling amorphous, shapeless, selfless, and he could tell, though he couldn't tell why; then he would rub and stroke her body all over, like a mother bear licking her cub into shape. And as he stroked she would take on the familiar shape of the day before. This wasn't one of those mornings. Today it was Jack, usually so serene and balanced, who seemed lost, stranded on the trail between dream and waking.

"Is it over?" she asked. "You had a bad dream. You were shaking."

"Was that it? I woke up with a terrible feeling. That must be why."

"What was it? Is the stuff on my walls freaking you out?"

"I don't know. I can't remember."

The floor showed its pattern of dappled light. It would be a very bright day. All the days had been bright lately, a blessing from the gods of weather. She took his hand and brought it to her stomach and pressed it down. "I thought you were fucking someone in your sleep. Me, maybe. So?"

He looked over at the clock. "I can't. I wish I could, but I have a meeting at nine-thirty and I've got to stop at my place first." They were sleeping at Renata's apartment because Jack had found an excellent parking space nearby, no small consideration in Brooklyn Heights. Most nights they spend together, they're at Jack's place a few blocks away. He doesn't care for hers, too weird, he says. Meaning the stuff on the walls. Her clippings, her lists. He doesn't like obsessions, though he likes her.

"Suit yourself." And she moved his hand away.

"That's what I need at my place, a suit, actually."

She groaned, as she was supposed to do. He makes such quips on purpose, to hear her groan. They indulge each other, Renata and Jack. They have their little games, their routines. Like Reality Tourism, Jack's game. For the traveler who's been everywhere: consider two invigorating weeks in Attica. Too much time sitting at a desk? Try a week's stint at a sweatshop. Or Renata's game, Redundancy, also known as Twin Titles. Kingshighway Boulevard. Perennial Classics. The real-estate ads are a good source. Summit Heights. Chateau Estates. She keeps a list. They have to be real, with data on where they were first sighted. The first time they slept together, Jack suggested Maison de la Casa, which he claimed was a new continental restaurant in Chelsea, but she wasn't fooled.

"Tonight, then?" he said. "Will it keep?"

"Whatever." Again on purpose. Jack dislikes that word. She doesn't like it much herself.

His cell phone, near at hand on the night table, bleeped, and he cursed as he waited for the message: "Jack, I just wanted to let you know I'll be late, sorry I forgot to tell you yesterday. I have to get Julio to day care myself because my mother and sister are in Puerto Rico for a few days. Anyway, in case you get in first I wanted you—"

"Carmen? I'm here. No, that's okay. I'm glad you called. Look, since you'll be right around there could you stop off at the Port Authority, I'm not sure which floor, the nineties I think, you can check in the lobby, and pick up those homelessness statistics? They promised to fax them but God knows when. . . . Thanks. . . . No, take your time."

"Carmen," he explained when he hung up. His stellar assistant.

"I figured that out," said Renata.

He dressed and bent to kiss her good-bye. "Don't forget to vote," he murmured, his hand lingering on her breast. "Primary Day, remember?" She called him an anarchist, but he was such a good citizen.

He was gone. A man not given to quick fucks. Everything he does is done with care and attention. A fine quality, but it has its drawbacks.

Not worth fretting about, though. The restless warmth inside would ebb away soon enough. Not worth sinking into the doldrums. The expression made her smile. Her friend and library colleague, Linda, a storehouse of arcane facts, told her about the doldrums last week at lunch.

"That old guy with the long yellow beard and the one earring, you know who I mean, who keeps hanging out at the Answer Lady desk? He told me he was in the doldrums, so I said he might like to know that the Doldrums are an actual place around 800 miles south of Hawaii. It's an area that's always covered with big dark clouds and almost no wind to drive them away. He liked that. I keep my customers happy. I see you like it too."

No doldrums today. Not a cloud in the sky. She was having lunch with Linda again—who knows what she might learn? She'd vote on the way home, not because she was a good citizen but because Jack would check up. Voting to please a lover—surely not what the Founding Fathers intended.

Before she left, she looked, as always, at the panels of Chinese calligraphy on the walls. The illustrations were small; the calligraphy dominated. The one she liked best had no illustration at all. It was from a letter written almost a thousand years ago by a local magistrate, advising a new colleague about how to govern. "A good magistrate must follow the people's wishes and help to spread a civilizing influence. He must clear his eyes and listen intently, so that he and his subjects may together be molded by the spirit and transformed."

She had studied the calligraphy hangings so long and so steadily that often she fell into dreamy wishful thinking and invented translations that resembled news bulletins. For the letter to the magistrate, she would imagine, "The child was found unharmed in the early evening, playing in a sandbox not far from the merry-go-round where she disappeared." Other times it read, "The perpetrators were apprehended in Chicago's O'Hare Airport and charged with kidnapping. The child was returned safely to her aunt in New York City." An alternate version of reality, the "what if" theory of history applied on the small scale.

That morning, the bad dream morning, Primary Day, the blessed weather morning, was when the sky burst into flame and paper rained down. No one voted.

But first—for isn't it natural to want to delay a disaster, to pretend for a while that it never happened?—what is a reclusive librarian sworn to solitude, or at least to emotional celibacy, doing in bed with someone she loves? Or is pretty sure she loves.

One

It started with a pick-up. She'd had pick-ups before, a good number, but nothing that ever lasted more than a few nights, or weeks. The men wanted to know too much, they wanted to exchange life stories, and they lost patience with her. This one would be different. He would become part of her life story, step right into it, even though he didn't know the early chapters. That took nerve. And he was patient. He could wait for the story. He would wait a long time.

A museum, a likely place for a pick-up, though neither of them had come for that. People do, it's well known, but Renata wanted to see what had so incensed the mayor that he threatened to cut off the museum's funds—an incident that became part of the urban folklore. The show, featuring young British artists with attitude, was called Sensation, and the offending painting, a Madonna, had dollops of elephant dung plastered here and there, elephant dung, in African tradition, being a semi-sacred object with spiritual over-tones. The mayor was unaware of the symbolic significance of the dung. In fact if he hadn't been informed to begin with that the black dollops were dung, the whole brouhaha might never have taken place. So much for the information age, for every ingredient in drugs and food and paintings being labeled.

But that painting wasn't what she was looking at when Jack turned up. After a quarter of an hour she was hardly looking at the exhibits at all; she was mesmerized instead by the writing on the wall, those informative little cards that make going to a museum like heavy-duty research—so much reading and cross checking is involved. She was copying what was on the cards into a notebook and would later transfer it to one of her folders—Absurdities, Banalities, or Meaningless Words, she'd decide later. The card before her accompanied an exhibit of a shark in formaldehyde. "Perhaps the shark is a cruel reminder of how even the most ferocious spirits—animal or human—are eventually brought low," it said. "Whether we feel weak or strong, we are all headed for the same end."

The words brought to mind an obscure language spoken in a small area of Lapland which she had learned last year for her work in the library. Bliondan was a language rich in near-synonyms, with an abundance of terms in the category of *prashmensti,* or "wrong words." The closest translation in English would be "lying," but *prashmensti* connoted a great deal more. The varieties of wrong words in Bliondan ranged from what we would call "white lies," told for convenience or to avoid hurt feelings, to words used imprecisely or insincerely in order to obfuscate (*prashmenosi*), to distract (*prashimina*), to mislead and thus avoid dangerous truths (*prashmial*), or used out of sheer stupidity, or to fill space when words were required—all derivatives of the root word, *mentasi,* speech. The words on the museum wall would probably be called *prashmenil-ala,* a combination of stupidity (*prashmenilis*) and the need to fill space (*prashmenala*).

"It's interesting," a woman beside her said to her companion, regarding the shark, "but I wouldn't want to have it in my living room."

Renata felt him come up behind her. He radiated sex. She didn't have to turn around to know that he'd speak, that he wanted something of her, for he stood there longer than it took to read the words. But she did turn. A casual look, no come-on, mere curiosity. He was large and burly, blunt features like carved rock, marvelous thick straight salt-and-pepper hair, dressed in jeans and a shaggy gray sweater, the kind of man who doesn't bother shaving on weekends. He met her eyes briefly. "'Whether we feel weak or strong,'" he read aloud, "'we are all headed for the same end.'" So they burst out laughing.

She ambled on and he followed, to a series of small photographs of the artist's family, to all appearances a sorry lot. "'How are we to judge the way they live?'" Jack read. Renata giggled, though usually she was not much of a giggler. "'We see emotional turmoil: In one photo, his alcoholic father is passed out by the toilet. In another, his mother shakes her fist in anger. The apartment is filled with clutter and filth.' Disgusting isn't it?"

"The filth, yes. I don't mind a bit of clutter."

"It's a matter of degree, I guess. 'But there are also moments of . . . joy. Do you think the artist is celebrating the people he loves, or is he asking us to pity or condemn them?' What do you think?"

"You're not supposed to think. That's the point. The answer is right here on the wall. 'The answer,'" she read, "'lies in our own sense of what constitutes a good life and family.'"

The next exhibit was a plaster cast of a child's bedroom turned inside out like a photographic negative: the spaces around the objects were made solid and the missing objects were represented by empty space. "The resemblance to a tomb is inescapable," the card read. "Could the artist be creating a monument to her childhood, perhaps mourning its loss? It's as though she has sealed off her memories. And we are locked out, left only with traces from which we might try to guess what once took place inside."

He glanced at Renata as if they'd known each other for some time. "Could she be doing that?" he asked. "What's your opinion?"

"My opinion is I've seen enough."

They were near the end of the show. He pointed to a final statement emblazoned on the wall. "'Do we let these artists offend us? Or do we just laugh and walk away?' Let's just laugh and walk away. And have coffee."

All right, but she had to copy some more cards first.

"Take your time. I wanted another look at the self-portrait in frozen blood anyway. Are you an art critic?"

"No, a librarian. It's for my . . . files."

"Whatever turns you on. I'll be in the vicinity. Find me when you're done?"

She nodded, then returned to the first item that had caught her eye, a painting of the notorious Myra Hindley, known as "the most hated woman in Britain," who, together with her lover, strangled at least five children and buried their bodies on the moors near Manchester. "The hundreds of children's handprints that define Hindley's face remind us of her victims, yet they almost seem to be stroking her face," she copied carefully and with repugnance into her notebook. "At the same time, the large scale of the piece implies a heroic status. But when we know Myra Hindley's history, the work suggests, and in a very powerful way, that the most banal face—the face of a friend or neighbor—can hide terrifying evil."

Twenty minutes later she found him in front of an exhibit illustrating the life cycle of maggots; the eggs, then the flies, were displayed on rotting cows' heads made of latex.

They got their coats and braved the January cold. The wind was bitter and they longed to cling together for warmth, but both were too discreet and too old for such impulsiveness, or maybe too young. Jack was thirty-nine but might be taken for older—a bit worn, a bit frayed, yet staunch and durable. Renata was five years younger but prematurely wary. Over coffee they discovered that they lived only a few blocks apart, in Brooklyn Heights. Kismet, he declared. But being careful people, they said good-bye at the subway exit and didn't go to bed until the following day.

At home, she curled up on the living-room couch with her Transformed Lives or Everyone Wants to Be Changed folder, her collection of metamorphoses—lives that took an unexpected turn. When she first began clipping those tales from the newspapers she wasn't sure why she wanted them. After a while she understood she was saving them as an act of faith, hoping the growing stack would prove that lives could indeed be transformed. By now she'd read them so often that their subjects had become her mind's companions. She liked to imagine herself leading their lives, owning their pluck and ingenuity. She wanted to change as they had changed. Like them, she wished to begin anew.

The one she chose for tonight was brown with age and shed tiny flakes when she unfolded it: "Shimmying Her Way Into a New Career." The photo showed a slim middle-aged woman with fuzzy auburn hair, dressed in a belly-dancing costume: beaded dark bra and long, flowing lavender skirt set low on her hips, rimmed by a broad cummerbund. Her finely muscled body arched sideways while her head remained erect. With her outstretched arms, the pose became a beckoning invitation. She was an inspiration: sexy, earthy, concentrated, serene. As she said in the interview, age was no handicap since belly dancing "is about the sexuality of a mature woman."

The caption below the photo identified Letitia Cole as a former composer of classical music, moderately successful but "swimming upstream" in the largely male world of classical composition, not getting the grants and attention she thought she deserved. In 1992, while working with Arabic rhythms for a sonata she was composing for a Palestinian violinist, she suddenly realized she would rather be dancing to the music than writing it.

There it was, the part of the story Renata liked best: "I suddenly realized." The certainty, the specificity. I won't be *this* any more, I'll be *that*. *There's* my future, in a flash. It wasn't that Renata wanted to leave the library and become a circus acrobat or a trainer of horses, the lives she'd dreamed of as a child, with her twin sister. It wasn't the future she wanted to transform so much as the past. She couldn't change the facts, but maybe she could change the way she told them to herself—different words, different emphases. Would that make a new story? Would it make her someone else?

Claudia and Renata loved their toy wooden farm, its buildings and figurines painted in bright primary colors, and played with it long past the time most children outgrow such things. They were eleven years old, they had formed an exclusive club with a half-dozen girls in their junior-high class who met every Friday night to gossip about boys and listen to Beatles tapes, they had their ears pierced in the mall and wore tight jeans and wished they needed bras, and still, in secret, they continued their saga of Farmer Blue and his family.

The farm had been sent to them from Montana one Christmas by their father's peripatetic younger brother. Peter was always trekking across the country on his motorcycle, from time to time phoning to ask for money, which their father always sent, over their mother's protests. The grandparents had died in a hotel fire in Atlantic City, and the older brother felt obliged to look out for the younger: after all, Peter had been orphaned at nineteen, barely grown up and still unsure about his path, while Dan had had a chance to finish college and business school, find work and start a family. Forever after he attributed Peter's waywardness to this bad luck, but his wife was unsympathetic. Nineteen was no baby, Grace snapped; Peter would have turned out a slacker no matter what. All the same, he never failed to send his nieces gifts on Christmas and birthdays, so that for Claudia and Renata he had the glamour of a fairy-tale benefactor, an eternally young knight on wheels. Then when the twins were ten years old, Peter and his girlfriend Cindy married and moved into a house just a few blocks away—the down payment supplied by Dan—in a doomed attempt at bourgeois suburban life.

The farm consisted of the house, the barn, the silo, the trucks, and the animals, and when spread out it covered sixteen square feet of the living-room floor. Farmer Blue and Mrs. Blue—named for the color of his hat and overalls and her apron—had three children, Sky Blue, Powder Blue, and Pastel Blue. There was also the hired hand, a deaf mute the girls named Hired Hand.

From the beginning, Claudia and Renata were entranced by their ongoing saga, a life proceeding alongside their own, and they remained entranced because the farm story unfolded in their private language, which their parents had banned. The language frightened Grace and Dan because they couldn't understand it. It was simple, really; it sounded alien only because the girls spoke it at top speed. They moved syllables around in patterns arrived at tacitly, but the patterns were consistent; mingled in were bits of the Sardinian dialect their mother's mother broke into every so often. Grace and Dan had loathed the language from the start, as do most parents of twins who devise a private language, which quite a few do. They tolerated it until Renata and Claudia were nearly eight, then demanded that they give it up. It was too weird, and if the girls persisted, they would become weird as well. Renata and Claudia obeyed when their parents were around, but they spoke it in the privacy of their room, and it flourished in their tales of Farmer Blue and his family, murmured in undertones, in breathy haste, with conspiratorial glee.

For years the Blue family had milked the cows, gathered eggs, planted and harvested in relative serenity. They had faced perils, naturally—drought, crop failure, the death of a favorite horse (lost in the backyard), and one fateful night the roof of the silo collapsed and had to be rebuilt. But things always turned out well in the end. Now, though, ever since they'd started junior high, Claudia had been pressing for something truly terrible to happen. She lusted for mayhem. She wanted strangers to ride in from the plains and steal the horses or kidnap the children. She got the notion that Hired Hand, who had served the family faithfully and mutely from time immemorial, was actually an ex-convict who was planning to destroy the farm and run away with the savings Mrs. Blue kept in a cookie jar. Maybe Farmer Blue would catch him and kill him in revenge. When Renata suggested an alternative—Hired Hand could turn out to be Farmer Blue's long-lost brother, Royal—Claudia just scoffed. Where was the fun in that?

She had always been the restless and impetuous one. This was only more restlessness, Renata thought; she didn't dream that Claudia wanted the game to come to an end. She herself would have been pleased to continue the lulling routine indefinitely, the family driving to town on market days, or watching the calves being born, or stacking up wood and bales of hay for winter—bundles of toothpicks tied with string, and the straw wrapping from Grace's new set of china. But at Claudia's urging, Renata had agreed a few weeks ago to a tractor accident in which Powder Blue lost two fingers of his left hand and had to be rushed to the hospital at the nearby county seat. Yet even that didn't satisfy Claudia for long. At last, to placate her, Renata consented to a lightning bolt that would set the barn on fire.

The roof of the barn erupted in flames—they hastily festooned it with strips of red crepe paper. Inside, the cows and horses set up a clamor and stampeded to the closed door of the burning barn. Renata banged a wooden block on the floor for the sound of the pounding, desperate hooves. "We have to hurry," she told Claudia in their secret language, "or they'll be trapped." Claudia was clutching Farmer Blue tightly in her fist. "Make him open the door. Where's Hired Hand?"

Asleep in the fields, Claudia reminded her. It was his afternoon break. With his deafness, he was capable of sleeping through it all.

"I'll wake him," Renata said, and began hunting for Hired Hand.

"No." Claudia grabbed her arm. "That's not right. He wouldn't hear it yet. We just have to see what happens."

Renata tried to pry Farmer Blue out of Claudia's fist but couldn't. Instead she grabbed Mrs. Blue and the children, who were in the house, clearing up after lunch. But when she brought them to the door of the barn, Claudia kneeled to block it so they couldn't get past. Renata set up an alarm, banging a spoon on the metal base of a floor lamp, to rouse the volunteer fire department. At the clamor, Fox came rushing in. He was a rust-colored Irish terrier their parents had given them when they were nine, but the girls had never warmed to him because he was too stupid to be much fun; he'd forget where he left things, then go sniffing around gloomily until someone took pity and found his plastic bone or his ball. Renata pushed him aside and ran to the kitchen to get the old whistle buried in a drawer full of junk. When she returned, Claudia still hadn't let the animals out of the barn.

"What's the matter with you?" she shouted. Their mother was out, so they could speak the language freely. "Do you want them all to die?"

"Shit happens," said Claudia. Still blocking the barn, she blew hard on the crepe paper strips to make them billow. Renata tucked Mrs. Blue and the three children deep in her jeans pocket to keep them safe from Claudia, then seized a miniature fire engine from the shelf and zoomed it up to the barn. She scooted it between Claudia's legs and managed to open the door and scoop up the animals, who came out gasping for air. Then she dragged over a hose—an oversized curly straw from a cereal box—and pushing Claudia aside, aimed it at the barn. The crepe paper strips sank down and Renata ripped them off the roof. Fox, having observed the scene in puzzlement, slunk out of the room.

Without a word, Claudia sat down on the floor with her back to the farm. The fire was out. Renata took Mrs. Blue and the others from her pocket, and while Sky, Pastel, and Powder tried to soothe the frightened, staggering animals, Mrs. Blue went to rouse Hired Hand so he could help. Claudia still hadn't let go of Farmer Blue.

"It's out," said Renata in the private language.

Claudia tossed Farmer Blue over her shoulder and he landed in the vegetable patch behind the house. They'd never treated the family so roughly. "But the farm is ruined," she said. Not in the private language. In plain English.

"Why did you want to kill them all? What's the matter?"

"They've gone on long enough." She got up and went out. From the window Renata saw her take her bike from the garage and ride off. Fox followed to the edge of the lawn, then stopped and gazed after her. Renata was left to put everything away.

That was the end of the farm. There was no sense in carrying on alone. They stopped speaking the language, too. Claudia wouldn't. She said it was silly.

After she "suddenly realized," indeed in the very next sentence, poof!, Letitia Cole had become a belly dancer. In life and not narrative, of course the change couldn't have been instantaneous. It turned out that she'd already studied ballet for years, an excellent foundation for belly dancing. By the next sentence, she was throwing away nearly everything from her old life as a composer. Here again, she probably didn't do this all at once but bit by bit. Yet how thrilling to picture her abandon—her fuzzy hair flying every which way as she tears up the scores, the reviews, the concert programs, the files, and hurls them out the window, raining paper onto the streets.

It was a vision both exhilarating and distressing to a paper-saver like Renata, with files of yellowing clippings stacked in folders and drawers, not to mention the ones hanging on the walls. Over the next months Jack would find the whole paper-hoarding business eccentric, and worse. Distasteful. Jack the tolerant, who unaccountably will find so much in Renata to love—unaccountably because she doesn't find herself lovable; sexy, clever, mysterious, maybe, but not lovable—can't abide that habit. It will be a constant test of his tolerance, or his need.

The day after the Sensation exhibit, at dinner in their local soul food restaurant, he set down his empty coffee cup with deliberateness and said, "Your place or mine?"

Renata wasn't sure if she was supposed to laugh, but she couldn't help it. To her relief, Jack laughed too. He was showing promise—a man who could deliver a cliché with a double edge, earnest and ironic.

That it would be one place or the other had grown evident through dinner; the urgency was that palpable. They hadn't yet touched, but they knew they would the moment a door closed behind them. Meanwhile they sat like civilized people, midway between his place and hers.

Renata had arrived first and watched him stride in, a man solid like a used car and showing the signs of wear, in jeans and a denim shirt, a man who in an earlier age might have worn a vest and watch-chain and leaned back in a swivel chair, smoking a cigar and giving orders in his grainy voice, kindly, authoritative, a man destined to grow portly with the years. Happily, he was not portly yet. He had a high forehead, and his dark hair, flecked with gray, was thick. He would not go bald for some time, maybe not ever. The thought surprised her, for usually with men she didn't anticipate the long run.

"Your place," she said. Outside, he took her arm and a fuse of warmth ran up to her shoulder as they walked fast through the snowy streets, sliding once or twice on icy patches. They didn't speak in the elevator, not a word until he locked the door behind them.

"You don't have any qualms about strange men's apartments?" he said as he unzipped her down coat and slid it off.

"I'll take my chances." She found herself in a spacious, high-ceilinged living room, lots of soft, old-fashioned furniture and big windows with hardware for curtains, but no curtains. "Mind if I look around?"

"Go right ahead."

The kitchen was large, with pots and pans hanging on a peg-board. It gave the feeling a woman had lived there. Or still did: she might be away for a few days. It wasn't merely the equipment and the full cabinets; it was the spice rack too, more than a dozen jars of assorted spices. She felt a stab of disappointment, again surprising. It wasn't supposed to matter. Except for the cumin and basil, though, the tops of the spice jars were dusty, as if rarely used. Later, more at leisure, she'd check out the bathroom; bathrooms were troves of information. She peered into a study piled high with papers, the only messy room. That was of no interest. She didn't care what he did, provided that he wasn't a drug dealer or a child pornographer: unlikely—he was so transparently decent. She saved the bedroom for last. The bed was bigger than she liked, bigger than required. Never mind, as long as it wasn't the kind with two single beds pushed together and a space in the center that widened during the night.

"So what do you think?" he asked, coming up behind her.

"Nice place. Are you unattached?"

"Very. Would you go home if I weren't?"

"I guess not. It's too late for that."

"And you? Unattached?"

"Even more than you."

And then he put his arms around her from behind and his hands were on her breasts. As she sank back and felt him hard against her she wondered how long he'd been walking around in that condition. The air was chilly as they undressed, and Jack pulled the covers over them and lunged at her. She liked the lunge. Her only misgiving had been that he might be too gentle; his manner was unnervingly kind. But he was not gentle through and through, and the bed was not the kind with a space in the center. He drew back just as she was ready for him. "Is this too fast for you?"

"No, go ahead. I want you there." It had been going on in her head all through dinner, all through the preliminary talk. No need to wait. They could wait later.

She'd never been a romantic. Her life had quashed whatever romantic tendencies she might have developed. But he kept surprising her. Being in his bed almost made her a romantic, for a few hours at least. She could almost believe certain people, certain bodies, were made for each other, designed and custom-tooled to match, perfect in every groove and fitting, timing perfect too.

He finally rolled off her and flung the covers off. "I want to look at you. Will you be cold?"

"No. Why, do I strike you as cold?"

He laughed. "No. You strike me as perfect. Especially now that I can see you. Perfect."

"That's nice. No one's ever called me perfect before."

"That's because I'm the person you're perfect for."

"But you don't know anything about me."

"I know all I need to know."

An excellent attitude. "It was lust at first sight," she said.

"I thought about you all last night. After the museum. I couldn't wait to do this. I almost called you around midnight. But I thought it might seem too, . . . I don't know, too much, and then this would never happen. Was I right? Would you have asked me over if I'd called last night?"

"Probably not," said Renata. "I mean, I wouldn't want to do anything rash. I'm actually a very cautious person."

"I can see," he said. "I can see how cautious you are."

"You're teasing me. I am."

"Okay, okay, now we'll make cautious love. Very careful."

This time he was painstaking, like a patient researcher. When it was over she rolled onto her stomach and he ran a finger very lightly from her neck all the way down her spine.

"Don't do that," she said.

He stopped. "What's wrong?"

"Just don't. I don't like it."

"All right," he said after a moment. "There are plenty of other things to do. We could even try talking. Like telling each other who we are."

"Don't tell me anything real yet. Tell me a fantasy. Who you want to be."

"Funny you should say that. Because I've been having this fantasy lately."

Maybe he was one of the Wall Street types she'd read about who chill out on weekends by working as sales clerks in upscale suburban home-furnishing stores. It's a fun way to relax, they say cheerfully, after logging fifty hours at a computer. They get to meet people, play with the cash register, wear a uniform. Strange as this form of recreation might seem to those exhausted by backbreaking work, or to the unemployed, Renata can sympathize. Her fantasies don't run to retail, but each time she reads the subway ads for training programs that promise a dazzling new future—computer skills, auto maintenance, physician's assistant—she imagines enrolling, until she remembers she's already been to school and has a job, indeed is on her way to it as she dreams over the ads.

"It's about running a travel agency. Reality Tours, or maybe Empathy Tours, if that's not too fancy-sounding. It's sort of a social protest agency. Bored by yet another vacation amid scenic beauty? Try something completely new, say, two challenging weeks on an Alabama chain gang. Dine on indigenous foods, meet new people, savor the fresh southern air, experience a lifestyle far from your daily routine."

"How about army barracks?" Renata suggested. "Or a navy submarine. The opportunity to learn new skills will more than make up for the cramped quarters. Or maybe old plantation slave cabins?"

"I could make you a partner. Have you ever been to Hawaii? There's a gorgeous out-of-the-way nook that used to be a leper colony. They brought the lepers there and pretty much abandoned them. It has a fantastic beach. The Kalaupapa Hilton. Or Hansen's Hilton. In the past, only lepers could bask in this isolated bay nestled in mountains created by ancient volcanoes. Now you, too, can live like a leper."

"On that note, maybe we can go to sleep? I have to get up early for work. By the way, how did you know which library to call?"

"I didn't. I thought I'd start with the main branch and work my way down."

"There are eighty-five branches of the New York Public Library, and that's not counting Brooklyn. Not to mention all the colleges and universities. How many would you have tried?"

"I don't know. A few dozen, maybe. A sexy librarian," he mused.

"It does happen. I have a colleague who's even sexier, or at least more preoccupied with it. Linda."

"All right, I stand corrected. Tomorrow," he said, "we have to find out who we really are. How about if I come over after work? I want to see you in your natural habitat."

"I'm not sure you'll like it. I want to sleep, all right? You wore me out. Come here." She turned over and opened her arms. "Put your head on my chest and let me sleep."

She liked him more, seeing how he slept. Some men, even ardent lovers, withdrew in sleep. They liked space around them. But Jack stayed close the whole night, and when she woke she felt wrapped in his body, like a shield against the daylight. He got up first and put on a robe. The room was chilly.

"Would you have an extra robe?" she called into the kitchen.

"There's one way back in the closet. I took it from some hotel. I'll be right in and get it."

"It's okay. I'll find it."

The closet was a shambles, with cartons and old shoes heaped on the floor, and more boxes on the upper shelves. She poked around till she saw the terry-cloth robe on a hook in a far corner, but when she reached for it, a large, flat, dark green box tumbled to the floor, scattering dust. She pulled it out. Layers of faded tissue paper parted, revealing a mass of white satin and gauze. A wedding dress. She was down on her knees staring at it, remembering her mother's, also kept in a box in the bedroom closet. Grace tried it on once to show the girls. "See?" she said. "I told you it would still fit." Then Claudia and Renata tried it on in turn, and it fit them, too. "Maybe you'll want to wear it some day," their mother said shyly. They were heartless at fifteen; they snorted and mocked. Who wanted to wear a dress like that? If they ever got married, they'd wear red. Or black. Besides, no one got married anymore. They certainly wouldn't. They had lots of things to do before they even considered marriage. So Grace folded it up and put it away. Renata relented. She was always the one to relent. "It's really pretty, Mom. You must have looked great." Grace shrugged and walked away—her instinctive response. Not long after, when undreamed of events shattered the family beyond her tolerance, she shrugged and walked away too, in a manner of speaking.

Jack came into the room.

"I'm awfully sorry," Renata said. "I've gotten the floor all dusty. If you give me a broom and dustpan I'll clean it up."

He didn't speak.

"It's a nice dress," she said, and waited. "They're back in style."

He spread it out on the bed. The dress was cream-colored, with long, narrow sleeves and a scoop neck ringed with seed pearls. A cocktail-length dress with matching pearls making a scalloped pattern just above the hemline. The woman who wore it must have been quite slender. It was too new to be his mother's. And what man ever saved his mother's wedding dress?

"I'm sorry I knocked it over," she said again. "But could you please say something? I mean, did she die, or what? What's it doing here?"

"She didn't die. She left it."

"Your wife."

"Ex-wife."

"Well, it's not the kind of thing you can get a lot of use out of. How ex?"

"Three years."

"And it's been here all this time? Is it a fetish or what? I mean, you don't parade around in it or anything?"

His lips tightened in pain and she regretted her tone. "I told you, she left it."

"I see that."

"On purpose. So I'd find it someday. Like now."

"Didn't you know it was there?"

"No. I never clean out the closet."

"She must have forgotten it."

"No. She wanted me to know she left it."

It was like a Jekyll to Hyde transformation: his face was pinched with rage. "It's not a good omen that you found it."

"It's not an omen at all. It was an accident. I was clumsy. Let's put it back and forget it."

"She left one day with someone she knew from before, who turned up out of nowhere. I came home and found all her things gone. And a note. I wanted to kill her. Sometimes I think I could still kill her. Such as right now. It was the worst thing that ever happened to me. The shock. More than missing her, it was the shock."

They sat down on the bed, next to the dress.

"You could throw it away," Renata said.

"Could you put it back in the box? I'll get it up on the shelf."

She folded the dress neatly. He brought a stepladder and put the box on a higher shelf than the one it had fallen from.

"I haven't stayed with anyone very long, since she left. Pamela, her name was. I can't let that happen to me again."

"I can understand that." So he, too, had the bad habit of clinging to past misery. There was a word for that in Etinoi, the South Seas islands language she was working on in the library: *bakiranima.*

"I'm afraid of what will happen with us," he said. "Are you the kind who leaves?"

"Isn't it too soon to be afraid? We barely know each other. We've just spent one night together."

"But it was good. Wasn't it?"

"Yes," she admitted reluctantly. She was about to add something dismissive, using the phrase "carnal knowledge," but his grim face restrained her. She brushed off the hotel robe and put it on. "Did you have any kids?"

"No."

Good. One less complication. Though she now knew more about him than she was ready for.

The dress was not the only thing Pamela had left. There were items on the top shelf of the medicine cabinet that she doubted were Jack's: a cream depilatory, the threads of its screw-on top faintly rusting, and expensive hand lotion. In the back of a drawer she found tweezers and half a dozen tampons, which she would use on future visits. In their sealed wrappers they were perfectly clean, and Renata was not fussy or superstitious. Otherwise, the contents of the medicine cabinet were banal. No mysterious prescription drugs, none of the ubiquitous Prozac, nothing stronger than Advil and cough syrup with codeine. A sound man.

Let air travel and wireless communication be the
two legs humanity stands on. And let's see what
the consequences will be.

VELIMIR KHLEBNIKOV

Two

It's such a perfect September morning, the city's most glorious
month, no clouds, no doldrums, that she'll walk across the Brooklyn Bridge. She walks across whenever she has time, almost every
morning this bright blue month, then catches the subway to the library on the other side. Today she has time because Jack left so
hastily to go home and change into his suit. The river and the skyline both lull and energize her; the rhythm of the serene parade,
the labor force snatching a bit of beauty before the day's rigors,
sets a good pace for her thoughts. Walking meditation, her friend
Linda calls it. Linda is an aspiring Buddhist originally from Houston. "For people like us, who sit a lot at work, it's better than ordinary meditation," she says.

But what Renata does can hardly be called meditation. It's more
like musing, drifting, enjoying the bustle of the Brooklyn streets.
She walks slowly, so slowly one might almost think she's trying
to delay something, to ward off the future. A child of the suburbs,
she's always found the city streets pleasing, calming. And soon

she'll be sheltered by the enormous stone weight of the library; nothing could be more solid or reliable. It waits for her across the river. The uniformed guards greeting her by name at the entrance are reassuring, guardians of her peace. The long, high-ceilinged, marble halls, where her clunky sandals sound an echoing click, are homey; her small office is a haven. She'll greet her boss, Denise, a monumental black woman whose long African braids form a bead curtain covering the telephone always at her ear. And across the hall is Linda, renowned in their third-floor coterie as the world's greatest research librarian. A large sign on Linda's door reads, "False language, evil in itself, infects the soul with evil." Socrates. Renata has passed it every day for six years and still finds it cheering. In her own office everything will be where she left it yesterday, the notepads, the books, the dictionaries, the computer waiting obediently to be animated. She can make the screen any color she likes, and she chooses different colors for different languages. Isn't that enough of a life? Any word one could want is right there in the building. Does she really need Jack? Is the feel of him pushing into her really so important, as important as she's let it become?

Lunch with Linda will be entertaining. Linda remembers, effortlessly, everything she reads, and she knows where to find anything else. Two days a week, Denise sends her out to play the Answer Lady. She sits at the information desk and people ask her questions. The rest of the time Linda reads and "fools around" with the computer, hunting down new troves of data, especially about love and sex. She is intrigued by the amorous customs of ancient and modern cultures. A bouncy chatterer, she offers obscure tidbits about these and about her own sex life, specifically, the odd venues in which it occurs. Linda was sympathetic to Bill Clinton's conducting his affair in the Oval Office and the adjacent corridors; she understood the lure of risky or physically challenging sites.

Her own preference is for moving vehicles: cars, buses, trains, and once, a rowboat.

Linda keeps Renata posted about her long and sporadic relationship with Roger, who works for a securities firm based in London and travels a great deal. They have had sex in the woods of the Adirondacks, on the beaches of New England, in the New Mexico desert, at the shores of Lake Michigan, and places in England that Renata can't recall. At last week's lunch, Linda reported that they did it on a plane returning from London.

"On the plane?" Renata asked in disbelief.

"In the bathroom."

"You're kidding. How?"

"It was a red-eye, because I had to be back at work Monday morning. It wasn't too full. We were in first class. They upgraded me."

"But—?"

Linda looked around. The café near the library was crowded, the tables close together. The waitress was approaching, and already a man at the next table was giving them curious glances. "I'd better tell you another time. It's almost worth buying a ticket for, though, believe me."

"Not for me. I hate flying."

"Exactly. This makes it bearable. Anyway, let's talk about something where we don't have to whisper." She reported on her unsuccessful search for information about a forgotten eighteenth-century composer, Giovanni Battista Pandolfi, whom Renata had asked about after she heard his violin sonata on the radio—or maybe it was a concerto, she can't remember anymore. The announcer had noted that very little information about Pandolfi was available; if not for the one sonata (or concerto) and a single reference to him as an employee in an orchestra, he might not have existed. He might even be an invention. Given her reclusive tendencies, this passage through life with no traces except one enduring piece of music would appeal to Renata, although many people have passed through life leaving even less.

"Nothing so far," Linda said. "It would help if you could remember whether it was a sonata or a concerto. How could you forget what you heard?"

"I don't know," Renata said. "But there's no rush. Take your time."

Maybe Linda will know more about Pandolfi today. Meanwhile, as Renata heads toward the bridge, she reviews her files in her head and lights on "The Long Unhappy Life of Miss Greff," one of the clippings in the Transformed Lives folder. By rights Miss Greff's is not a transformed life at all and doesn't belong in a folder of that name. After decades of extreme frugality, Rosalind Greff, a child of the Depression, died at ninety, leaving $105,000 in savings accounts to be distributed among the fire department, the rescue squad, and the youth recreation program in her Pennsylvania town. According to the newspaper account, she worked in a shop as a jewelry polisher from the age of thirteen and remained there, "taking overtime whenever possible," until she retired in her sixties. "Miss Greff lived her first 45 years with her mother, who dominated her. After the mother's death, she lived the next 25 years with her brother, who also dominated her." When he died, she was alone. Her only human contact, after her retirement from the jewelry store, was with a neighbor who kept an eye on her and did occasional shopping and errands. Among Miss Greff's fears were bugs, thunder, and men. In the manner of such eccentrics, "she made aprons from old dresses, and after her brother died, she made blouses from his shirts. She caught water that dripped from the kitchen faucet and used it to wash dishes. . . . She dusted with a mop she fashioned from old underclothes and a hanger," and, no surprise, she sat in the dark to save electricity, finding her way around by the light of a street lamp. Her existence was noted only when the heirs to her largesse realized they had no idea who she was, nor did anyone else in town, except for the one neighbor. She was a woman whom no one knew.

Why should this story mean anything to Renata, other than to evoke the expected pity and dismay? It certainly hasn't the zing of Letitia Cole's happy metamorphosis into a belly dancer. Renata's life in no way resembles Miss Greff's, nor is she especially frugal. She wasn't a Depression child but grew up in the relative plenty of the '70s and '80s. Her mop comes from the hardware store on Court Street and her clothes from good shops—she favors a blend of arty and expensive classic; her parents were not domineering but rather permissive, in the manner of baby-boomers. She doesn't fear bugs or thunder and has not avoided men. During the two years after her father died and her mother was institutionalized, she slept with a great many men, until circumstances required that she stop. Later, when she was free to resume, she was more selective, being a bit older. Then she stopped again—it became unrewarding—until eight months ago and the advent of Jack.

She studies Miss Greff's life because she used to imagine her own life might be one in which nothing would happen. Early on, in a short span, a great deal happened. Enough to fill a much longer span. Then nothing, or nothing worth thinking of. Then Jack happened, and that happening confuses her.

After the events of her early youth, there was comfort in the prospect of no powerful emotions ever again. She liked, or had persuaded herself that she liked, contemplating a peaceful stretch of blank years, broken only by obscure new languages with evocative new words, often words so subtly shaded that they have no adequate equivalent in English, words for feelings and sensations we have not named, and as everyone knows, what we haven't named we cannot see or take into account. Like *iranima,* for instance, from Etinoi, the South Seas island language she'll be learning this week. *Iranima* means the faint melancholy we feel at the attainment of a longed-for wish. The closest way to say it in English is "nostalgia for longing," the bittersweet parting with a familiar craving, and the resulting emptiness of the soul grown used to crave. *Bakiranima,* its derivative, was what she had noticed in Jack their first time together—a clinging to past misery or an unwillingness to embrace good fortune when at last it comes round in the Etinoian cycle.

Still, the desire to live—to live for two, her dead sister as well as herself—would keep asserting itself. And when Jack turned up, that desire gained the upper hand, as apparently it never did in Miss Greff. Does she want to risk it or fight it? But fight for what? Emptiness?

A week after the disaster on the farm, twenty dollars was missing from their club dues. Renata was the treasurer.

The seven girls sat on the basement floor, and Renata opened the dues envelope as she did every Friday night, always a titillating moment. Children on the cusp of adolescence are fascinated by cash; they don't know quite where it comes from, yet they have an inkling of its powers. But that wasn't what made the blood rush to Renata's face. There should have been seventy dollars in the envelope—two dollars a week from each girl, five meetings so far. Last week she'd brought the mound of crumpled singles, some of them soft as rags, to her father and asked if he could give her bigger bills. Monday night he handed her three new twenties and a ten, which she stroked over and over for their crispness and put carefully away in the envelope in her bottom drawer.

"What's wrong?" asked Abigail, the president, a haughty girl with ivory skin and a long blonde ponytail she liked to toss about. "What are you waiting for?"

"There's money missing. A twenty." Renata rubbed the stiff bills between her fingers in case they were stuck together. She even slid her thumbnail along their edges, making a nasty squeak, as if she could force their minuscule third dimension to split.

The club was saving up for a trip to the city. One day soon, when they'd accumulated enough, they would take the bus in and have adventures. Any kind of adventures; the mere words "the city" set off fantasies all the more alluring for their vagueness. None of their parents would allow them to travel into the city alone, so they would lie. They relished planning their lies as much as they relished the coming adventures.

The girls didn't accuse or sulk. They were girls raised to be civilized, the brightest and prettiest girls in the class, girls who moved and spoke and dressed with ease, who knew already how to negotiate in the world. The club's unspoken purpose was to declare their distinction, to include and exclude. From the first weeks of junior high they'd sorted themselves out: girls like that can spot one another at a glance, just as they can spot their opposites—the clumsy, the ill-defined, the inarticulate, the hesitant. And so on that first evening, they honored a tacit allegiance. If they were suspicious, they remained polite. "It'll turn up. It's got to be somewhere." Besides, Claudia and Renata possessed a mystique. It was a point of honor to be able to tell them apart; mistakes were embarrassing and could reduce one's standing in the group. The other girls studied them, trying to find subtle differences. They interrogated them about twinhood. Did each one know what the other was thinking? When did they stop dressing alike? Who was smarter? Who could run faster? Would they get their periods at the same moment, or at least on the same day? (Everyone awaited this milestone with a mix of eagerness and apprehension; the two girls who'd already reached it were envied.) Did they like the same foods? Did they always agree? Did they ever fight?

Foolish questions. To Renata and Claudia, being twins meant something of quite another order. It meant relief, immunity, from what they imagined as a painful isolation: living as the only one bearing *this* particular face, *this* body. *They* each knew what it felt like to live behind the same face, and they marveled that others could bear their singularity. Everyone could look in a mirror, but mirrors abandon you the moment you turn your back. Mirrors couldn't be companions. They two were faithful mirrors, companionable mirrors. Other people, Renata learned later, are uncomfortable meeting someone who resembles them: they feel eerily exposed, found out. As she grew up she noticed that women can be vexed to find someone wearing the same dress: the sign of identical taste is obscurely mortifying. Also, the same dress on different bodies points out the oddities and flaws of each. But she and Claudia had nothing to hide. Their identical bodies relieved them of the shame of carnal secrets.

Above all, there was the secret language, at least there had been until the fire in the barn a week ago. None of the girls in the club knew the language existed. And because in this language they confided everything thoroughly, their memories merged and became common property. They couldn't say anymore which one had seen the dead cat floating near the edge of the river, its matted fur giving off a foul smell, or seen the English teacher, Miss Pryor, and the biology teacher, Mr. Jimemez, kissing in the front seat of his red Volvo. And so they had double memories, a richness of scenes witnessed that was like an extra layer of consciousness, each one possessing what the other had seen or heard.

It was that way for Renata, and she had never thought it could be otherwise for Claudia. But she was wrong. Claudia was changing. For her the common face and common memory had become oppressive. She needed to escape from twinhood. From her twin.

Their mother helped them look for the money. The next day, after they'd searched every closet and drawer, every pocket and backpack, she spread newspapers on the kitchen floor, shooed Fox away, and dumped out the vacuum cleaner's bagful of clotted dust. Down on their knees, the three of them rummaged through the week's worth of filth, raveling it with their fingers. Renata blushed with shame as the dirt formed black lines under their fingernails, as if she really were a thief putting her loved ones through this ordeal.

Grace sat back on her heels. "Think, both of you. Think back to everything you did since the last meeting. Maybe one of you borrowed it for something and forgot to put it back?"

"I never use that money. I just put it in the envelope," Renata said.

"How should I know?" Claudia said. "She's the treasurer, not me."

Then Renata knew for sure, from her voice, her sullen withdrawal. It had occurred to her the night before, when Claudia went to bed without a word, but she'd stifled it; she wouldn't think the unthinkable. Now she couldn't even tell their mother: she and Claudia never told on each other—that, too, was unthinkable.

All the latest studies of twins illustrate the uncanny affinities that persist even when the twins are raised apart. They turn out to have similar tastes and aversions; they eat the same foods, play the same games, choose the same sorts of lovers. When they're brought together they fly into each other's arms. In the face of such research, the old examples from enduring myth tend to be overlooked, the betrayals and the murders—Cain and Abel, Jacob and Esau, Romulus and Remus.

Renata saw the club members at school every day. Their civility eroded. A few hardly bothered to hide their suspicions. She felt marked. There was no way to explain. Her father gave her a new twenty to replace the one that was lost, and stroked her hair and said the girls would forget about it soon. In the locker room she handed the dues envelope to Abigail, the president. She didn't look Renata in the eye, just accepted the envelope silently and turned away with a faint toss of her head.

That was a cloudy day in late November. After school Renata went down by the river, alone. "Down by the river," for the girls in their group, meant a special spot. High above the Palisades walling the river was a park with a playground and picnic tables where the local kids congregated. Surrounding the park was a wooded area, and a little ways in past the trees was a path that led to a bare ledge of the Palisades. From there a steep path wound down the rock face to the shore. Not many kids knew the path, no one knew who made it, and no one ever told any parents about it. Below, the space between the rock face and the water's edge was no more than eight feet wide, and had always struck her as too humble a gateway to such a broad river. It should have an enormous, regal frontage all the way along. All it had here was a dilapidated, narrow wooden pier, its approach overgrown with weeds; it stretched far out into the water, much of the railing gone, the planks rotted and broken in places. Birds would perch on the rail and leave their droppings.

The ground down by the river was mucky, with faded tufts of grass and sickly reeds. Nearby were three abandoned rowboats, leaky, their paint peeled off to leave a dingy, mottled gray; beer cans and empty cigarette packets and condoms littered the bottom. The appeal down there was privacy. They could watch the cargo ships pass, and the barges, and on summer weekends occasional sailboats; they could even glimpse, far in the distance, the Circle

Line from the city below, at the highest tip of its orbit. They could walk out onto the pier—not too far out, because there was a point at which the rotting planks couldn't bear their weight—and gaze out at the town on the opposite shore, at the bridges, the great one to the south and the low sleek one to the north, and on a clear day they could spy the beginnings of the city they'd been saving their money for.

A few times, Claudia and one of the wilder girls had gone far out on the pier and threatened to jump in. "Come on, I dare you," Claudia called one hot day in September, while Renata and the others hung back. "What are you afraid of. It's just water. We'll swim." "It's filthy," Abigail said. "It's disgusting. And you don't know what's underneath. The whole thing is falling apart." "I dare you," Claudia repeated, but when no one took up her dare, she and the other girl slunk back. It was filthy. Every kind of debris drifted past: a boot, a wire hanger, a blender, a man's briefs, an alarm clock, a soap dish, fruit peelings, a dog collar. They were suburban girls, envious of the city, and they liked to blame it for the defilement of the river, though it was really the upstate factories oozing their waste that did the more serious damage.

It was a secret place, uncontaminated by adults. There might be other kids from school there now and then, sometimes a couple fooling around in one of the old rowboats. But mostly it was empty. Mostly it was their own.

That November day, Renata walked through the park among the deserted picnic tables under the arching elms and climbed a special tree she and Claudia loved. She entered the woods, took the path, and scrambled down the rocks to the edge of the river. No one was there. She walked out onto the pier and skipped some stones on the water and acknowledged that something had ended. Claudia wouldn't play with the farm anymore or speak the language.

She never mentioned the missing money, though she must have known Renata knew the truth. She didn't care. Renata didn't know why she was being abandoned, not yet. A large ship went by, then two barges. Across the wide span of water, the houses of the town opposite were as tiny as houses on a Monopoly board; the boats docked at a small landing were toy boats. She peered south and glimpsed the northern edge of the city under the gray sky. She must learn to be alone, she thought. Like everyone else.

She couldn't face the club meetings anymore, and after a few weeks Claudia dropped out too. "Boring." But Claudia remained part of the group of girls. She and Renata had been seen as virtually interchangeable, yet somehow Claudia was not tainted by suspicion.

Renata became a loner. Things might have changed two years later when she went to high school, a large school with new people who didn't know or care anything about the childish club. But by then she didn't care about being one of the popular girls. She had lost her sister and no other company could make up for that.

At the same time, a pair of British twins, just a few years older than Renata and Claudia, were adolescents locked in a struggle of such potent mutual love and loathing, need and revulsion, that they ended in a mental institution. Neither one was complete without the other. They were each other's lifeline and torment. "Like twin stars," their biographer described June and Jennifer Gibbons, "they are caught in the gravitational field between them, doomed to spin around each other forever. If they come too close or drift apart, both are destroyed."

Not so, Renata protested when she read it—for of course she would read it. Look: she was not destroyed. She might even be considered fortunate, since Claudia didn't turn the full force of her resentment on her, no more, that is, than by betraying her and estranging her. Claudia might well have destroyed Renata, but instead she destroyed herself.

She was so sunk in memories, moving like a sleepwalker toward the bridge, that at first she didn't recognize the short old man with the leathery face who approached her on Court Street. He didn't recognize her either. "The subway?" he asked in a Spanish accent. His appearance should have been enough: he always wore loose brown pants with a belt and black suspenders, a plaid shirt, a battered brown fedora, and thick square glasses. Renata started answering in Spanish, and as soon as the words came off her tongue she knew who he was. The bookman. She'd never seen him away from his table of used books on the corner of Montague Street with his cronies keeping him company, lounging on the ledge of the apartment building.

And he'd never seen her anywhere but walking past his table. When he heard her voice they smiled in recognition and gave the usual greetings: how are you today, how are you, beautiful day. Indeed, the Technicolor blue of the sky kept deepening, and a light breeze wafted from the north, rippling her flowered skirt against her bare legs, reminding her of how Jack had left her unattended to an hour ago.

"I have to go to a court building on Centre Street in Manhattan. I'm a witness in a case," he explained in his genteel way. "But, you know, I hardly ever leave the neighborhood. I don't know the subways very well." Like most people who are forced to speak an adopted tongue and speak it poorly, in his native Spanish the bookman sounded smarter and more competent.

At his corner table, the bookman would welcome everyone like a long-lost friend, even first-time visitors. Renata never used to stop there because she was surrounded by enough books at the library, until one day last year, as she neared his post, he headed straight toward her holding a banana in each hand, smiling as if he'd been expecting her. He thrust the right-hand banana at her and the left-hand banana at another woman passing by. She tried to say she didn't want a banana but there was no refusing him, so she took it with thanks. The other woman did, too. He flashed his toothy smile—cheap, gaudy dentures—and said "God bless you," the words with which he ended every encounter.

He wasn't pleased about testifying in court—who is?—and Renata commiserated. "Is it a serious case? Criminal?"

"No. My brother slipped on the ice in front of a building and broke his hip. I was with him, so I have to tell what I saw."

"Oh, I'm sorry. I hope he'll be all right."

"He's fine." The bookman smiled benignly. "It was two years ago."

"Ah, the wheels of justice. . . . Well, it's only a few stops. Go to the corner." She pointed. "Cross the street, turn left, walk one block, and it's right there." She was glad to help him out: the bookman was a local saint who inspired saintliness in others. He was at peace with the world and emanated a sense of the benign; everyone in the neighborhood felt it, at least those who wanted to make the world a better place. Or thought they did, but regretted having so little opportunity. Even a sense of the divine, one might say, were one inclined in that direction.

Helping him out was a small recompense for the banana and the many books he'd sold her at absurd prices from his jumbled inventory of cheap romances, how to find your inner child, *The Iliad*, John Le Carré, how to play golf like Tiger Woods, how to make a great toast at a wedding, *The Book of Laughter and Forgetting*, Louis L'Amour. People gave him the overflow of their shelves, and the bookman accepted all contributions indiscriminately. Happily.

A happy man. Her best find on his table was the book about uchronies.

Uchronies are stories that imagine history taking a different course through some small but not inconceivable turn of events. The "what if" theory of history. Or, in the fancier language from the library's recent exhibit on utopias, a uchrony is an "apocryphal historical sketch of the development of European civilization such as it never was, such as it could have been." Let's say Hitler accidentally drowned on a camping trip as a boy, what would German history have been? Gandhi ducks the fatal shot. Truman slips getting out of the tub and can't give the order to drop the bomb. And so forth. Closer to home, what if Claudia had been careless and left the twenty dollars she took from the club's treasury at age eleven— the theft for which Renata was blamed—in the pocket of her jeans, and she, Renata, had discovered it? Or, four years later, when her Uncle Peter ran one finger gently down the back of her neck and between her shoulder blades while she was bending over her bike in the garage, adjusting the kickstand, what if she had understood right away that he was mistaking her for Claudia, was in the habit of caressing Claudia (which would account for Claudia's recent moodiness), and what if, despite the lacerating shame, she'd gone like a good girl to tell her mother . . . ? Would they have believed her? Would they have banished Peter? Would everything have turned out differently, Renata herself, altogether different?

She'd wanted an obscure book about uchronies, a book she couldn't find in the library, and there it was on the bookman's table. It's true all kinds of things turned up there. Everyone who knew him suspected the bookman was in touch with a higher power. Not that Renata flattered herself that any higher power would care whether she found a particular book, not with so many more weighty matters on the agenda. Still, it was uncanny.

She pounced on the book. Just what she was looking for, she told the bookman, who grinned. "God bless you." He charged a dollar. She wanted to give him more, he'd never make any money charging such low prices, she told him, but he wouldn't take more. He said he'd rather have friends than money: "*Mas valen amigos en plaza que dineros en casa.*"

He wishes the world well. He would rather give than receive. How has he gotten so far along—in his seventies, it seems—without growing embittered or wary? It's unnatural. Renata is much younger and very wary, especially of people who aren't wary. Maybe the bookman is slightly soft in the head—all those God bless you's. Who is he, anyway, when he's not at his stand? Some days she imagines him in a shabby room with one grimy window and a hot plate, staring at an ancient black-and-white TV, and other days, blue sunny days like today, she thinks that for all she knows, besides the brother, he has a wife, children, a nice apartment with pictures of the Crucifixion and the Virgin all over the place, a retirement pension, the book table his twilight-years hobby. As it happens, as he will shortly tell her when they have occasion to speak more intimately, that latter, better fantasy is very much the way it is for the bookman.

One way or another, he has an effect. She feels better after she talks to him. He brings news that the world is benevolent, and though she doesn't trust the message, she trusts the messenger.

"Take the number 2 or 3 and get off at Chambers Street," she told him. "It's only a few stops. Once you get there, walk east on Chambers, four or five blocks, and you'll get to Centre. All the court buildings are there, a block or so north. Just ask when you get there."

He thanked her and set off. She waited to be sure he got it right. He stopped for the light at the corner, crossed, for a moment was blocked from view. When next she saw him, instead of turning left he turned right. What to do? Call out and run after him? *No, no, Señor! Por allí no! Por allá!* The other way! Even though she was faster and could catch up, she shrank from making a spectacle of herself, shouting and dashing through traffic in her flowered skirt and sandals. Was he still her responsibility? He must have changed his mind, decided to buy a paper or make a phone call. Or spotted one of his many local friends. But let's not rationalize, let's be frank: chances are he made a mistake.

Her directions were perfectly clear. Then again, what's clear to one person may be complicated to another.

He was getting farther away. She'd have to run pretty fast to catch up now, and the longer she waited, the more foolish she'd seem when she did catch up. He'd know she'd been watching him. Well, so what? He'd chase after her, for sure, if the roles were reversed.

She carries on like this, makes every moment a life-and-death matter, because she knows what a seemingly trivial decision can mean. To go after someone or not, to go after Claudia, for instance, the night she went out so late. As in a uchrony, such decisions can change the course of history. What if, what if?

Oh, never mind, he'd get there sooner or later. He'd ask someone else. His brother's case had waited two years; it could wait another half hour. He'd probably conclude that her directions were wrong, that she was one of those insufferable people who couldn't admit ignorance; it's a matter of pride to have an answer to any question put to them. No, he was so good, he'd understand.

He was long out of sight. She continued on, past the new-agey medical establishment for pregnant women, Birthing Renaissance, a favorite addition to her Twin Titles or Redundancy list. The neighborhood was propitious; only last week she'd spied a delivery truck speeding down Remsen Street appropriately bearing the name Velocity Express.

She climbed the stairs to the bridge. She'd be late getting to the library, but no one would care. Or if they cared, they wouldn't say, because she's indispensable.

The library receives books, pamphlets, reports, and every variety of written what-not in hundreds of languages from all over the world, some of them in danger of extinction. Renata's job is to figure out what these cryptic publications are about so that they can be properly catalogued. She also helps anthropologists translate taped oral histories in unwritten languages and devise systems of transliteration. She has a freakish gift, or that's what she calls it. (Would Claudia have shown it, too? she wonders. Would identical twins be alike in every anomalous tangle of their brain cells? But Claudia didn't live long enough to find out, and wasn't studious while she lived.)

Renata can look at a language and very quickly, within hours for simple languages and days for complex ones, decipher its structure and vocabulary. A dictionary helps, but if need be she can manage without one; a few clues will do. She doesn't know how it happens, a glitch in the neurons, most likely. It's like some musicians' perfect pitch, or their ability to reproduce any melody on an instrument, only it's rarer. Or like those wizards you hear of who can multiply six-digit figures in their head, or tell you how many marbles are in a jar. Often the latter are autistic or otherwise not quite right, which makes her suspect such idiosyncratic talents may go hand in hand with peculiar deficits. If brain space is limited, that is, perhaps the perfect pitch or the marbles-in-a-jar cells are taking the rightful place of more crucial skills. In any event, she's made good use of the gift: unless a more efficient freak turns up, the job is hers for life. It would be hard to find a replacement who'd be content to remain in the library forever. Any possible replacements are traveling to exotic places for the United Nations or pursuing more lucrative academic careers. Renata barely finished college.

What she thinks about all day long, as she pores over Cochandi (from deep in the Amazon jungle) or Etinoi or Bliondan, isn't the mechanical task of finding equivalents in English, but why language functions at all. Why, and this is true of every known language, does a series of words in a certain order make us laugh, and in another order make us cry? The ready, now universally accepted answer that we're hard-wired for grammar, syntax, and connotation isn't enough: she accepts it, then dismisses it. The puzzling question is, Where is the bridge between sounds or marks on a page and our emotional apparatus? What makes us respond to ink strokes with a quickening of the heart or a surge of adrenaline? Why couldn't her mother understand the jokes in the language she and her sister spoke, and why did those curious syllables make Grace feel angry and excluded, while they made Claudia and Renata laugh?

Reading all those endangered-species languages, she comes across dozens of fine distinctions absent in English. To take a simple example, Etinoi (pale green on the computer) has three words for brother-in-law, denoting a sister's husband, a husband's brother, and a husband's sister's husband. It has words for the parents, brothers, and sisters of one's children's spouses—our inadequate "in-laws." It distinguishes between aunts and uncles by blood and by marriage, all embellishments on the root word. Etinoi also has separate words for the varieties of loss: loss of a small object (most likely misplaced); loss of a large object (most likely destroyed or stolen); loss of a person, exactly as we mean it in English, by death; loss of a situation or way of life—one's job, for example, or social standing or place in the world; loss of a state of mind or being, such as security, contentment, success. And each of those distinct words for loss can be modified by suffixes that indicate whether the thing lost can possibly be regained—*tanfos-oude*, the misplaced object found, or *tanfanori-oude*, success somehow regained—or whether, in the case of death or destruction, it is lost for good: *tanfendi-noude.*

Social life among the speakers of Etinoi is based on an elaborate system of obligations, both within families and in the larger social group, obligations regarding the rearing of children, the distribution of land and food, the allotment of tasks, or relations with neighboring peoples. The most serious obligation of all, which embraces and supersedes all others, is the obligation to live one's life, that is, not to shrink from it. The word for that is *ahmintu.* It's an easy enough principle to understand in the abstract, but not so easy to follow when it comes to action. Miss Greff, for instance, did not fulfill her obligation to live her life. She did not enter the world and take up any of its opportunities and challenges. Letitia Cole, in contrast, the composer turned belly dancer, obeyed the principle of *ahmintu.*

The task that awaits Renata today is decoding five pages from a taped account of an Etinoi creation myth. She'd love to hear the speaker's voice, even though that would make the work go slower, but she hasn't been sent a tape. She has to rely on the anthropologist's murky transcript. The earth began in fire, the story goes. She can't tell yet how the fire began. Out of the conflagration from nowhere came an enormous mound of ashes, and out of the ashes plants began to grow, as they do on landscapes scorched by volcanoes. Trees sprouted, and insects and worms crawled out of the ashes. As best as she can tell, everything else came about through some sort of evolution. The story suggests—again she's not quite sure—that the world will end as it began, in a conflagration. And that this constant cycle, from fire to fire, is unending, with each new universe more precarious than the last, as if the materials are exhausting themselves with each round of flames. A disheartening prospect, but she's enjoying the work. Looking forward to getting to her office haven.

Those who walk across the Brooklyn Bridge in the morning do it out of love. Love for the bridge and the skyline and the water. So there's a nice camaraderie among the walkers. Today she was early when she started out, because Jack didn't have time to make her late. The bookman made her late. Jack had a meeting, he didn't say where. Something he needed to wear a suit for. She appraised the men striding past and fixed on one, a black man in a tan suit, carrying an attaché case. Just speculating, idling away the walk. . . . Liking him. Liking the way the breeze rippled her skirt against her legs. Wondering if he noticed her too. . . .

So, adrift in her erotic fantasies, she didn't see it happen, although she's seen it so many times since that it feels like she saw it. People around her screamed, so she looked where they were looking, at a huge marigold bursting open in the sky, across the river, flinging petals into the blue. Everyone stood frozen on the bridge, as in a game of statues, gasping statues. Then, like an army suddenly given the order to retreat, they wheeled around and ran in the other direction, back to Brooklyn, back across the bridge and down the stairs. To put the river between them and the bloom of fire.

She felt stuck in place while people rushed past her. She didn't want to go home. There was nothing at home. She headed for the Promenade, in the running crowd. By the time she got there, another grisly flower had burst open in the sky. The people with cell phones and Walkmans told the others what the radio and TV were saying. It was nothing comprehensible. Rumors, conjectures, scraps about planes, flight numbers, nothing compared to what was happening in the sky.

All at once, as she stood gazing across the river, she couldn't tell for how long, the blooms were extinguished, replaced by a pillar of smoke. An instant later came a sound like nothing she could place, more muffled than thunder and more alive, almost like the roar of a great herd of beasts, but muted, far in the distance. As the sound subsided, the pillar of smoke began surging across the river, walling the skyline, making it seem there was nothing behind the wall.

The bookman!

If he found the subway . . . If he found the subway right away and got on, he could be underneath the pillar of smoke. Or he might be out by now. If he dawdled or walked farther astray, was that better or worse? Maybe he was so slow or befuddled that the subways stopped before he tried to board. He was a slow walker. So what had she effected by not chasing him? Good or bad? What if?

After the pillar of smoke came a hurricane of paper. The sky rained paper, and later some of the papers would be picked up as relics and sorted out—office memos, bills, jottings, computer printouts, resumes, stock reports, the daily menu of corporate life mingling with private scrawled hieroglyphics—while other papers would be left lying in the ash to devolve back to pulp under trampling feet and the wheels of sanitation trucks. Any other day, the papers would have been a treasure trove for Renata, with her collections of linguistic artifacts, of demotic speech, examples of brain and tongue parting company. But not today. Not hurricane day.

People were in motion all around her but she remained, rubbing her smarting eyes, shielding her head from the gale, trying to see past the smoke. They were all coughing, covering their faces with hankies and scarves and tissues. Some people bent to pick up bits of paper as they ran, the way people do peculiar things in a catastrophe. Renata bent down too. Then stood up, for it felt too stupid, as stupid as trying to see through a pillar of smoke. Then bent down again, an impulse she would never fathom, to riffle through the papers gathered at the edge of a grilled sewer lid coated with ash. Among the papers, as if she had been hunting for it, she found the twenty-dollar bill.

Whatever is happening, she thought, whether it's the end of the world or simply the end of the city, it's not right to profit from it. What kind of people would want to profit from this? Well, maybe some. Later, indeed, would come the profiteers. Still, the twenty-dollar bill was too powerful to resist. Not out of greed; she's not greedy. She had the absurd notion that it might be the same twenty dollars that went missing when she was eleven years old, causing the estrangement from her now-dead twin sister and lasting grief. Changing the course of her life.

She is thirty-four. The chances that this is the same bill lost more than twenty years ago, come back to her, are nil. She knows that. But she picks it up and brushes it off against her flowered summer skirt—useless; the skirt, like the bill, is covered with ash—and stuffs it into her purse. Then joins the crowd and goes home, for surely there would be no work at the library today, if ever again. All the while, a thought nags at her, only it's not even a thought, more of a flicker, a wisp, a feather just past her range of vision. She wants it and doesn't want it. She heads toward her Spartan apartment, where she'll throw her clothes in the garbage—her favorite skirt!—and stand under the shower to rinse off the ash that has bleached her black hair white, and only after that, turn on the television like everyone else.

Meanwhile she walks as fast as she can. Instead of the elusive flicker, something she and Linda laughed at during lunch comes to mind, a question Linda was asked during her last stint as the Answer Lady. Earthquake boxes. Renata didn't know what they were. "In San Francisco and other earthquake areas," Linda said, "people are advised to keep a box near their bed with anything they might need to take with them in an earthquake. You know, like a toothbrush, medication, address book, extra pair of glasses, whatever, for some types maybe their Palm Pilots and cells. Aren't you glad you don't live there?" She's ashamed to be thinking of it now; it's wrong to be remembering laughter. The other thing, the flicker, the feather, is more important, but she's reluctant to grasp it.

Once she reaches her apartment, she gazes out the window at the smoke. Everything else is still there, river, sky, a few boats. She puts the bill under a blue vase on the square oak dining-room table, sturdier than her other things, a table she took from her childhood home after her family broke apart and her mother relinquished memory, which is why Renata wound up with the table, to remember the family dinners of childhood before all those things happened that were not supposed to happen to happy families. The vase sits next to a pile of magazines and the folder of clippings, and the twenty dollars will remain under it for some time. It is not money to be spent.

Only as she stands under the running water does the thought finally cohere and force itself on her. At which point she turns off the water and sits down on the edge of the tub digging her teeth into a towel. A nine-thirty meeting, Jack said. But where? Where? He works near there, under that stretch of ravaged sky. She knew it, she knew it, it's no good to get close, to love people. Maybe she doesn't love him if she hasn't worried about him till now. Too busy feeling guilty about the bookman?

Now the flicker is a bright light, blinding. Jack. Mad Mom. They're the only ones left. But however many times she tries, the phones aren't working. They're experiencing technical difficulties. Already they have words for it.

Even the grief-stricken can't sit on the edge of the tub all day. She needs to put some clothes on, first of all. It's wise to be dressed in an emergency, utilitarian clothes, jeans, T-shirt, sneakers, good for running. She dresses in the living room, in front of the TV. Watching the thing happen over and over feels ghoulish. Even so, she tapes it, more ghoulish still. But if Jack is still alive he'll want to see. He's the sort who'll definitely want to see and hear everything. She's known that since their very first, no, their second night together, when she was finally willing to hear who he really was.

Three

He came over, that snowy night in January, out of curiosity: to see her natural habitat, smaller and less cozy than his own. Renata lived in a fourth-floor walk-up in a brownstone, sparsely furnished but closer to the river. A large patch of river and skyline was visible from the bedroom window, and at night the lights made an abstract follow-the-dots pattern against the dark sky. First thing, Jack admired the panels of Chinese calligraphy on the living-room walls.

"Do you know what they mean?"

"Yes."

"Well, what? This, for instance." He pointed to one with a drawing of a bleak landscape of pines encircling a field under a wan moon.

"That's part of a letter from the late fifteenth century. 'For several tens of days my hands and feet have been numb. I get up in the middle of every night and sit. The fortune-teller says it will be around the Great Snow before the illness can be pacified. In Pao-an

Circuit, people have been killed in broad daylight. . . . Friends are all scattered.' And more of the same. He was a complainer."

"There's no personal symbolism, I hope. You're not numb, are you? Do you get up in the middle of the night and sit?"

"Well, I didn't last night, that's for sure."

He pointed to another. "And this?"

"'Mulberry fields and green oceans interchange in an instant. Where once were the golden stairs, the halls of white marble, we now see only the green pines remaining.'"

He liked that. He kissed her as if she'd made it up.

"But you could say they mean anything and I wouldn't know the difference," he said. "You could make anything up."

"I could. And you're not sure you trust me?"

"I'm not too trusting, no."

Pamela's doing. He was a slow healer. He might never get past her. Meanwhile his hands were under Renata's shirt. "Are you hungry?" she asked. "Do you want some dinner?"

"You do dinners?"

"I'll throw something together. Come in the kitchen with me." The calligraphy was an easy test. Other men had liked it too, the ones with a smattering of taste. The kitchen was a greater challenge.

"Jesus, what is all this stuff? 'There are always going to be people who find it necessary in one form or another,'" he read, "'to find a way of being able to try to gain an advantage by virtue of doing something like this.' Like, no shit."

She set some water to boil and got out a box of spaghetti. She started washing lettuce for a salad. "I collect bits of language. Bad language. You know, misused. Socrates said that false language is evil and infects the soul with evil."

"You don't say."

"It's kind of an obsession." Language mutilated and bent out of shape. *Prashmensti,* in Bliondan. Wrong words. Language used to obfuscate and lie, language used mindlessly, in ignorance, language perverted to anti-language. . . .

"Each pre-fab phrase is a means of delay, because he doesn't want to say anything. It becomes a habit. 'Find it necessary.' 'Being able to try.' 'By virtue of.' It's a kind of disease, that sort of talk." *Prashmenosi,* willful deceit. *Prashmenala,* filling space. *Prashmenilis,* stupidity. . . .

Jack was looking at her strangely. This wasn't a habit you could justify to a stranger. She concentrated on the salad. Tomatoes. Scallions.

"I see you put up a few from that museum show. Some Comfort Gained from the Acceptance of the Inherent Lies in Everything. I remember that. 'Can we find comfort in looking at these cross sections of cows?' I sure didn't. 'And does this suggest that, in a larger sense, our other ways of understanding the world around us are arbitrary and absurd?'"

"Don't make me laugh, not when I'm close to a pot of boiling water."

"Can I do anything?"

"No, we're not intimate enough to cook together. Just keep me company."

"Can we find comfort in lies? Of course not." He came very close, which wasn't hard to do in that tiny kitchen.

"Look, I'll drop the strainer if you keep that up. Can we eat first?"

She turned on only a low lamp in the bedroom.

"It's funny I haven't seen you around the neighborhood." He pulled her over on top of him.

"Maybe we have seen each other and just didn't notice."

"I would have noticed you," Jack said. "You're unique."

She wasn't unique, she thought as she shifted her weight to accommodate him. She was a twin. He was curious; some time soon he'd be asking about her past, her family. She'd have to be evasive, and everything would turn sour. Sometimes there is comfort to be found in lies. She would keep silent as long as she could, to make this feeling last. Not that she expected much from it beyond the pleasure of the moment. Ever since she'd lost Claudia, she hadn't wanted to be close to anyone else. Not what passed for closeness, what she saw around her. Not after what she had known closeness to mean.

She fell asleep underneath him, and when she woke, the bedroom light was on and he was sitting up, reading the wall near the bed, the Outrage wall. There were several clippings about the Joel Steinberg and Hedda Nussbaum case—the couple who left their adopted and abused child to die on the floor, choking on water. He'd filled her with water because water was healthy, he claimed. There was a clipping about a four-year-old who'd been kept in a cage for his entire life. There were clippings about children shaken to death or found starving in closets. Not all the stories were quite so brutal. "Couple in Jersey Are Accused of Trying to Trade in Their Baby for Used Sports Car." The car was a 1999 Toyota station wagon valued at $9,500. The car dealer called the police after the couple approached him about the trade, and they were waiting at the scene to make their arrest. The charges were endangering the welfare of a child and giving a child for illegal adoption. At first the car dealer considered agreeing to the trade because as a boy he had lost a brother in a fire. But then he changed his mind. "How could this kid cope with life knowing he was traded for a car?"

Jack turned around. "What is it? Did you have a child and lose it?"

"No," she said. "I've never had a baby."

"Why, then?"

She shook her head and tried to lure him back.

"You sleep every night surrounded by this stuff?"

"I sleep fine. How about some ice cream? I have a weakness for ice cream. Do you like butter pecan?"

They sat up cross-legged in bed, knee to knee—Renata's apartment, unlike Jack's, was overheated—and ate bowls of butter pecan ice cream.

"The way you feel about language," he said, "I feel about bureaucracy."

Renata was contented, eating the ice cream and waiting for more love, but now it was coming, the biography part. He ran a social services agency in downtown Manhattan. Not a government agency but his very own. No forms to fill out, no red tape. "I get people around the red tape."

"A social worker?"

"I don't have a degree. But I know my way around. I know everyone," he said, smiling. "I can get anyone to do anything."

"Your charm?"

"No. My focus. You'd be amazed how simple things can be if you skip the official routines. Just go to the right people, ask one small thing for one person at a time, and things get done, little by little."

"An anarchist."

"You could say that, but I wouldn't. I have no ideology. People turn up with nowhere to sleep and I find them a room. They're sick, I find doctors. They're hungry, I find food and food stamps. They need to learn English, I find tutors. Jobs are harder, but I try. It's all out there if you know where to look. The city is too bogged down in paperwork or computer files. It doesn't work. My place works."

"You must have a big staff."

"Only a few people. But we're all hands on. You take care of each thing as soon as it comes up. You don't put anything off. One thing at a time, start to finish. And fast."

"Hands on," she echoed, and put her hands on him. "Where do you get the money for all this?"

"Foundation grants. And, uh, I have my own small foundation."

"Money? I'd never have pegged you as having money."

"Yeah, it's embarrassing. My father's in real estate in Santa Fe. So I use it the way I like."

"A regular saint." In bed with a fucking saint, she thought. My first.

"I'm good," he agreed. "I'm not embarrassed by that."

"If it's so simple, why doesn't the government do it the way you do?"

"The first business of government is to perpetuate itself. Taking care of people is far down on the list."

"Did you ever think of running for office?"

"Never. If you run for office pretty soon all you care about is getting reelected. Anyhow, I like doing things my way. At my office I can be a benevolent dictator. Look where elections have gotten us. This last election? They hijacked the system. It'll happen again, too. No, you can't look to government for anything."

"Private money," she said. "Well, what about people who want to do good but don't have the money and need to earn a living? What are they supposed to do?"

He smiled. "Let them come and work for me."

"There's some deep flaw in all this."

"In theory, yes. But in practice it works, because I do it right. That's the only way anything ever works, if someone does it right."

"Did you ever hear of a guy called Franco Donati?"

"No, who's he?"

"He did something right, the way you'd like, I think, but he had no money, so in the end it didn't work." She told him about Franco Donati, a thirty-two-year-old Italian photographer whose story was in her folder. "Chronicling the Homeless, A Photographer Meets Their Fate." Franco Donati came to New York City to work on a book of photographs documenting homeless people, but not in the usual dreary, generic guise, hunched and ragged on the sidewalk beside an overflowing shopping cart. He shot them in portrait-photography style, against a blank canvas, in poses that showed each sitter's distinctiveness. In the sample photo in the paper, an old, white-bearded man reclines on the ground, draped in biblical-style robes; his outstretched arm, holding a staff, forms a triangle against the blank upper center. He resembles a figure from the Sistine ceiling. The newspaper head shot of Franco showed a mustached young man with a bright smile and classic Latin sexiness, though Renata knew better than to mention this. He was definitely on to something, she said. He'd even won a Guggenheim Fellowship for $35,000. But the publisher who'd strung him along for many months finally decided not to publish his book. By that time, Franco Donati had become so immersed in his subject that, according to the article, "he gave up other work assignments, maybe even a bit of common sense." Meaning he used up all his money and couldn't make his rent. He ended up, in the words of the reporter, "a homeless man . . . with a cell phone."

"And then what happened to him?" Jack asked. "Is he still out there?"

"He moved back to Padua to live with his father."

"He needed a patron. He needed one rich person who believed in him."

No. Jack didn't get the point of the story. Franco Donati was no simple do-gooder. Franco Donati was a visionary who was transformed. He got so close to his vision that he became his material.

"Now we know a little something about each other," Jack said after they made love.

"Mm."

"Or you know a little something about me. I still don't know much about you. Except your obsessions. But a person can't be made up only of obsessions." He waited. "Or can they?"

She knew how to handle this moment, when it came. It was a pity to have to "handle" anything with Jack—she liked him too much. But since there was no other way, she gave him a few facts, nothing that wasn't technically true. She'd learned how to evade without ever uttering an untruth. Her skill with languages helped, but really, it didn't take much skill: you simply chose your words with the utmost care, like politicians. Their specialty was convolution and distraction; Renata's was omission, a form of minimalist art. She told him she grew up in a suburb across the river. She told him her mother was not well and lived in a halfway house north of the city, where she visited her as often as she could. She told him her father was killed seventeen years ago in an auto accident. The police records would add that he'd been at the wheel in a state of extreme intoxication. Blind drunk, in plain speech. But she didn't want to describe her father as an alcoholic; he wasn't, not until the last year of his life. She told him about her work in the library—nothing to hide there. And because she didn't want to have this conversation again, because she wanted to get this ritual telling done and be with him—for however long it lasted—as if nothing had ever happened to her before they met, she told him she'd had a twin sister.

"Had?" He shifted the pillows so he could face her. "What happened?"

"She died."

"Oh, Renata." He drew her closer. "Was she the child . . . ? Was it like one of those stories on the wall?"

"No. Not like that."

"What happened? How old was she?"

"It was a long time ago. We were sixteen."

"So now she'd be . . . ?"

"Ah, so you want to know how old I am? She would be thirty-four."

"That's all?"

"Why, do I look so old?"

"No. God, women's vanity. Only you seem older. You sound older. Was she sick?"

"She drowned. Can we stop now?"

In a little while he was sleeping. She watched him, this man she hadn't even known two days ago who now lay naked and trusting in her arms, and thought of all she hadn't told him, or anyone. She gave herself up to past misery, to *bakiranima.*

It was an ordinary school night. They sat on Claudia's bed doing trigonometry—Renata's worst subject, but Claudia had a friend who gave her the answers. Fox lay dozing on the floor, breathing hoarsely. All at once Claudia leaned back against the wall and drew her knees up to her chin. "I'm pregnant."

"You're what?" Renata said.

"You heard me."

"Are you sure?" The words were shocking enough, but even more shocking was Claudia's speaking them aloud. Since the lost twenty dollars, five years ago, they hadn't told secrets.

"Stop being dumb," she said. "I'm sure."

"How?"

"God almighty, Renata."

"You know what I mean. Who?"

She was raped, she said. Then amended—well, sort of—and spun out a story about going in to the city with two girlfriends a couple of months ago. They met some guys in a bar, ended up in a dorm room, drank too much. . . . She didn't want it to happen but it happened anyway.

Renata didn't believe her. Not that the story was impossible; it must happen all the time. And for all she knew Claudia might be having such adventures. Sometimes she said she was sleeping over at a friend's. Sometimes she went out late at night, with the excuse of walking Fox. She might have been going anywhere. Still, Renata knew her well enough to recognize a lie. What stunned her most was that she hadn't noticed a thing. The missed periods, extra weight, morning nausea? Renata was no expert on pregnancy but she knew a few things. There must have been signs. She'd missed them.

"Have you told *them*?" Code word for their parents.

"No."

"I don't believe you. About the rape, I mean. You just don't want to say who."

"Why don't you believe me? Because I didn't come home bleeding with my clothes ripped off? It's not always like that."

There were things Renata wanted to ask but no longer could. It was as if a screen hung between them and Claudia raised and lowered it at will. Was it your first time? What is it like? What's it like now, with something growing inside you? What do you feel that I don't feel? That was the crucial question. And what do you know that I don't?

Instead, words she never expected came out. "Not true," she said in their old language, the first time she'd felt the words on her tongue in years. She shuddered, afraid Claudia would mock.

She didn't mock. "True," she answered back, and Renata felt a thrill of victory. She'd spoken the language.

The air lightened, as if all at once they were younger and light-hearted. "Not true." They fell into an infantile taunting match. True. Not true. True. Until they began giggling as they used to years ago. Fox woke up and, hearing the commotion, leaped up between them and yelped in his own tongue, while they nudged him back and forth between them as in the old days. Renata was the first to stop. "This isn't really funny. What are you going to do? You'll have to get an abortion. Won't you?"

"I don't know." She tilted her head and frowned. "I don't care what happens anymore."

"Claudia! This is unreal. What's with you?"

"I can just . . . be pregnant. Then I wouldn't have to go to school."

"That's crazy. You can't have a baby. We'll figure something out."

"I'm afraid."

"They use anesthesia. It'll be okay." They stared at each other for a long moment. "What does it feel like?"

"Nothing, mostly. Sometimes sort of gross. Let's do the trig."

"It's not going to go away, you know."

"I do a lot of exercise. Maybe it will."

"Sure, or maybe you want to try a wire hanger." This Renata said in plain English. This was not for their childish language. "You have to tell them."

"Soon. And don't you tell. Just keep your mouth shut, okay?"

"Oh, you want *me* to keep your secret? You don't have any right to ask, after what you did. Why did you take the money?"

She couldn't deny it, not now when they were speaking truth. "You really don't know? To be separate. To get away from you. I couldn't take it anymore. You were always . . . *there.* You wouldn't let me be a person on my own. I used to envy everyone else, the ones who were separate. Everything I felt or did, you felt or did. It was creepy. It was like I had nothing of my own." The dog nestled on her lap and she stroked him.

"I never felt that way."

"I know," Claudia snapped. "Don't I know it."

"It was so mean. Couldn't you find some other way?"

"So I'm mean, okay. Maybe that's how I'm not like you. Maybe that was the only way I could be different. I'm not even sorry. Sorry, but I'm not sorry."

"You're awful."

"So what?"

"So nothing. Where'd you put it?" Renata asked.

"What does it matter? You want it now?"

"I was just wondering."

"You see, you want to know everything I do."

"Oh, go ahead and have your stupid baby. I don't care. You'll make them miserable, you know that. But you don't give a fuck, do you?"

Claudia didn't tell their parents until three weeks later—too late for an abortion, the doctor said. While Grace sat crying in the living room, Claudia came upstairs and undressed and showed Renata her stomach, which was starting to look round and puffed. "Show me yours," she said, so Renata did.

"You see? Now we're really different." Claudia was triumphant.

They were close again. Not especially loving, just close. Their words were bare, crude translations of what they felt. That was what Renata wanted, what she had missed. Claudia could be nasty, but there were times when she cried in Renata's arms. And Renata was satisfied. Her sister needed her after all. The dreadful solitude was over, like a prison sentence she'd served. She was released. Claudia got bigger and moved more slowly. She stopped going to school, toward the end, and Renata had to bring home the assignments.

Their Uncle Peter volunteered to arrange for the adoption: a nice couple he knew in the city, he said, young, longing to have a baby, but they couldn't. Leave it simple, he said, no papers, no lawyers, no waiting or red tape. It was much better that way. Dan went into town to meet them. Grace and Claudia didn't want to go and Renata wasn't asked. He came home satisfied. The neighborhood was slightly run down, he reported, but the apartment, on the upper West Side, was clean and neat. They seemed responsible. They had jobs; they showed him paycheck stubs. And that was that. Soon it would all be in the past.

In the hospital, Renata had one look at the baby in the nursery: they were all pretty much the same, lined up in their cribs. Only later did she begin thinking about the child given away so cavalierly, handed over like a package in the hospital parking lot. No lawyers, no red tape, keep it simple. Only later, when her mother sent her to visit every month to see how the child was doing. Only later, when she started calling her by her name—Gianna, the name Grace chose; when she grasped that Gianna was as real as she herself was, as Claudia had been, not merely the product of a mistake, something to be disposed of.

When Claudia came home from the hospital, opened the door of their room, and flung her backpack on the bed, Renata hugged her tight. They both cried. She was truly back now, Renata thought. They could start fresh.

The doctor promised she'd have her figure back in a couple of weeks, Claudia said. Ten days later, she was lost again. *Tanfendi-noude.* Lost for good.

Four

The President's face appeared on the screen from an undisclosed location. He was going to "hunt down those folks who committed this act." Renata pulled up her jeans. He thanked "all the folks who have been fighting hard to rescue our fellow citizens." She tugged the shirt over her head and tried calling Jack again, but got the message about technical difficulties. She tried calling her mother.

The President said, "Freedom itself was attacked this morning by a faceless coward. Freedom will be defended. Make no mistake, the United States will hunt down and punish those responsible for these cowardly acts." There was no point trying to find comfort or enlightenment in the words. It was a public moment, that was all; the occasion required that his mouth move and English syllables emerge.

She dialed Jack. Dialed her mother.

"The resolve of our great nation is being tested. But make no mistake: we will show the world that we can pass the test."

Again she tried Jack. Her mother. Her hand felt dusty when she replaced the phone; a fine film covered everything, like a light sprinkling of talcum powder.

"I want to reassure the American people that the full resources of the federal government . . . " The alternative to his words, turning the set off, was impossible. A shred of useful information might arrive. And who could resist the pictures of the burning, the running, the crushed vehicles and the concrete beams? Already barely an hour in the past, it was becoming theatrical; it was irresistible.

On the eighth try she reached Grace.

"I'm fine. What's the trouble?"

"Do you have the TV on, Mom? Don't you know what's going on?"

"Oh, that. Yes, it's terrible. But it's not anywhere near where you work, is it?"

"Mom, thousands of people were incinerated. The towers crumbled. Didn't you see?"

"I saw. What a thing to happen. But up here, you know, it doesn't really touch us. It's quiet here in the country." Westchester, she meant. Her country. Unlike Franco Donati, the photographer of the homeless, the man who became his material, Grace wanted to be as distant as possible from the scenes that greeted her eyes.

"Mom, remember that book about the cave people Claudia and I used to read? The one we acted out?"

"You know I can't remember much, Renata."

"You don't? I used to think it would be so terrible to live in cave times, with all the dangers, and you and Dad laughed?"

"I don't remember."

"I can't reach Jack. I don't know where he is. He could be dead." The oblivious made ideal listeners—you could say anything.

"He's probably fine. That's your new boyfriend? The one who's divorced?"

"He works right near there. Sometimes he has appointments in the towers. I don't know what to do. What should I do? The phones here aren't working. It took me eight tries to reach you."

"He'll turn up. Are you calling from work?"

"There's no work today, Mom. The city is covered with smoke. Nothing is running."

"Tsk," Grace clucked. "And the air is so polluted to begin with."

Sometimes Renata tried to shock her out of her oblivion by reminding her of everything she wanted to forget, but today she didn't make the effort.

"Okay, I'll call you later, Mom."

Up From the Caves, the book was called, and she still kept it on a shelf in her bedroom. When she and Claudia were eight or nine they were entranced by it; they read it so many times that they knew it by heart.

"The early cave man and his family led a hard life. Their home was a dark, cold, stony place, with none of the comforts we enjoy today. In winter, when night fell early, there were no lamps to read by, no TV or tapes to pass the time. Luckily the cave people had fire. Families would sit huddled around the hearth dug into the cave floor, watching the eerie shadows cast by the flames flickering on the stone walls."

Renata and Claudia turned out the lights in the basement and shone their pocket flashlights on the wall to make eerie shadows. But all they saw in the beams of light were the beige mesh curtains at the high window, the Bruce Springsteen poster taped to the wall, and an enlarged photo of Grace and Dan, impossibly young, not yet parents, jauntily dressed in white shorts and shirts, standing on the deck of a boat and holding between them an enormous fish. Nothing to inspire any fear.

When they first began to play their cave games, Claudia brought down a box of kitchen matches and lit them one by one, waving them in the air to create eerie shadows, but their father, suspicious of the dark and silence, came down and found them. He snatched the matches away and said if they ever did that again he wouldn't let them share a room. That was enough to stop them. Being separated would be more eerie than shadows on a wall could ever be.

The President was back. "This will be a monumental struggle of good versus evil. . . . It's not a war against the United States, it's a war against civilization."

The book featured a cave family: Bodo and Zuna, their son Jiddi and infant daughter Samu. They had only "rudimentary language," it said. How could they have names, then, if they barely had language, Renata asked. Her father couldn't answer.

Bodo and Zuna were stocky but gracefully built. The boy, Jiddi, was lean and bony, and Samu was chubby and ruddy in her little leopard bunting. Except for their faces—low-browed, deeply ridged over the eyes, wide-mouthed—and their animal skins, they might have been a TV sitcom family on a camping trip, the Flintstones spruced up and slightly hairier. The illustrations showed them bathing in a stream, sitting around the fire eating hunks of charred meat skewed on sticks like the shish kebab in the Middle Eastern fast-food place in the mall, and curled up at night with other families nearby, each in its own sleeping area, as in a Red Cross shelter. Renata's favorite picture showed Zuna kneeling at the fire, cradling Samu in her arms as though she were about to sing a lullaby, which of course she couldn't do without language. Maybe she crooned wordlessly.

The book was a gift from their Uncle Peter's new girlfriend, Cindy. Peter had met her in Mexico and two weeks later brought her to meet the family. Later on, Grace, who was always skeptical about Cindy, used to say Peter "found" her, not "met" her, in Acapulco, as if she were some rare, gaudy shell he picked up on the beach and tucked in his suitcase. Despite Cindy's good intentions, the book was far too advanced for six-year-olds—crammed with information, as such books always are: the Neanderthals' tools, habits, burial rituals, and more.

The girls must have accepted her gift apathetically, for Cindy shook her head, making her fluffy curls bounce and her long copper earrings sway. "Jeez," she said, "I guess maybe it's not the right thing. I mean, I don't know many kids and Peter said they were smart for their age. I could return it and get something else."

"Not at all." Dan was always quick to allay discomfort. "They'll love it. They just have to grow into it. I'll read it to them until they can read it for themselves. Girls, say thank you."

He was right. They grew into it. Two years later they were stomping around the basement on all fours, zooming through millennia in their reenactment of humanity's ascent from the apes. That first illustration showed a single file of shaggy creatures, becoming successively more erect and less hairy. At the head of the line stood Cro-Magnon man. With his finely-cut features, proud stance, and full brown beard flecked with gray, Cro-Magnon man looked remarkably like Mr. Killian, who drove the school bus.

As for the benighted cave family, the book's tone was distinctly patronizing. It's only human to want to feel superior to someone, after all. But multiculturalism, just coming into fashion, left few groups one might scorn. If not Neanderthals, who else? "They had no washing machines or dishwashers, no toasters or blenders. They had no furnaces for cold weather, no air-conditioning for summer. They had no planes or trains or cars. Anywhere they needed to go, they went on foot."

"Where would they need to go?" Claudia said. "The mall?"

Each day, Bodo and Jiddi went off hunting, hoisting long spears. "Their diet was not varied like ours. They hunted reindeer, wild boar, buffalo, leopards, and hyenas to bring home to their families. The women foraged for seeds, nuts, and berries."

"Would you like bison for dinner tonight, dear?" Claudia asked, wearing a towel arranged to resemble a loincloth. "Or boar? How about a nice little, um, otter? I could pass by the stream and pick one up on my way home."

"I was thinking of something light," Renata replied. "Like bunny or squirrel." She was the cave wife; her towel covered her chest. "With a seed and berry salad."

"Often they trapped their prey in pits disguised by leaves, or forced whole herds off cliffs." The illustration showed chunky men in loincloths at the top of a high cliff. Using thick stripped branches, they prodded a herd of bison down into the ravine far below. One large horned creature fell through the air upside down, its face poignant with shock. In the ravine, more hairy hunters waited to spear the fallen beasts.

"The hunters headed home in the dusk, carrying their prey, fearful of what might lurk nearby. The land was mostly open plains and prairie, where wild beasts roamed freely. Often they had to find their way home by the stars."

"Turn right at Sirius, then left at Cassiopeia." The girls knew the names of all the stars from *The Book of the Night*, a gift from their father. "Two blocks from Orion." They staggered through the pitch-dark basement, their eyes fixed on the ceiling, where their mother had pasted glowing stars in patterns she hoped corresponded to the constellations. Grace had used *The Book of the Night* as a guide, keeping it open on the shelf of the tall ladder she perched on. She was a girlish, whimsical mother; she undertook odd projects in sputters of enthusiasm.

"Besides the struggle for food, shelter, and clothing, there was illness. There were no doctors or hospitals, no corner drugstores. Any minor illness could turn serious. Neanderthals didn't live nearly as long as we do. Most died before the age of fifty. The less hardy babies might not live past infancy."

"Wa, wa, I'm dying. Help me," wailed Claudia. But mostly the cave people communicated by grunts, sighs, and moans. Tears? The babies would cry, like all babies, but what about the grown-ups? They'd cry when their children died in infancy, Renata imagined. But they wouldn't cry from hunger or cold since those were the pervasive conditions, and even at nine she understood that people don't cry, or at some point they stop crying, over given conditions. She wasn't sure grown-ups cried anyhow. She'd never seen one do it.

"I do believe that child is breathing her last," Renata said mournfully. "If only we had a doctor or hospital, like they'll have in more advanced times."

Claudia choked, gagged, let out a long, gargling rattle, and collapsed on the floor. Renata rocked the corpse in her arms. "Uh, uh, uh," she grunted. When the death throes were over, she said, "Well, that's one less mouth to feed."

Outsiders were a constant threat: one picture showed Bodo and his mates advancing with rocks and spears against a bunch of strangers who'd wandered into their territory. The book didn't say what would be done with the spoils of battle.

"They'll eat them," said Claudia. "What else?"

Renata gasped in shock.

After Claudia fell asleep in the other bed, Renata lay awake with her sister's steady breaths lulling her through her fantasies.

She liked to scare herself. She liked the clutch of fear, the verge of disaster, and there could be no real danger with Claudia six feet away. Renata joined the cave family. One evening, when Zuna sent her out to gather fallen branches for the fire, she got caught on the prairie in a snowstorm and had to find her way home in the dark, startled by every crackle underfoot, mesmerized by a whiteness so vast it blocked out the stars. She came down with a fever and tossed on her bed of skins, while all Zuna could offer in relief was water heated over the fire, with a fistful of bitter herbs thrown in. In her delirium she cringed at the shadows on the wall, certain they must be a lion prowling at the mouth of the cave. She longed to huddle close to Zuna and have her fears eased. But how could she, without words? If there were words at all, they were words for food and sleep, bear and rock. No words to express fear or ease it, especially fear of what might not exist—no words for fantasies. What would she be without words, only fears and feelings? Could she have thoughts? Could she even think "lion at the mouth of the cave?" It might be an image in her head, a series of images like a movie: the lion rushing in, splitting the darkness, bounding over to dig his teeth into the flesh of her thigh. . . .

The whole cave family caught Renata's illness and died. She had to bury them with elaborate rituals, with food and tools, as if they were setting off on a journey. She was left on her own to join the men in their hunts, chasing the bison off the cliffs, then tearing the dripping meat from the bone and stuffing it into her mouth before the vultures swooped.

When at last she had made herself thoroughly terrified, she would stop to breathe, and listen to Claudia breathe.

The most terrifying thing about her cave life was living it without her sister. And yet she didn't take Claudia along on her fantasies; she wasn't sure why. Maybe she wanted to go someplace alone, feel herself as separate, the greatest thrill and greatest danger of all.

Renata took firmly to heart the book's plain message: Aren't we lucky to be living now and not then? To live in houses, not caves, to wear sweaters and not skins, to eat steak grilled on the backyard hibachi instead of raw hyena? She didn't care about the lack of TVs and telephones; what she brooded over was forever living in peril. Imagine being unable to step outside and walk freely, carelessly, feeling the sun on her skin and catching the river's gleam in the distance. Life must have felt like a mysterious sentence of one pain after another. Happiness, if there was happiness, would be a rare moment of grace, maybe tinged with portent. Sometimes, padding down to the kitchen at night for a dish of ice cream, glimpsing her parents watching TV in the dim living room, she'd feel a surge of gratitude that she hadn't been born in cave times. She managed gratitude even when bad things happened—when she sliced open her knee on a piece of broken glass in the driveway and had to go to the Emergency Room for stitches. In cave days her leg might have blackened and withered. Of course in cave days there wouldn't have been glass or a driveway. Still, everything was better now. Compared to cave days, the small jolts that came her way were nothing.

Strange, she thinks now, how benign the cave people were, at least in the book. Bodo and Zuna never quarreled about doling out the food or about who would sleep closest to the fire. Zuna never sulked when Bodo failed to bring home the dinner; Bodo never raged if Zuna accidentally let the meat fall into the ashes. They never dashed their children against the stone walls of the cave when they cried too loud or too long, never crept on top of them under the animal skins for a bit of variety. What peril there was came from outside. Perhaps the author thought the other kind of peril would make too threatening a story for children.

Up from the Caves rolled to a sonorous close: "Think of the vast changes over thousands of centuries as the human race progressed from cave times to our own. Think of man's striving to order Nature for his own well-being. Above all, man's ability to invent tools to meet his needs is the trait that enabled him to reach his present level of civilization."

Those words made Renata and Claudia giggle. Girls—women too—always laugh at pomposity. Then Renata grew up and moved through her life, and she did think.

Suppose Bodo and Zuna really had no dark side, she thinks. Suppose they were as impossibly goodhearted as the book implied, keeping their children alive through illness and danger, living in harmony with their neighbors, their only aggression reserved for predators. It must have been because the powerful darkness of the caves, of their lives, sucked out their individual darknesses and absorbed them, leaving them innocent and light and buoyant. If that was so, then our passage up from the caves and into the light would return our darkness to us. As the light struggled to grow and spread, it left the darkness with no place to retreat. It got compressed in the air and we breathed it in. We accumulated darkness within.

"If Bodo and Zuna were magically to return and visit a large modern city like New York or Chicago or Pittsburgh, they might think themselves in a different world. They might not even recognize us as beings like themselves."

Maybe not, Renata thinks. Maybe they wouldn't be so shocked at a city where homeless people live in underground tunnels or in large cardboard boxes and warm themselves around fires in wastebaskets. They might not recognize the boxes that once held refrigerators or washing machines, but they would surely recognize the pervasive conditions of human life, the conditions you stop crying about eventually.

But today, yes. They'd be startled if they magically happened to return on the day paper rained from the sky. They wouldn't comprehend, any more than the rest of us did, the pair of high buildings swaying faintly like giant stalks, then bursting into bloom. They'd stand watching in bewilderment, as Renata and her neighbors stood across the river, watching the huge shudder, the withering into smoke and ash—great dandelions gone to seed. Something blew on them, hard, and the gray clouds scattered their seeds over the city.

"In the same way," the book ended, "thousands of years from now, who knows what dramatic changes we ourselves might find? We, too, might not recognize human life or the earth as we know it."

Well, all such speculation is moot. As she learned later in school, Bodo and Zuna were not our ancestors. The Neanderthals were an evolutionary dead end. Our ancestor, Cro-Magnon man, was another species entirely. Bodo and Zuna's kind died out; no one knows exactly why.

On the TV screen the President was declaring for the tenth time that he would find the folks who did this and smoke them out of their caves. Granted, he had not the gift of gab; vocabulary and syntax did not leap at his command. Renata tried to make allowances: there were no proper words. Bliondan had a much richer spectrum of words for shock: five degrees, ranging from mild dismay, *dradosk,* through stronger and stronger stages—*dradoska, dradosken, dradoskona,* to ineffable shock, *dradoskis,* which was first used to describe the response to a solar eclipse centuries ago. But even if the President were fluent in Bliondan, the task would be daunting.

"This battle will take time and resolve," he said. "But make no mistake about it, we will win." Make no mistake? Why "make no mistake?" Who was likely to mistake him?

She looked out the window at the stained blue of the sky, then, for relief, studied the Chinese scroll on the wall: the thousand-year-old letter of advice to the newly appointed district magistrate who was urged to spread a civilizing influence. "He must clear his eyes and listen intently, so that he and his subjects may together be molded by the spirit and transformed."

Transform us, she pleaded to no one. Change us back to what we were three hours ago.

"In Pao-an Circuit, people have been killed in broad daylight. . . . There are many calamities in the area, and friends are all scattered."

The sound of the phone jarred her as it would have jarred Bodo and Zuna in the cave. She leaped to it.

"Renata? Are you okay?"

"You're alive!"

"I've been trying to call you for hours."

"Me too. Where were you? I didn't even know where you were."

"I was uptown. And you? On the subway?"

"No, the bridge. I was late. I met the bookman. He was going to . . . Where are you now?"

"Walking over the bridge. It's hard to talk. Meet me at my place."

"But—"

"Please, just do it. And listen, buy some milk."

"Milk. Okay."

"Not regular milk. Baby milk. You know, like formula."

"Are you sick?"

"No. I'll tell you later. Get there, will you?" He hung up.

Outside, the cars were draped in ash, the streets strewn with paper. The air held a sweetish, smoky smell, like sausages in a distant oven. Some people had paper masks, others held handkerchiefs over their faces. She had a key to Jack's place and let herself in. When she heard his heavy tread in the hall she rushed to the door. He was filthy and bedraggled and in his arms he held a baby in a pale blue terry-cloth sunsuit. Incredibly, the baby was sleeping. Over Jack's shoulders was slung a powder blue plastic baby bag.

"Take him," he said, then dropped the bag and fell onto the couch.

"What—?"

"It's Carmen's kid. Julio."

"But why . . . Oh, no."

Jack started to cry. "She was in there. Remember, I sent her? Remember she called when we were in bed? I asked her to go. I did it. She wouldn't be there if I hadn't—"

He sat sobbing. Renata put the baby down and held him. "Maybe she'll be found. Maybe she escaped." Maybe she was one of the bodies plummeting through the air.

"It was too high up. No one up there could have gotten out. It'd be a miracle. I sent her."

All she could do was hold him in her arms, while Julio slept peacefully on the floor.

"I tried to go look for her," he said, "but there was no way. I couldn't get near. Then I started to come home, and then I remembered there was no one to pick him up. I know the place. I arranged it for her, so they let me take him. Carmen. She's under there, Renata. It wasn't so urgent, just some papers. Why did I even pick up, when she called? Then she wouldn't be under there. Why didn't I go myself? Why did I have to send her?"

It's only the minutiae of life that are important. . . .
Confronted by the truly microscopic, all loftiness is
hopeless, completely meaningless. The diminutive
of the parts is more impressive than the monumen-
tality of the whole.

JOSEPH ROTH

Five

So of all things, on this singular day Renata has a baby to see to.
On a day when the city's entire attention is consumed by bewilderment, grief, rage, and fear, she has thrust on her this diversion. It
happens that she's not totally new to child care, but she's never
tended a baby of this age, around six or seven months. Jack should
know his age. In a more lucid moment he would remember when
Carmen took maternity leave, but Jack is not lucid. He's lying face
down on the couch wearing a towel, having just emerged from the
shower, and, like others who were within a mile of the attack,
stuffed his clothes into the garbage. He plans to get up and start
phoning right away, but he needs a few moments of inertia first.
Before the shower he called his parents in Santa Fe and his brother
in Albuquerque to let them know he was alive. Soon he'll try a
wider circle, as far as "technical difficulties" permit. Through it all,
the TV plays. "We are prepared to spend whatever it takes. . . ."
"We hunt an enemy that hides in shadows and caves. . . ." The
President's features have shed their merry, cartoon-rodent aspect

and rearranged themselves into lines of sobriety, as if by a few swift strokes of the animator's pen. "Make no mistake, the United States will hunt down and punish—"

With the baby in her arms, Renata stares out the living-room window. One of the panes in the casement window is flawed: the glass is wavy. It makes everything seen through it wavy too. On the street, alone or in small groups, people have slowed down, drifting through the ashes underfoot like sleepwalkers. They shimmer through the wavy glass; their shapes are uncertain, tentative; their bodies ripple. The sidewalks ripple too, and the moving cars, the signs on the shops across the street. The walkers are moving through a new medium, not quite as fluid as water, not quite as vaporous as air. It is a fluttery, trembly ambiance, and they're not used to it; behind the wavy glass, they move with hesitation. From what Renata can see, they're not talking much, probably not only from shock but because the rancid air makes them reluctant to open their mouths. Only on TV is there no shortage of words. "This is total war, real war. This is a wake-up call for America." "Make no mistake, we will win."

"I have to get in touch with Carmen's mother," Jack mumbles. "To tell her. And that the kid is okay."

Renata is in no hurry to give up the baby, now that he's here. Somehow having the baby with them makes it more bearable. Thousands are dead, the TV says, thousands more injured, doctors and nurses are gathered at the hospitals waiting for the onslaught of the wounded, downtown is ankle-deep in rubble and dust, the unthinkable has happened (though the instant after it happened it wasn't unthinkable at all, simply no one had had the wit to think of it), and on top of everything, another kind of butchery is in progress, not bloody but insidious, an assault on the common lan-

guage. With all that, Renata lingers in this unlikely niche of pleasure, this baby she has never given a thought to in her life.

"I forgot his name. Isn't that stupid?"

"Julio." Speaking the name sets Jack to weeping again, so Renata
sets Julio down in a nest of blankets on the floor, then joins Jack on
the couch and strokes his back.

"Just a few more minutes, then I have to get started. I can't just
lie here."

"Take your time. The phones are no good anyway."

"I'll go and give blood. I'll go down there and do something.
What about your mother?"

"I spoke to her. She's okay. Look, before you go anywhere,
could you stay with him while I get some things from my place? I
didn't even bring a toothbrush. I can't take him out in this, at least
until . . . " Until the dust settles, she was about to say, but the
cliché is too apt. She and Jack always get a laugh out of those
cliché-come-true moments. Not today, though.

"You're staying?" For months he's been trying to persuade
Renata to come live with him, but she's hedged.

"It's better for him here than at my place, isn't it?"

"Is this what it takes to get you to move in? A national disaster?
International."

That sounds almost like the old Jack. But again they can't
laugh, barely smile. Not yet. Maybe in countries where they're used
to flying steel beams and pulverized concrete, choking air and
compacted cars draped in dust, they can joke more readily. Not
here, not yet. Not till they discover how many bodies are under the
rubble. Not till she knows what happened to the bookman.

It's not hard to take care of a six-month-old baby, she finds.
Easier than the last time she was called on to care for a child. That

child was older, with questions, fears, the beginnings of a history. They talked. And as so often happens when words come into play, lies and dissimulation come with them. The child, her dead sister's child, asked where her parents were, and Renata had to make up a story. The child was too young to understand the true circumstances. I'm your aunt, Renata told her, and for the three-year-old Gianna, that was sufficient. At first she asked a lot of questions about the couple she believed were her parents, then after a while, when they never reappeared, she stopped asking. So many of the answers Renata gave were lies anyway and weighed on her conscience; they still do. She felt more honest when they played with the toy farm she'd saved from her childhood, making up fantasies about Farmer Blue and his family. With Julio, now, it's simpler. No chance for lies; nothing much is needed beyond affectionate murmurs that earn a gurgle and a smile. Julio doesn't know he's bereaved, bereft; if he misses his mother he can't say so; his cries might mean anything and are quickly soothed. Renata picks him up, gives him a bottle, changes his diaper from the supply in the blue bag, so efficiently crammed with bottles, nipples, Pampers, and extra clothing, demonstrating what a provident mother Carmen was, so briefly.

People are helpful, too. The ashes and rubble and thousands dead and injured remind them to be kind to the living while they can. Back at her own apartment, for instance, when she checks to be sure the neighbors are alive, she gets a warm greeting from Mrs. Stavrakos, the habitually snarling widow on the first floor. Today Mrs. Stavrakos is ashen-faced, smoking, with an open bottle of gin beside her chair and the TV on. ("This will be a monumental struggle of good versus evil. But good will prevail." "Make no mistake, we will hunt down and punish those folks who . . . " Already it's beginning to sound like a rerun.) Renata accepts a quick drink of gin though she doesn't really like it. Thanks, but she can't stay; she has a baby to take care of. To her astonishment, Mrs. Stavrakos produces four jars of baby food she keeps in a cabinet for when her daughter visits from Astoria with the kids. "Who knows if any stores'll be open. Take them." She dusts the lids with a dish towel. The gay couple on the second floor who run the antique shop on Remsen Street answer the door together, holding hands and crying. And here Renata always thought they were unnaturally cheerful. But everyone appears to be transformed—it's like the *Metamorphosis,* where tears are the universal solvent, rearranging every accustomed shape. Gerald and Henry are both fine; their shop is a mess but never mind. The thing is, though, they have a close friend who works for Cantor Fitzgerald and they can't get him on the phone. She steps inside and they all embrace. She's never been in their apartment before and, no surprise, it's crammed with antiquey knickknacks from the shop. She tells them about Carmen and Julio. Gerald, the tall, thin black one with shoulder-length dreads, insists on giving her one of their collection of stuffed animals, a panda, and Henry, the short, white, moon-faced, balding one, ties a red ribbon around its neck. The Polish woman on the third floor is fine, too, only all her English has departed from the shock. When Renata speaks to her in Russian she's overjoyed. On any other day she wouldn't be eager to converse in Russian, language of the despised oppressor, but today she won't let Renata leave, recounting over and over how she would have been on the subway except she was getting one of her migraines and stayed home. And now, believe it or not, the headache has gone away. Imagine that! Usually they last for days.

So far, so good, but the smartly dressed young couple who'd just moved in on the fifth floor and begun noisy renovations aren't home and that's worrisome: they seem like the type who might work at one of the big investment houses.

Her apartment is exactly as she left it a couple of hours ago when Jack called. Hours that feel like days, everything is so altered. It's a bit more dusty than usual—yes, all the surfaces are covered by the fine film that leaves a grayish patina on her fingers (such a splendid day that she'd left the windows open)—but nowhere near as dusty as those apartments in lower Manhattan that she'll soon see in the newspaper, where each object is shrouded in white, everything suddenly a plaster cast of itself, like the inside-out plaster cast of the child's bedroom at the Sensation exhibit where she met Jack and they laughed together at the captions. "The resemblance to a tomb is inescapable. It's as though the artist has sealed off her memories. And we are . . . left only with traces from which we might try to guess what once took place inside."

She tosses some things into a backpack, clothes, makeup—can't start letting go now—and a few of her folders; she needs to have her clippings and scraps of language nearby. If she ever did move in with Jack, she'd have to do something about that unseemly habit. Keep the stuff out of sight, at least. Jack wouldn't want it around. He thinks her paper-hoarding is foolish, obsessive, irrelevant.

She will miss the calligraphy hangings, the boldness and delicacy of the writing as well as the stories of rescue and recovery she invents for their meanings, but they will wait for her. What she does need is the Transformed Lives folder. It seems prescient, as if she's gathered its tales just for today, when transformation is rife, most of all beneath the fallen towers. All flesh evolves to the condition of dust, but slowly, slowly, so that each generation, which has to learn the lesson anew, can get used to the idea. Today's shock was its speed, flesh transformed to instant dust. The stories in the Transformed Lives folder, whose characters have become her silent companions, seem more than ever valiant today, so hopeful that life can renew itself in a fresh guise. Take Letitia Cole, the former classical music composer who now belly dances in Morocco. She "likes being a Jew in an Arab culture," especially as "her father's family was originally from Palestine. 'It's all Semitic. It's all the same. It's terrible we're not brothers.' Belly dancing is her 'little gesture of peace.'" Where is she dancing now? Renata wonders. Is anyone watching her gesture of peace?

At the door, she glances at the twenty-dollar bill under the vase on the table, the bill that turned up at her feet in the paper storm. Let it lie there. Just as she's about to leave, the phone rings.

"Renata? Are you okay? Oh God, Renata, you can't imagine what . . . " The voice is sobbing, hysterical.

"Linda? Is that you? Are you okay? Take it easy."

"I'm okay. I was at work but . . . Oh God."

"What is it? Who?"

"Roger."

Roger, the boyfriend, transcontinental sexual athlete, in-flight stud. "Oh my God, where was he? Not—?"

"He was supposed to, . . . he was almost on that plane from Boston but, . . . he got a—" She can't speak, can't stop sobbing.

"Tell me! Is he all right?"

"Hold on." Linda coughs and clears her throat. "He was in Boston and he was coming down for a quick visit but—"

"Please, just calm down. I can't understand you. Is he okay?"

"He was waiting for the plane but he got a call on his cell that his mother had an aneurysm so he . . . he didn't get on and he booked a flight back to London. And now—"

"Linda, stop crying. He didn't get on the plane, is that what you're saying?"

"No. I mean yes. He's still in Boston. He didn't get on, but he was supposed to. He almost did." She's sobbing again.

"Pull yourself together. He's all right. You'll see him soon."

"He can't fly anywhere now. Not even here. He could have been on that plane."

"But he wasn't. Got that? He wasn't. He's fine."

"Okay. Okay. He wasn't. That's the thing, right?"

"Right."

"Okay, I'm better now. Is everything okay with you?"

"Yes. Well, not exactly." She tells her about Jack and Carmen and Julio. "What about everyone at work?"

"I don't know. They all went home. I sat for a half hour because I thought he was on the plane and I couldn't move. Denise stayed with me a while, till she reached her son—he's okay—then she left too. Then Roger called and I sort of collapsed and then I walked home through the park. Coughing all the way. The air."

"I saw it. From the bridge. Look, I'd better go. The baby, . . . I'll call you later. I won't be able to go to work for a while."

"Don't worry, there won't be much work going on. He wasn't on the plane. I have to remember that. And then his mother, . . . well, she'll have to manage without him."

Back at Jack's place, he fills her in on who's accounted for and who's not. Everyone in his office, accounted for. Most of the people he knows at the Port Authority, missing. Others, he's not certain yet.

"I'm going out. I've got to do something."

"How? There are no trains."

"Somehow. Are you okay here with him?" he says at the door. "You don't mind?"

"No, I'm okay. Be careful." More than okay. She likes it. She doesn't ask if he tried calling Julio's grandmother in Puerto Rico. Anyway, no planes are flying, the skies are eerily silent, so she has a few days.

After he leaves, Renata hears voices in the hall and wanders out with Julio in her arms. The neighbors are commiserating and exchanging things—bread, aspirins, towels, milk, a bottle of bourbon, Valium. For an instant she has that sensation of watching through wavy glass again, but in the bustle of ordinariness it quickly passes and everyone solidifies. A gray-haired woman is pleading for Prozac, Paxil, anything, but the younger people explain. "It takes weeks to work. And you can't just take anyone's. You don't know the dosage. What you want is the Valium." An Indian woman from across the hall gives Renata an outgrown stroller and bassinet she was saving for Goodwill; another woman gives her a sling for carrying Julio on her chest. The man from next door whom she's never seen but knows by his voice—he clomps through the hall day and night, talking loudly to his dog, "Attaboy, Merlin, how's about a run along the Promenade?"—turns out to be a balding fifty-year-old with an eye patch and a withered arm. He coos at Julio. "Merlin loves babies, here, let him pat Merlin, he's very gentle." Everyone likes a baby. The bookman would like Julio too. As soon as she ventures out again, she'll bring him to show the bookman. If he's still there. He wouldn't be daunted by the smoky air or the littered streets; if he's alive, he'll be manning his table, handing out bananas and saying God bless you. If not . . . No, don't think about it. Don't go there.

By the time Jack returns in the early evening, it's clear that the throngs of the injured will not materialize after all. Only a small number have been brought to the hospitals: burn victims, broken limbs and abrasions. Shock. Any others still living will have to be dug out, extracted like precious metal. Very soon, in a miracle of modern efficiency, huge machines that resemble prehistoric creatures will be stretching their steel necks, baring their teeth and claws and preparing to mine the rubble.

No one wanted his blood, Jack tells her. He left a case of water with other contributions near the site. Indescribable, the piles of tortured steel, the fires everywhere, the buckling pavements and the smoke, the smell. Above all, the strewn paper. He couldn't get to his office—the streets were cordoned off. While he was looking for a path he saw another building collapse, a smaller one. "Just sank into itself. One minute it was there, then it wasn't." He's restless, frustrated that all he can do is watch TV, and how many times can you look at the same images. The stream of ashen people trudging across the bridge, the man being laid on the stretcher, the woman sitting on the curb with her head in her hands. . . . The plane drilling into the tower, the explosion of flame. Innumerable times. Then something new: the President's address to the nation. "We are the brightest beacon for freedom and opportunity in the world. And no one will keep that light from shining."

Julio starts to fret and Renata warms a bottle of formula. She can hear the TV from the kitchen. "Today our nation saw evil. . . . Our financial institutions remain strong, and the American economy will be open for business as usual—"

"Not exactly inspiring," she remarks as she prepares to feed Julio. "But at least he didn't say 'Make no mistake.'"

"What'd you say?"

"Didn't you notice, earlier? How many times he said 'Make no mistake'? Why does he keep saying 'Make no mistake'? I mean, who's likely to make a mistake?"

"Renata, come off it. It's just an expression. What does it matter? There are more important things to worry about. Oh, and the footbridge across West Street collapsed on top of God knows how many people."

Still, it matters, and will matter more in the days to come, but now is not the moment to explain, assuming she could explain.

Not the moment to quote Socrates emblazoned on Linda's door: "False language, evil in itself, infects the soul with evil."

"I guess you're right. Shh, Julio, your bottle is right here."

She stays in Wednesday, cocooned with Julio and the TV set ("I have directed the full resources of our intelligence and law-enforcement communities to find . . . We will make no distinction between the terrorists who committed these acts and those who harbor them"), deferring the moment she must step outdoors and into the reality of the altered city. For now, she's glad enough to wait for Jack and greet him with a kiss and a drink like a 1950s suburban wife.

He's exhausted. He's carrying three newspapers under his arm and a mushroom pizza. He had to wait a long time for the pizza. Half the neighborhood was lined up, it seems no one's up to cooking, and they were shorthanded because the main pizza-maker's brother, a cop from Staten Island, is missing. Jack reports that he hooked up with a group of young guys who got past the barriers to bring things to the men on the machines that appeared out of nowhere—sandwiches, coffee, work gloves, boots. Seventy-five people from the Port Authority are gone, many of whom he knew, so he has to be there doing something, doesn't he? And of course Carmen. "They're looking for survivors. Yesterday fourteen people were found trapped in a stairwell. The cops and firemen went wild when they came out. Since then, nothing." Later he went to his office. Dozens of people turned up, asking for temporary housing, child care, what-not. He grows animated as he describes it all, a foot-soldier in the perpetual campaign to bring order out of chaos. Tomorrow he'll shop on the way; the construction workers need all sorts of odds and ends—batteries, safety goggles, throat spray, Chapstick—and no one's yet organized enough to supply them. If

Renata has a minute, she might pick up a supply of chocolate bars and cigarettes and Tylenol; they need those, too.

The site is worse than it looks on TV. "You can't grasp it from what they show. It's huge. Thousands of tons of steel tied up in huge knots. Crushed cars and fire engines all over the place. And the smell. It's all still burning. It'll burn for months, they say. Shoes strewn all over. That was the worst, the shoes. Some of the things I saw, I can't even tell you."

"You mean, like . . . bodies?"

"No bodies. Parts. I saw a foot . . . Never mind."

This while they eat the pizza and drink a bottle of wine. Jack coughs a lot, eats a lot, even finishes Renata's crusts.

Maybe Franco Donati, she thinks, the hapless Italian who took extraordinary photos of homeless people, could return from his father's house in Padua and photograph the site. He could do it justice, he has the right kind of eye. No one can find the right words, but through his lens it would be more than seventeen acres of tangled metal and concrete and shoes and unspeakable body parts; it would enter history and become a symbol of something. Of what? Not the brightest beacon for freedom.

Talking relieves Jack, helps distract him from his guilt and grief over Carmen. He's spread the newspapers out on the table, on the remains of the pizza. Already he's looking at things on the large scale, what he likes to call the big picture. Already he's making pronouncements about not giving in to rage, not making things worse than they are. He's reading the papers in indignation.

"Look at this *Post* headline. 'BOMBS AWAY.' 'Who are they? Who cares? Cast a wide enough net, and you'll catch the fish that need catching.'"

"It's just words," Renata says. "What people say when they feel impotent. It's just crude. It doesn't mean anything."

"Crude? You're calling that crude? You mean 'Bombs Away' is only bad manners but 'Make no mistake' is really offensive? It seems to me 'Bombs Away' is dangerous. It'll lead us into a war before we know it."

"Bombs away" has its appeal. Renata has known impotent rage and the lust for revenge, directed at anything handy. It's tempting. But no doubt Jack is right. She's never been one for the big picture. Today in particular she can see only thousands of small pictures, the faces of the dead in the newspapers. And the faces of the living. Julio is one. The bookman? She'd like to tell Jack about the bookman, how she didn't chase him when he took the wrong turn, and where is he now? But Jack is so tired and guilty and desperate to talk that the right moment doesn't come.

"And this letter in the *Times* today. Just listen. 'Now is the time to call to mind our mighty heritage, to turn our plowshares back into swords to defend our time-honored freedoms. Now every heart must beat as one, every spirit pledge itself to the heroic challenge before us. Let us not waver from the duty that calls. . . . '"

"It's the same as 'Bombs Away,'" she says. "In fact I prefer 'Bombs Away.' At least it has no pretensions. You want some coffee?"

Jack shakes his head. She's not helping him.

Just before they go to sleep he flicks on the remote for a last look. Overnight, it's become everyone's favorite disaster movie: the plane boring into the tower yet again, the crowds running, the woman sitting on the curb with her head in her hands, the President's face straining to appear grown-up: "Make no mistake, good will prevail." This is the trailer. We've all seen the complete version already, yet we can't resist seeing the highlights over and over.

"Come to bed, Jack. You've seen it a dozen times."

He doesn't move. He stands naked, the remote in his hand, watching the talking heads. A representative from the Washington

Institute for Middle East Policy is heard from: "You can't bomb these guys into the Stone Age because they already are in the Stone Age."

"Did you hear that? Is that kind of thing going to do any good?"

Nothing will do Carmen any good. "Please," she urges. "There'll be more tomorrow."

Finally he turns it off and falls into bed with a heavy arm flung over her. She lies warmed by his arm, the bassinet with the sleeping child a few feet away, and for the short while it takes to fall asleep they feel like a makeshift family, strangers thrown together by disaster or war.

In the morning Renata resolves to get moving too. She can't hide forever. They've been living like Bodo and Zuna from her old cave book, Jack braving the perils of the world while she hangs out in the cave, tending the baby. Enough. The air may be foul but the sky is so blue, a sky like a summons: come out, enjoy me.

First she calls Denise, her boss, at home, since the library is closed, along with other nonessential services.

Denise's news is mixed. The good: her son walked down from the forty-eighth floor of the South Tower. "They told them to go back up, can you believe it? Thank God they were smart enough to keep walking. Most of them, anyhow." But Tanisha, the cleaning woman for the linguistics division, lost her husband, a window washer. The sister of a guard. The nephew of someone in the Periodical Room. And that's only so far. Lots of people haven't yet been heard from.

After they go through everyone they can think of, Renata explains about Julio. "I'll have to be out a few more days at least."

"Don't worry about it. We'll be open tomorrow, but your stuff is not exactly high priority. Oh, but wait, I almost forgot, there is something and you can do it at home. Guess who called—the State Department. They started at the top but it worked its way down to me. They need people who can read Arabic. They don't have enough of their own. How's your Arabic?"

"*Nada.* But I suppose I could learn. What am I supposed to do, be a spy? Intercept secret messages?"

"Very funny. They want to find out how this is going down in the Middle Eastern newspapers. That means Standard Arabic, of course, not any of the national dialects. And don't go spreading this around. You know how they are in the government. So what shall I tell them? I mean, how long before you could read a paper?"

"Arabic is hard. It's a totally different alphabet. Better make it a couple of weeks. You really mean they haven't got people in Washington?"

"Apparently not. And the university professors don't have security clearance and can't take the time off. So they came to us. They'll have to check you out. I presume you're not a security risk?"

"Not that I know of. These guys work fast, don't they?"

"Not fast enough," Denise says with a snort. "There are rumors that they had warnings of this, you know, coded messages, but they didn't put it together. Or something. Maybe it would've all been different. For Chrissakes, Linda could have put it together if they'd let her into their computers."

Arabic, okay. It's notoriously difficult to speak correctly, but reading should be manageable. She'd find a book. There's Rashid's Book and Record Store on Court Street. Or maybe the bookman has a basic grammar; it wouldn't be the first time he'd anticipated her needs. Of course for that, he'd have to be alive.

The air can't be good for Julio but he'll have to take his chances like everyone else. Stroller or sling? The jaunty sling, connoting independence as well as a back-to-the-land earthiness, is what all the women use these days. But it suggests pregnancy, a condition Renata has never experienced nor desired, not after watching Claudia endure her pregnancy with loathing at age sixteen. She straps Julio into the stroller.

Outside, there's an odd sense of freedom, ghastly parody of a holiday, all daily schedules disrupted, all ordinary obligations rescinded. No way to get down the street without stopping every half block to talk. For this is her turf, these are her neighbors, and though she's usually reserved, just a nod and a smile, she's as transformed as all the rest. Each shopkeeper has a story of someone who was trapped or who escaped. The shoemaker's shop bears a hand-lettered sign: "Closed Due to Tragedy." When she buys a paper, the newsstand man explains that the shoemaker's wife was a cook in the top-floor restaurant. Lost. Definitely lost. The hot-dog stand man's son is a fireman but he's all right, or rather, he has a dislocated shoulder because a falling body grazed him, and the hot-dog man is giving away pretzels out of gratitude. Renata takes one to share with Julio, breaking off little salty bits. Everyone fusses over Julio, and he gives his brightest smiles as people murmur their sympathy for his loss. Through it all Renata keeps her mind on her destination. She's always been far-sighted. She'll know a block away.

Just before she turns the corner from which she'll spot him, or not spot him, she pauses to breathe, cough, and prepare herself: It won't be your fault, how could you have known? Don't exaggerate your importance. The bookman himself wouldn't blame you. But it's no use. Logic is rarely any use against guilt. She rounds the corner.

He's there, straightening the books on the table. Such a happy surprise, maybe even the fourth degree in the Bliondan spectrum of happy surprises, *kol-dradoskona.* Instead of going weak in the knees and teary, she feels a surge of adrenaline and starts to run, stroller and all. Whee! Hang on, kiddo.

The bookman is surprised to see her with a baby and even more surprised when she throws her arms around his neck.

"You're all right! I was so worried. I saw you going the wrong way. What happened?"

He doesn't know what she's talking about. He wants to talk about the baby. "Beautiful baby. I never knew you had a baby. God bless you, little one," he says, bending down over Julio.

She has to remind him, and spills it out in hasty Spanish with grammatical errors, very unlike her.

Oh, that. His brother's case. It's been postponed. His daughter called and found out the court buildings are closed.

"But the subway! Remember you didn't go the way I said? And I was so—"

Oh! Now he remembers. Yes, he understood her directions perfectly. But he realized he was early so he stopped in Starbucks for a cup of coffee.

Starbucks, she thinks. Saved by Starbucks.

And in Starbucks he met a friend and they got to talking. Then just as he was getting ready to go, it happened. All of this he recounts with a happy smile. Now she goes limp and has to sit down on the ledge of the building. At last he understands.

"You worried about me? God bless you."

"Thanks," and she bursts into tears.

He lets her cry, makes no attempt to soothe her, merely entertains Julio till she can compose herself. He understands that the tears are the accumulation of the last two days; maybe in his wisdom, he suspects they've been accumulating for the last two decades. In any case, he doesn't need to know, and nothing surprises him.

He must have a life beyond the book table. Are his family and friends all right? It turns out he has a wife, four children, and nine grandchildren, all living nearby, and he recites all of their where-abouts at the moment of the calamity. None of them anywhere near the site, which strikes Renata as nothing short of miraculous—so many, and all safe.

He has no Arabic grammars. His featured selections today are antique comic books, *Captain Marvel, Wonder Woman, Archie, Tales from the Crypt,* and if Julio were older she'd buy a few. Instead she buys a Raymond Chandler mystery for Jack. One dollar, as always.

In between the chats and groceries and errands—chocolate bars, Jack said, cigarettes, Tylenol, Chapstick, cough drops—exactly like a young mother pushing her stroller through the day, she notices the words that have sprouted on the walls. Missing, Eileen Sefaris, wavy auburn hair, wearing gold chain and gray pants suit, burn scar on inner arm above right wrist. Colin Jones, 5'10", heavy-set, Spider-man tattoo on left thigh, missing first upper left molar. Concepcion Delgado, black eyes, black hair, round light-brown beauty mark near left shoulder, bites fingernails. Scrawled, hand-lettered, computer-generated, all with photos: wedding pictures, graduation pictures, birthday parties—Albert V. Hirsheimer blowing out the candles on a frosted white cake with blue and green flowers—vacation photos, passport photos. Stefania Pignarelli, worked on 87th floor of South Tower, wearing striped miniskirt and black top, mole on right cheek, yin-yang tattoo on lower back. . . .

Signs, what a good idea. It never occurred to her to put up signs for her missing. Claudia: age sixteen, 5'7", slim, long black ponytail held in a wide chrome barrette, dark eyes, olive complex-ion, wearing jeans and Nike sneakers, striped tank top. But Claudia is not literally missing, not like the people on the walls, who might still be found: *tanfendi-oude.* Claudia was last seen alive in their shared bedroom on a hot June night—hot enough to have the windows wide open—eighteen years ago.

They were going over the assignments Claudia had missed. She'd decided—their mother had decided for her—to make up the work and take the final exams so as not to lose the whole term. They were in their junior year of high school. Renata had the task of bringing her up to date. They sat on her bed, Claudia on a pillow because she was still sore. She wasn't cooperating.

"If you're going to be that way let's just forget it," Renata said.

"I've got to do it some time."

"Then pay attention."

During the months of Claudia's pregnancy, they had been close again—a truce. The stolen money and the five years of estrangement could not be forgotten, but they were set aside. Claudia had needed her sister. Now, with the baby gone, she was once more a stranger.

"Look, just give me your Spanish notebook, okay? I can do it in five minutes."

Claudia handed it over and Renata filled in the blanks for verbs in the past conditional. "Okay, now the history. You can copy mine but you need to change the sentences. She'd get suspicious. Not that she has half a brain. She spent so much time on the Civil War that we hardly had time for the twentieth century. I left class one day to change a tampon and when I came back I'd missed the Vietnam War."

Claudia barely smiled.

"All right, I'm going to bed," Renata said. "It's all here if you want it."

She crossed over to her side of the room, dropped her clothes on the floor, pulled the sheet over her head, and fell asleep instantly. In the old days it was Claudia who fell asleep in three seconds, while Renata lay listening to the sound of her breathing, scaring herself with cave fantasies. Now each night she escaped as fast as she could; she never knew how long Claudia lay awake.

She woke to the sound of rustling. Footsteps, drawers opening and closing. The room was pitch dark but she sensed Claudia moving around. After a moment she could make her out, sitting on her bed and putting on her sneakers.

"What are you doing?"

"I can't sleep. It's so hot. I'm going out for a while."

"Now? What time is it?"

"Go back to sleep. I need some air. I'll walk Fox. He's pacing like he needs to go out."

"But it's so late."

"So?"

She opened the door and Fox bounded in. Claudia shushed him and attached the leash. Renata rolled over to look at the clock on the night table, a babyish clock in the shape of a teddy bear that she'd had ever since she could tell time; on Claudia's night table was its identical companion. Nearly eleven-forty. Had it been two in the morning, she might have tried to stop her or threatened to wake their parents. She might have changed history, as in a uchrony. No, Claudia wouldn't have paid attention. Renata had lost whatever influence she used to have. Let her go. It was hardly the first time—though rarely so late as this. She was old enough to go out as late as she liked. After all that had happened, she wasn't a child anymore. Renata was the child.

Sleep had been her friend these last months. Now it turned enemy. When she next looked at the clock it was four-thirty and Claudia's bed was empty.

She should have been on the alert even in her sleep. She should have slept lightly, the way mothers of newborn babies do, ready for the cry. But even in her sleep she was furious at her sister. She'd been furious ever since Claudia broke their pact. They used to be intertwined like clasped hands. But Claudia had yanked her hand away. Now Renata was tired of her too, tired of her troubles being the family melodrama, everyone fussing over her because she was the bad girl. Nobody fussed over a good girl.

She searched the whole house, even the basement they hardly used anymore. Long ago it had been their special retreat, where they played secret games and spoke the secret language. When she couldn't delay any longer she knocked on her parents' door, then pushed it open and called out. They pulled apart from the clinch they slept in. Renata turned off the TV they'd left on, some old black-and-white movie, people dressed in tuxedos and satin gowns, drinking champagne in a nightclub.

"What's the matter?"

In the midst of the frantic questions, Dan noticed the dog wasn't around. They were downstairs by that time. He flung open the back door and found Fox curled up on the deck. Stupid Fox. Why hadn't he scraped and battered at the door? Why hadn't he barked? He'd found his way home from wherever Claudia had taken him and dropped off to sleep. His fur was caked with dried mud; he shook himself off all over them, and Grace made a sharp shrieking sound and dabbed at her white nightie. Finally Fox barked. He wanted them to follow him somewhere and they were willing, but when he got to the corner he stopped and walked around in circles, pawing at the ground as if he didn't know which way to turn.

The police wouldn't look for missing persons until twenty-four hours had elapsed. Call her friends, they advised. Grace paced the living room, making little mewling noises. They called a few of Claudia's girlfriends, or rather, they had Renata call, although those weren't her friends. She and Claudia no longer had the same friends.

She never said she saw Claudia go out. She said she fell asleep early—not exactly a lie but not the whole truth, either. She didn't want to be blamed. The last time she was blamed, five years ago, it skewed the world. The world tipped on its axis and had remained atilt ever since, so she'd turned inward. She wouldn't be driven further inside that cramped space. Anyhow, she didn't know any more than they did.

They got dressed and drove aimlessly around the neighborhood, Renata in the back seat with the mud-caked dog. He was getting her filthy.

"Oh. The river," she said.

"What do you mean, the river?" said her mother.

"Down by the river." Like everyone else in town, Grace and Dan knew the playground and the picnic area along the Palisades, but they didn't know the narrow strip down by the water where the teenagers hung out, where they sat on the ancient rowboats with their feet dangling over the mucky ground and watched the barges go by, or walked out on the rotting pier to look with longing toward the city. No one would risk climbing down that steep rock face to the shore at night. It was too forbidding. But there was no telling what Claudia might do.

Renata told them there was a place they sometimes went. They parked and found the path, using the flashlight from the car. Fox panted behind them. The barest tinge of light showed in the sky. They all climbed down the rocks, but found nothing except the old rowboats.

"This is a waste of time," Dan grumbled, so they climbed back up and went home.

Three days later the police dragged the river. They didn't want to; there was no evidence of a drowning, only Renata's insistence. She was very insistent. It wasn't any mystical intuition, none of the uncanny vibrations that undulate between twins—they didn't have that anymore. Simply, she knew what the place meant. Like the basement, it was a retreat, a place for secrets.

She and her parents stood on the shore with Fox alongside. It was near noon, bright and hot. Peter and Cindy were there too, along with a local reporter and several cops. With all those people, the place was ruined. Up at the top were police cars and half a dozen more cops. The sun was so strong they had to shield their eyes to watch the boat and the device used to trawl the depths. The boat wasn't very far from shore, just a ways past the pier. They could make out the figures of the men on board quite clearly. One of them waved toward shore and a cop spoke to him on a walkie-talkie. "You might want to go back up," the cop said. "They may have found something."

Her father's eyes had a look she would remember forever. The brown of his irises darkened till she thought they were turning purple. "We'll wait here." Then he motioned to Grace. "Unless you want to—?"

"No, we'll wait." She had had three days to compose herself. She'd stopped whimpering and settled into a kind of torpor.

They dragged in something big and dark and caked with mud, hauled it onto the boat and headed to shore. When they came closer and Grace saw the striped shirt in tatters, she sank down into the muck. A cop raised her up. A terrible smell drifted to shore; soon they could see Claudia's face, green and bloated, her hair tangled with mud and reeds, her clothes shredded, her leg bent back at a crazy angle. To Renata it was like seeing herself, the way she might look, dead. They had to cover their mouths and noses because of the stench. Claudia's stomach was puffed up, as it had been when she was pregnant. She'd just had the baby ten days before.

Her leg was broken, they were told the next day. Splinters from the pier were found in the gash in her knee. And there was a head wound; she must have hit the concrete abutment beneath the pier. It might have knocked her unconscious, it was hard to tell. But with the leg, she couldn't have swum to safety in any case. It was judged an accident. A foolish girl taking a foolish risk. That was as far as the police hinted. What could she have been doing down there at night, all alone? they asked, but no one could answer. Not all alone, was all Renata could say. She didn't know who or why, but not all alone. She was sure of that.

For a while, she would make up scenarios in her head, but she knew too little to speculate. The scenarios were like old silent films, blurred, with gaps, the film breaking at the crucial moments: Claudia on the pier, taunting, daring someone to dive in, the other person just outside the frame, casting a faint shadow. It's just water. I dare you.

She was found, but she would forever be among the missing. She and the child she bore, the child Renata made her own, both missing.

In the book about June and Jennifer Gibbons, the British twins bent on destroying each other, she read that the Yoruba people of West Africa carve small figurines to mark the birth of twins. "If one twin dies, the figurine is cared for by the surviving twin, who feeds, dresses and treats it as his living brother or sister." This is not something Renata would do. But Julio and the twenty-dollar bill, both brought to her by Tuesday's tragedy, have elements of pretend, like Farmer Blue, like figurines.

When she gets home after her errands she turns on the TV first thing. There is the President, surveying the ruins of the Pentagon. "Make no mistake about it," he says, "this nation is sad."

Six

"I can't talk no more about how I came up. It hurt to think about it." The speaker is Leola Pettway, one of a group of extraordinary quiltmakers, poor black women from Gee's Bend, Alabama, a small settlement of a few extended families, descendants of slaves, where each generation of women teaches the next how to quilt. Renata saw their work at the Whitney Museum over the summer—a show mercifully free of any writing on the wall. The quilts, made of discarded household scraps, spoke sufficiently. The women used to hang them on clotheslines near the road, where passersby would stop to look and buy. After a while someone realized that the quiltmakers were great artists.

It is difficult, just now, for Renata to recall clearly anything she did before Tuesday, but she has the catalog to help her; she bought it for the women's oral histories and reads it to hear truth in language that refreshes, now that the ambient language is so stale and sour that it reeks. "It was when Daddy died. I was about seventeen, eighteen. He stayed sick about eight months and passed on." The speaker is Arlonzia Pettway, who lost her father at the same age Renata did. "Mama say, 'I going to take his work clothes, shape them into a quilt to remember him, and cover up under it for love.' She take his old pants legs and shirttails, take all the clothes he had, just enough to make that quilt, and I helped her tore them up. Bottom of the pants is narrow, top is wide, and she had me to cutting the top part out and to shape them up in even strips."

There's no getting around it: Renata wants her mother. She thinks of Grace day and night. When she pictures the body parts being sorted from the smoking rubble and placed by gloved hands in biohazard bags to be transported to ferries at the river's edge, she thinks of her; when she smells the carnage in the air, she thinks of her; and she thinks of her when she reads the papers ("You don't want to know," says a firefighter, "you don't want to know the things we stepped over") or hears the TV reports: "The body of a flight attendant was discovered with her hands bound, in the wreckage of the aircraft downed in Pennsylvania." When she finds herself loving Jack as never before with a piercing, apocalyptic urgency—is that love or fear? When he comes home gray-faced and disheveled, strips off his clothes, and runs into the shower before even reviewing for her his lists of the saved and the immolated, she thinks of her mother. She needs her. She wants to be with her. She's still young enough to want a mother, after all, even though she's had to grow up fast, even though she's been on her own for a long time. Because this, what has happened, is utterly new. From the moment she saw it, her mind has been a jumble; pieces of past and present jostle roughly; time has unhooked from its moorings; nothing is firm. The explosion has flung her in the air like a chunk of debris from the fallen buildings and she's still aloft, tossed and battered by air currents.

She knows her mother can't give a fraction of what she craves. The most Renata can hope for is to be called by her name and offered a few words. Yet against all reason she wants to sit in the same room with her mother and be reminded that she comes from someplace and has firm outlines. That the past is more than a strewn graveyard. With sorrow thickening the air like humidity, she wants to return to something benign, before. Not only before the attack. Before everything. When she was young enough to sit in her mother's lap. She'd sit there now, if Grace were still that kind of mother.

She doesn't like to admit her longing, naturally. She tells herself she ought to pay a visit for her mother's sake. It's not enough to phone every day. The clinically depressed, or selectively amnesiac, or whatever Grace can be labeled, are not at their best on the phone. It's only right to go and see how she's bearing up in this painful time. And the instant that sentence frames itself, as she kneels at the tub bathing Julio, she hears its hollow, lying ring. Wrong words. *Prashmensti.* A sentence that comes from watching too much television. "It's only right. . . ." A sure warning not to trust what follows. "This painful time." Words like that, pre-fab, pulled from a file in the more primitive parts of the brain, spoken to distract, *prashimina,* or to avoid, *prashmial,* can't be trusted. Anyway, Grace sounds as if she's "bearing up" as well as usual. The event, calamity, tragedy, attack, Renata hasn't yet fixed on the right word to use in her head (the media say "monstrous deed" or "evil act," not false, yet not words one uses in the privacy of the mind), seems not to have touched her mother. "You keep asking," Grace says on the phone. "But you know, up here, we're so far away it doesn't really touch us."

So far away? Seventeen miles out of the city? Jack has had calls and e-mails from people much farther, people who were touched.

How could anyone not be touched by five thousand people, no matter where, dead at one stroke? Or four thousand. Three? No one knows yet.

Renata's fury at Grace is infantile. She of all people knows Grace has twisted some screw in her head to ensure that nothing more will touch her. She's managed to "forget" so much of what once touched her closely; she has, unlike Renata, utterly renounced *bakiranima*, clinging to past misery (which, by the addition of the negative Etinoian prefix, "tal," *tal-bakiranima*, would mean an insufficient acknowledgment of the past). So how could she be touched by the deaths of strangers? By the crater downtown. By the future suddenly shaken into a new pattern, as if someone rattled a kaleidoscope.

There's something else, too. Julio. Like a child with a new toy, Renata wants to show him to her mother. No, not a toy, rather like something she's achieved. Like bringing home a trophy earned, or a project made in school, the way she used to do, full of pride, before the twenty dollars was lost: a wooden tray, a clay pot. Look what I made! And her mother would lavish praise, her pleasure radiant. There's not much pleasure Renata can bring her mother now; Grace is determined to ward off pleasure along with everything else. But she doesn't mean to shock Grace into pleasure, only to display Julio as proof that she can do it. It's exploitation, maybe, but surely he's too young to mind. Look how she's kept him healthy and safe these last three wretched days! Look at him splashing around in the tub right this minute! He's happy, he's getting used to her. He's chortling as he tries to grab the rubber duck from her hand. Doesn't that count for anything? Does it count at all, can it begin to make up in some minuscule way for the child given to her care years ago, whom she failed to keep safe?

All this she wants to bring to Grace. She wants the reassurance only a mother can give.

So on Friday morning she borrowed a baby car seat from the woman across the hall—Aruna, she was called, as Renata learned when she knocked on her door for baby advice. Aruna, not long arrived from New Delhi, peered through the peephole and opened hesitantly; she was worried for herself and her family, afraid they'd be mistaken for Middle Eastern or Muslim and be assaulted. Renata tried to assure her everything would be fine, New Yorkers weren't like that, but Renata was mistaken. On the very day she borrowed the car seat, Aruna's husband, Vikram, would be jostled roughly on the subway by a bunch of teenaged boys, no real physical damage done but the family would be heartsick. Still, this was mild compared to incidents reported in the papers. In Arizona, a turbaned Sikh owner of a gas station, shot dead. In California, shots fired into the house of an Afghan family. In Dallas, a Pakistani grocer shot at. And right here on Atlantic Avenue, a mere stroll away, a woman walked up and down the street hurling invective at the Arab shopkeepers, telling them to go back where they belonged. And lose all those great restaurants?

Renata packed Carmen's bag with baby supplies and hustled Julio into the back seat of Jack's car, quickly, because it was raining. There had been a thunderstorm Thursday night. The noise had woken them up, and Jack had turned on the TV to see what the site looked like in the rain, but there was no coverage at 2 A.M., so he watched a few minutes of an old submarine movie instead.

She hadn't ventured out of the neighborhood since Tuesday, and with the bridge closed, she had to take a circuitous route to reach her mother. Flicking on the car radio, she found that a few AM stations had resumed ordinary programming. During a discussion of the evils of alcoholism a caller described her father's dismal condition as "psoriasis of the liver." Normally this would get duly entered in Renata's records, but it hardly mattered anymore. And after Tuesday's events, was civilization endangered because the radio host said "between you and I?" She turned it off and watched the city glide past. Julio was getting quite a tour—three boroughs in less than an hour. He was a calm baby. When she glanced back every few minutes to check, he was gazing out at the sedate, low buildings of Queens, or the span of the East River under the Triborough Bridge, or the suburban gentility of Westchester, with his fixed, tolerant baby stare. So different from what Grace would describe when asked what it was like to raise twins. "A handful," she used to say. "What a handful. They were never still for a minute." And Renata would picture herself and Claudia in miniature, the size of newborn mice, squirming their wee limbs, overflowing from their mother's upturned palm.

As she approached the broad two-story building overlooking the Hudson, sitting on its low hill with placid dignity, she was pleased all over again with the place she'd found for Grace. She couldn't have managed it when she was eighteen and left on her own: she didn't understand enough about money; she didn't realize the house had to be sold and the proceeds invested. All that took time. Now the job at the library helps, too, although Grace never asks where the money comes from to keep her in such comfortable retirement.

At first Renata was hesitant to settle her in a house with a view of the river that had cradled her dead daughter, but Grace made no objection, and it was such a splendid view, such a perfect house. A former mansion redone as a group home. It had turrets and bowed windows, a broad covered porch with potted plants like an old-fashioned resort, with the upper-story balconies removed, to offer no temptation. A few of the residents were simply old; others were old and a little crazy; a few weren't old, just crazy, but no one so far out that you'd notice right away. No one who'd disturb the peace.

They managed fine under the care of their keepers; had today been sunny and not drizzling, Renata would have seen several people sitting out on the lawn. It wasn't unusual for the younger ones to use the tennis court. She'd played tennis with them several times, when her mother wasn't in the mood to talk and it seemed a pity to waste the trip and the sunshine.

Grace had been here for seven years, and it was a great improvement over the hospital she came from, before the medications got so efficient. That place was large and institutional, not anywhere you'd want to bring a child, although it might have suited Jack's Reality Tourism fantasy: the Bedlam Marriott. Sample a new kind of cocktail in a safe, secure environment. Round-the-clock service available. In that place, before you got to the elevator you had to navigate a corridor lined with ancient people strapped in wheelchairs, heads lolling on their chests, or worse, the wide-awake ones who stared accusingly, a stare conveying the message that though you may walk with a sprightly step now, you'll come to the same end. Upstairs, Renata would nod to Mr. Zelniker, drooling into his beard and shouting obscenities, and to Mrs. Baird, clutching her rag doll to her face, kissing it and murmuring, "There, baby. There, there, baby." One woman used to call out, "Help, please, get me out of this chair. I didn't do anything. I've been punished enough." What a clamor she made. And then Renata had to pass the gauntlet of the locked-up. Behind plate glass they drifted in clouds of smoke—this was back when smoking was permitted—some pressing their palms and glaring faces to the glass. In the hazy background a young woman in a white shift was forever dancing to inaudible music, a slow, syncopated dance with raised arms and snapping fingers and undulating shoulders, a quasi-belly dance of the kind Letitia Cole learned to do after she gave up composing classical music.

Renata had brought Gianna there once during the four brief years she'd cared for her. She'd wanted to show Grace her grandchild but realized right away that it was a mistake. Gianna was scared, and Grace was not having a sociable day. In fact she was having such a bad day—somnolent and savage in turn—that Renata looked around for an attendant. She finally spotted a hefty, fiftyish woman reclining on a couch in the lounge among the patients, wearing a name tag on her chest and engrossed in a copy of *Allure.* "What's that you're saying?" She removed her earphones. "No, there's no doctor on duty today. It's Sunday. No one's here."

"What about us?" asked a girl in a Chinese silk bathrobe staring out the window. "We're here. Aren't we anyone?"

No danger of anything like that here. Renata set up the stroller and hoisted it up the porch stairs, and Mrs. Hernandez, reading the *Times* in an Adirondack chair, got up creakily to have a look, to coo and goo. Everyone loves a baby. Well, not everyone. A new woman, youngish, sitting at the far end of the covered porch, leafing through a comic book, looked up and called out, "Look at the white tramp with her black baby."

"Don't say such things, Helene," Mrs. Hernandez scolded. "We've all told you before. If you can't say something nice, don't say anything at all." The woman was silenced. Renata looked down at Julio with his honey skin and fuzzy hair. He was fairly dark, but then she was on the dark side herself. People had mistaken her for Latina. It wasn't impossible that she could be his mother.

"You weren't pregnant the last time," said Mrs. Hernandez. "What did you do, adopt?"

"No, his mother was killed in the attack so I'm taking care of him." She hadn't the stomach for lies, and Mrs. Hernandez was quite sane, just old and alone with diabetes and arthritis. She could take it. She'd have to.

"Oh, the poor little thing. Look how he smiles. How he doesn't understand a thing. I've been watching the TV day and night. I'm just taking a little break. Dr. Schaeffer's daughter was in there, but she got out."

"Really? I didn't know he had a daughter."

"He took off the Walkman when she came yesterday," Mrs. Hernandez said wryly, and Renata smiled too. Dr. Schaeffer never took off the Walkman except to shower and shave and change the tape—Mozart and Bach exclusively, so loud you'd hear it when you passed by, though as a former doctor (or did one remain a doctor forever?), he should have known it could damage his ears.

Cecilia was in the front room when she entered, setting up a checkerboard for two men in wheelchairs. On the TV mounted on the wall, the President was saying, "I'm a loving guy. And I am also someone, however, who's got a job to do and I intend to do it."

"He's a loving guy. Now don't you feel better knowing that?" Cecilia was the attendant Renata liked best, a pert black woman of about her own age, with amber cornrows and outrageously large earrings, who behaved as though she were the social director of a cruise ship rather than the keeper of the declining. "Well, what have we here? Whose little cutie is this?"

As Renata explained about Julio, Cecilia's face darkened. She stroked his cheek and her eyes filled with tears. Her boyfriend's brother was a cop, she said. She turned off the TV; it was too loud to tell truths by. He was missing. And he didn't even have to be there. He was off duty but went anyway. "He had no idea. No one knew what they were getting into. He's probably lying under a piece of concrete. Or wandering around somewhere, you know, totally freaked." Then she shuddered and looked around quickly— she wasn't supposed to use that kind of language here.

But the men at the checkerboard didn't seem to have noticed. "Put that back on, would you?" one called. "What'd you turn it off for? We're watching."

She turned it back on. The President was confronting the ruin of the Pentagon. "I am overwhelmed by the devastation," he said. "Coming here makes me sad on the one hand. It also makes me angry."

Renata inquired about her mother.

"The same. No worse for wear. She doesn't seem upset by what happened."

"I know. When I call, she says it's too far away to touch anyone here."

"Yeah, well, I wouldn't quite put it that way." Again Cecilia lowered her voice. "Most of them get it, pretty much, especially the ones with family in the city. They're yakking on the phones all day. Lillian almost had a fit before she heard from her son, but he's okay. None of them had people actually die. You know Dr. Stevens, the one who's here weekends? He was in town and went to help at St. Vincent's but hardly anyone turned up. A few burn victims, that's all." She sighed, and on a breathy exhale, said, "Oh well, what're you gonna do?"

"Kill the bastards," one of the checkers players declared, an old man in an NYFD baseball cap and suspenders. "That's what to do. Nuke them all back to their caves. They want to hide in caves, then let them."

Renata might have told him what the TV pundit said: "You can't bomb these guys into the Stone Age because they're already in the Stone Age," but she restrained herself. Maybe the caves of the perpetrators were near the caves of Bodo and Zuna, the Neanderthals of her beloved book. They were so impossibly good-natured, they wouldn't have been capable of anything like this, even if they'd had the speech and technology. Though if they'd had speech and technology they might not have remained so good-natured.

"Yeah, Freddy, well maybe we should leave that to the government to decide," said Cecilia.

"It's a free country. I can express my opinion."

"Sure, be my guest. How about a cup of coffee meanwhile? Go ahead up, Renata. Your mom was in the TV room when last seen. Bye-bye, cutie-pie," and Cecilia leaned down to wiggle Julio's chin. Then she whispered, "My personal opinion? I think your mother knows more than she lets on."

"I think you're right." Renata laughed bitterly. How right you are, Cecilia. She knows plenty. But she keeps what she knows hoarded in a vault, and only alone in the dark does she take out the tiny key and creep inside to sort through her treasures. Griefs stored up, accruing interest. She lives off the interest, if you could call this living. Never touches the capital. There was really no need to hide it. No one would want that tainted fortune. It was only by a fluke that Grace possessed it herself. She was to have had the most ordinary of lives, the birth of twins her only singularity. But by some alchemy of fate, look what her gold has turned into.

Renata picked Julio up while the President said, "More than acts of terror, they were acts of war," parked the stroller behind Cecilia's desk, and started up the broad, curving staircase with the oak banister. The abstractions followed her up: "Unite in steadfast determination and resolve. Freedom and democracy are under attack."

She knew the upstairs TV room, a large squarish room with windows facing the river, a Turkish rug on the floor, sofas and chairs, a coffee urn on the sideboard. The management had tried to avoid the institutional look and had nearly succeeded. This was

Grace's favorite room. And there she was, in a straight-backed chair, arms folded in her lap, staring at the screen six feet in front of her, rapt in a commercial for anti-wrinkle cream. Grace's face was remarkably wrinkle-free for a woman her age, fifty-eight, though her skin was sallow and lifeless. Her hair was still dark, cut short. Her eyes, very dark. She'd never needed glasses. She had good, firm bones, a handsome woman with full lips and chiseled features. She looked well-rested, and why shouldn't she, thought Renata. She chose early retirement and had the lax face of someone on whom no demands were made. If any were made, she'd refuse them.

Two middle-aged women sat on a sofa, one knitting, the other picking at her fingernails. Each was as separate as if she were alone or in a movie theater. Grace never sat on the sofa because she didn't care to be too near anyone. She was wearing green polyester pants and a man's shirt, a Hawaiian shirt splashed with gaily colored toucans. It was a mystery, where Grace got her hideous outfits; Renata brought her nice things to wear but never saw Grace wearing them. She suspected these were old clothes from some grab-bag arrangement in the hospital of years ago. Maybe they came from dead inmates. Back when Renata and Claudia were teenagers, Grace wore tight jeans and miniskirts and hippie beads, even after she got her real-estate license and started meeting with clients. She could still have worn tight jeans and short skirts; she was slim, though her body was slack from lack of use. But the legs lasted. *Le gambe sono le ultime ad andarsene,* Renata's grandmother used to tell the girls. The legs are the last thing to go. If you have good legs, you almost don't need anything else. This turned out to be an exaggeration, but it had a grain of truth, like most folk wisdom.

"Hi, Mom." Renata placed herself between her mother and the screen.

"Renata?"

A good start. Excellent. On bad days Grace didn't call her anything. Back in the hospital, in the beginning, she sometimes called
her Claudia, and Renata didn't always bother to correct her.

"How're you doing?" She bent down to kiss Grace, awkwardly,
because she was holding Julio.

"All right. Could you move over a little, dear? You're right in
front of the screen."

She moved. She pulled a chair close to Grace and sat down.
"Hey, Mom. Look what I have here. Isn't he adorable?"

Grace glanced over perfunctorily. "He's a nice baby. He's not
yours, though, is he? You didn't mention you were having a baby.
You're not even married."

"Look, Mom, I'd really like to talk to you. Can we go somewhere more private?"

"Shh, in a minute." The commercial was over, replaced by a
soap opera, an angry confrontation between a man and a woman
with flawless faces: "I'll find out whether you tell me or not, and
when I do I'll kill him." "I'll never tell. You can't threaten it out
of me."

"But Mom—"

"Would you mind keeping your voice down?" That was the
woman on the sofa picking at her nails.

As if he'd been scolded, Julio let out one of his rare wails,
drowning out the quarrel on the screen.

"Why don't you wait in my room?" said Grace. "I'll be there as
soon as this is over."

Renata obeyed. She popped a pacifier into Julio's mouth and
went down the hall to Grace's small, neat room, quite bare of personal effects aside from a hairbrush on the dresser and a crossword
puzzle book and a pencil on the night table. Renata indulged in

crossword puzzles too, but seeing the book on her mother's night table she vowed, as she did on each visit, to kick the habit. She jiggled and nuzzled Julio to settle him, and together they watched the river out the window. "See the big boat? Isn't that a nice big boat? Someday I'll take you for a ride on one. That'll be fun."

She could take him to visit Mrs. Gertrude Stiller on the *QE2*. Mrs. Stiller's was her favorite story in the Transformed Lives folder, a woman who had found for her old age a setting even more beneficent than this placid house on a hill. A widowed octogenarian from Darien, Connecticut, she took up permanent residence in a cabin on the *Queen Elizabeth 2*. Until 1999, the Stillers had enjoyed many cruises on the *QE2*; it was on one of those cruises that Mr. Stiller died. Afterward, Mrs. Stiller decided that making the ship her home would be "the best way to deal with the loss of her husband." Her life on board, she noted in the *New York Times* article, was no more costly than a retirement community would be. "It's a lot of value for your money." She was kept busy dancing, playing bridge, going to shows and lectures, handling her e-mail, strolling on deck, and meeting celebrities, of whom her favorite was Nelson Mandela. "Mrs. Stiller is very definitely a member of the family to the crew," said the hotel manager of the *QE2*. "It is a very warm and close relationship."

The deck, as Mrs. Stiller made her way across it in a photograph, looked vast, although Renata didn't think she herself would care for the cramped living quarters. She didn't play bridge, either, or long to meet celebrities, though who would not make an exception for Nelson Mandela? Strictly speaking, he wasn't a celebrity anyhow, or not merely a celebrity. She would enjoy the ship's library. Come to think of it, she might very well get a job there; her skill at languages would give her a leg up, especially with the *QE2*'s international clientele.

At last Grace shuffled in. Why this shuffling? Pick your feet up, for heaven's sake. She sat on the bed and Renata joined her, with Julio on her lap.

"I'm so glad to see you, Mom. You've been on my mind, you know, with everything that's happened. . . . I told you Jack was all right, didn't I?"

"Yes. That's nice."

"I thought you might like to see Julio."

Grace sighed. She understood that a demand was being made on her attention, her curiosity. As if it were an immense labor, like heaving rocks, she said, "So, where'd he come from?"

"Jack brought him home the day it happened. See, I got him these little sneakers, even though he's too young to walk. I thought he needed something for outdoors."

Grace glanced absently at the sneakers, bright blue with white Velcro straps and specks of red light that blinked on and off. She folded her arms tightly around herself.

"He's just able to sit up. It's a good thing, otherwise I couldn't take him around in the stroller," Renata continued, her voice rising in desperation. "He doesn't crawl yet, though. If we put him on the floor he just lies on his belly and waves his arms like he's swimming."

Grace's face was changing, looking more as it used to in the hospital, remote, sealed, the eyes vacuous. She was falling down some rabbit hole in her head. Renata had to catch her before she vanished entirely.

"What happened is . . . His mother worked for Jack. She was killed when the towers collapsed. She was in there. We don't know who the father is. So Jack brought him home."

"Oh, stop! Why do I have to hear all this?" Grace cried.

"Because it's about me, too, that's why. You're still among the living, so you have to."

Grace turned away. "I really don't know what you're talking about," she said in what Renata used to call her dead voice. When she would play dead, in the hospital. Pretending she'd never had a life, pretending that, like Miss Greff from Renata's folder, she knew no people, had never gone anyplace, simply walked around in the dark fearing bugs, thunder, and men. But Grace's hollowness was a lie; she'd had a life, she had honored the principle of *ahmintu*, living one's life, only now she refused to acknowledge it.

"That first year, remember, after Claudia's baby was born and Peter gave her to that couple he knew in the city?"

The family never liked to use the couple's name. It was as if speaking the name aloud would give its owners a public existence, and then the shame of disposing of the baby so readily would have a public existence too. On Peter's recommendation, they did it. No lawyers, no red tape. They had jobs, her father made sure of that. A nice young couple.

"Remember," she continued, "you sent me to go see her every month, you gave me little presents to take, you asked all about her, but you would never go yourself. I was sixteen years old and you sent me to see how she was doing. I went because you couldn't. Wouldn't."

"You know I can't remember. It's my sickness. It's why I'm here."

"I'll help you remember. And then, after—" No, she wouldn't recount how her father crashed the car into a tree, accident or suicide no one could say for sure. She didn't need to be brutal. Or brutal only up to a point. Selective brutality, to counteract selective amnesia. "I going to take his work clothes, shape them into a quilt to remember him, and cover up under it for love." No, Grace did nothing like that. On the contrary. So, no mention of her father, or of who she supposes the father of Claudia's baby to be, a slow knowledge Renata has arrived at over years, through mists of denial almost as dense as Grace's. "Then when you were in the hospital, I had her with me. Remember, they gave her to me when they left town? She was three. Bigger than Julio. I told you all about it. I brought her to see you." You scared the shit out of her. Your glaring. Your not talking.

"I want to go back to the TV room." Grace was starting to get up.

"Later. Here, do you want to hold him? It feels nice. Try." She set Julio down on the bed and opened Grace's arms so she could have the feel of him. But Grace's arms were limp. They'd drop him.

"Please!" Renata cried. "I took care of her for four years. I did it all myself. I tried hard. You didn't want any part of it, of anything. And on that day, . . . I just did what everyone else did—I put her on the merry-go-round, on a horse, and stood there waving each time she went past. All the other parents were doing the same thing. It was so crowded, such a nice day. And then, . . . I only turned away for a minute, two minutes, and . . . When it stopped she wasn't there. I've told you a dozen times. Listen to me! Claudia wasn't your only child. I'm your child too."

"All right, all right. Stop yelling," Grace said. She held out her arms and Renata placed Julio in them. She stood right in front of Grace in case she decided to go limp again.

Grace held him in silence for a long time and finally looked down at him. "This can't be the same baby."

"No, Mom. That was years ago. That was Gianna. This is Julio."

"Gianna?"

"You named her. Remember, right after she was born you decided you wanted to give her something from our family so you gave her your mother's name? You made Claudia write it on the birth certificate. You had to spell it. Remember, Claudia started writing J-A-N-A and you fixed it? She said, what's the difference, they'll probably call her Jane or Jenny anyhow. But you said no, make it the Italian way."

"Where is she now?" Grace whispered.

"I don't know." It killed her to say it but she had to. She couldn't lie about this.

"Don't cry," Grace said. "Enough crying. You can't change the past."

"I really tried to take good care of her." Renata wept. "I really tried."

Grace raised Julio and nuzzled his cheek against her own. She smiled. Then she cried too. Renata moved to take Julio so she could weep freely, but Grace clutched him tighter, clasped him until he whined in protest. She rocked back and forth on the bed, weeping. "Take him," she said. "I don't want to scare him."

So Renata took him.

"Where is she?" Grace asked again. "Gianna."

"I told you, I don't know."

"So find her."

Seven

Find her. If only she could. Gianna would be nearly eighteen now. She is even more lost than Renata was at seventeen, or eighteen or nineteen.

After the morning when they stood on the banks of the river and watched Claudia being dredged up, her face pale green like some kind of sea monster, her leg twisted and her body puffy—from languishing underwater, from childbirth—her father began pouring bourbon steadily month after month. Her mother retreated into some shelter of the mind from which she emerged now and then to watch television or push a cart through the aisles of the supermarket, buying a bizarre assortment of things she tried to turn into meals. But that was usually too much effort. Lifting a cup of coffee was too much effort. "It's so heavy," she said when Renata brought her coffee in bed each morning. "Since when did cups get so heavy?" So Renata took over. Grace was more than willing to yield up credit cards and authority. She'd stopped selling real estate, a pity because she'd worked so hard to get her license and was good at it. If any of her old clients called, Renata was to say she was on leave. Every few weeks Grace urged her to take the bus in to the city and see how the baby was doing—Gianna, named for Grace's mother, Giovanna. She was with the couple Peter had found, friends, he'd said, who'd wanted her when no one else did.

Did Renata imagine it, or did her parents really wince when they looked at her face, the image of Claudia's before it underwent its sea change? Well, let them wince. If that's how they feel, let them go to hell, was Renata's mantra. Let the house tumble down around them. She'd be getting out, going away to college. She'd arranged it all on her own, catching her father in sober moments when the bills arrived. He was kind when he remembered she was there, though at times he seemed faintly puzzled when he passed her in the hall or the kitchen, as if he considered her dead along with Claudia, as if twins were so inseparable that they couldn't be in such antithetical states as dead and alive. Other times he cried at the kitchen table and wanted company; she obliged at first, then stopped. He was sickening.

Her first thought, when the police came to the door that rainy April night with the news that he'd rammed his car into a tree, was that now she wouldn't be able to go away to school. Her mother wouldn't survive on her own. Her next thought was that he must have done it on purpose. It happened less than a mile from their house, at the sharp bend in the road, near the turnoff for the park where they'd fished Claudia from the river. Everyone knew to watch out for that bend. Renata had just learned to drive, and her father had warned her about it himself. She was so mad she could kill him. How could he? she thought when she went to identify his body. If he ever dared to open his eyes, she'd pound him senseless.

Instead, when Grace refused to stir from bed, Renata wrote a letter withdrawing from college. When Grace refused to speak or to eat, Renata wished for the first time that pain-in-the-ass Peter was still around. But Peter and Cindy had decamped from the house three blocks away just after Claudia died—Cindy first, leaving with not so much as a goodbye, then Peter. "Disappeared without a trace," said Grace in her I-told-you-so voice. And Dan, who doted on his younger brother, who always defended and protected him, frowned and poured another inch of bourbon. As for friends, well, they'd been scarce lately, especially as Grace and Dan hadn't led anything resembling a social life for some time. So Renata called an ambulance and packed Grace's bag.

She saw her mother before she was moved to a bigger hospital, farther away, where she might have to stay for a while, the doctors said. A pointless visit—Grace was not inclined to conversation. Renata had seen a lot by then, yet the sight of Grace scared her: she was sitting in a chair and breathing but looked dead. Dead not in quite the way the others had looked. You'd expect death to leave a uniform imprint, but each of Renata's corpses had had a distinct way of being dead, and Grace's was arguably the worst because it wasn't real, only a perverse pretending.

Renata was left with a house, a car, three credit cards, and a high-school diploma. More than some teenagers possess, yet she didn't know what to do next; she didn't feel like doing much of anything. She did know that if she stayed in the house she was in danger of going her mother's route. Already she was spending too much time imagining Claudia climbing down the rock face in the dark (was Fox behind her or did he stay up above?), running out onto the pier. Tripping on the broken planks? Or jumping in? I dare you.

If she went on this way, who would call the ambulance for her? She got a handyman to look after the house—her last sensible act—and packed a bag and went to the city. That was where Claudia used to sneak off, to escape.

It was the cheapest apartment she could find, just one room. The windows were dirty, so the light coming in through the fluttery, once-white curtains looked dirty too. Two small lamps were fixed to the wall, their lampshades the color of old yellow dog's fur. A small scratched wooden coffee table sat in front of the studio couch she slept on. There was a large wing chair upholstered in a fabric of pea-green leaves and brown flowers, flowers long past their prime. The beige rug was dappled with stains, one patch like a map of Europe connected by a narrow strip to Africa below. Sitting in the wing chair, she would try to pick out the shapes of countries she remembered from the maps on the walls at school. In one corner of the room, a stove, refrigerator, and sink projected from the wall like lumpy, cracking tumors. The kitchen table was covered with a light green plastic tablecloth that had a tart, acidic smell when it was damp. Her one concession to gracious living was to throw away the tablecloth. She wasn't seeking punishment, only oblivion. She hadn't done anything wrong, after all, unless it was wrong not to stop Claudia from going out that night. Could anyone have stopped her? But of course it was wrong. Of course the apartment was a punishment.

As she lay awake in the first light, she studied the cracks in the ceiling. They made a graceless calligraphy, ugly, yielding nothing, not like the hangings she would buy later, when everything was transformed yet again. The walls were pinkish-beige and needed a paint job, which the landlord might have provided if she'd asked. But she didn't like to ask—he was a gruff man with a thick Russian accent—and she didn't want anything so intrusive as a paint job marring the void of her life. She quickly got used to things as they were. She got used to the room as if it were her fate, and soon she even felt she belonged there, as if her earlier life had been a mere prelude, as if everything had happened in order to lead her to this room. All she brought from that earlier life were her memories and her body, and she really didn't want either one, not her memories because they pained and confounded her, and not her body because it was barely eighteen years old and hungry to live.

One habit did remain from her old life, and that was visiting Gianna. Every few weeks she went across town and pushed the stroller through Riverside Park, gazing at the river, imagining how nice it would be to have her niece for company, but that was only a fantasy. She had no idea how to take care of a baby, and anyway, Gianna's new parents would never give her up. They loved her, or showed all the signs. It was working out, just as Peter had promised. It was good of them to let her visit.

She got a job in a bar down the street. Drinking held no appeal, but it felt familiar watching the men drink, and soon she started letting them come to her apartment after work. In this way she learned all about sex, and sometimes the sensation of Peter running his finger down her spine in the garage came to mind like a scene from a movie she'd seen long ago and nearly forgotten. If the men bought her dinner or offered her money, she accepted. It came in handy. She slept with them to keep her body quiet. It was loud, her body; it set up a clamor only she could hear. She did it because she wasn't busy and wanted to think as little as possible. She did it because it made her feel safe. When the men were inside her she was stopped up, less liable to spill out, leaving a crumpled skin. The man inside her was like a cork holding her together. She did it because Claudia had done it, to keep something of Claudia close by, though she wouldn't have admitted that.

Sometimes it was the same man for weeks at a time, then he would change. But really there was no change at all. Sometimes when she opened her eyes she was confused by the face she saw. The men were older. The bar wasn't a young singles hangout but an old-fashioned place where men came to chill out, shoot pool, watch ball games. In her room, sometimes she made them coffee. Sometimes the man would want to talk. She let him. She could wait. Soon enough he would touch her and then her body would get what it wanted. It had to be fed the way you feed an impatient animal. She, or rather her body, became ravenous. The men were surprised. Some were amused and some didn't like it much; those didn't come back. When she came, she kept her eyes closed and pretended she was alone, that the flesh against her skin was a part of her. Or that it was the whole world, everything that was not her, pressing in to offer her life. It made her delirious—she'd never felt so alone or so alive. Everything else was a great exertion, an arduous victory over inertia, but to this she leaped effortlessly. Later she'd look at their naked bodies, amazed that they were the instruments that could shock her into life, and so much more pleasantly than the doctors who were shocking Grace. But after the men left she crashed. Her memories came sweeping in, tsunami-style, and she was overwhelmed with fury at what life could do, and loathed her hungry body that insisted on living in its primitive way.

Soon the money machines stopped spitting out cash when she stuck the card in, and bills she didn't comprehend kept being forwarded. She had to think like a grown-up. She called the agency where her mother used to work and said she wanted to sell the house. With everything in it? they asked. No, not everything. She put some things in storage but hauled the carton with the toy farm back to her room. She went through her father's desk and figured out that she was not destitute. She learned what power of attorney was, and on one of her hospital visits shoved a pen into her mother's limp hand and told her to write her name. Here, here, and here, and Grace obeyed. By the time it was all taken care of, Renata knew a lot about personal finance, enough to grasp that she could afford a better life. But she'd grown used to things as they were, with so few reminders of what had gone before.

One day the woman who had taken Gianna—Renata couldn't bring herself to call her Gianna's mother—phoned to ask if she might bring her over for a couple of days. "You'd be doing me a big favor." She came in leading Gianna by the hand and carrying an armload of kiddie paraphernalia. Gianna was three; she wore blue jeans and an "I Love New York" T-shirt, and her black bangs reached down to her eyes. She knew Renata. She shouted her name and barreled into her arms. They had to go out of town, the woman said, a family emergency, and Renata was the person she most trusted. Renata was afraid she'd stop trusting her once she took in the grimy walls and stained rug and shabby furniture, but she was too distraught and hurried to notice anything. She clasped Gianna tightly, then ran away.

Renata had the oddest feeling that she'd never see her again, and she didn't. Her half-hearted, ignorant stabs at locating the couple, at locating Peter and Cindy, were in vain. Why find them anyway? Suddenly she had a child, Claudia's. And what was Claudia's was virtually her own. Suddenly the two years she'd spent in the room with the gray light and the stained rug felt not like years of blank oblivion but years of waiting. Waiting until Gianna arrived.

She bought a small bed and put it in a corner of the room with a sheet hanging up for privacy; she knew the latest man, Joe, would turn up if he didn't find her in the bar. He was about forty and seemed domesticated, a mild, affable man who could make love endlessly; Renata liked anyone who could wear her out. He didn't want any more of her than she wanted of him, so they got along nicely. A few times they'd gone to a movie—a gesture to the social niceties—but basically they fucked. She didn't know much about Joe except that he came from Queens and drove a furniture delivery truck. He used to operate a backhoe, a job that required a lot of control and precision, he said with a grin, and she smiled back to show she got the joke. After she moved away she could no longer remember how he dressed or what he drank at the bar or how he first approached her. She did remember his body. She remembered— still does—many of their bodies, though she'd rather not. At inconvenient moments they parade before her eyes like girls in a beauty contest, and she tries blinking or shaking her head to make them go away. Joe was an inch or so taller than she, stocky, slightly paunchy, an athlete's bulk gradually softening. He had a blond crewcut, blue eyes and a thick nose he said had been broken when he was an amateur boxer. He had full lips and perfect teeth and small ears and large, warm hands and a round birthmark the size of a silver dollar on his left calf. After they made love he would fall asleep on top of her and stay inside her for ten or fifteen minutes; that might have been what she liked best about him, that and his mild nature.

A few days after Gianna arrived, Joe rang the bell late, close to eleven. They had to be quiet, Renata said; a friend's child was staying over. He grunted in a way that implied he knew all about accommodating to children. The apartment was overheated and the radiator valve was stuck, so she opened the window. The curtains stirred and cool air rippled over them. After the first time, while he lay dozing on top of her, Renata stared at the ceiling and traced the cracks that resembled calligraphy, wondering dreamily if you could devise a rudimentary language, a message, out of cracks in a ceiling. Joe woke, rolled over and combed her hair with his fingers. Her hair was very long; it had had plenty of time to grow since Peter had run his finger across the bare nape of her neck in the garage. Joe draped her hair over his face and they laughed softly. Next thing she knew, she was impaled on top of him—so luscious she would have died happily then and there. Joe's lips were curved in a half-smile. That would change quite soon, she knew: he would get a look of intense concentration, self-absorption, and when at last he opened his eyes, he'd look faintly surprised to find her, but friendly. Oh, so it's you! Just now, though, the half-smile showed his perfect teeth. His blue eyes were pleasantly vague. As he moved inside her, she felt he was grating her the way you grate an onion, scraping back and forth like a reliable machine. Fine, she thought, grate away, scrape me till there's nothing left. She gave herself up to it.

A whimper came from behind the curtain, then a louder cry, like a beginner's bow scraping across a violin. Her heart thudded against her ribs and she stopped moving. But when she stopped, a protest rose in her gut, a cry to match the child's cry. It wouldn't let her stop. It was the crucial moment; she had to keep moving.

"The kid," Joe whispered as he pushed into her. "Maybe you should go to her." She shook her head, shook her hair. No, no. Gianna screamed and Joe moved to nudge Renata off him. No. She turned and glimpsed Gianna, who'd come out from behind the curtain and stood staring, clutching a plush dog to her chest, her mouth wide open. Still Renata couldn't stop. A minute later she collapsed on his chest. "Go on," he said. "I can wait." She sprang up. It was hard to run across the room with the pulsing not yet abated, but she forced herself. She picked Gianna up. Her face was hot and wet, Renata's thighs were hot and wet, the radiator sizzled, everything was dripping, tropical. "It's okay, it's okay. I'm here. He's a friend of mine. It's okay," she kept saying.

"I want my mommy," Gianna wailed.

"Yes, yes, she'll come very soon." A lie, the first of many. They would get easier as time went on. "It's all right. I'm here."

She gave Gianna some water and took her to the bathroom, then rocked her against her naked body till she quieted down. Between gasps, Gianna said she dreamed there was a monster on the other side of the curtain, so Renata told her there was no monster, only she and her friend. We were playing a game.

Once Renata got her settled in bed she returned to Joe. "Sorry about that," and she offered to start all over, for him. "Nah, I better go," he said with his grin. "Shit, kids. I've been there. Maybe you could, uh, just give me a quick hand with this?" So Renata did what he asked and he left soon after.

She was ashamed that she'd waited, ashamed that her voracious, impatient body had won out over a child's crying. She sat up far into the night and knew she must change everything about her life. She would move to a decent apartment suitable for a child. She would learn to take proper care of her. She would send her to nursery school. Maybe she'd even go to school herself. She would transform herself into one of those staunch single moms everyone marveled at, deft and responsible and competent, however overtaxed.

And she did exactly that.

The next morning, though, before going hand in hand with Gianna to buy a paper and check out the apartment ads, Renata made one small gesture of reclamation. She spread out the pieces of the toy farm on the stained rug and explained to Gianna all about the buildings and the animals and the farm family. Gianna took to them right away, though every now and then she would stop to ask if her mother was coming back soon.

"Soon," Renata said. "Look, these are the children. Sky, Pastel, and Powder." She lifted each one in turn and handed them to Gianna. "This is their horse. This is the silo where they keep the corn."

They made up a long story about a happy day at the farm. In the years to come, as Gianna stopped asking about her parents, it became their favorite game.

Eight

Once she's come home from visiting Grace and settled Julio in for his nap, Renata finds several surprises. Not pleasant. Blasts from the past, as Linda would say. Messages she could do without.

She's given Jack's phone number to several people, so it's only natural to play his messages. She's living here, isn't she? At any rate for the duration. The first three are business, skippable, but then comes a woman's voice, light, trembly, cajoling.

"Jack? It's me. I know it's been ages and you probably aren't thrilled to hear from me but I just had to find out. . . . I've been obsessing about you ever since it happened. Are you okay? Please, Jack, could you forget everything that happened at least for now and give me a call, okay? I've had visions of you down there and . . . Well, so just please, please call? I'm praying you're okay. I'm fine, in case you want to know." And a Manhattan number.

The fabled ex-wife. Pamela the petulant, the impossible to please, the faithless, who left her wedding dress on a shelf in the closet and her tampons in the back of the bathroom cabinet. Renata, not usually the jealous type, has to sit down, she's shaking so. She almost misses the next message and has to play it again: her neighbor Gerald of the dreads and stuffed-animal collection. "Renata, love, I hate to tell you this but the news is not good. Or only half good. The couple upstairs? He came home but she didn't. Call back if you want to know more. Hope the little guy's doing okay."

While the little guy sleeps she leafs through her folders for solace. No Mrs. Stiller on the *QE2* today, nor the exuberant Letitia Cole. They make her envious. Instead she reads about the mermaids. The mermaids provoke envy, too, but they are so far beyond anything she might attempt that the envy remains abstract. Ever since Claudia was dredged from the Hudson River, Renata hasn't been lured by water. Looking at the ocean is fine, only not getting wet. Too many imaginings, the sensation of struggling, unable to move her leg, the sinking, the disbelief, then the panic, then the knowing.

In a tiny town off U.S. Highway 19 in central Florida, tourists can watch through acrylic panels as mermaids in colorful, glittery fishtail costumes swim and cavort acrobatically in an underground spring, dodging fish and the occasional turtle. The whole act takes months to learn: the trick is using the air hose properly. In a photo accompanying the story, the mermaids look quite beautiful as they sit chatting around the tube from which they enter, their long hair streaming, their legs tightly swaddled. How do they get into this line of work? Renata wonders. She'd like to go and see the mermaids; she's even planned a fantasy trip, driving down, maybe with Jack, to watch women who can endure underwater, far from the strains of the upper world. Frolicking in the medium that killed Claudia.

Since Tuesday, though, travel is no longer enticing. She slams the folder shut, irked at her own idleness. There's so much she might be doing while Julio sleeps. Cooking a real dinner for a change. Reviewing the Arabic alphabet; she found a dictionary and an elementary-level grammar in Rashid's bookstore, showing four columns of variations for each of the twenty-eight letters, depending on their position in the sentence. In normal times, this discovery would delight Renata, but in a national emergency and with a baby to boot, it is dismaying.

Visiting Grace always saps her energy. All she manages to do is turn on the television, just in time for the replay of the President's speech at the memorial service in Washington earlier today, words he must have spoken right about when Grace accepted Julio in her arms and wept. "Our response to history is already clear. To answer these attacks and rid the world of evil." While Renata is dutifully trying to wrap her mind around that ambitious project, ridding the world of evil, she's distracted by the bulletin slithering across the bottom of the screen; the crawl, they call it, and she has to admire the apt name. The crawl says the representatives of fifteen Arab nations were instructed that "the time has come to choose sides." Presumably between good and evil. But what if they have different notions of good and evil? That's something to think about, for sure, but the crawl doesn't permit thinking. It's designed to fracture attention and ensure that nothing lodges in the mind long enough or firmly enough for thought. "Grief and tragedy and hatred are only for a time," the President continues. "Goodness, remembrance and love have no end," and the camera pans the somber, familiar faces of many political leaders at the service. She can identify a handful and is working on the others, but again the crawl grabs her attention: the State Department demands that the Arab nations "wrap up and prosecute terrorists on your own soil." She's a trifle dizzy; the crawl has had its inevitable effect; her mind is in little pieces.

Still she listens politely till the end of the speech, then goes into the kitchen to forage for a snack. When she returns it's playing

again, from the top: "We are here in the middle hour of our grief,"
he says. And she has just enough of her mind left to know that although the words have a nice ring—good job, whoever came up
with that line—they are quite mistaken. Make no mistake, she
thinks, we are nowhere near the middle hour of our grief. We've
barely begun. Is she splitting hairs again? Does it really matter, so
long as the sentence rolls along well and offers comfort? That's
what Jack might say. Linda would understand. She'll have to call
Linda later just to hear her exclaim, offended to the core, The *middle* hour of our grief? The *middle*? Give me a break! In the calligraphy hanging in Renata's apartment, the fortune-teller said it would
be around the Great Snow before the illness was pacified. This may
take many Great Snows.

She can't watch anymore, she's so sleepy; the crawl has con-
quered, pulverized her brain. Her body is leaden, her eyes droop-
ing. She'll take a nap, like Julio. But first, she might as well pick up
her own messages.

"Renata, now don't keel over in shock, but it's Cindy. Long
time no see, right? Are you okay, I mean, I hope you weren't anywhere near . . . you know. Isn't this just the pits? Look, could you
give me a call, please? I, uh . . . " The bright voice quavers and dissolves. "I need some help, is the thing. I really need some help."

Cindy. Renata's once-aunt, her Uncle Peter's wife, who split for
unknown parts after Claudia's death. No way was Cindy ever aunt-
like, a giggly, daffy girl with a mop of red curls. Lucille Ball, Grace
used to call her behind her back. Silly Cindy, Renata and Claudia
called her to her face, even though she was their occasional
chummy babysitter who fixed their hair in the styles she'd learned
in beauty school and let them play with her makeup and taught
them the latest disco dances and joined them in cooking gross
concoctions involving peanut butter and flour and apple juice.

Even though she gave them the precious book about the cave family. If Cindy happened to drop by at the right moment—after she'd finished at the hairdressing salon in town, say—she'd curl up beside them on the floor to watch *Gilligan's Island* or *Batman,* and she begged them to let her play with Farmer Blue and his family, but that they could never allow, for it would mean admitting her to the sanctuary of the private language. Renata might have succumbed, but not Claudia. "Even if we wanted her," she said, "she's too dumb to learn it." Silly Cindy, always with a glass in her hand.

Eighteen years since Renata's heard that piping Southern California voice, though not for lack of trying. When she was nineteen and got Gianna back and wanted someone—anyone—in the family to see her, wanted to create some facsimile of a family for Gianna, she had looked in the phone book, tried a dozen beauty salons, but Cindy had disappeared without a trace. Maybe returned to San Diego. Later, after Gianna was gone, when the stifled suspicions began creeping into Renata's nighttime vigils, when she thought back to the time Peter ran his finger along her spine in the garage as she bent over her bike—the dreadful, unspeakable thrill of it, and the shame—she realized that Cindy, of course, silly Cindy who took off like a shot, would be the one to know for sure. And she looked again. Nothing. And now? Cindy needs help? Who doesn't, now? Renata jots down the phone number, kicks off her sandals and curls up on the couch. After eighteen years, a few more hours can't make much difference.

She wakes to the sound of Julio's loud happy nonsense syllables coming from the next room, the mystery tongue no linguist has yet decoded, though Renata believes if she had the time and patience she might decipher something from those gurgles. It's only another language. Indeed, speakers of Cochandi, who live in the Amazon jungle, believe that a baby's inchoate burblings are the fading remnants of the language used in the spirit world before birth, among those waiting to be born. The physical shock of birth erases much of the language, clearing the mind for its destined earthly speech. If those few vestigial sounds could be deciphered, they would give valuable clues to the world of the spirits, but no one has yet succeeded, which suggests that we here in the earthly realm are not meant to know.

She's just finished changing Julio and is snapping up the denim overalls when Jack comes in, sweaty and grimy. It must have been the office first, today, then the rubble.

"So, how'd it go?"

He falls onto the bed. "Come keep me company." They all three lie down together, Julio on top of Jack, belly to belly. Today he dished out food in the Red Cross tent and handed out a shipment of heavy socks donated by a sporting goods store in Delaware. A few bodies turned up; he saw them go by. A fireman was unearthed. When the firemen's remains are carried out everyone stands at attention, helmets off. Not so for the civilians, hierarchy persisting even in immolation. The engineers discovered that the careening steel beams punctured the subway tunnels and possibly through to the water mains. No one can yet gauge that damage. Four construction crews are on the job. It's not clear who's in charge, if anyone, and the construction workers, firefighters, and cops don't get along all that well. But somehow the work is getting done. Slowly. "It has to be slow, because of the, you know, the remains. They can't just go in and blast. They have to pick it apart by hand. I doubt if they'll find anyone alive at this point. But no one wants to believe that."

People can still say "lost" or "missing" for their loved ones, Renata thinks, implying that they might be found. If they spoke Bliondan (though this attack would never have happened in Lapland), they would have to distinguish between lost-but-may-still-be-found and lost forever. Their loved ones would be in the process of turning into *tanfendi-noude,* from the more optimistic *tanfendi-oude.*

The air is very bad, Jack goes on. Everyone's coughing. A volunteer herbalist—God knows how she got through the barriers, maybe a construction worker's girlfriend—came around distributing homeopathic pellets supposed to be good for the lungs. Everyone wants to do something. Oh, and the President dropped by, after the memorial service in D.C. Jack didn't see him up close but heard that he spoke a few encouraging words, standing shoulder to shoulder and hard-hatted with the mayor, the governor, all the election-winners who got more than they bargained for.

"Did you catch that on TV?" he asks.

"No, I wasn't here. I went up to see my mom. I took your car. I forgot to ask, I hope you don't mind."

"No, that's fine, but where'd you park it?" Like many in the neighborhood, Jack is obsessed with finding parking spots. So community-spirited in other ways, when it comes to parking he's tooth-and-claw competitive.

"Just around the corner. No restrictions, remember?"

"Oh, right. So how was she?"

"The same. She held Julio for a few minutes."

"Really? That's something, isn't it? Could be a good sign." Just as Renata finds signs in language and speech, down to commas and pauses, he finds signs in tiny permutations of behavior. Good signs. One day soon he may even unearth a good sign from the attack: besides unrestricted parking, how well-behaved and generous New Yorkers have become in crisis. Already, several among the glut of newspaper articles have suggested that tragedy will improve our moral fiber, wean us from our addiction to the lifestyles and court trials of the rich and famous, catapult the entire nation into sobriety and adulthood. This notion Renata dismisses. She distrusts those who are so ready, so soon, to assemble and package their thoughts for public delivery. But newspaper pages have to be filled, obviously. She has not yet read (it's a few days too soon) the *New Yorker*—the cover showing the barely discernible black towers fading into deeper blackness—with its collection of responses from famous writers, but when she does she will toss it down in disgust. The soon-to-be-famous words by Susan Sontag, attacking the "self-righteous drivel . . . being peddled by public figures and TV commentators," will make her cringe. Not because the words are not true. They are true and Renata thinks the same thing. Their placement is what makes them cringe-worthy. She knows from her own past. It's not so much what you say. It's what you choose to say first that reveals character. Even when a voice speaks truth, it can speak it in a tone that destroys trust.

As far as her mother, she shrugs. Good signs, bad signs, she can't tell anymore. And since she can't, or won't, tell Jack how or why her mother wept, there's nothing to say. "I got a message from Gerald. You know, my downstairs neighbor? The woman on the top floor is missing. I had a feeling she worked there."

They've run out of words for these exchanges. He squeezes her hand. "Did you know her well?"

"No, hardly at all. But still. There're a few other messages. One of them . . . I'm sorry, I didn't mean to, . . . I was just listening in case there was something for me. One was your ex, I think."

"What!" He rolls Julio off him and sits up. "What?"

"You heard. At least I think so. Unless there's someone else."

"Oh, Christ. Is she all right?"

"Yes. She's worried about you."

He looks ready to spring up, then lies back again. "I'll listen later." He strokes her hair absently for a while. "I got a call from

Carmen's mother today, in Puerto Rico. I must have told you I've been trying to reach her."

"No, you didn't."

"Well, anyway, she called back. I had to tell her about Carmen. It was terrible."

"I'm sorry."

"She sort of knew anyway because she hadn't heard from her. But now it was definite. At least I could tell them Julio's okay. She and Carmen's sister are coming back as soon as the planes are flying."

Renata is silent. She knows what this means.

"So next week they'll be coming to get him. You can go back to work. You've really been great about—"

"No!"

"What, no?"

"We could adopt him," she says wildly. "I mean, maybe they can't take care of him."

"He's theirs, Renata. Why shouldn't they take care of him? It's not like they're impoverished or anything. Carmen's sister is a nurse. Her mother does something in an office, I forget what. Look, you knew it was only for a few days. Don't you want to get back to your life?"

That's what the mayor keeps counseling on TV: get back to your life. Its imprecision grates. Whatever you're doing at the moment is your life. You can't get back to your life because you can't have been away from it. "It's not fair," she cries. "I'm taking such good care of him. He loves me."

"Renata, you're not making any sense."

"Why does everything have to make sense?"

Love should not categorize, but even Jack, lavish in love, cannot help thinking the obvious: a thirty-four-year-old woman, childless, with hermit-like tendencies, obsessive, eccentric. Surely a child is what she's been needing all along.

"Okay, so you've gotten attached to him. It's only natural." And there Julio lies between them, discussed in the third-person invisible, looking very fetching as he kicks his bare feet in the air. Jack gives him an absentminded tickle on the chest. "But we can't keep him indefinitely. Babies don't just get passed around like . . . He has a family. You can visit him, they're nice people, I'm sure they'll appreciate all you've done."

She just weeps.

Finally: "Look, Renata, if it's a baby you want, we can have a baby. We'll get married and have a baby. If that's what you want."

"It's not that I want a baby!"

He's never seen her cry like this. He's never seen her cry at all. Except for Tuesday, but that doesn't count; everyone cried on Tuesday. "I don't. I mean, I don't long for a baby. I just don't want them to take this one away."

He studies her curiously, almost professionally. "What is it? You had an abortion? A miscarriage? What?"

She shakes her head. Stupid, stupid. Sometimes his simplicity makes her want to scream. It comes from the supply-and-demand principle of his work. No, demand and supply. If someone turns up hungry, give him food. Ignorant, give him schooling. Sick, find him a doctor. Need, gratification. Problem, solution. She can't bear to give up the baby, so he'll give her a baby of her own.

"I'm sorry, sweetheart, but you must have known all along," he says. "Listen, everyone's half out of their minds right now. You're stressed out. You're irrational."

"You don't understand!"

"No, I don't. Maybe you can explain it to me."

Just what she doesn't want to do. She doesn't want that to be part of Jack and her. She doesn't want Jack to be part of *it.*

"Okay, I tried." He goes into the kitchen, returns with a can of beer, plops down in front of the TV, flicks it on, pops the can open, and yet again: "We are here in the middle hour of our grief."

Renata dries her tears and begins composing a letter in her head. Dear Mr. President, With all due respect, I must point out that your phrase, "the middle hour of our grief," is inaccurate. This is the third day after the attack. If this is "the middle hour of our grief," and if the stages of our grief will be roughly equal, it logically follows that the end of our grief would fall somewhere around the sixth or seventh day after. You know as well as I do that this is not true, and that our grief will last much longer. Granted, the beginning, middle, and end stages of our grief (assuming it has an end) may not be equal. The middle may last longer than the beginning, which your words suggest is now over. Even so, my point still . . .

No. No, no, what is she thinking? She'd never send a letter like that. Jack is right, she must be out of her mind. It's not only crazy but probably dangerous as well. Wasn't someone fired from a TV network for challenging the President's use of the word "cowards" for the hijackers? Didn't they pass some law just yesterday, increasing the government's surveillance powers? Soon it might be illegal to criticize his prose. Soon it might be illegal to say anything at all that might be construed as less than thoroughly vengeful. Even to belly-dance might be construed as unpatriotic. Watch out, Letitia! What was that story she heard on the radio two years ago: in Argentina, during the worst of the despotism of the 1970s, a wildly popular singer was banned from singing his signature number, a political protest song called, "All I Ask from God." The song was so well known, though, that he didn't have to sing it: he could simply sit onstage and strum the chords on his guitar and the audience would sing it for him. Soon we all might be speaking to each other through silence.

She goes over to Jack and rests a hand on his shoulder, a half-hearted gesture toward peace. "I didn't get around to cooking anything. How about if I phone for some Indian food?"

"Sure. Whatever." He's so hypnotized by the screen, she might just as well have suggested elephant dung: "Grief and tragedy and hatred are only for a time. Goodness, remembrance and love have no end."

They eat in front of the TV while Julio lolls happily on the floor in a round, cushiony contraption Aruna brought over. The news, like the Indian food, is a melange of sour, bitter, tangy. Caves, rumors of war, vows of revenge, more assaults on Arabs, and scenes from the Armory in midtown, where relatives of the missing fill out forms and have the soft inner tissue of their cheeks swabbed for DNA samples. A psychologist urges parents to hug their children more than usual and assure them that they're safe; Renata picks Julio up and holds him on her lap, lets him taste a few grains of basmati rice. The crawl continues but she tries not to look, to preserve her brain cells. At intervals the mayor appears at the site in his hard hat. He's ennobled by tragedy, all his notorious sins gone up in smoke, his mind far from elephant dung. Go to restaurants, he says. Go to theaters. Go shopping. It's good for the economy. The covert message: shopping can distract, alleviate pain, maybe even ward off further disaster. Shopping is the best therapy.

"I'd better get him changed and into bed," she says. "Then I have to make a call."

It must be money Cindy wants, she thinks as she settles Julio in the bassinet. (On his back to avoid Sudden Infant Death Syndrome—she's noted the warning signs in the subway.) What else, after so long? Okay, she'll give it for old time's sake. But as it happens, her thinking, like Jack's, is too simple: problem, solution; problem, solution.

"Can you stay with Julio tomorrow?" she asks after she's hung up. He's on his second beer, or maybe the third, his eyes still fixed on the screen. "It's Saturday. You won't be going to work, will you?"

"We'll be open but I can take a few hours off, sure. What's up?"

This takes a bit of explaining. First of all, she has to explain who Cindy is. "I just spoke to her. She wants me to meet her tomorrow."

"How'd she find you after all these years?"

Exactly what Renata had asked. "In the phone book, she said. But it seems she knew all about me through my uncle. They're still in touch on and off. It's weird—I've tried to find him myself over the years, but I never could. And all along he was keeping track of me." Weird is hardly an adequate word, but she's too dazed to find a better one. It's frightening, enraging, sinister, like something out of film noir. How could he know all about me? she asked Cindy. People like Peter have their ways, she said. Trust me, it's better not to know.

"So why call now, all of a sudden?"

"It's about her boyfriend. He's been missing since Tuesday. He works at a deli right near . . . " She can't bring herself to say "Ground Zero," which sounds like a computer-game locale. Nor can she use Jack's term, "the pile." That's an insider's word, for the initiated. She hasn't earned it. "She wants me to help her look for him, in the hospitals for starters. She has this idea that I'm competent. She may not know many people who are."

"You mean to say she hasn't done anything about it in three days?" Such negligence rouses Jack's interest. Just as a senator is declaring, "We should be prepared to take warlike activities," he clicks the mute button, leaving the senator's mouth working in vain.

"She says she's been out of it. Knowing Cindy, at least the old Cindy, that could mean drunk. She's the sort of person . . . She doesn't know how to do anything. Except cut hair—that she does very well. I don't know how she's managed all this time."

"I'd try St. Vincent's first. It's the closest," says Jack. "And go there rather than call."

"Okay. What about Pamela? Are you going to call her?"

"I don't know. Not tonight. What do you think? You think I should call?"

"All she wants to know is if you're dead or alive. That's pretty simple. It shouldn't take long."

"With her nothing is simple."

"Oh, are you afraid of getting back in her clutches?" An odd dialogue to be having, she thinks, while the silent screen shows two dozen firefighters lined up, hats off, hands on hearts, forming an aisle down which four more firefighters carry a stretcher. It's pointless to let the coolness between them continue when Jack is the only source of pleasure around. She sits on his lap and reaches inside his shirt.

"Her clutches," he says. "You're really funny. She'd have to get me out of your clutches first."

"You could be lucky and get her machine. Do you want to go to bed, maybe?" They haven't made love since it happened. It has seemed an impossible act. Not since before the blue-sky Tuesday morning when he was late for a meeting. She should have made him stay; it was within her power, she just didn't try very hard. Then he might not have gotten on the subway at all. She wouldn't have been alone that whole morning. Wouldn't have met the book-man (which might have been worse for him), wouldn't have found the twenty-dollar bill. Like a uchrony, what if, what if? But the important facts wouldn't have changed. The planes would still have crashed, the buildings fallen, the kaleidoscope shifted. Suddenly she wants Jack just as he is, not at his most appealing, can of beer in his hand, unshaven, surly, gray-faced. "Come on. It's better than arguing."

"Coax me."

"All right. Turn that thing off, though."

He targets the disaster site with the remote and she pulls him to the floor instead of bed. It wouldn't do to wake Julio. Even though it's very quiet love, very muted, no talking. They're different, not the lovers they were. Like Bodo and Zuna, maybe, after a strenuous day of hunting and gathering. No, that was probably a quick, grunting grappling. This is ponderous and silent, not mechanical, only enervated. It takes a long time, like a slow-motion dance, or like climbing a mountain. The view at the top is as grand as expected, but it's been so arduous, you almost can't appreciate it. You almost wonder whether it was worth the climb.

Afterward, when Jack is in bed, she can't sleep, so she wraps herself in a shawl and curls up on the living-room couch with a magazine. Global warming, faulty voting machines, the elusive Pinochet—last month's magazine. All from before. All these matters sound prehistoric. At last something catches her interest. A group of psychologists at Cornell designed a series of experiments to study whether the testimony of children in abuse cases could be trusted. "Some say children can recall events very accurately. Others say their memories are unreliable. . . . Research psychologists deliberately set out to plant the seed of an imaginary event in the minds of young children, to see if it would take root and grow into a false memory."

A group of three- to six-year-old children were asked, individually, if they'd ever gotten their hands caught in a mouse trap. Ninety percent of the children said no, which was the correct answer. A week later they were asked the same question again. "We want you to think real hard, did this ever happen to you? Now it's not quite ninety percent, it may be eighty-five get it correct."

By rights Renata should grab a pencil and fix the errors, but her heart is pounding too hard for that.

"We bring them back a third week. We ask the same question. We bring them back a fourth, a fifth, an eighth, a tenth, a twelfth week, each time just asking the same question. Think real hard, did this ever happen? By the tenth, eleventh week, the majority of 3- and 4-year-olds will claim that getting their hand caught in a mouse trap really happened."

In a related experiment, "over 2000 professionals—pediatricians, psychologists, social service workers, judges, lawyers—were asked to watch videotapes of these children.... The professionals were unable to pick out which children were describing true memories and which were describing a false implanted memory."

Apart from strangling these experimenters with her bare hands, what Renata would enjoy is waking Jack to vent her fury. Telling children deliberate lies? Mindfucking in the service of justice? Even Bliondan's abundance of terms for every variety of wrong words, *prashmensti,* is not adequate for this outrage. But telling Jack would bring no satisfaction. Jack the ever-reasonable, even after sex, would point out that yes, while the experiment might be morally dubious, its goal is worthy. Consider the falsely accused, blah, blah . . . Arguments of means and ends. Who first made that up anyway, about the ends justifying the means? Who ever thought of separating means and ends? Every means becomes an end. There is no end to means.

Nine

Cindy is predictably late, so there's plenty of time, the next day, to study the south entrance to St. Vincent's Hospital, which has become a kind of wailing wall plastered with photos of the disappeared, the *desaparecidos*, ordinary home photos, nothing arty of the kind Franco Donati might have done, along with their descriptions and *marcas corporales*. Kevin Moore, lightly freckled, gold wedding band, mustache and goatee, broken nose. Janice Chun (pictured holding a toddler), ponytail in tortoise-shell barrette, navy-blue blazer, white skirt, missing tip of right index finger. Tashiko Tayahashi, bald spot on back of head, rimless glasses, vertical chest scar from bypass surgery. If the televised images of suited pundits have been oppressive, these notices are an antidote, so much more eloquent than the public words: hunt them in their caves, the full resources of our law-enforcement agencies, all necessary security precautions, a monumental struggle. These words—mastectomy scar, left eye turned in, feathery salt-and-pepper hair, shamrock tattoo on left buttock—sear the eyes. She moves from one to the other of the smiling faces—school photos, posed for a dive, proudly displaying a six-foot fish—imagining how they might have looked in their last moment, contorted by fear.

She's not the only one reading the wall. Half a dozen people glide slowly past, stunned like sleepwalkers, but the one who draws her eye is a skinny, waif-like girl of seventeen or so in a sleeveless flowered shift, the flimsy kind that hawkers sell on the street, and pink rubber flip-flops. Seen in profile, her body, held very still as she edges along the wall, has a feline grace, like a dancer suspended between spins. Her hair is a brassy blonde, short and uneven, as if chopped carelessly with a kitchen knife. Its color is just short of garish, too blonde for her skin, which is olive, Mediterranean. The black roots show here and there. She wears small, thin gold hoops in her ears, the kind Renata got for Gianna when she was seven, much too young for earrings, but she begged to have pierced ears like the Dominican girls at school, and Renata gave in; Gianna sat bravely biting her lip as the girl in the jewelry shop sprayed her earlobes numb and aimed the needle. The olive skin, the earrings, the lithe body and that elegant Botticelli profile are so eerily familiar that Renata shudders, the way they say you shudder when someone walks over your grave, still empty.

There's something else odd. She doesn't carry any purse or backpack, nothing at all. She must be homeless, a street kid, yes, with that look of no place to go, all the time in the world to do nothing. When their paths cross, her glance falls on Renata and becomes a bland stare. She looks like she's about to speak but she doesn't. Renata acknowledges her with the tiny nod she's given the others at the wall, the sign of communal sorrow. The girl stares longer than she should and Renata wonders if she ought to give her some money. She almost expects a hand to be extended, the pale lips to murmur some plea, but that doesn't happen. When the girl reaches the end of the row of photos she starts drifting back in the other direction. As she does so, Renata feels she's watching her through the wavy glass of Jack's window; the molecules that make up the girl shiver and reassemble, again and again, so that she never quite keeps her firm shape. She's about the age Gianna would be now, and come to think of it—but truly, the thought has been there from the first instant—it's uncanny how much she resembles Claudia at that age (and me, too, Renata thinks), especially in the first months of pregnancy, a stricken, vulnerable look. Only this girl is more still, doe-like, as if her own movements might startle her.

She's made uneasy by the girl's stare. Last night Jack called her irrational for wanting to keep Julio, but this notion, absurd and powerful, is even worse. It challenges common sense. Renata wheels abruptly, blinks to clear her vision, and turns the corner to find Cindy.

There's nothing puzzling or shapeless here. She would have known Cindy anywhere. After so many years, there's more of everything, especially honey-colored hair. Cindy is chubbier, blowsier, more flying apart. Her cheeks are pinker, her eyes blearier. She wears a loose print shirt over white capri pants and sandals. They hug, and Renata remembers the pillowy embrace. Cindy brushes away a tear.

"Sweetie! You look beautiful! You're all grown up."

"Well, what did you expect? Where've you been all these years? I looked for you a few times, when I was a kid, but I didn't really know how."

"I know I should have kept in touch," Cindy says. "I'm sorry." She wipes her forehead with a fist. It's a hot day. "I went back to San Diego for a while, then Mexico. But I've been here in the city for years. I like it. And now there's this shit. Who would've thought . . . ? Anyway, how's your mom?"

Renata tells her, the short version.

"So she never got over it," says Cindy mournfully. "I guess there's nothing like losing a child. And the way it happened."

"She was managing until my Dad . . . He was, . . . he died in an auto accident about a year later. He started drinking a lot after Claudia . . . We were never sure exactly how it happened. Anyway, after that she just gave up."

"The poor thing. Well, listen, we have a lot to catch up on. My life hasn't been a bed of roses either. But I'm in better shape now. I'm in AA. That's where I met Hal. We were doing great together. It was really working. Then the other day, when he didn't come home, I crashed. I didn't want to call anyone in the group, the shape I was in, so I got the idea of calling you. I didn't know what else to do. Later maybe we can sit down and have a cup of coffee. But meanwhile, you said on the phone your boyfriend knows how I can find Hal?"

"He said to go around to the hospitals, and to start here."

"Oh God, if he's gone I don't know what I'll do. I can't face it. You do the talking, okay?" Cindy's eyes are streaming.

"Okay. Tell me his name and where he worked. But you might have to describe him."

Their task proves surprisingly easy. Renata had foreseen a day of traipsing up the island from hospital to hospital, but here is Harold Brody, age fifty-two, on a list at the front desk. He's in the burn unit. His condition is serious, not critical. Yes, they can see him.

"Oh my God. So he's alive?"

"Yes," the clerk answers. "At least on this morning's list he is."

"But why didn't anyone call or anything?"

"It's been very hectic around here."

"But—"

"Let's just go on up," Renata says.

As soon as they step off the elevator, at Cindy's insistence—
she's sure the clerk said seven—it's clear this is the wrong floor, not
the burn unit but the children's section. Small chairs, kids' draw-
ings on the walls. A shelf with picture books, Dr. Seuss. A small
boy, six or seven, is darting up and down the hall with a pull toy on
a cord, a horse that makes a clickety-clack noise, and at first he
looks perfectly healthy, it's hard to imagine why he's in a hospital,
but as they stare, disoriented, they realize simultaneously that the
boy's right leg is plastic, perfect leg color, perfect, that is, for his
fair skin, and he moves very agilely on it; he doesn't evoke pity but
admiration. A triumph over disability. What makes Renata's heart
flip is not the leg at all but the sock, a horizontally striped blue and
white sock, which lies absolutely smooth on the plastic leg, not
wrinkled up or askew like the sock on the other, the real, leg. The
sock almost undoes her. She quickly turns away.

"I told you she said ten," she snaps at Cindy.

"Sorry, sorry. God, these kids. Makes me glad I never had any."

When they get to the right floor, it's obvious why Hal hasn't
called himself. He's in a room with three other men and no private
phones. He looks heavily sedated, either asleep or in some deeper
state; one arm is in a cast, and both legs are swathed in bandages.
There's a bandage over one eye, as well as tubes in his nose and his
good arm. Harold is a black man with graying hair, a broad face
and strong cheekbones, a thick mustache and full lips, dried and
cracked and slightly parted. He breathes noisily. Cindy starts to
rush over, then stops. "Shit. And I was blotto all the time he suffered like this. Hal? Baby? Can you hear me?"

The one good eye opens, bloodshot, and stares. He wets his
lips with his tongue. "Where you been all this time? You okay?"

"Oh God." She's about to collapse on his chest but Renata
holds her back.

"Careful. You could hurt him."

"It's okay. That side is the good side," he says. His voice is phlegmy and forced, like it's pushing past obstacles. "It's not so bad as it looks."

Cindy leans down on the good side and strokes his face and sobs.

Renata gazes out the big picture window. From up on the tenth floor, she has a superb view of downtown. There's empty space where the towers should be, framed by the window. Down below is the panorama already familiar from the TV screen, only at this height it resembles a scene from a movie about interplanetary travel. Amid the acres of jumbled metal and concrete, the yellow machines move slowly, like enormous, menacing bugs, and helmeted people, tiny as dolls, tiny as the figures from Farmer Blue's farm, inch along carrying equipment. Strands of smoke rise wistfully into the air. It's like a wrecked village, a mining town where they mine for bodies.

"I'll wait down the hall," she says.

"He used to be a wrestler back in Barbados, and then a cop for a while. He's a strong guy. So he thought he could, you know, help?" Sitting across from Renata, Cindy sips iced coffee, black, through a straw, in a coffee shop on Sixth Avenue. Out the window, soldiers in camouflage patrol the streets, their guns at the ready, faces sealed, so there is the feel of being in a foreign country. Not this country. "He wasn't real clear about it, he's still foggy, he doesn't even know what day it is. He saw the whole thing from outside the deli, it's like half a block away—he and his partner were pulling people inside, out of the smoke. He saw people running and tripping and a bunch of them fell in a heap, with the concrete flying, so he ran to get them and this ball of fire got him in the legs and he fell himself, that's how he must've broke his arm, and the next thing he knew someone was dragging him and stomping on his legs to put out the fire and that's all he knows. He must've passed out and they brought him to the hospital." She drains the glass and hides her face in her hands.

"It's okay." Renata reaches out to pat her awkwardly. "It's okay. Did you speak to a doctor?"

"A nurse. She was nice. She thinks he'll be okay. They did two skin grafts and may have to do more but it's only the bottom part of his legs. He'll be able to walk. There's two men in there in really bad shape, worse burns. And the fourth, a construction guy, just happened to be in a small fire where he works. You sort of forget there's ordinary life going on in the middle of all this. It's a miracle that we found him alive. Thanks, Renata. You really saved my life." She wipes her eyes, orders another iced coffee, and settles back in the booth.

Now, Renata senses, they are about to "catch up." She braces herself. She is having an attack of *iranima,* the vague letdown on the realization of an almost futile wish. For so long she'd tried to find Cindy, and now that she's here, it feels too casual. There was more texture in anticipation.

"So," Cindy says after a pause, "I guess you had a rough time, I mean with the little girl and all."

It's as if a weight has plummeted from her throat to her groin and knocked the breath out of her. A minute or so passes before she can speak. "You know about that?"

"Yeah," Cindy nods. "I do."

"I don't get it. Maybe you could fill me in. I could use another coffee too," and she waves to the waitress.

Now that Cindy has relaxed, she slips into using the rising in-flection, every sentence a question, which gives her voice the care-less, light, uncertain tone of a teenager. "He used to call me every few months? Peter, I mean? He would never say where he was. It was creepy. Just out there somewhere? He always knew where I was, though?"

The rising inflection hurts Renata's ear. She has to keep herself from giving an encouraging nod with each statement.

"How?"

"I told you, people like that, they know everything? They have connections? Your father must have known what he was. Or if he was too dumb to see—sorry, I mean blinded by brotherly love or something—your mother certainly could see. Peter was involved in all kinds of things."

"You mean like drugs?"

"Drugs, other stuff. How do you think he knew those people he gave the baby to? They weren't such bad types, basically, and they really did want a baby, but they were in it too. You know, selling on the side? That was partly why I left. I didn't like being around all that. That was why I drank so much? Well, no, I can't blame anyone for the drinking, I know that now. That's my responsibility. Anyhow . . . He didn't like it when I joined AA five years ago. He'd rather have me drinking? He even sent me money. Not that I asked. I'm not into blackmail. I did take it, though, I have to admit."

"I'm totally confused. I can't put all this together. Why would he want you to drink, first of all?"

"Well . . . " Cindy looks at Renata as if she's a little slow, a little stupid, exactly as Renata and Claudia used to look at her when they were teenagers, so certain of being smarter than silly Cindy. "He didn't want me talking about any of it. What happened. If I sobered up, I might say things. . . . That's why he kept in touch and sent money. It wasn't because he cared about me or anything like that."

Renata can't speak. She will have to let it all spool out, then sort it through later.

"Look, I'm really sorry, Renata. I acted like a shit. No one knows it better than me. I should have helped you out when you had to take care of her all on your own. What was her name again?"

"Gianna," she whispers.

"Gianna. That's it. For your grandma, right? Yeah, I knew it was some odd Italian name, I just couldn't remember. Peter told me they left her with you? The Jordans, I mean."

Renata winces when she hears the name. The people her parents handed the baby to like a package in the parking lot, who returned her three years later like a package.

"They had to get out of town," Cindy goes on. "They were in trouble. They didn't want to leave her, but what could they do? If they got caught, where would she be then? Like maybe in foster care or worse? They figured it was better to give her to someone who would at least take good care of her."

At least. I did better than "at least," Renata thinks. Up to the day I didn't. Maybe Gianna would have been better off with them, with the Jordans, in the long run. Better off with parents hiding out than whisked from a carousel in broad daylight. They loved her. They must have suffered, leaving her behind. But she cannot work up any interest in the Jordans' suffering. There is enough to think about without that.

"You know, in AA, one of the twelve steps is when you make amends to all the people you harmed? I was going to do that. I had you down on my list to call and make amends, but when I told Peter, he got mad and threatened me. First I paid no attention, but then I came home one day and my apartment was trashed? That was scary. So I'm saying it now. I don't know how I can make amends, but I am sorry."

"Sorry you didn't help me with Gianna?"

"Well, that too. But sorry I didn't . . . I knew about when your father died. *He* knew. And about Claudia. I'm sorry I didn't tell you all I knew."

Cindy is sorry. Renata sits like a stone. But maybe she's being too severe. At least Cindy is apologizing on her own. She's not resorting to second-hand intermediaries as one can do now in Tianjin, in China, a nation that, according to a recent news article, is "apologetically challenged." The Chinese dread the loss of face that apologies provoke, and so they avoid them. To help out, the Tianjin Apology and Gift Center will, on behalf of remorseful clients, write letters of apology and send gifts at the reasonable rate of two dollars and fifty cents per apology. If that doesn't do the trick, the Apology Center offers personal visits, made by their soberly dressed and scrupulously trained representatives. (Related services, designed to relieve stress, include "whacking a large blonde female mannequin with a stick," one dollar and twenty-five cents for five minutes.) For Cindy, suddenly brave, loss of face is not an issue.

"I mean, not *knew* like I saw it with my own eyes," she goes on, "but still—"

That is bad enough but it can wait. The dead can wait. One thing at a time. "Do you know where she is?"

"Gianna?"

"Yes." Who else? There's no doubt where Claudia is.

Cindy sips through her straw and shakes her head, no. She has both hands around the tall glass. Renata notices that most of her fingernails are bitten and ragged except for, inexplicably, one thumb and both pinkies.

"So he took her from the merry-go-round. I always thought so." Would Peter want her back, though? What for? Far more likely that the Jordans took her, with or without Peter's help. Or neither.

Strangers. All these conjectures have been hurtling around in Renata's head for years, bumping and bouncing like balls in a pinball machine. An infernal clanging. She can hear it right now.

"Oh, was it a merry-go-round? I never knew. I only knew she was missing. That's all he knew, too. Really. He knew you didn't have her anymore and you were in touch with the cops. He swears he had nothing to do with it."

"And you believe him?"

"I think so? Because, like, why? I mean, sure, there's a lot of traffic in kiddy porn and stuff like that, everyone knows that. But I don't think he would. He's a sleaze, all right, but there are limits."

"Limits? What kind of limits does he have?"

"It happens a lot, Renata. Kids disappear. He felt bad about it."

"You said he has so many connections. So did he try to find her?"

"I don't know. But you tried, didn't you?"

"Of course."

"And nothing?"

"What do you think, Cindy? You think I'd be sitting here asking you these things if they'd found her?"

"Okay, okay, take it easy. Look, you said limits. I'm pretty sure he wouldn't, you know, do anything really gross because, . . . well, you do know, Renata, don't you? That she was his kid? I mean, it's not like I'm telling you anything you don't already know, right?"

This has never been spoken aloud before. Only thought in the dead of night. Even now, Renata can only murmur about it. "Claudia said she was raped in the city but I never believed her."

"Raped, give me a break. I'm sorry, I know rape is no joke, but really. I knew all along, but I never dreamed—"

"Hold on. You knew all along?"

"Well, I knew there was something going on, sure. He was out a lot, late at night. And then when Claudia got pregnant and wouldn't say, . . . I put two and two together. Tell me something. Why in hell didn't she have an abortion? Wouldn't they let her?"

"She didn't say anything till it was too late. I don't know what she was thinking. She wasn't thinking. It was like her brain switched off. You knew and you didn't say?"

"I thought it would pass. Before she got pregnant, I mean. I tried so hard to get him away. I hated that town. I wanted to go back to California but he wouldn't. How could I know it would end like . . . ? That day at the river, with the body, . . . after that, I freaked. 'Cause he was out that night. I remember he came home with a twisted ankle. He said he tripped in the driveway. Later he said if I said a word he'd—"

"But what did he tell you? What happened?"

"Nothing. He was shocked, you could see that for yourself. He didn't do anything, he said. It was an accident."

"So why didn't he go for help? What happened down there? You have to tell me!"

"Renata, if I knew I'd tell you, believe me. Don't you think I wondered too? Why do you think I left? I'm surprised you look so shocked. I thought you must've figured it out, I mean, what was going on with them. If not back then, at least by now. You were a smart kid. Smarter than your parents."

She'd figured it out, of course, but couldn't frame the words that would make it real. You can know something and refuse the words for what you know. Words are dangerous. Once something is in words, it's in the world, in the common language. It's registered in history.

She was smart back then, but not smart enough to put two and two together, like Cindy. That moment in the garage was more than enough evidence for any smart girl, even if she was only fifteen. But she let it go. Too stunned by the feel of it to take the next step and imagine what it might mean. And even now, after all the men she's known, the feeling is as searing as it was then, his fingers running down her spine, bare in the halter top. Her shuddering with fear and a shocking pleasure.

It happened on a Saturday afternoon in the fall, unusually warm. The weather, like Claudia's news, had been oppressive, and on impulse, Renata had cut her hair short. She was crouched down in a corner of the garage fixing the kickstand on her bike and didn't hear the footsteps. When a hand came down gently on her neck, she started with fear.

"I haven't seen you in days," he said softly. "Where've you been keeping yourself? What'd you do to your hair?"

It was a relief to recognize Peter's voice, even though it sounded different. Lower. Not the usual flippant nonchalance. Her muscles relaxed, then she shivered in the stuffy garage. She didn't turn around right away.

He stroked her shoulder. "What's up? No hello?" And ran a finger horizontally across the back of her neck, which wasn't yet used to being exposed, then down her spine. It made her shiver again, not with cold but with an unfamiliar warmth, a tingling pleasure that ran through her nerves like a flame on a fuse. She stood up to make it stop.

He was looking down at her with a wry smile that made him younger than his thirty-three years, almost boyish, but as she turned to him his face changed. She can still remember the peculiar shift in his expression: the arrangement of the muscles, the cast of the eyes, all transformed him. For an instant he'd been a stranger, and then with that reconfiguration behind the skin, he metamorphosed back into her familiar, useless, pain-in-the-ass uncle.

"Oh, sorry, I didn't mean to frighten you, Renata." He looked sheepish. "I thought you heard me come in."

"I didn't."

"Going for a ride?"

"What does it look like? You could have said something. You scared me to death."

"Sorry. So what's up?"

They weren't supposed to tell anyone about Claudia's pregnancy. "Nothing. Same as usual."

"I dropped over to see your father. Is he inside?"

"Yes. Maybe you should knock first."

He ambled off with his vague, undirected gait. His walk was like his life, apparently going nowhere, yet with something offensive in it; without any swagger, his walk managed to be an affront. She felt hot and feverish and her stomach pulsed. She rubbed the back of her neck to wipe away his touch. She could still feel the pleasure of it though not for a long time would she identify it as pleasure, only as a sensation that made her confused and unsettled. There was something very confident about the touch, but that was as far as she could go. She didn't want to know more.

Cindy lifts an ice cube onto her spoon and sucks it. "You'd feel better if you confront what you know. It's no good living in denial, Renata."

"Oh, spare me the new-age jargon. How do you know what's good for me? After all these years."

"All right then, forget it."

"Why are you telling me all this now, anyway? Aren't you still afraid of him?"

"No, because he's sick. Too sick to do anything."

"I see. Well, good. I'm glad. Do you know where he is?"

"You really want to know?"

"I'm asking, aren't I? I really want to know."

"In a hospital in Houston. He'd never say before, but now he's begging me to visit. He wants to see someone? Anyone. But I'm not about to go."

"He can see me. I'll go."

"Are you serious?"

"Very. I'll pay him a visit. As soon as the planes start flying."

"Well . . . " Cindy shakes her head and pushes her hair back from her forehead. Her skin is quite smooth, remarkably unchanged. It's her eyes that show wear and tear; tiny red lines, like meandering little rills, run through the whites. "I guess that's your business. I don't know what you hope to accomplish. I mean, you're not thinking of, like going to court or anything? He won't live long enough for that. Besides, you have nothing, no evidence."

I have you, Renata thinks. "I don't know what I want to accomplish. I'll see when I get there. I should go home. I can't talk anymore."

"Me too. Thanks a million. I mean it. You really came through for me."

"Are you okay, otherwise? Are you working?"

"Yeah, I have a job in a salon three days a week, and a few private customers. We manage. It was worse before I met Hal. I had some bad times, but I try not to think about them."

"I would have helped you out if you'd asked."

"I know you would. I appreciate it. I guess you got something from the sale of the house, right?"

"Yes, but it took a while." Because she didn't know how to deal with real-estate and insurance agents and lawyers when she was eighteen years old. Because it was all she could do, arranging her father's funeral and coping with her mother's collapse. She's had some bad times too. In any case, the expected appeal for money is not forthcoming. She feels a grudging respect for silly Cindy. "I'll call you to get the name of the hospital in Houston. And I want to know how Hal does. Now that we're back in touch—"

"Yes," Cindy says. "Let's not wait so long. I think I'll go back to the hospital and see him again."

"My subway's on the corner. I'll walk over with you."

So they part amicably, after all that. Again the pillowy hug, again a few tears. Their goodbye on the street, at the wall with the Missing notices, under the gaze of the young warriors in camouflage uniforms, seems strangely pacific to Renata, considering the brutalities they spoke of. It's true that much of what Cindy told her was not news, but then again, much of what we call news is merely confirmation of what we already know. Or have envisioned between sleep and waking, then banished in daylight. For once the words are articulated, they press for thought. Even so, words do ease the burden. They bear part of the weight. The stone is definitely lighter now. Moreover, she's going to do something about it.

Again she reads the notices, studies the faces and descriptions of the Missing. *Cicatrix detras de la canilla,* gold stud in navel, vaccination scar on right upper arm, cornrows, pockmarked face, blackened big toenail on right foot. . . . Among the others edging up and back along the wall are several she can identify as tourists: they carry cameras, backpacks, wear pastels and polyester or speak foreign tongues. She wants to shoo them away, tell them they don't belong, like crashers at a funeral. A few are actually snapping pictures; it's Jack's Reality Tourism come to life. As her fingers itch to seize the cameras and dash them to the pavement, she sees again the thin girl with the chopped blonde hair, who might have been drifting along the wall all this time. Waiting. She does look very much like Claudia at that age. Like Renata herself. The girl might be suffering from amnesia or shock, after the attack. She might have been orphaned. She might be related to one of the Missing she peruses so intently, or she might herself be one of the Missing. She might be anyone. A runaway girl from hundreds of miles away, lost in the city. A drifter, a prostitute, a junkie, a homeless girl, a mental patient who in the general confusion of that Tuesday wandered out while the doctors and nurses were busy preparing for the onslaught of the injured that never came. Or a foreign tourist who got separated from her family or her school group. (But why would a tourist be walking around in flip-flops?) She might be anything. And anything might be made of her.

She notices Renata and gives the merest glance of recognition. Not a smile, just a faint livening of the dark eyes. There's something raw about her, not a girl who's been tended or cosseted. Raw and lost, so lost that impulsively, Renata goes up to her and says, "Are you all right? Do you need any help?"

Her lips part in the beginning of a smile, as if she's pleased to be addressed, but she says nothing, gives no sign in answer. Deaf? Dumb? Retarded?

"Do you have a place to go? Are you hungry?"

Nothing, only the half-smile lingers. An intelligent smile. Not retarded. Renata tries speaking to her in French, Spanish, German. "Are you lost? Where do you come from?" Nothing in response except a faint look of puzzlement. Not deaf. Not a tourist. Simply mute.

"Here. Please, take this." She pulls out a twenty-dollar bill and holds it out. The girl looks confused, as if she doesn't know what it is or why Renata is offering it. She doesn't reach for it. Renata takes her hand and places the money there. Her hand is warm and soft, larger than expected, finely articulated. She has nowhere to put the money, no bag, no shoes, no bra. Renata doesn't know what else to do.

"Can I help you get home? Call someone for you?"

Nothing. But her fingers curl around the bill.

"Tell me what I can do. I want to help you. What about . . . Can I get you a sandwich or something? Come on."

Nothing. She won't move.

"Okay, then. Good luck."

She could be anyone at all. What was she before? What has she been turned into? She could be Gianna, turned up after all these years. Why not? Gianna must be somewhere. Why not right here?

Ten

Jack's first words on Sunday morning were ill-chosen.

"They're coming to pick him up tomorrow. I spoke to Teresa yesterday, while you were out. Carmen's mom. They've got a flight from San Juan."

"Good morning to you, too." It was a loveless night. A happier night might have tempered her sarcasm. All three slept densely, even Julio.

"I'm sorry it came out like that. It's because I've been dreading telling you."

He was padding around the living room barefoot, wearing a black satin Chinese robe Renata had bought him at a local thrift shop, the kind of robe suave movie stars sported in their penthouse apartments in 1940s films, ambling toward the living-room bar to pour a couple of martinis. But Jack didn't wear it with the same aplomb. The robe was open to the waist, revealing matted chest hair and an incipient paunch; the sash hung down to his knees; his hair was rumpled from sleep, his voice was thick, and it wasn't an hour for martinis even if there had been a bar in the living room. Ten o'clock. He was generally an early riser, but he was exhausted after days of hauling crates of work clothes, picking his way over mounds of smoking rubble, breathing bad air, and dashing to the victims' services clearinghouse over at the West 55th Street pier, then back to his office to cope—without benefit of Carmen and on phones that worked intermittently—with hysterical or near-catatonic clients who needed clothing, shelter, day care, and Valium, many of them locked out of their Battery Park City apartments, which were shrouded in ash and littered with glass. He could have used some sympathy, but Renata was not in a giving mood. She sat, freshly showered and neat—a sharp contrast—on the rug next to Julio on his belly, trying to learn to crawl. "Attaboy," she cheered him on. She was pleased with herself because she'd found the will to turn off the TV after a few words from the Medical Examiner's office on the usefulness of DNA samples in determining the identity of the victims, then a snatch of the President's latest speech ("My message is for every-body who wears the uniform to get ready"), and settled down with her Arabic grammar and dictionary. She didn't wear the uniform, felt far from able to rid the world of evil, but if there was something she could do to help, she'd do it. If it meant puzzling out the welter of diacritical marks above the Arabic letters, so be it.

"Well, I don't want to be here when they come."

"You don't want to meet them? I'm sure they'd like to meet you. To thank you for—"

God, he could be so obtuse. "I prefer not to. Anyway, I have to go out of town." Until this minute it had been a vague intention: in a few days or weeks, once she'd checked with Denise at work, once boarding a plane didn't feel suicidal. Peter could hold out that long. Now, in her pique, she decided she had to go immediately. Grace had said, Find her. She'd listen to her mother for once.

"You do? Where?"

"Away."

Like a seasoned working mother, with one hand she jiggled Julio's rattle and with the other, turned the pages of her book. She'd never had so much trouble with an alphabet before; the letters were cursive, and half a dozen of them looked alike. The vowel signs were perversely arbitrary, in fact the whole language was a masterpiece of arbitrariness. Yet she was catching on, hunting down the elusive designs. She was helped by some translations from the British papers she'd found on the Web. A mullah speaking in an Islamabad mosque: "This is the wrath of God. . . . The demolition of such a huge structure was not caused by the suicide attack. It was God's work, who intensified the impact of the crashing jet aircraft." Not so. The mullah ought to read the papers she read, the engineers' and architects' technical reports, their rueful hindsight: he'd see how mistaken he was. The killers had learned from their 1993 attack that the towers were more vulnerable at the top than at the bottom. The wrath of God simply didn't figure.

"Away where?" Jack repeated.

"Does it matter?"

"Yes, Renata, it matters."

"Houston."

"Houston." He started winding the satin belt around his index finger, winding and unwinding, tightening it so the finger turned white, then letting the belt drop. "Now? With the airports in chaos? There were two bomb scares yesterday. I mean, what's in Houston that's so urgent?"

Ah, just because they'd been sleeping together for eight months, he thought he had the right to know. As a romantic, he wouldn't like seeing their relationship defined in such graphic terms, but Renata liked it. It was lucid and simple and factual. In any case, he cared where she went and what she did and what she thought and felt. None of her evasions could change that. And she cared the same about him. Most of the time. Only not right now, as he was preparing to take Julio away from her.

Did eight months of bed and companionship—she resisted calling it love—give him the right? How would she know? Before Jack, she'd never stayed with any man long enough to learn the web of rights and obligations. Or long enough for anyone to know much about her beyond the dailiness. With Jack, she'd been drawn into an ominous coziness, especially since Julio arrived: a little family huddled against the savagery outside, like Bodo and Zuna and their children.

"I asked you what's so urgent, all of a sudden."

"These are too many questions for me, Jack."

"You really don't know how to do it, do you?" He tightened the belt around his waist, twirled one end in circles in front of him.

"Do what?"

"Life. Be with someone."

"I told you that a long time ago."

"You also told me you were interested in learning how. One thing is, you let them into your life."

"This, these last few days, isn't ordinary life."

"All the more reason. But all right. All right. What about Julio? What am I supposed to do with him while you're away?"

Hearing his name, Julio raised his head and chest and gave a happy grunt. Renata leaned over to chuck him under the chin. "Yes, that's you! You know your name! That's great!" For Jack, she shrugged and finally closed the book. Were they about to squabble like a married couple? Whose turn to stay with the baby? "Day care. That place he was in when you picked him up."

"They can't still be down there. The street is cordoned off."

"I'm sure you can find out where they've moved to. If anyone can do that, it's you."

"What is this trip? Something to do with the Arabic?" He waved vaguely at the book.

Why not make it easy and say yes? How about that, posing as some kind of latter-day Mata Hari. What was in Houston? NASA. Oil wells? Arabs? Never mind. It was too silly a lie, not even serious enough to merit a place in the Bliondan hierarchy of *prashmensti.* Silence was better. Silence—*emenast*—was a form of lying, too, but at least it was clean, it wasn't wrong words.

"No, nothing like that. I just have some business. It should be quick. I'll call as soon as I'm back."

"Sounds like a man is involved."

"No! Well, yes, a man, but not in the way you mean."

"Someone from the past."

"From the past, yes. But not—"

"But now it's become the present again? You might have told me. I'm fed up with your mysteries, your past, whoever's waiting for you down there. I won't go through this a second time."

"You are so wrong about this, I . . . I just can't tell you. I'm not like Pamela and you know it." It was perverse not to tell him, only now was not the moment, not when she needed her strength to face Peter after so long. Not with Julio squirming around on the rug—and on this last try he almost succeeded. He'd be crawling any day now, but she wouldn't see it—he'd be with his grandmother by then.

"Look, it's my uncle, my father's brother. He's sick. Dying. I have to go see him. Cindy told me yesterday. He's her ex-husband."

"Your uncle. Funny you never mentioned any uncle before."

"I mentioned him the other day. Did you ever call Pamela, by the way?"

The tiniest hesitation. "No." She knew he was lying. For spite. He turned away and hunted for the remote.

"Can't you trust me for two days? This is some kind of obsession with you."

"Trust." He gave a nasty laugh. "What can you trust nowadays? We trusted that it was safe to go into Manhattan."

"I'll explain everything after. If I leave tomorrow, I can be back Tuesday or Wednesday."

"You'll have a hard time booking a flight. They're all backed up."

"I'll manage."

He was already in front of the television for his fix, the latest installment in the Reality TV hit series.

"This is a new kind of evil," came the voice. The lines of the President's face, the taut, small quivers of his lips, were so familiar by now, it was as if he'd moved in with them. "We will rid the world of the evildoers. They have roused a mighty giant, and make no mistake about it, we're determined."

Renata was determined. And she did manage to book a flight. She pleaded a medical emergency and cited the name of the hospital she got from Cindy. It wasn't very hard. Maybe no one was eager to fly to Houston on a Monday morning; New York in fall was so beautiful, despite all. September is its finest month.

What does a family with a young baby do on a glorious September Sunday afternoon? They were so glutted with TV it was like poison in their eye sockets. Only the real world could clear it out. The park? The Promenade? Maybe a drive to the country? But it was a pain to drive anywhere. So many streets and bridges were still closed, like quarantine. The great temptation was to drive across the Brooklyn Bridge, just reopened, to the site, where they could stare their fill. It was enticing, the unimaginable made palpable; it was where they belonged, like the widowed who can't keep away from the graveyard. It was Reality Tourism, the game they couldn't play anymore now that it had turned real. Already, sightseers were drawn there in flocks, if they could find a route, with the subways so haphazard. You could see them on TV, creeping around the periphery, peering for a view through their cameras, restrained by police barricades and the armed men in camouflage. Surprising that apartment-dwellers with the best views hadn't begun selling tickets—or perhaps they had. Yet who could blame the tourists: they needed to see for themselves. However bad the stench, the real was healthier than the TV screen.

But it wasn't a place to take Julio. Instead, as a parting treat, they decided to show him the ocean. Coney Island. Honky-tonk. He was too young for the rides or for a hot dog, but they let him lick an ice-cream cone and he was overjoyed. He lived in the present. Would he ever remember his mother? Renata wondered. Of course not. What was an infant's memory? Even now, his mother had become a dimming blur; she was the face of love just beginning to detach from its surroundings. Love would take on other faces. He wouldn't remember Renata's face either.

Despite the glitz and the noise of the rides and the Skee-Ball galleries, everything was subdued. No soldiers in sight. The faces on the boardwalk were grim: the old fat Russians with their sturdy laced-up shoes and their canes, the women powdered and bleached, the men balding—what horrors were they recalling?—and the teenagers skittering lithely on their skateboards. The few happy faces, the handful of people cavorting in the water, must have been from another planet. Hadn't they heard? Jack was tense and withdrawn as he walked beside Renata, pushing the stroller. They went down to sit on the sand. He stared out at the ocean. Julio tried to eat sand. They barely spoke. This was what they had come to, in only a few days.

In a coffee shop on the boardwalk the TV was on, no escape even at the edge of the sea. "What this war is about is our way of life, and our way of life is worth losing lives for." The secretary of defense, channeling Gertrude Stein.

It was a relief when the outing was over, even for Julio, fretful in the back seat. Just as they were getting out of the car on Jack's block—that ease of parking a sad reminder, a benefit any car-owner would gladly have sacrificed if only the world could revert to its pre-Tuesday state—Renata glimpsed a familiar figure sidling along. It was the girl from yesterday who'd stared at the photos of the Missing on the hospital wall and stared at her. In an instant, the figure vanished around the corner. It might have been a trick of the sliding-down sun or a memory of the optic nerve, but no, Renata was certain: same flowered dress, same short, brassy blonde hair, same floaty, aimless gait. She was carrying a plastic bag, maybe for the money Renata had given her. She must have seen them, too, the sullen little family. She must have been waiting. Lurking. Why did she run away, then? Renata thrust Julio into Jack's arms, raced to the corner and looked, but she was nowhere in sight.

"Where'd you run off to?" asked Jack.

"I thought I saw someone I knew."

With the world turned surreal, notions of the supernatural were tempting, notions of transformation. Had the girl metamorphosed into a tree, perhaps? A parking meter? But Renata wasn't yet so far gone. The simplest explanation was, the girl had ducked into a building or a shop. Although God knows what transformations she'd been through in her young life.

Another simple explanation: she must have followed Renata home on the subway yesterday.

Eleven

Monday morning, preparing Julio for his big day is serious business. Babies don't travel light. "Back to school, Buster," Renata murmurs as she gets him dressed and fed. She stuffs his things into the bag he came with, like returning an article that didn't fit properly. Later on she'll return the baby equipment to Aruna across the hall, or better still, let Jack do it. As she works, the radio drones on. "We plan a comprehensive assault. . . . We are planning a broad and sustained campaign to secure our country and battle the evil."

She's trying to wean herself from the incessant news, but she can't give it up entirely; like everyone else, she's hooked. Groggy with sleep yet primed for the apocalypse, everyone turns on the TV or radio first thing, to see if anything's happened. The broadcaster's tone, rather than the words, is the tip-off. If it lacks the edge of excitement, of controlled panic, then nothing's new, so far. Today the announcer seems almost bored as he introduces another presidential sound bite: "I will not settle for a token act. Our response must be sweeping, sustained and effective." Without the face to accompany it, his voice comes across as petulant. The more it strives for certainty, the more uncertain its timbre. "Find them, get them running and hunt them down. They hit and run, they hide in caves. We'll get them out." That prospect seems to liven him up, the thrill of the chase.

Fine, then. A new day and all is well. But surely something will happen soon. It's only a matter of time. So with each morning's relief there's a shameful dash of disappointment: let it happen, bring on the worst, so we can be freed of the asphyxiating suspense. Ever since the image of the plane drilling into the flat face of the tower drilled itself into the collective memory, the range of possibilities has widened beyond imagining. Like everyone else, Renata has been caught unawares, a condition slightly different from the five degrees of Bliondan shock, and like everyone caught unawares, she feels a bit foolish. Innocent. Not politically innocent. It's too soon. The professional analyses, the smug I told you so's, have barely begun. Existentially innocent: we should have known this is what life can offer. We should have known from infancy, from the instant the light of day hit our bemused eyes.

She doesn't want to be around at the leave-taking, so she throws her own things together hastily and bundles her folders into a backpack. She gives Julio a quick, crushing hug, then rubs her cheek against his and pats him all over as if to leave the imprint of her hands. A careless kiss for sleepy Jack, and she's at the door.

"Hey, hold on." He grabs her arm. "This is it? You're taking everything?"

"I need my things. I've got to get home and pack."

"When will you be back?"

"Wednesday. I told you."

"I'll be over that night."

"Okay."

"Careful on the plane," he says.

"How can you be careful on a plane?"

"You know what I mean. Take care."

"Okay. You too."

"Come back in for a minute." She steps in and he gives her a long passionate embrace. It goes on so long and becomes so elaborate that she thinks he wants her back in bed. She pulls away, though not quite out of his arms.

"I've really got to go."

"Thanks for all you did. Taking care of him."

"You don't have to thank me."

"It was good having you here. This was the longest you ever stayed here. I liked it."

"It had its moments, yes."

"So maybe you'll come back."

"Mm." The very suggestion makes her retreat. And yet he's the kind of man most women her age would treasure. Lock him in and throw away the key. For her part, she feels like a nun who's taken a vow of chastity. Emotional chastity. It was safer to lavish her love on Julio.

The sky is that same bright blue again. Sunlight rinses the streets and buildings, the shop windows, even the passing faces, to a high gloss. The carrion tinge hasn't quite evaporated, but the air seems better. Well, marginally better. She's not yet ready to agree that we are in the middle hour of our grief, but it's not as bad as it was two days ago, or three. The shock on awakening is not quite as great.

She walks briskly, thinking of what she'll find in Houston. Suddenly, rounding the corner near Birthing Renaissance, there's the girl again. Today she's not furtive. She comes right up and smiles shyly, barely parting her lips.

"Hello," Renata says. No reply. "I saw you yesterday too. You followed me home, didn't you?" She pauses as long as it would take for a brief answer, but the girl doesn't give answers.

"You must need help. Don't be afraid to say. What can I do? . . . Is it that you can't remember anything? . . . Well, let's walk a little bit." Somewhere, maybe, someone spoke words like that to Gianna. Someone offered help. If she was fortunate. "I bet you're hungry. I haven't had anything either. Come on, we'll pop in here for breakfast."

Renata has coffee and a donut and orders French toast for the girl, who ignores the menu. Is it possible she can't read? Anything is possible. Gianna could read by five years old. Gianna loved French toast. They made it together every Sunday morning; she would dip the bread in the beaten egg and milk, then lick her fingers. Mary Elizabeth Kennedy, one of the Gee's Bend quilters, said, "When sometime there was a question about who the real father was, the response was, 'If the child don't look like you, if you feed him long enough he'll be starting looking like you.'" French toast proves a success now too. The girl smothers it with syrup and eats it down to the last crumb, along with two glasses of milk. "Thank you," she mouths, no sound. She may have amnesia but she hasn't forgotten her manners. Someone taught her. Past the barrier of whatever reluctance or inability or perversity keeps her mute, those two reflexive syllables push through.

"So. Okay. It's just a few blocks to where I'm going. What will you do now? Do you have anywhere to go? Is there someone I can call for you?" Renata is starting to feel rather stupid. Obviously the girl is not about to answer, and if she had anywhere to go or anyone to call she would have done so. There's nothing for it but to leave her, or else take her to the police. But for this matter the police, despite their recent display of courage, do not inspire confidence. Jack might have some ideas, but she doesn't want to get Jack involved. Forget Jack. This has nothing to do with him.

The notion grips her more tightly with each step: Gianna might have ended up exactly like this girl. She might well be this girl. Common sense, again, is yielding to slippage. The girl's presence is like a mind-bending drug. Gianna must be someplace, right? Renata has never accepted that she might be gone for good. Why not in this place? If she were to imagine Gianna at seventeen, she would imagine a face very like the one in front of her. She's the right age, too. Well, perhaps a trifle younger, but with teenagers now, who can tell? With the kind of life Gianna might have led, the transformations. . . . Although the kind of life Renata pictures when she lies sleepless would have made Gianna look older, not younger. But— and here she tries to revive common sense—the point is not whether she recognizes the girl. The girl recognized her. That's what's convincing. Why, out of all the people walking through the city, would she choose to follow Renata unless she recognized her?

Common sense aside, she can't leave her behind quite yet. They walk another block in silence until they come to the bookman's stand. *Hola!* Good morning, good morning. It's a relief all over again to see him. He's not buried in a subway tunnel after all. It will be a happy relief each time she sees him, maybe for the rest of her life.

"And where's your little baby?" he asks.

"He's going back to his grandmother today."

"*Bueno, bueno.* But you'll miss him."

"Yes, I will."

"And who's this?"

Who is she? Renata is weary, too weary to explain how she found her wandering on the street, and all the rest. Stick with the simple. "My niece," she says. "*Mi sobrina.*"

"Your niece? Yes, she looks like you, I can see."

"I haven't seen her for a long time."

"A pleasure to meet you," he says, and Gianna smiles back politely.

"She's very shy. She doesn't talk much. So, what do you have today? I have to take a trip. I can use something for the plane."

She picks out a novel that promises enough plot for a few hours, then turns to Gianna. "Would you like a book? Do you like to read?"

Gianna surveys the wares and finally chooses a pulp romance from a stack with shiny, lurid covers. Renata buys the books for a dollar each. "Thank you and God bless you," says the bookman, and they walk on.

Now that she's identified Gianna publicly, and to the bookman with his connections to a higher authority, she can't just leave her on the street. That would be unconscionable. If she's her niece, she must be treated as such. And even if she isn't. . . . Like a good Etinoian, Renata is simply honoring the concept of *ahmintu,* being an *ahmintesh,* yielding to the circumstances that come her way, incorporating the vagaries of chance into the loftier principle of destiny. You can't leave a child alone on the street in a city in chaos, with nothing but the clothes on her back and a paperback book and the remains of twenty dollars in a plastic bag. Not even a cell phone, as Franco Donati had at his lowest point.

"You need some clothes. You've been wearing that same dress for days." In the global village there's always a Gap within spitting distance, so they find it and step in. It's a patriotic act. Why, just last night the paper carried an exhortation from the elusive Vice President: "I would hope the American people would, in effect, stick their thumb in the eye of the terrorists and say they've got great confidence in our economy, and not let what's happened here in any way throw off their normal level of economic activity." In other words, keep shopping—the most potent weapon. The attack was a finite event; shopping is forever, like goodness, remembrance, and love.

Gianna seems familiar with the layout. She goes for the jeans first and knows her exact size; she hasn't forgotten everything. Maybe she's forgotten nothing, but finds this new adventure prefer-able to her old life. With Renata's encouragement she also picks out a few T-shirts, a pair of khaki shorts, a windbreaker. Everything fits her fine—she tries on each item and shows Renata. She turns and preens in front of the mirror, already possessed of the absorbed self-scrutiny of a woman trying on new clothes. Like Julio, she lives in the present. If she's truly forgotten the past, she doesn't know what she's lost, and if she remembers, it's not of any concern for the moment. She doesn't seem worried about the future, either. Simply a girl let loose in the Gap.

"Oh, and you need some kind of bag, a pack or whatever. You can't carry money around in a plastic bag." Gianna picks out a small canvas shoulder bag. Renata would have chosen something larger; every bag she owns is big enough for a book. But she doesn't inter-fere. They stop in a lingerie shop for some underwear. "Shoes." Renata glances down at the rubber thongs, their soles flattened to a quarter-inch thickness. How long has she been traipsing through the city in them? "A decent pair of shoes." Gianna picks out sandals that don't look at all suitable for the amount of walking she does. "Okay, but we'll have to get you something better later. Sneakers, maybe." In Duane-Reade, a toothbrush and comb, then Renata hands Gianna the basket and tells her to get whatever she needs. Her tastes aren't expensive, only odd, at least for her present mode of life. Three lipsticks, bright red nail polish, hair conditioner, gel. "Is that it? You sure?" Gianna shrugs, and as if yielding to sugges-tion, selects a bag of miniature Snickers bars. That reminds Renata of food for the next two days, so they make a quick stop in the corner grocery.

Laden down with their loot, they proceed toward Renata's apartment. Gianna appears willing to follow wherever she's taken. But first there's one more essential stop. Gerald and Henry's antique shop, a couple of blocks out of their way.

At the tinkling doorbell, Henry looks up from the catalog he's studying. "Renata? What brings you here? Coming back home?"

"Yes. How are you both doing?"

Henry grimaces. "As well as we can. Gerald just went out for coffee. He'll be sorry he missed you. Where's the baby?"

"Going back to his grandmother. Jack took him this morning. How's the guy upstairs? What's his name again?"

"Philip. He's a wreck. He wanders around the streets holding up one of those photos. You know, Missing? I mean, it's six days already. They're not going to find anyone alive now. He can't go back to work because there's nowhere to go yet. We had him down for a drink yesterday and he just cried."

She can only shake her head. "Henry, this is my niece, Gianna. Gianna, say hello to Henry. He and his friend Gerald are my downstairs neighbors."

Gianna's been wandering about, staring at the assortment of antique telephones, lamps, tapestries, vases, and general clutter, but she turns and extends a hand.

"Hi. Looks like you guys have been shopping."

"Yes, she, uh, needed a few things."

"I can see that," Henry says wryly.

"I'm going out of town for two days and Gianna's going to stay in the apartment. So if she needs anything, is it okay if she calls—" No, she wouldn't call. "I mean, is it okay if she rings your bell?"

"Cool. Or if we're not in she can try here. Okay, Gianna?"

She nods.

At home, Renata shows her how to use the keys, guiltily, because she's never given Jack a set, and here she is giving them to a total stranger. Well, not quite a stranger anymore. She's her niece. This is the real Gianna now. Renata will make herself believe it. Why else would the girl follow her? She remembers her. Maybe she remembers everything since the afternoon at the merry-go-round, and one day she'll tell.

"This one is for the front door, and these two are for the apartment. Here, you try, so I'm sure you know how."

Renata shows her around the place. "I have to leave but I'll be back in two days. Okay? Do you understand everything?"

A nod.

"You can sleep here on the living-room couch. It opens up. See, it's easy. Make yourself at home. You can watch TV if you want, and there's a VCR. I'll put the food away—make sure you remember to eat—then I've got to pack and get to the airport." Talking to herself, almost.

Now that she's getting used to it, Renata finds it oddly relaxing to speak to someone who never answers. No disagreement or conflict or strain, no wondering what the words might be concealing, no nuances or misunderstanding, at least on this simple level of keys and groceries. No ambiguity. No lies. She almost wishes Gianna would never speak, so she'd never have to figure out who's behind the compliant face. Silent, she is wholly benign and uncalculating, merely a child who needs help. Perhaps she was punished for the words she spoke. Possibly she's known and felt things for which there are no adequate words, so why bother with any at all? "I can't talk no more about how I came up," Leola Pettway, the quiltmaker, said. "It hurt to think about it." Everything they've accomplished today has been done without her uttering a single word.

"Well, I'm off." Gianna's been curled up on the couch reading her new book while Renata packed. Last thing, she tucks in her purse the Arabic grammar she found at Rashid's, and an unexpected find from the library, *201 Arabic Verbs.* "Will you be okay for two days?"

She nods.

"When I get back we'll figure out what to do next. Here's some money. Use what you need. But leave that twenty on the table, okay? It's . . . sort of a souvenir. If you need the phone, if you decide to start talking, it's over there. And if you like to read, there're lots of better books." This makes Gianna smile. She must have heard it before. Okay, no reforms yet. Stick to the basics. "Oh, and don't go out late at night, okay? I don't want to have to worry." This advice is even more absurd: Gianna's been wandering the streets at least since Saturday. It's a miracle nothing has happened to her. Assuming nothing has.

At the door, with the taxi waiting downstairs, Renata takes one last look over her shoulder. Her voice comes out shaky. "Will you be here when I get back?"

Gianna nods.

Renata knows that in the eyes of any sensible person, Jack, or Denise, or even flaky Linda, she's done something outrageous. Mad, even. To give a stranger off the street the run of your house. . . . You never know, are you out of your mind? In Hawaii no one would be shocked. In Hawaii it's an age-old custom to take in children of relatives, friends, any child who needs a home. The practice is hallowed by tradition and by love, with no need for formal adoption procedures. *Hanai,* the custom is called. The child is called a *hanai* too.

Twelve

How different is flying from Renata's fantasies of life on the *QE2* with Mrs. Stiller. In their heyday, the old ocean liners, grand and humane, were traveling communities that lent themselves to metaphorical use: ship of fools, ship of state. They rocked and swayed in the cradle of waters, lulled and lulling, gentle as very large, slow things can be gentle. They were a vacation from the commonplace yet didn't extinguish its memory. Ordinary events continued, made lustrous by the sea and the lulling and the luxury, while unexpected winding stairs and crannies allowed for small, safe adventures, for losing and finding one's bearings—the kind of adventures Mrs. Stiller must be relishing on the *QE2*. People ate dinners at linen-covered tables, made friends and enemies, stretched out in the sun, played cards or sports or music, had love affairs, even married. They bore children and died. The captain invited to his table the most illustrious or gracious members of the community, for even at sea the innuendos of social stratification persisted; people accumulated histories and reputations; some were sought out and others avoided, but everyone belonged somewhere.

Flying, even in the best of circumstances, is a refined form of torture. So Renata believes. Does she really exaggerate? The cramping and claustrophobia and bad air and wretched food are the least of it. A commercial airplane is a sealed autocracy, with its pilot the invisible despot, benevolent, we have to hope. Carrying out his will is a staff of uniformed "flight attendants," as ubiquitous as the police in an autocratic state and as swift to point out infractions of the rules. In olden times the attendants—stewardesses—had to be female and beautiful and ingratiating, but equal opportunity changed all that. Now they need only be enforcers. So many rules! So many announcements, sing-song voices nagging in ridiculous euphemisms. Surely the rules can't all be necessary. Surely some primitive gratification is at work, some glee in regulation for its own sake. Where to sit and how—upright or reclining—where to put "personal belongings," when to eat and drink and use the bathroom. (And speaking of bathrooms, she wonders, as she finds her seat and stows her bag, what Linda and Roger's punishment would be, were they discovered in some contorted sexual posture in the cramped bathroom. Would they be mildly admonished, or be seated far apart like naughty children in school, perhaps even put off the plane in an unscheduled stop? For that matter—and it's strange that this hasn't occurred to her before—were there any couples having sex in the bathroom on those four doomed flights, anyone interrupted mid-climax, blown to bits while . . . ? No, such thoughts are blasphemous. Cut it out, she scolds.)

On the ground, self-reliance is prized, but up in the air the prime virtue is passive obedience, the sacrifice of self. Identity is siphoned off: here is equality at its tackiest. Everyone endures the same tyranny, never mind the linen napkins and wider seats of first class. Individual features of dress or speech or gesture mean nothing; everyone dissolves into a shared impotence at the far reaches of anonymity. And it does no good to remember that soon enough we'll be picking up our identities along with our luggage. It feels as though we are no one, have never been anyone, and never will be again.

Now, of course, these complaints felt frivolous. On Renata's flight to Houston, as on all flights since they resumed two days ago, everyone on board was simply frightened of being hijacked and blown up. Some less, some more, depending. Renata more, not because she was more cowardly than others, but because her need was greater. She had to get to Houston; she had to see her uncle. After all this time, she could not be thwarted by some zealot's passion. She had a passion of her own—to confront, to avenge.

Her Houston-bound neighbor, a thirty-something body-builder who smelled of aftershave, poked at his teeth with a green plastic toothpick he kept in his shirt pocket. She leafed through the morning paper. An extremist group in Birmingham envisioned a future Britain as an Islamic state, and one of its leaders addressed young Muslim men: "When the attack comes then every Muslim in the world should take it as an attack on themselves. This is a war that the west cannot win. Muslims love death more than life and they will never understand that." The plane began taxiing toward the runway and she braced for the sickening roar of takeoff. Suddenly they stopped short. Captain Farrell, whose accent proclaimed him from Wisconsin ("aboot twenty minutes more"), explained that they were pausing to fix a valve on the door of the luggage compartment. Renata imagined the door catapulting into the blue somewhere over Kentucky, baggage overflowing as from a cornucopia, hurtling through the sweet southern air to settle in swaying blue grass.

"That's no joke, a loose door," her neighbor snarled. He had mean little green eyes. "A door's loose, flies open, the air pressure in the cabin changes, ruins the whole balance of the plane." He made a diving motion with his hands and brought them down between his knees.

"One more thing," Captain Farrell said, "while I have the attention of you folks. This aircraft is not—I repeat, not—going to be hijacked. Anyone makes a suspicious move, I want every able-bodied man aboard up on their feet to take him down. Able-bodied women, too, let me add. Anyone with ideas, consider yourself warned. This aircraft is going to land safely in Houston and I wish you all a pleasant flight."

She didn't look up from the paper. "Dying in the name of Islam is the ultimate sacrifice and you will be rewarded in heaven. If the alliance of the Devil attacked the Taliban, then it is every Muslim's duty . . . " She shivered in the frigid air (outside, the temperature was enviably balmy) as the attendants jiggled down the aisle to make sure everyone was properly belted. "Straighten your seat back," they ordered, and she obeyed.

Yet even in the oppressive cylinder of the plane, she recalled, once in a while a kind of camaraderie does spring up (not today it won't, not with the dreadful man beside her). It can happen when the plane lurches and feels out of control, and everyone searches the attendants' porcelain faces to see if they're worried too. Strangers clutch each others' arms, whoever is alongside them, as Mrs. Amalia Gutierrez of Queens, mother of four, clutched Renata's arm last winter when they hit a series of air pockets. She and Jack were flying home from a weekend escape to Puerto Rico, in their first flush of lust. "It's just air pockets," Renata told Mrs. Gutierrez. "It's nothing." On her other side, Jack was sleeping through the turbulence. Mrs. Gutierrez was not consoled, and in between sobs she related her life story, so that it should not go unrecorded. It was a happy story, for the most part. She had a lot to lose. For those fifteen minutes, Renata was her confessor and her confidante, the bearer of her closest secrets.

The most intimate moments can be the most ephemeral. When the crisis is over we're strangers again. It's not like a stupendous crisis, where the two who clutched hands will greet death together, like those who leaped from the flaming towers, or, if they live, will forever honor the memory of what they endured and what solace they gave. It can be a small crisis of mortification, of having unwillingly bared, under extreme pressure, the intimate self. As they filed out, Mrs. Gutierrez just nodded, eyes lowered.

Still, those few poignant moments when the plane plunges and thrashes—driven by the currents, driving us into each others' arms—are a paradigm of love. We're solitary, sealed off, and then out of the blue comes an impulsive rushing together, preternaturally intense, swiftly erased.

Ships offer the illusion of a life of ease, free of toil. No wonder they figure prominently in movies: they are susceptible to being romanticized. The unlovely airplane can't evoke very much. It's too clumsy and stiff for a bird; at night it may be mistaken for a star, but only briefly. The only films about airplanes are satirical farces or disaster films. And soon, after a decent interval, Renata supposed, would come a spate of terrorism movies featuring dark bearded men who love death more than life.

She must have dozed, for when she opened her eyes the plane was bouncing unpleasantly through an ash-white sky. She peered past the man beside her, perusing *Sports Illustrated* and stirring his Scotch, to catch a glimpse of another plane in the distance, a silver speck that stubbornly remained stationary and parallel. Just let me get there, she prayed. If I have to die, let it be on the way home. After.

"You missed the drinks," her seatmate said. "But they'll be coming back to give me my change, so you can get one."

She nodded and raised the paper again. "Oh, there will be times when people don't have this incident on their minds," the President said yesterday. "There'll be times down the road where citizens will be concerned about other matters, and I completely understand that. But this administration . . . will do what it takes . . . " The attendant was back. "Marcia," according to the tag pinned to her maroon uniform, looked as though she would rather have been at a PTA meeting. Middle-aged, brown-haired and stocky, she would never have met the weight and beauty standards required in the coffee-tea-or-me days. She gave Renata a Coke, then addressed the muscular man.

"Your change, sir."

He counted the bills. "I gave you a twenty."

"I'm sorry, sir," she chirped. "You gave me a ten."

"I gave you a twenty." His lips curled in a smirk.

"I'm pretty sure it was a ten, but let me check. Sandy," she called down the aisle. "Seat 18C, was that a ten or a twenty?"

"You've got to watch out for them," he muttered to Renata. "Bitches always trying to gouge you."

"A ten," Sandy called back.

"I gave you a twenty and I want my change. Now." Along with the smirk, he tilted his head almost coyly, but Marcia was too old to be impressed.

Her voice dropped one octave. "Let me go back and check again, and I'll do my best to straighten this out."

"Lucky it wasn't a hundred." He laughed and slapped his thigh. "They better watch their step. No one messes with me or screws me out of my money."

"Are you sure?" Renata said. "They're usually pretty careful."

"Of course I'm sure." Now she got the smirk.

Marcia returned. "I'm sorry, sir, but we've tallied up and . . . Maybe if you checked your bills again?"

He half-rose from his seat and leaned over. Renata could feel his breath, the Scotch. "Listen up, Marcia. If I say it was a twenty, it's a twenty. Hand it over before I get really mad."

Marcia looked at Renata appealingly.

"I'm sorry, I was sleeping." She hoped Marcia understood that they weren't traveling companions.

"One moment, sir." Marcia scurried away and a new attendant appeared, "Doug," a hefty black man in a crisp white shirt and tie. A bouncer type, but where could anyone be bounced, so far up?

"I hear there's been a misunderstanding," said Doug in an operatic bass.

"Misunderstanding, my ass. I gave your girl a twenty and she gave me change for a ten, man. Just give me my money and everything'll be fine."

After a pensive moment, Doug strode off and returned with a crisp ten-dollar bill. As Renata's seatmate tucked it into his shirt pocket next to the toothpick, he gave her a quick wink.

She should have lied, she thought, and stuck up for poor plastic Marcia. She knew how it felt to be wrongly accused. Sure it was a ten, I saw it. It would have been the most innocuous form of wrong words, *prashmon,* a negligible lie. Except if her neighbor strangled her, she wouldn't get to Houston. She closed her eyes, but it was hard to sleep with him beside her.

Last winter, on the flight to Puerto Rico, Jack had put his hand under the blanket and up her skirt (her favorite flowered skirt, now in a garbage heap with other debris) and dug his fingers into her. Not so bold as Linda's flying escapades with Roger, but bold enough. Renata was barely awake but opened her eyes to find Jack looking composed, innocently Jack-like. She stirred in the seat to help his fingers, suppressing all sounds, only a long sigh at the end. They didn't look at each other. After, they held hands. His hand was sticky and hot. "I was so bored," he murmured. "There's nothing to do." The memory made her warm, and made the brute next to her worse.

Out the window the flat, brownish landscape—a converted swamp bed—rose at a tilt, upended, threaded with a maze of highways and low buildings sprinkled here and there. The land climbed up closer and clouds of dust climbed with it, shimmering in the heat. Then the awful bump as they hit the runway, the rush forward, the plane galloping out of control, the pilot in the saddle gripping the reins to hold it back. Everyone gasped in relief. They were still imprisoned, but one danger was gone. They would no longer crash into a building.

Welcome to Houston. A voice thanked the passengers for choosing to travel with them and hoped they'd enjoyed their flight. The voice spoke English, but the syllables didn't make words Renata could recognize. They were pieces of familiar words, but something about the pacing was off. It was the stresses—all wrong, a stress every few syllables regardless of sense, making a repetitive, opaque little tune. "Ladies *and* gentlemen, please remain *in* your seats *with* your seat belts fastened until the aircraft *has* come to a complete *stop* . . . " Words and melody had never been introduced. It was like hearing Cole Porter sung in rap mode.

As the passengers filed out, the attendants at the door bid them farewell like ministers greeting the worshippers after a church service, except they greeted only every third passenger. Renata emerged from the tube to see the approach of four armed guards in camouflage flanked by two plainclothesmen. What have I done!

"Come along with us, please."

They were addressing her seatmate, right behind her. "What's going on? What're you talking about?" he said.

"Let's not have any trouble. Just come along." Two of the guards reached out to take his arms.

He tried to wrench away, while all around them the passengers froze. "Hey listen, I'm no fucking terrorist. I just wanted my fucking change. They tried to give me the wrong change."

"You'll have a chance to explain everything. Just come along quietly and there won't be any trouble."

"That cocksucking cunt," he shouted as they escorted him away swiftly. "Do I look like a fucking Arab? I'm an American citizen, goddammit." He had to be dragged off. "What about my bags, eh? I want my stuff."

It was almost six and the light outside was fading. The moist heat was a relief after the plane's frosty air, but that relief was brief: the bus to the city was air-conditioned to a fault and smelled of fake leather. Out the window was flat desolation. Webbed highway as far as the eye could see, forty miles of serpentine gray stripes and broken white lines. Finally the city, a distant glitter of green and glossy black. The closer they got, the more splendidly it glistened, an emerald city, each sleek glass skyscraper mirroring another's surfaces. A few showed signs of architectural wit, stony ornaments, bits of cornices and friezes borrowed from the past, the only acknowledgment of a past. The highway snaked around the buildings as if to display them at different angles; the facets shifted, appeared, disappeared; the light flickered.

From where she sat, in the third row on the aisle, Renata could glimpse her face in the round rearview mirror at the front of the bus. Her face appeared to be vibrating. Trembling. The surface jiggled, as if its features were loose, its planes readjusting. She touched her face but it felt quite still. It took her a moment to grasp that the mirror itself was loose on its frame, and the speed of the bus was making it shake. Only another minor delusion but eerily true, as if the mirror were reflecting not her carefully composed face but a layer behind it.

Her hotel was in a downtown empty as a desert. The room, large and depressingly neat, was freezing. Outside, tall buildings stalked the dark, sending out gleams like animals' eyes in the night. Plastered on a building across the street, far below, was a poster advertising the Academy Art School, but she didn't even bother to note it down. When she called the desk to ask how to turn off the air-conditioning, she was told it couldn't be turned off. And why on earth would she want to? the voice implied. The cold was built in and everlasting.

She ordered dinner from room service. The TV was tempting, like something you know is bad for you, but she fought it; she'd promised herself a day off, like a smoker giving her lungs a rest. If anything happened she'd know soon enough; it wasn't likely to happen here. She tried to study Arabic, but both the plural forms and the mysteries of the fifth verb conjugation defied her powers of concentration. Mrs. Stiller, amid the luxuries of the *QE2*, came back to mind, and then, inevitably, Miss Greff. Miss Greff would have felt at home in this room, this place, because nothing reeked of life. No need for *ahmintu*. Here you could play dead. It was worse than the room Renata had lived in when she first came to New York, for that at least was dingy, and dinginess was a form of life.

Around midnight she looked again out the window she'd tried in vain to open. Far down below, a passel of slender figures dressed in black—shorts, tank tops, knee pads—swept back and forth on the empty street. Skates or blades, she couldn't tell, but wheels for sure. The figures were spinning and swirling, looping and leaping, a dozen or more, moving too fast to count. They made no pattern, each one moved in isolation, yet they were clearly a group, a clan, a tribe. When they skimmed under the hotel's light, she could see their hair standing straight up and out in spikes, like Gianna's hair but more colorful. Chartreuse, pink, teal blue, gold, and silver. A flock of lurid birds on wheels, a nighttime species, they prowled, crouched, darted. They swooped from one end of the broad street to the other in their entropic ballet, defying the dead streets. They were a pack of abandoned children protesting their abandonment, protesting those hot, empty streets, insisting on motion and color. If she'd been able to open the window, she would have cheered them on. In the king-sized bed, she piled on all the blankets she could find, tried to imagine Jack's body curled around hers, and slept.

Her taxi came promptly the next morning. After a quick gust of warm street air, she was refrigerated again. This city renowned for its unbearable heat from May to November was the coldest place she'd ever been. And at nine-thirty on a Tuesday morning, where were the people?

"*Abajo.*" The driver was Mexican. Down below.

"*Abajo?*"

In the underground passageways. You could go from your car to your office, he explained, or from one building to another, without ever risking the air. You could eat lunch, do your shopping, go to the bank or the gym. A subterranean stratum of city lay hidden from the glare of the sun. This would never be the target of a terrorist attack. Everyone was already buried. This was the right place for Peter, the rat. How fitting that he'd ended up here.

She navigated the frigid labyrinth of the medical center for fifteen minutes before she found the right section. A nurse with hair slicked back in a bun sat staring at a computer screen. Renata asked for him by name, the words an irritation on her tongue, like a bit of grit. Peter. But not his real surname. A new name, the one Cindy said he went by; he found it best to change from time to time.

"Down this hall." The nurse raised her head. She sat very erect, shoulders back, neck long and straight like a dancer's. "Make a right, then the third door on your left."

"Is he . . . ? How's he doing?"

"Rather poorly." She studied Renata. "He hasn't had any visitors since he's been here. Are you a relative?" Her skin was very dark and her eyes were a startling shade of green. Like jade, like the jade brooch Renata's father gave her mother on their anniversary a week before the twenty dollars was lost, smoky green fading into gray. She and Claudia had exchanged a grin as he pinned it on their mother's blouse because his arm brushed her breast. Maybe this nurse's great-great-grandmother had attracted the green eyes of a slave owner who bequeathed them. When the nurse looked in the mirror, did she see her eyes as a sign of violation? Did she cling to old outrages? Surely not. Surely she liked her eyes; they were beautiful. Only Renata saw violation everywhere. The nurse was waiting for her to answer, the green eyes blinking with impatience.

"His niece."

"I could let him know you're here. So he won't be shocked?"

"I'd like to surprise him, if that's okay. I only just learned he was sick."

The nurse turned back to the screen. "You'll see his name on the door."

She saw the false name, and beneath it, H. Chang. Mr. Chang occupied the first bed, a slight, wizened Chinese man of about seventy, with graying hair carefully combed straight back. He sat propped against pillows, looking proprietary in crisply ironed striped pajamas—his own, not the hospital's standard-issue gown—reading a Chinese newspaper, his glasses low on his nose. He looked up and nodded at Renata in regal fashion, as if she were a tourist come to gawk at his estate. At his bedside, in a pink plastic chair, sat Mrs. Chang, she presumed, a plump, round-faced woman in a polyester pants suit, also proprietary, but not regal. A placid knitter. A long red skein unfurled from her rattling needles. On the bedside table was a vase of purple irises, along with a white telephone and a few paperback books. But for the high white bed and the plastic water pitcher, the Changs might have been spending a peaceful morning on the patio, enjoying their retirement.

"Good morning," Mrs. Chang said. "Are you here for the gentleman in the next bed?" She gestured toward the drawn curtain dividing the room.

"Yes. How is he?"

Mrs. Chang shook her head. "He doesn't say much. He doesn't want to eat. The nurses try to make him eat. I try. But it's no good. Maybe you can make him eat."

"Maybe I can." What a glutton Peter had been. When he and Cindy came over for dinner her mother used to cook in great quantities. He eats like there's no tomorrow, she would say. He's a growing boy, Dan would joke. To you he'll always be a boy, that's the trouble, Grace muttered.

Well, fine. Renata was glad he couldn't eat. Let him starve. Her mother didn't sit down to a meal for a month, after Claudia was fished from the river. They ate crackers and cheese and apples and pizza until Renata began cooking, from a book. Only now that she was here to see how thin he'd grown, she couldn't seem to cross the two yards to the curtain that separated them. She hated to leave the Changs' well-ordered domesticity. They were the family she should have had. When Mr. Chang recovered—and surely he would recover, he didn't seem very ill—maybe they could adopt her and take her home; she could forget and start a new life. She'd once had a smattering of Chinese but just now it eluded her. With a bland smile at Mrs. Chang, she forced herself to step to the other side of the curtain.

What she saw resembled a photographic study in shades of white and gray. The sheets were blinding white in the sunlight beaming in from the window. The body on the bed was asleep, at least the eyes were closed. Peter's hair, once so black, was a steely gray, matted from sleep, his face a sickly ivory, the skin blotched with grayish spots. The stubble on his chin was white. His lips, greenish gray. The hospital gown was yellow-gray and his hands, long and smooth, the family's hands, were the color and texture of used waxed paper.

The only color in the room was the salmon pink of the visitor's chair, where she sat down and gazed out the window. Low, drab houses were strung out in rows, laced by highways with billboards advertising auto parts and barbecued ribs. She could almost feel the sky's white heat, though the air inside was modulated to a slight chill. The sensible Mrs. Chang had worn a cardigan.

He stirred. She cleared her throat to make him wake, driven by the predator's thrill, a flutter behind her ribs, a low whir in her head. He was in his early fifties, but he looked much older, older, even, than Mr. Chang. Hollows had carved themselves out under the cheekbones. With his head flat on the pillow, the flesh sank down to drape the bone. His lips trembled with each faint, blowing breath, a syncopated rhythm. A tube snaked into his nose. Another, attached to the inside of his elbow, delivered a colorless liquid from a bottle suspended near the bed. A third tube, thicker, emerged from under the sheets and carried a brown liquid that emptied into a large, narrow-necked jug on the floor. The flesh of his arms was loose, like fabric. The body hardly rose above the mattress, as though the bed were concave, and his feet rose up in sharp points.

Her sister, with this? Claudia was willful; she didn't give in easily. He must have played on her boredom, her restlessness.

She stared hard until his eyelids began to twitch. His eyes opened slowly, black marbles with blacker dots for pupils. They opened straight onto her, and the look in them, gathering terror, was worth years of grief. The same look as in her father's eyes when they dragged the river. In her own, in the mirror, when she entered their bedroom and knew she would sleep there alone from then on. Never in her mother's eyes. Her mother refused terror; she closed her eyes and hid.

Renata sat perfectly still while he stared. She felt relaxed, more than she'd been since last Tuesday. For the little while she sat here with Peter, she didn't have to think about that. His Adam's apple jerked as he tried to swallow. He was confused, naturally. She'd changed in eighteen years, as Claudia would have changed, though not so much that he wouldn't know her. Them. He closed his eyes as if he'd made a mistake and opened them onto the wrong decade, then tried again. It was the same a second time. He'd seen a ghost.

"No," he croaked.

"Yes."

"But—"

"I'm not a ghost. I'm Renata." Not destroyed, like a twin star slipped out of orbit. She is lost but I will not be destroyed.

He gave a groan and put a papery hand on his chest. "You nearly scared me to death." His lips parted to show yellowish teeth—an attempt at a smile. "You came to visit me? That's good of you."

"This isn't a social call. I've been looking for you. You're not easy to find."

"How, then? Cindy? Ah, Cindy. Always the sentimental one. Well, how are you? How've you been all these years?"

He had nerve. She had to grant that. Nerve enough to keep up the pretense.

"Are you okay after what happened, . . . you know, last week? You weren't anywhere near, I hope?"

"No."

"What a terrible shock. Especially living in New York. And your mother?"

"Not quite in tiptop shape. What can you expect? But then, you know all about her, don't you? Don't you know all about everyone? I heard you've been keeping tabs."

"I don't know what you mean. I'm sick. You can see that."

"Oh, cut it out. I didn't come to hear more lies. It's incredible I didn't realize right away. Incredible. Don't you think so? An imbecile would have understood. It just goes to show what people can refuse to see. All of us. We're all guilty."

"I don't get it. I'm sick, I told you. I can't listen to all this."

"I'll make it quick. Remember the time you came on to me in the garage?"

"You're all mixed up, Renata. I know you've been through a lot, but—"

"Of course you remember. You were the one who was mixed up that day. You put your hand on my neck. And when I turned around and looked up at you and you realized, you said you were sorry, you didn't mean to frighten me." That's what she should have said a moment ago. Oh, sorry, I didn't mean to frighten you. Maybe he would have recognized his words.

"I don't remember anything like that. I think maybe you should go now." He looked to the left, at a cord with a nurse's buzzer.

"That buzzer can't do you any good. I can get to it quicker than you can. I always knew she didn't go down there herself. She'd never have done it alone. You were so close, we just didn't see you. Now I have to know how you did it."

He started coughing, spat up into a tissue, then reached for the buzzer, but she got there first and held the cord away from him. In the silence came the pages of Mr. Chang's newspaper rustling. "Do you want a cup of tea, Herbert?" said Mrs. Chang. "Shall I get you a cup of tea?" They heard her leave the room.

"Why are you saying such things?" Peter muttered. "Are you mad? It's made you mad."

"You arranged to meet her that night. I know. I saw her go out with the dog. How did you do it? Did you push her off the pier and then go home to Cindy?"

"Stop it! I was home all night. I was as horrified as you were. When people can't accept things, they rearrange them in their minds."

She could have hit him, helpless as he was. "Cindy remembers. She said you used to go out a lot at night."

"Cindy." He was wheezing with every breath. "Cindy makes up what she likes. She always did. She's a drunk. Can you trust a drunk?"

"She's not drunk anymore. She's quite clear." She tossed the cord behind the bedframe and leaned over him. "Tell me how you did it," she whispered. "Just say it. That's what I came for. I need to hear you say it."

"I can't say what isn't true."

She sat back down. "I can wait till you're ready." Moments passed. "What about Gianna, meanwhile?"

He raised his head an inch from the pillow. "What about her?"

"Did you arrange that with the Jordans or do it yourself? That day at the merry-go-round. How did you manage that? It couldn't have been easy. You must have had help."

"I had nothing to do with that."

"I don't believe you."

"I swear it. I lost touch with the Jordans after . . . after they moved away. I never saw them again."

"How many other children did you sell? Was that one of your sidelines? Or did you just sell your own?"

He spit up again. "It's pathetic, what you've turned into. I'll call for help."

"You won't call for help because I'll tell everything I know. Cindy will talk if I ask her to. You have no hold over her anymore. Do you want to die behind bars?" Mrs. Chang was returning, so she spoke more softly. "Do you want your nice neighbors here to know what you are? They might not want to share a room with you."

"Stop," he whimpered. "I'm in pain."

"What've you got? AIDS? Cancer?"

"Lymphoma. They can't do anything. It won't be long. Give it up, Renata."

Pleading for mercy. It was what she'd envisioned, what she'd made the trip for. But she didn't feel the satisfaction she'd envisioned along with it. *Iranima* again: the melancholic unease on the attainment of a long craving. She was torturing a dying man. But dying doesn't exempt people from anything. While we live we have to answer, isn't that justice? She bent lower over him till his stale breath made her lip curl. Sick people exude rot, or maybe it was the smell of guilt. Her mother hadn't any smell, just neutral, dry and clean.

He sank deeper into the bed. "Give me a drink of water."

She held the glass as he drank. He might have spit in her face, she was prepared for that, but he sipped carefully, like a well-trained child. A good patient.

"Listen, Renata." He gripped her wrist tightly. Surprising strength for a man so sick. "You hate me. So do it. Now. Hold your hand over my mouth."

Her heart pounded so hard it shook her chest. "What?"

"You understand. Please. You won't get caught. They expect it any minute. Pull out the tubes. Do something. You know you want to. You'll be satisfied and I'll be done with everything."

"Shut up. Do you know what you're asking? I'll be like you then."

"You'll be righteous. You always liked being righteous. Remember the time you lost that money? You were miserable because you lost your righteousness. So do it. Have your revenge."

"I didn't lose the money. Claudia took it. She stole it and let me take the blame."

"Whatever. Does it matter now? Just let me go."

She studied the tubes and imagined yanking them out. It would have to look like he'd done it himself. No. Not yet, anyway. Not until she knew.

"I'll think it over. Maybe I'll come back and do it tomorrow." Help rid the world of evil, why not? But revenge didn't feel sweet. It felt like more to add to the past.

He held up his hand. "Don't, don't come back anymore. I don't want to remember. You're cruel to come here."

"I am. When she was stolen, it made me cruel. Tell me what happened to her and I won't have to be cruel."

"I don't know," he gasped. "I told you. People take children all the time, but I was never into that."

"What people?"

"You know. People. They . . . " He turned his head to one side and closed his eyes. "I wouldn't do that to her."

"Not to your own child. To others, maybe. All right, so tell me about Claudia. Go on, I'll wait as long as it takes."

"Please go away. If you won't help me, go away."

"I didn't say I wouldn't help you. Did you plan it? Did you know that place down by the river? Or was that her idea?"

"I didn't plan anything." It was as close to a shout as he could manage. Then at the sound of Mrs. Chang's soft murmurs, he lowered his voice. "Why would I go climbing down those rocks in the middle of the night? I only wanted to talk to her."

"But somehow she went out on the pier and you pushed her."

"You're all wrong. Nothing like that. We were up in the park and we argued. She said she was going to tell. First she went along with everything, but after the baby she got scared. She couldn't take it. Any of it. Us, the secret. She wanted the baby."

"She asked you to get the baby back?"

"When I said no she went wild and started running. I chased after her, I was afraid she'd hurt herself, but I couldn't see, and those rocks, . . . I slipped and twisted my ankle and by the time I got down there she was out on this, I don't know, sort of broken-down jetty. I could barely see her out there. She must've flipped out. She was calling me—she wanted to swim. A midnight swim." He crumpled the tissue and dropped it on the sheet. "Totally crazy."

That part Renata could believe. She could hear her. I dare you. It's hot out. What are you afraid of?

"Go on. I want to hear it all."

He rolled his head on the pillow. "I yelled to her to come back, I would do whatever she wanted. And then, it was so dark, I don't know how it happened. She didn't jump in, she just . . . disap-

peared, like she fell through." Tears oozed out the corners of his
marbly eyes and down the grooves in his face.

The planks were rotted. She couldn't see in the dark. Anyway, it
was only water. He thought she was scared? She'd show him who
was scared. I dare you. In the silence came the click of Mrs. Chang's
knitting needles. Renata waited.

"There's no more," he said.

"You mean you left her there to drown." If it was true, this was
worse than she'd imagined, worse than if he'd pushed her in.

"No, I was . . . I figured she must be hiding underwater to
frighten me, it couldn't have been that deep, and she'd come up on
the other side and get back up another way."

"You figured she was better out of the way. She was too much
trouble. She wasn't trouble before, but she was trouble now. You
figured they'd never find her. Who would ever think of the river?
Well, I thought of it."

He coughed. "Can't you just shut up? You're terrible."

"No, you're the terrible one. And you lived this long. Too long.
You don't know what you've done." She stood up.

"I know what I've done. Don't you think all my life—"

"Don't tell me about your life. I don't want to hear about your
rotten life. I'm going."

"Don't go."

"You were just begging me to go. What should I stay for?"

"You promised. That's why I told you."

"I might come back. You won't know. You might be sleeping.
You can lie here wondering if I'll come back to release you." She
heard Mrs. Chang moving about and raised her voice to a conversa-
tional pitch. "Goodbye now. By the way, I heard you're not eating.
Try, Uncle Peter. If you're going to get well, you have to eat. You always enjoyed a good meal."

The Changs were sitting as before, and Mr. Chang was sipping from a Styrofoam cup. Renata smiled as she passed.

"You told him to eat?" Mrs. Chang said.

"I told him, yes, but he's always been very stubborn. A stubborn old goat. I hope you're well very soon," she said to Mr. Chang, who looked up over his glasses and smiled remotely.

She asked the taxi driver to take her to a park. Any park. They must have one. Somewhere away from tall glass buildings. The place he brought her to was scruffy and flat as far as the eye could see. The grass was wilted, but not from the trampling of feet; no one was around. The few benches looked mournful, in need of a paint job. Only the trees showed a sense of pride: magnificent, widely spaced live oaks with dripping Spanish moss. The outdoors was a vast steam bath, the kind of heat in which the body goes limp and the mind follows. Everything was hazy and shrouded in damp. Far off, the glass buildings, shimmery in the heat, looked like shoe boxes with windows cut out, the kind of houses children make after they've gotten new shoes. Renata and Claudia did that, made shoe-box cities.

She walked on and soon heard a rhythmic barking voice. In the distance, a group of forty or fifty boys and young men were doing calisthenics, their leader shouting orders like a drill sergeant with a platoon of new recruits: push-ups, jack-in-the-boxes, somersaults. They marched, too, and executed smart military turns. As she approached she could read "YAC" on their shirt fronts, Youth Athletic Corps spelled out on the back. Around them rained a fine mist of sweat. They must be one of the paramilitary groups she'd read about in the papers—the antithesis of the flock of nocturnal birds, the anarchic skaters skimming the streets last night. The skaters had an ironic, somber gaiety. These young warriors were earnestly cheerful, like a local team giving their all for the honor of the school. They had heard the President and were heeding his call. "My message is for everyone who wears the uniform to get ready." They were zealous. They were dedicated, disciplined, and sinister, as all groups of marching men are sinister. A reminder that any minute now, tomorrow, in a week, or a month, would come the war. The sheer eagerness could not be suppressed. And here she'd forgotten for a little while. It was just what the President had predicted, one of those "times down the road where citizens will be concerned about other matters." Watching them, she flushed with shame. What an ignoble scene she'd played in that hospital room. No wonder she couldn't bring herself to tell Jack of her plan. It was too shameful. She couldn't have done it if he'd heard it out loud, the impotent rage of it.

But she did do it. And she was glad.

Linda, who came from Houston, said there were three things worth seeing. The only one Renata remembered was the Rothko Chapel, and so she spent the rest of the day in that octagonal space staring at the black paintings on the wall. Not vacant but a rich black. Black that turned the city's blankness inside out like an empty bag and filled it with all that was missing. Black not for oblivion but for remembering, so dense with memory that the colors of the spectrum deepened and merged.

Back at the hotel, she changed the next day's flight for an earlier one; her business was done. She checked out, unwilling to spend another night in that tall cavern. She chose a cheap motel on the highway near the airport, overlooking a parking lot. It was spare but adequate—no thick towels or tiny bottles of shampoo and body lotion, but the bed was fine and she'd sleep well. Just to make sure, she drank half a bottle of wine with her steak at the roadhouse across the highway.

At three-fifty—she checked her watch; this kind of motel didn't supply a bedside clock-radio—she was awakened by men's voices and clattering feet. The voices were so loud, the sound of the key in the lock so close, that for a moment she thought her own door was being opened. But its placard outlining the fire regulations didn't move; she could see it from the light insinuating through a crack in the curtains that didn't quite close, as they never do in cheap motels. Drunken chatter broke through the cardboard wall. Young voices, four or five of them. Or two or three, making enough noise for five. Things banged around. She pictured burly, suntanned college boys with opaque eyes and incipient beer bellies. Boys like the iron-pumper on the flight in, who was probably locked in a cell right this minute, trying to explain he wasn't a terrorist, just trying to get his change. Careless rich boys on a spree. Or, given the motel, careless poor boys, much the same thing.

"Now I call that scoring," one of them said.

She could hear everything, though in the haze of sleep it didn't make sense at first. How about that tall skinny one who put away the beer like a pro? And that one with tits like watermelons. The one with the slit in her skirt. A litany of the girls they'd just left.

"I forced her," the loudest one said, laughing raucously. Those words were clear; they made her sit up in bed. "She was more loaded than me, and I was pretty loaded. I forced her."

I should do something, Renata thought. But first she got up to make sure her door was securely locked.

"I forced her," he kept saying, and the others joined in his laughter, like a sitcom laugh track. "She tried to get out from under but I was inside before she even knew it was happening."

Would a man knock on their door and confront them? And say what? She could ask Jack what a man would do. In a uchrony, Renata would bravely apprehend the criminal and change the course of history in the direction of justice. But righteousness was out of the question here in the middle of the night, in the middle of nowhere, in nothing but an old T-shirt.

There was a smudged white phone beside the bed. She could call the police. Even out here in the wilderness, there must be police. She could say she overheard a confession. She was lying in bed and heard voices through the wall. Would they bother to come when they heard that story? A woman alone, dreaming in a motel bed. Dreaming of rape?

She could wait till morning. Knock on their door with the desk clerk beside her and say she'd heard it all. And then? Tie them down till the cops arrived?

Or she could go outside and write "Rapist" on their windshield. She tiptoed to the window to scan the parking lot. Were she a car expert, she might figure out what a bunch of rowdy boys would be likely to drive. A pickup? SUV? Suppose she wrote "Rapist" on the car of some law-abiding family man, taking his wife and kids to see the grandparents. Wouldn't they be surprised. And what would she use to write with? She must remember, in the future, to travel with Magic Markers or spray paint for just such contingencies.

She could watch for them in the morning, take down their license plate and report them. She could try worming their names out of the desk clerk. She could rent a car and follow them, find out where they lived, and begin a campaign of retaliation. Another chance to rid the world of evil. They'd never know who sent the threatening letters or phoned the dean. But that was elaborate, and she had a plane to catch.

It was one rape out of many. It happened every night, many times a night. The girl was home by now. Crying. The way Gianna might have cried, how many times? Until she stopped crying altogether, and stopped speaking too. The girl might have cried herself to sleep by now. She wouldn't report it. Too mortifying: I went to a bar with my friends, met these guys, we had a few beers, they said they knew a great club not far away, we got in the car. . . . Bingo.

And if they'd brought the girls back to the motel room? Would she have banged on the door then? Called the police? A boy could push his way into a girl faster than the police could arrive.

She'd never see their faces. Or if by chance she saw them in the morning, checking out, she'd never know which was the one. But somewhere not far away, a girl was having a bad dream.

She called for a cab early in the morning and left a note on the night table: "I heard a boy in room 112 next door say he raped a girl last night," she wrote. She had to use the pad she carried around: cheap motels don't provide writing paper. The maid would find it. She'd throw it away. It was a pathetic gesture that would change nothing. The whole trip had been a pathetic gesture, an orgy of *baki-ranima.* Still, it was better to have come than not. Better to have something to cling to, than nothing.

Thirteen

All the way home in the taxi, she imagined what might await her. The apartment colonized by a gang of street kids stomping around to ear-shattering music. Converted into a crack house. Trashed and looted, everything stripped from the walls—the calligraphy hangings, the good magistrate spreading a civilizing influence, the long, numbing illness to be pacified by the Great Snow. And the irate neighbors assembled out front. . . . But visions of mayhem were a weak diversion. What she feared most was finding an empty apartment.

She paused to listen before inserting the key. Quiet as a grave. If Gianna was gone, the past few days would become one more troubled dream of the many raining down on the city, last Tuesday's charred petals still sifting earthward. If the girl was gone, she would not go looking for her. Not any more.

Gianna was sitting on the floor, wearing her new shorts and a T-shirt, a can of Coke beside her. She smiled when she saw Renata. After two nights in a real bed, with a roof over her head, her face was less taut, her eyes less wary.

You look better, Renata was about to say. But she couldn't speak. For spread out around Gianna were Farmer Blue's family and their worldly goods—the house, the barn, the silo, the cows and horses on the square of green turf, the trucks, the tractor, the antique plow. Even the faintly suspect Hired Hand was there, not asleep as he so often had been, but setting up a ladder against the side of the barn, perhaps to repair the roof. Claudia had always wanted to make him a villain; she said they needed a villain, everything was too perfect. But here he was, benign again.

"Where did you find that?" she whispered.

Gianna pointed to the closet and the overturned carton. Her eyes narrowed, worried that she'd trespassed. She began gathering up the pieces.

"No, it's okay. It's fine. Leave it."

Renata set down her backpack and knelt alongside her. Gianna was clutching Farmer Blue. Renata picked up Powder Blue, who had been her favorite, and stroked him.

"Do you remember all this?"

Gianna stared.

"Do you remember we used to play with it?"

She looked confused, then finally smiled. A girl who tried to please, who'd learned that was the safest way. Or perhaps she didn't know she remembered; only her hands remembered how to spread the pieces out.

"His name is Farmer Blue," Renata said, pointing. "This is Mrs. Blue. And the children—Powder, Sky, and Pastel. You might not remember their names after so long. We used to make bales of hay and pile them on the truck. You liked to make the horses gallop. But they're not really racehorses. They work in the fields. See? They pull the plow."

Gianna studied the plow, then attached a pair of horses and nudged it through the field.

"That's right. That's exactly how we used to do it. Mrs. Blue used to bake pies in the kitchen. We used pennies and dimes for the pies. You do remember, don't you?"

Gianna's fixed smile was blank. She must be embarrassed, Renata thought, to be caught out at such a childish game. It was one thing to have played with Farmer Blue for hours on end when she was five or six or seven. But she was far too old now for a toy farm; no doubt she'd unpacked it out of boredom, poking around for something to do.

"Think," Renata pleaded. "Think hard. Don't you remember?" And what she couldn't bring herself to say: Your father gave it to us, to your mother and me, when we were little children. We loved it. We played with it until she got tired of it and wanted to destroy it. You and I played with it years later. Even after I learned to despise the giver, I loved the gift.

There was no telling whether the girl's stare hid a rag of memory. Her life, whatever it had been, would have made her cunning. She would have tried to obliterate the past, during the ordeals of the later years. She would have needed every bit of strength for what those years served up. To recall a patch of ordinary childhood might have weakened her.

"You're safe now. Try to remember," Renata urged. She couldn't help wondering if she was doing what the psychologists had done in their stupid mouse-trap experiment. Implanting false memories, wrong words. Were they wrong words if the memories were harmless, even good?

At last, with the plow and horses still in her fist, Gianna nodded. Renata put her arms around her and drew her close. Gianna sank into her. How long since she'd been embraced in safety? How many unwanted embraces had she endured?

⌐

Since last Tuesday nothing in daily life has seemed as urgent as it used to. Only the essentials matter: caring for the children who've fallen into her hands, hearing the latest news, learning how many bodies were incinerated or crushed. That number changes every day and will keep changing for two years before it settles into a definite figure, like the arrow of a roulette wheel, vacillating, hesitating. Of the half-dozen phone messages since Monday, nothing is essential, not even the one from Denise suggesting in her wry way that it might be about time for Renata to return to work. Only the last message matters. "Hi. I'll be over later, just wanted to remind you. I'll bring dinner. Hope the trip was okay." She'd forgotten Jack was coming. Or rather, pushed him and his visit to a far corner of her mind, something at which she's adept. But now that she's home, he's crucial again. If she wants to keep him in her life—and she does, she does—she will have to take his demands seriously.

Meanwhile Gianna's turned on the TV. She flipped past the news and found a *Law & Order* rerun. It's one Renata's seen, a prominent local politician accused of raping a campaign worker. Because of his connections at City Hall, it's difficult to pin the crime on him. Gianna sits transfixed.

If Jack is coming, she has to hide Gianna. Anything connected to that part of her life must be kept separate from Jack for as long as she can manage it. Jack is new and clear and good; he gives her a chance to be new too.

Henry and Gerald are reliable and would be glad to entertain Gianna, but Renata has a better idea, more mischievous. Cindy. She was so brimming with apology for not helping out all those years. Let her help out now. Let her make her sober amends.

She goes into the bedroom to make the call. "Cindy? How are you?" Not hitting the bottle, I hope? No, that's not the way to ask a favor. "Good. And Hal? . . . Oh, that's great news. I'm so glad. . . . Two weeks? You must be relieved. . . . Yes, I'm fine." She omits the real news: I went to Houston. I saw him. I told him . . . He told me . . . "Cindy, I wonder if you could help me out with something. I'd really appreciate it."

Cindy is slightly puzzled but agrees willingly. "Sure, okay, I could use the company. What's her name? Jane?" She won't know who the company is until Renata is good and ready. Unless she recognizes Claudia in Gianna's face. Renata will take that chance; she almost enjoys the risk.

She waits to tell Gianna until the trial on television is over. She understands the need to complete the arc of justice. Guilty: that's satisfying. Like Cindy, Gianna is puzzled but agrees. She hasn't got much choice.

"It's just for tonight, because my boyfriend's coming over. Cindy's an old friend and very nice. You'll be fine. I'll pick you up in the morning. Okay? Let's get your things together."

Nothing much to stash away to conceal Gianna's presence. She's not a girl who leaves many traces. As a matter of fact, the apartment seems neater than Renata left it, and the twenty-dollar bill still sits under the vase on the table.

Thank goodness the trains are running again, after a fashion. There's just time to get there and back. Cindy's three-room walk-up in the East Village is a mess and smells of stale smoke and hairspray, but Cindy is good-humored and welcoming. "Your hair, sweetie! Who did *that*? Maybe I can fix it for you." She doesn't remark on any resemblance. Is Renata the only one who sees it? No, the bookman saw it too.

At six-thirty Jack rings her bell, the pressure and duration of the ring meant to chide her for not giving him a key. He lumbers in, holding a takeout bag from the soul-food place around the corner.

"Ribs?" she says. "The way to my heart?"

"The way to something. I need real food, anyway. I was up at Pier 94 this afternoon, eating donuts. You have no idea how many donuts people have contributed to the war effort."

She reaches up to kiss him and he lets her, but with no enthusiasm. She knows why. He thinks she's spent the two days with someone else. He'd sully himself.

He's brought everything she likes. Besides the ribs, collard greens, yams and cornbread. Ice cream. To soften her up. That's intimacy, is it not? When a man knows what you like to eat.

They sit at her folding table in the kitchen, and he rolls up his sleeves as if preparing to assault the food. The thick, hairy arms remind her that she's missed him. She'd like to reach out to touch, but he's not in the mood.

"So how was your trip?"

She thought he'd give her more time, but evidently Jack angry, Jack threatened and in distress, is not the patient man of every day. She's rarely seen him angry, and even now he speaks casually, as if she's been on vacation. But his face is unforgiving.

"Fine."

"Oh. Fine. So that's how it's going to be."

"Can't we slow down a bit?"

"How slow? After dinner?"

"Look, I . . . First tell me how it is down at the site. Were you there this week?"

"Yesterday. Still chaos, but more organized chaos. No one's expecting to find survivors anymore. They've cleared a road for the trucks so they can get the debris out quicker. That helps. Soon they'll be demolishing what's left of the smaller buildings. It's hard to keep the construction guys in shoes. The shoes get soggy and stiff after a few hours. Some of the firemen don't even wear masks, some kind of macho thing, I guess. They keep coughing. They take risks they shouldn't, but so far so good."

"I want to go down there and see. Now that I don't have Julio, I can go. Maybe you can get me in."

"It's not a tourist site, Renata. There are too many people already. And it's dangerous. You can't tell where the ground might give way. Or things could fall. The worst is underground—the engineers aren't sure what's going on down there. Like if the walls are cracked, the river could start pouring in. A group of them went down to have a look Monday, a couple of engineers and two guys I know from the Port Authority. I hung around until I saw that they got back okay. Like going into an inferno. I don't want to talk about it anymore."

"Tell me about Julio, then. Did he get off all right?" All the while they keep passing the food around, filling their plates, reaching for the cornbread, gnawing at the ribs like famished people.

"I met Teresa and Carmen's sister, Pilar, her name is, at the day-care place around three. I didn't want to go in the worst way. I had to drag myself." He tosses aside a bone and takes another. "I knew I'd have to tell them I was the one who sent her there."

"But how could you know—"

"Let me finish, okay? I went. It was one of those dreadful scenes like I've had at the office for days, only this time I was right in the middle of it. Julio cried. They cried in Spanish. I didn't cry. I'm not sure he remembered them. Do you think babies that age remember?"

"I don't know. Probably a little. Did you tell them . . . what you said?"

"Yes. They're very decent people. They tried to make me feel better. They said the kinds of things you keep saying."

"And did you? Feel better?"

"No. But at least I could tell them what to do, you know, to get around the red tape. I can make that easier. But in the end, dead is dead. I can't get around that."

He'd like to, though. Beneath the amiable manner, such a lust for power. Not money, not high office, just control over life and death.

"Do you want some more collards?"

"Okay. So how was your uncle? You did say it was your uncle, didn't you?"

"Yes. He's half-dead. But we managed to talk some."

"I'm sorry he's so sick. But why the big secret?"

"You don't need to be sorry. I don't like him. I loathe him."

"Then why'd you go? I don't get it." He leans back and begins folding his napkin into small and smaller squares. "Why, just at this moment, when I need you, did you have to go see someone you haven't seen in years and you loathe besides? I'm not sure I even believe this uncle story."

"Come on, am I in the habit of lying to you?"

"That's a joke. If you don't lie it's because you don't go near anything worth lying about. You just sort of leave out everything important."

Not pleasant words to hear, but he's correct. Just now she's leaving out the important fact that she picked up a stray girl on the street and decided it's her long-lost niece who disappeared ten years ago at the age of seven from the Central Park carousel, where she rode a rearing white horse with a red and black saddle and halter, not stationary but the better kind that goes up and down; they'd had their eye on that very horse and raced to get it when the music stopped. Disappeared—kidnapped, lost, evaporated into thin air, transformed? how do such things happen?—under Renata's very eyes, though her eyes were averted at the crucial moment, a fact she'll never forget. She also can't forget that although she wanted to go on the carousel too, on the green horse beside Gianna (duller, stationary), the child begged to go all alone—"You always come with me. I want to go myself! I'm big enough!"—and Renata relented. "Okay, I'll wave when you pass. Hold on tight." She watched and waved, hardly ever looking away, only now and then glancing at a dirigible up in the sky advertising tires. Round and round spun the carousel. She'd promised Gianna ice cream from the cart a few yards away as soon as the ride was over. Gianna had wanted the ice cream first, but Renata was afraid the motion might make her sick. She turned away from the whirling carousel to gaze at the cart; the crowd around it had dispersed. The sign showed the varieties of ice cream, so vividly she could almost taste it on her tongue. The ride must be nearly over. She'd get it now, when there was no line, and have it ready when Gianna came off. By the time she returned holding the ice-cream pops, the carousel had slowed down. The parents milling around to collect their kids made it hard to find Gianna on her horse—it was on an inside row. When she couldn't spot her the next time around, Renata leaped onto the moving carousel and raced to find the rearing white horse. She bumped into a child climbing down and dropped the ice cream. There was the horse at last, but it was riderless. She yelled Gianna's name. She lost time, running frantically around the carousel while it circled in the opposite direction. She called for the operator to make it stop. Stop it, stop it! My niece! But it took forever to stop, and all the while she elbowed through the crowd screaming Gianna's name. When the crowd thinned out there was no Gianna anywhere.

It was June, a week before school would be out for the summer. Gianna was finishing first grade. Another important fact she's left out is that for nearly four years before that day, she had been virtually the child's mother, taking over from the adoptive parents (unofficial, no papers, Peter said; it's simpler that way), having had motherhood thrust upon her when she was nineteen and hardly knew how to begin. She learned by doing. That for nearly four years Gianna was her reason to live, her closest blood relative, not counting her mother of course, who could not be counted on for much in those days, less even than now. And that for over ten years the child has been one of the missing (though Renata never thought to walk around the streets holding up a photo as everyone's doing now), a child in a police dossier who merited a brief article in the paper: more notice than if Renata had been a poor ghetto mother on welfare, less than if she'd been a rich and prominent corporate executive. One child of many, the police told her, as if that were any consolation.

She's left out that even now, every month she phones the precinct, Captain Sheridan who took over six years ago from the retiring Captain Riley, to be told ruefully that nothing has turned up; there are sophisticated new techniques nowadays but unfortunately the trail is quite cold. It was never warm. Still, never say die, Captain Sheridan says. Where there's life there's hope. In other words, still *tanfendi-oude,* lost-but-possibly-not-forever. That she's registered with the National Center for Missing and Exploited Children, and although the woman who answers the phone is invariably sympathetic—it was just three weeks ago, in fact, that Renata last called—the news is always the same. No leads have turned up. She calls from the library, where there are people around, where she can't dwell on the fact that while Gianna was being whisked away in the crowd, she, Renata, had deserted her post, too impatient for her ice cream, busy making up her mind—pop or cone or sandwich? No, she hangs up fast and dashes into Linda's office for a bit of diversion.

Incredible, how a child could vanish into thin air in the midst of a boisterous, jostling Sunday afternoon crowd, the first nice Sunday after weeks of rain and gloom, everyone in the city, it seemed, converging at the merry-go-round. "It sometimes happens that way, in crowds, the confusion, . . . " the husky black cop with the mustache said after Renata had screamed her head off and people nearby ran to call the police, not so easy in the days before cell phones. He bundled her into a cruiser and they sped through the park while cops on foot fanned out (she remembered that phrase, "fanned out," and pictured them later as she lay in bed, dark-blue-uniformed men streaming out from the carousel like spokes furrowing the park), but they found no one furtively carrying a seven-year-old child, and no bodies in the bushes, as they regularly turn up on *Law & Order.* "What will they do with her?" she cried in the station, and the husky cop patted her shoulder. "How could this happen? I haven't got any money, they can't want money." "We don't really know, miss." "Who would know? Who can I ask?" "We're the police. We'll do what we can." "But how can I go home without her? How will she find me? She's too young to find her way around." She told them about Peter—even then she suspected him—and she told them about the Jordans, but they couldn't find them, either. What were they good for, then, these obliging policemen? Whom could they find? They're brave, they're staunch, they pulled bodies from under the concrete beams of the towers, but they couldn't find one seven-year-old.

She's leaving out the fact that the girl reappeared on the street a few days after Tuesday's disaster, reborn from the big bang. Five thousand people killed and one returned to life. Found. Find her, Grace said, and she did. That the girl has spent the past three days here in this apartment and was sent over to Cindy's tonight precisely so Jack wouldn't tell Renata she's lost her mind, how can it possibly be the same girl, half the city's hallucinating in one way or another. Poor Renata, the attack's driven her round the bend, he's been so busy he didn't realize. Now he'll get "help" for her.

All she said in her defense, lamely, was, "I've told you about my parents."

Jack stood up. He looked so tired, slumped and creased. "You haven't told me about *you*. You have no idea how frustrating . . . it's like being with someone who came out of nowhere. It's . . . I only know there's something, you're obsessive, with these words pasted all over the place. As if the way people talked were some kind of moral issue. You think this administration would be better if they all took a course in grammar? I doubt it. But never mind that. All this time I was waiting. I thought it just took patience. Because I loved you. But what did I love? Look, I'm not at my most patient. I'm exhausted. Maybe I should go."

"Please sit down. Please." Already he was using the past tense. Loved. She couldn't watch him walk out. "It's nothing like what you're thinking. You think all women . . . because of Pamela. There's no one from the past. It's really my uncle. I had to see him. I wanted him to see me."

He'd leave if she didn't give more. He hadn't even hung up his jacket; it was draped over the sofa, his battered briefcase beside it. She threw the remains of the dinner in the garbage while he stood waiting, then straightened up and leaned on the sink. This was the moment she'd dreaded since the first time they went to bed. She'd known then that if she ever took her clothes off with him again, it would eventually come to this. Everything in between had been postponing.

"You'd better sit down," he said. "You don't look too good."

She sat. "I'm not the person you think you love. I've made so many mistakes."

"Well, what does this uncle have to do with it?"

"It's because of him that Claudia's dead."

"I thought your sister drowned."

"She did. But he was there with her, down by the river. He saw it happen. She fell through a broken pier and hurt herself, and he just watched."

Jack had heard a lot. He was used to weeping women and their sad tales. He found them lawyers or doctors, jobs or apartments. He knew how to talk to them. The last thing she wanted was to hear his kindly, professional tone. The kindness would be real, but kindness can be the hardest thing to bear.

He didn't go professional. "Let's go into the bedroom," he said. "Tell me lying down. Everything is easier lying down."

So they went into the bedroom and took their shoes off—no more than that; she didn't want to be any more naked—and she told him. Selectively. The suburban life. Claudia's pregnancy. The baby. The bloated body in the river. Not the hours spent trying to reconstruct the scene, with Peter a blurred shadow on the margins. Not the secret language, not the stolen money. The loss of her sister to death by drowning, yes, but not the loss while she was still alive. "I can't talk no more about how I came up. It hurt to think about it."

"She had a baby?" He looks around at the clippings on the wall about the lost or abandoned or abused children. "You never mentioned any baby before."

"Yes, well, there was one. A girl."

"What happened to her?"

"We gave her up for adoption. My uncle arranged everything. He had connections, he said. We didn't understand then what he meant by connections. We didn't know half the things he was into. My father was an innocent. He didn't want to know. Peter was his baby brother and he always took care of him, ever since their parents died. He couldn't let himself think anything bad about him."

He'll straighten out, Dan used to tell Grace when she complained about Peter's irresponsibility, his laziness, shiftiness. That was Grace's term, quaint but apt: shifty. Never any real job, though he was always driving into the city. Appointments, interviews. Give him time, Dan said. He'll come around.

"It took me a long time to figure it all out myself," Renata says.

This is the part she wants most to omit: how long it took. She doesn't even have her father's blind affection as an excuse. She simply willed herself to remain ignorant, while Grace willed herself into darkness. For surely Grace figured it out, and when she couldn't look at what she knew, she chose the dark.

Renata's ignorance took a more canny path. Even with her sister's belly growing every day, she kept the scene in the garage in a separate niche of memory, a place to store anomalies, mistakes, exaggerations. But the truth lodged in her chest like a stone and grew, a living stone that got heavier all the time. She might have yanked it out, but she was afraid of what it would look like. What she would be once she'd seen it. She got used to the weight of it. She can still feel the touch of the fingers whispering down her spine, and the feeling makes her shudder and reflexively shift her body an inch away from Jack lying by her side.

"I should have known from the beginning. That it was his child. I don't know how I didn't. That was another reason I needed to see him, to tell him I knew now. And to find out what happened, that last night."

"So did you? Find out, I mean?"

"Yes. Sort of."

"Was that good? A relief?"

"Relief? I don't know about that. What he said, . . . I'm not sure how much to believe. But I can put it together better." Come on, I dare you. What are you afraid of? Yes, she believes that.

"What about the child? Did you ever see her afterward?"

"Oh, yes." And she tells him how, after Claudia died, her mother sent her to see how Gianna was doing. Just check things out, Grace said, sitting in front of the mirror absently brushing her hair. She'd let it grow very long and wild, until she looked like a witch. Why don't you go yourself, Renata said, but Grace only kept on brushing.

"She didn't have the guts so she sent me. The parents—I hate to call them that but I guess they were her parents—they were okay with my visiting, once they realized I wasn't trying to take her away. They lived on the upper West Side. They seemed okay. They had nice things. Expensive stereo, furniture, stuff like that. She was a secretary, I think, at an interior design business, and he worked in a store that sold musical instruments. What did I know? I was sixteen, seventeen years old. I didn't pay much attention to them. I just wanted to see her."

Jack shakes his head slowly. Though he must have heard far worse, he didn't expect anything like this.

"I know what you're thinking. How could we do that? But people do. We did. You have to imagine how it was. My mother couldn't take it all in. At the beginning, she even wanted me to go and take the PSAT's for Claudia when she stopped going to school. She wanted me to pretend I was Claudia. I could have pulled it off, too. But I wouldn't." Not because she was scared of lying or of being caught. Because she didn't want to be Claudia, even in pretend. It was complicated enough being herself. Grace was angry. We have to stick together, she said. You're not doing your part. Renata felt guilty, and then in the end Claudia didn't need any PSAT scores.

"We didn't even realize there must have been money involved, at least I didn't. But there must have been. Some kind of deal."

"Ah," says Jack, and reaches out to touch her, not a light finger running down her spine—he knows better than to do that—but a broad hand stroking her back, hard. Not someone testing her but someone who knows her. "I see now, about Julio. I'm so sorry."

No, he doesn't see at all. He only assumes he does. She can't bring herself to tell the whole story, the stages of collapse, the family caving in not all at once but buckling stone by stone. Claudia. Then Cindy left and Peter moved away, and her father started drinking and her mother unraveling. But she accepts Jack's caress. She wills him to keep his hands on her skin; it makes it easier. He knows something now, and this should hold him for a while. I can't talk no more about how I came up. . . .

"Where is she now? Do you still see her?"

The man is insatiable, but she answers calmly, evenly. "No. Look, this is enough for one night." She reaches out to touch his face. "And now will you stay?"

He pulls her close and she lies with her head on his chest. His arm is around her; she can feel his slow, steady heartbeat. Even after what he's heard, he still wants her near. He murmurs the generic, soothing words you say to someone who's just unearthed a boulder from her chest and is feeling too weightless, too excavated, to move. "It's all right, it'll be all right." Meaningless words; it's the voice that matters, and she loves his grainy, sexy voice, that odd, bumpy New York mixture of rough and smooth. She's so soothed, it's such a peculiar feeling to have cast off some of the weight, that her usual discipline is faltering. It's like the lassitude after love, where you have to be careful what you say, you might be sorry later, you might be giving someone ammunition. . . . She even thinks . . . She can hardly believe it, but she thinks she might tell him about Gianna, the almost grown-up Gianna staying in her apartment. Maybe he wouldn't find her crazy after all. Maybe he'd help. He could be the dad. Or something close to it. Not "uncle," though. That is not a role or a term she can even consider.

It's so peaceful, lying here with him, she won't plan whether to speak or not. She won't shape any words. She'll wait, and if words come out, fine. They may be assembling themselves on their own, as she rests. There's more, she might say. Or maybe not. There'll be plenty of time now. There's something I need to tell you, she might say.

"There's something I need to tell you," Jack says, as if he's so close he can echo her thoughts. That would be the closest she's ever been to anyone, since Claudia.

"What?" she says lazily, and smiles up at him.

"It's about Pamela." His voice is all grain, no smoothness.

"Oh, did you call? I totally forgot. Is she all right?"

"I saw her."

"So?"

"I, uh, went to bed with her."

Renata can move after all. She can spring away so they're not touching at any point. "You . . . what? What'd you do that for?"

"I, uh, . . . I don't know. She wanted to. I was pissed because you went away like that. Everything's so crazy these days. She was so . . . distraught."

"Distraught? Distraught! You fucked her because she was distraught? Waved the magic wand? So did it help? A mercy fuck? Was she less distraught when you finished? Traught? No, maybe tractable. How thoughtful of you. Always ready with a good deed."

"I'm sorry. It didn't mean anything, really."

"Oh, please. Everything means something. How was it? Good? Great?"

"Not bad. I mean, I do know her. . . . It was better than right before we broke up but not as good as when we—"

"Stop! Do you have to be so literal? Oh, Jack." She's sitting up cross-legged, and very glad she's fully dressed.

"I thought it would be better to tell you," he says sadly. "Because you were so open with me."

"Open!" she spits out. "Well, you thought wrong. It's always better not to tell. Silence is better than wrong words." *Emenast,* any time, rather than *prashmensti.*

"No," he says in that tone of utter certainty, a tone she both loves and hates, depending on the circumstances. When he says, No, forcing people to sleep in a shelter or leave their kids to work for a minimum wage is not a good idea, she likes it. Just now she hates it. "You feel that way right now, but in the long run—"

"Don't tell me what I feel, okay? Just go away. You couldn't bear to keep your stupid little secret so you had to lay it on me. Ease your conscience at my expense."

Restraint is like a muscle. It requires exercise. If you train it, it will carry heavier and heavier weights. "It's harder to keep your mouth shut than to spill it out. Believe me."

"I understand," he says. "But I wanted things open between us."

"Will you stop saying that moronic word? You sound like a parody, you know? Next thing you'll be talking about your inner child. Plus your timing is awful, to put it mildly. After what I just told you? Now?"

"I see that. I shouldn't have said it just now. You're right about that."

This ability to be in the wrong and feel undiminished is something else she usually loves about him. He's firmly rooted. Admitting a mistake won't make him topple over. Only right now all his lovable traits are turning ugly. To be so firm is maddening. Is there no way to get at him? He can't be torn to shreds as she's torn other men, just to be rid of them. He's like some miracle fabric designed for heavy-duty wear.

"I thought you went away to see someone. Not that that explains anything, I know. Look, Renata, is it really such a big deal? Considering how we are together?"

"I'm not sure. It was a big deal for you, wasn't it? When you thought I was with someone in Houston?"

"Okay, so I'm inconsistent. At least I'm telling you. So it won't come between us."

At this piece of idiocy she can only roll her eyes. "Where did you do it?"

"Where?"

"Yes, where?"

"At my place. In my bed. Why?"

"I just wondered. Look, I'm exhausted."

"Me too. Let's go to sleep and deal with it in the morning."

"It's too early to sleep. I have to do the dishes. In the morning I have to go to work. Denise called, she wants me back. What does that mean anyway, deal with it? Get used to it?"

"Get past it. In the scheme of things—"

"If you say 'the big picture,' your life is in danger. Maybe you want to get back together with her."

"No. I don't even like her anymore. What I really want to do is sleep."

"Go home to your own bed, then. Maybe it's still warm."

"You don't really want that."

"I don't?"

"No."

He's right. She doesn't want him to go home. She also doesn't want to tell him anything ever again. Just let him stay. Don't leave me alone with the words I dredged up. Drown them out, she thinks. Fuck me like you fucked her. Ram me into oblivion.

"You want me to stay and hold you all night. That'd be much better." She lets him hold her. It is better. After a few minutes he says, "This is the longest, this last hour, that I've gone without thinking about . . . you know. It's almost a relief to have a fight. At least you remember there's a private life."

"Mm." It was that way when she saw Peter in the hospital, too. Exactly as the President predicted, in his words that leach gravity from all they touch. "There'll be times down the road . . . " But she doesn't feel any relief. Being held in his arms is a pleasure and a pain. She did as he asked, told him what he wanted to know, so he would stay. And in return, look what she's had to hear. Now he has his hand on her breast, he wants to make love, and in a moment he'll be murmuring in her ear, he'll be making her pulse and quiver. She'll be rocking and gyrating like a belly dancer, slithering all over him like a mermaid, and that will be a pleasure and a pain too. A way of forgetting, however brief. And a way to ensure sleep.

The dream offered itself as a gift of color and motion, as if to compensate for the somber colors of the past week. She was part

of a crowd gathered on a great lawn transformed into a fairground:
balloons, streamers, music, booths where sausages were grilled and
brightly colored fruit drinks were churned, and of course, rides. A
Ferris wheel, a parachute, a carousel with prancing horses. She had
on her favorite flowered skirt, brand new again, and she stood waving at the children on the carousel. Suddenly everyone stopped and
turned to watch a new attraction, an enormous, slender rectangle
made of particles of mist, or perhaps it was tinsel or glistening
raindrops, suspended in the air, hovering a few yards above the
ground. In the midst of it, a couple held hands and danced, kept
aloft by the mist, swirling and dipping, their clothes billowing. It
was so splendid and magical an image, so alluring, a tower drifting
in air, its shimmering vertical streams like a delicate waterfall, that
other couples ran to dance inside it too. Hand in hand they leaped
up and were gathered into the tower of raindrops. Renata began
running toward it, but something held her back. She was reluctant
to make the leap alone and she retreated, disappointed in herself,
her lack of adventurousness. She couldn't accept her own dare. The
tinsel rectangle rose and rose, with the floating couples dancing inside it, and gradually disappeared into the upper air. Everyone
who'd remained below waited eagerly for it to return, to drift back
down; they waited to hear the dancing couples describe what they'd
found in the upper air. They waited and waited, Renata among
them, until after a while they grasped that the tower would not
reappear, and the dancing couples were not coming back. And then
a wondrous horror came over them, at what they had witnessed.

Fourteen

"You seemed a million miles away when I called yesterday." Jack reaches for Renata's hand in happy couple walking mode, but his grip is tentative, as if he's afraid she might resist. She doesn't. "What were you doing?"

"It's hard to talk at work. I was deep into Arabic. Remember? To see what kind of press we're getting, find clues, God knows what. Can you believe, there aren't enough people in the government who can read the newspapers. Maybe if I'm good, later on I can get to see secret documents. Maybe I can be a spy."

The afternoon air is balmy and wonderfully clear. On the Promenade, the Saturday strollers in their bright colors are out in force, with skaters and bikers darting among them. The trees sway in full regalia, flaunting their abundance before the leaves start to turn and fall. The river carries blotches of sun and miniature patches of rainbow on the underside of wavelets.

"You'd make an excellent spy. I'll vouch for you. So how's it going. Are you fluent yet?"

"No, speaking is another thing entirely. But I can read some, if I use a dictionary."

One of the important words she's learned is *shahid*, which means "martyr." Once a suicide bomber has pledged to carry out his mission, once he's written the letters of farewell to his loved ones and maybe made a videotape with greetings, he's called *al-shahid al-hai*, which means "the living martyr." At that point he is considered, for all practical purposes, dead already.

"Say something, anyhow, so I can hear how it sounds."

"I lost my niece when she was seven," she says haltingly in Arabic, "and now I've found her. So many dead and one brought back to life." This is not only badly pronounced but contains several grammatical errors. It doesn't matter, since Jack can't tell the difference.

"What does that mean?"

"We will fight the evil ones to the death to preserve our sacred way of life."

"That sounds familiar. Didn't we hear something just like that recently?"

"We hear it all the time. But I think you mean what we heard at Coney Island last weekend. In that coffee shop. 'What this war is about is our way of life and our way of life is worth losing lives for.'"

"Right, I remember now. You have total recall?"

"Well, no. Actually I wrote it down after we got home."

"So I'll see it hanging on the wall soon. Listen, Renata, I called you at work because you were sleeping when I left. Then on the phone you were so quiet, I thought maybe you were still mad and you'd . . . you know. Call it quits."

It's a novelty to see Jack uncertain, awkward. "I was busy, my first day back. Anyway, this is no time for major decisions. It's like when women get their periods. Not a time to decide to break up. Especially when everyone else is looking up long-lost friends."

"Good. I'm glad you feel that way. But I know you. You'll never forget, even if you never say another word about it. It'll go into the permanent file."

"That's probably true," she says lightly, and rewards him with a smile. "I'm not good at forgetting. Why don't we drop it? Isn't it a gorgeous day?"

A few sailboats drift idly by; two kayaks glide and bounce. Just ahead parades a large family returning from a birthday party, to judge from the balloons that bump overhead. A typical late September Saturday, Seurat's dotty paradise transplanted to the Brooklyn riverbank, and if not for the gaping hole in the scenery—the Manhattan skyline—everything would be perfect. Well, not quite perfect. It's not just the absence of the buildings, the two tall, thin rectangles the promenaders knew intimately: heads keep turning to the empty space. It's the impromptu memorials, the chaotic little shrines sprung up along the railing, with candles, ribbons, scrawled messages, bunches of wilting flowers, some already twelve days old, pathetic, touching, hopeless. It's the mood of the crowd, subdued, slow, a bit dazed. Yet the old habits of trust persist. The kayakers are bundled in lifejackets, the bikers helmeted, the skaters armored in knee and elbow pads. As if those could keep them safe. Meanwhile the ubiquitous posters lure the eye with smiling photos, happy faces posed on the beach, holding up a bowling trophy, standing in front of the Eiffel Tower. Missing, our brother, our father, our daughter: Movado watch, long dreads, dark birthmark at left breast, scar from left ear to chin, brown hair with frosted tips. . . . Let's not look, Renata said when they began their walk. We look all the time. Let's take a day off, okay? Jack was willing. So they don't join the others in contemplation; they merely glance at the posters in passing, the breath that sticks in their throats already an accustomed ache. What they can't control is gazing every few moments at the blank parallel bars in the sky, like everyone else. Just checking, in case the buildings might suddenly reappear.

"Didn't you ever do anything like that?" Jack asks. "I mean, hurt someone you love?"

"No. Or not in that way." That's the truth. She never loved anyone, is why. "Let's not talk about it anymore." She has another agenda in mind. She can't go on keeping Jack away or sending Gianna to Cindy's. Even at the best of times he needs attention—high-maintenance, Linda would call him. If she keeps putting him off he'll have Pamela back in bed in no time. Bad news all around. She's got to tell him. Not about the lost child, never; not after the other night. But about this new Gianna, risen from the rubble, living in her apartment for the past week, like old times.

You can hide lots of things, as Renata well knows, but it's hard to hide a real person. Gianna is very real. She likes Mister Softee and pizza with extra cheese, she watches far too much television, especially MTV and Nickelodeon reruns, she reads mysteries and concocts fruit drinks in the blender. She still doesn't speak but sometimes mouths "Yes" or "No" or "Thank you," which Renata considers fine progress for only a few days. She wanders around the neighborhood while Renata's at work, drops in on the bookman and perches on the ledge, watching his customers come and go, or hangs out at Henry and Gerald's shop, maybe sits in Starbucks with a movie magazine and Renata's Walkman wrapped around her absurd brassy hair, evened out by Cindy into a semblance of order. This can't go on indefinitely. A girl needs a real life. And yet time, under the forever blue late-summer sky, seems held in abeyance, freighted with uneasy expectation, the way it felt when she lived in the shabby room down the street from the bar,

barely older than Gianna herself. And while they wait for the unexpected, she's safe and cared for, maybe safer than she's been in
years. Renata takes good care of her. They listen to music, they
play cards, they rent videos. Gianna has a taste for fluffy romantic
comedies, just like her aunt. *When Harry Met Sally. You've Got Mail.
Sleepless in Seattle.* Harmless little tales, from before.

"Are you missing Julio?" Jack says out of the blue.

"No. Maybe a little. It's okay, though." She feels a pang of
guilt—she's hardly thought of Julio in days, yet when Jack speaks
his name the warm feel of him in her arms comes back, the smell
of laundered terry cloth and baby spit and talcum powder. He and
Gianna are alike in their lack of words. And Renata, with all her
languages, has become a devotee of silence these past twelve days,
when so many of the words spoken, read and heard are meaningless. Right now she'd be content to walk holding hands in silence,
but as they approach the northern tip of the Promenade, strains of
music drift into the air.

A horn, the rich, juicy wailing of a jazz trumpet. The melody is
familiar but she can't place it. Each time she tries to predict its
path, the tune veers off on a detour. Where's it coming from? She
and Jack turn to each other, smile, and keep moving toward the
sound, an elusive, bluesy music, luscious music Letitia Cole could
dance to. Then she sees him sitting alone on a bench, facing the
river and the lopped skyline opposite: a stolid, paunchy man with a
gleaming brass trumpet. Everyone nearby stops to listen. Everyone
understands this is music that can't be ignored or interrupted. But
they don't dare get too close. He's playing for all of them, but he's
playing in solitude, too, sending his furling riffs through the
bluish-gold air like a gift, like water to the parched. If they get too
close he might stop. So they move quietly, the way you move so as
not to disturb a deer or a rabbit. The player looks somewhere be-

tween fifty and seventy-five, it's hard to tell, just as it's hard to tell
whether he's black or white: his skin is the color of tea, or old
pages in forgotten books that never see the light. His face is as impassive as a buddha's, a buddha in dark glasses and a New York
Mets baseball cap, only his expression isn't mild. Concentrated. He
wears a short-sleeved white shirt that strains at the donut of fat
around his belly, checked rayon slacks, white socks, and shiny black
shoes, supremely respectable shoes. Nothing about him could intimate the wry, apocalyptic music he makes. He's not playing for
small change, no hat or open leather case at his feet; he's no student
or beggar. He's playing for the pleasure of it, but he's also a thickset herald, playing to announce what's happened to all of them,
playing for the blue glory of the sky that Tuesday morning and
how it broke apart, playing the beauty of that day and the horror,
oscillating them like figure and ground. He's playing for the city in
mourning, for the lost and for those remaining, an elegy and an
appeal, playing an antidote to the ugly, nonsensical words that have
been the public response. His feet are firmly planted on the
ground, and one glossy black shoe softly taps the beat.

No one is walking now; even the pair of armed soldiers in
camouflage have stopped their pacing. Everyone is still, stopped in
place. Renata squeezes Jack's hand. The music lasts a long time, but
it can't go on forever, much as they'd like it to. One last wail of a
cadenza and it's abruptly over. The trumpeter lets the hand holding
his instrument descend, and he gazes out across the river. Then he
puts the trumpet in its case and gets up and walks away toward the
streets. A mass holding of breath is released and people start moving again. Renata and Jack go over to sit on the bench the musician
occupied. He rests his hand in her lap.

Now, she thinks. Now with the music suspended in the air,
now is a good time. So she tells him about the speechless dark girl

with the bleached blonde hair she found wandering on the street after the attack and brought home to live with her. Her *hanai*.

"A total stranger?"

Oh don't, Jack, don't get all social-worky on me. "Not anymore. She's a good kid. You'll see. I want you to meet her. You can come meet her right now."

"But . . . Her parents must be looking for her. Someone must be looking for her. And she needs medical care. You say she's mute. You have no way of knowing what—"

"Don't do that just now, okay?"

"Renata, look, you're upset. Everyone's upset. Everyone's doing weird things. But think—"

"Do you want to come over? We could get something to eat."

"Sure. Okay."

They're no longer holding hands. The sky is as blue as ever, but the sun has begun its descent; the light is less glorious.

"Have you asked her," Jack says, "what happened to her that day? If she remembers anything?"

"No. I'm not a member of the helping professions."

"But that may be what she needs. Mutism is a common symptom of trauma. There are ways to treat it. It's usually a sign of—"

"Jack. All I asked is if you want to have some dinner with us."

"Right. Okay, not another word."

At her corner they run into Henry, carrying two shopping bags. "Hey, Renata. How're you doing? Jack, right? Say hi to Gianna for me. She's a help in the store, did you know? Dusts, puts things back in place. Nice kid."

"I will. Thanks."

Jack looks puzzled but says nothing, as promised. Anyway, they're distracted by a sidewalk runner bounding blindly forward, a lanky, bare-chested man in jogging shorts and an Indian-style headband. This is Philip, the man whose wife was incinerated at her desk. He seems to have given up shaving and doesn't notice them in his path. "Hi," Renata says. They've never exchanged much more than that, but she's got to say something, even if it's trite. "Hi, we've met before. I live downstairs—" But he's pushing ahead as if he's gone deaf as well, arms pumping wildly.

"Who was that?" Jack asks.

"He's the guy whose wife . . . "

"Oh."

Upstairs, she turns her key, then knocks so as not to take Gianna by surprise. She's curled up on the couch reading *The World According to Garp*, the Walkman installed on her head.

"Hey, Gianna. Everything okay? I want you to meet my friend Jack."

Jack moves forward in his most charming manner, not condescending as some men are around teenagers, but with respect, as if she's a real lady; his right hand is extended. Gianna looks up reluctantly, unplugs her ears, and takes him in. She tugs at her shorts, spreads the open book on her lap, and shakes hands as if she knows she has to. This isn't the sweet, shy way she greeted the bookman, or Henry and Gerald. She's suspicious, Renata can see. She may even be frightened. Of Jack, of all people! The self-appointed minister to the needy. Wouldn't hurt a fly, far less a waif. But he's a man, and Gianna feels the sex that radiates off him in waves as Renata first felt it, appreciatively, that winter day in the museum. She knows what it is and it scares her. Renata's heart starts knocking against her chest but she can't, not now, stop to conjure up what Gianna is scared of and why, what past misery she might be clinging to, or if she might even harbor a toddler's shred of memory: Renata impaled on top of Joe, ignoring her impatient shrieks. There were never any men invited over after that.

These thoughts will have to wait. Later, in bed, she'll have time
to think about lives transformed, of Gianna's lost years from age
seven to now, and of God knows what was done to her to put that
mute glaze in her eyes.

It's okay, sweetie, he's quite harmless. He can be a bastard, sure,
he was just the other night, but not in any kinky way. Those, of
course, are impossible words. Could the girl possibly be thinking
. . . ? Could she be taking fright at Renata as well, could she imagine she's been set up? This is so appalling a notion that Renata
gasps, dashes over to Gianna and hugs her tight.

"We just had such a nice walk on the Promenade. We heard the
most fantastic music, a guy with a trumpet. Now we'll get something to eat. That's all. That's all."

Jack understands, too. He backs off and sits far away from her.
He clears his throat. "We really like that Indian place down the
block. Have you ever had Indian food?"

It's no use trying. Gianna barely nods.

"We've known each other close to a year," Renata says desper-
ately. "We met in the Brooklyn Museum." What is she doing, she
thinks wildly, establishing his cultural credentials? Gianna sits
impassive—nowhere to run.

"Look, you can read in the bedroom if you want," Renata says.
"We interrupted you. We'll call you when the food comes."

After she's fled, after Renata calls for takeout, comes silence. Finally, "How do you know her name if she doesn't talk?" Jack asks.

Very smart. Renata's stumped. He doesn't push it.

Gianna comes out when she's called and relaxes enough to eat
her share, but the meal is not a success. She seems less frightened
now than sulky; there's even a perverse provocation in the way she
gives Jack sidelong glances or reaches past him for another helping,
as though safety might lie in using what she knows. If Jack notices,

he doesn't let on. He makes conversation about school, his high-school days, how he was so hopeless at languages while Renata here is such a whiz. His best subject was history. Casting about for a way to put her at ease. Gianna eats quickly, then moves to the couch and turns on the TV, a rerun of *Bewitched.*

"I think I'll walk Jack home," says Renata. "I'll see you later. We can finish our game of Hearts. You were winning, remember?" She hopes she'll see Gianna later, hopes she won't have fled for good. Yet she can't simply dismiss Jack. If she sends him home alone, he might call Pamela for company. Besides, she doesn't want to send him home alone. She's seen him anew through Gianna's eyes, and what scared the girl is just what Renata wants.

It's growing darker outside. Behind them the buildings are becoming silhouettes against a pink sunset. Ahead, the sky is turning a pewter color.

"You haven't said a word all this time," she says when they reach his apartment.

"I thought that was what you wanted. You know what I'd say and you wouldn't like hearing it."

"You think I'm nuts, is that it?"

"I wouldn't say nuts." His tone is maddeningly judicious. "Just not acting entirely rationally. Like a lot of people."

"You think she'll murder me in my bed?"

"That didn't occur to me. What I think is that she needs to be taken to a doctor to see why she's content to sit around watching TV in a stranger's apartment for a week. What exactly happened to her that day and why she doesn't talk. People who turn mute—there's usually something they're too terrified to say."

It's not so unusual, Renata thinks. There's even a verb for it in Arabic, *tabakkama,* to be struck dumb. If there's a word, it can't be so rare.

"I think somewhere her parents must be frantic," Jack goes on. "I see people like that every day. You can't imagine what they're feeling."

"I can so imagine. How do you know what I can or can't imagine? And what makes you so sure she has parents? Maybe she's been wandering the streets for a while. Maybe she ran away."

"Maybe. In that case she might need foster care."

"Foster care!" she bursts out. "You, the rich anarchist do-gooder, recommending foster care! I thought you were the sworn enemy of bureaucracy. Shit. She doesn't need foster care. She needs me."

"Look, I didn't start this. You asked me. I didn't think you came back here to fight. Can't we—"

"All right, I'm sorry I blew up. I just wanted you to—"

"Support you in this? I can't. I don't believe what you're doing is the right thing. For her, anyway. I can't say what's right for you."

So reasonable, so sensible, and she hates him for it. They've been standing up in the living room all this time, Jack puttering around, straightening things up. "Sorry about the mess. I wasn't expecting you."

"Don't bother," she mutters as she sinks into a chair, deflated. Was it Pamela who left this clutter of newspapers, books, coffee cups and ashtrays? Things were neater when she was here with Julio. "I don't think I'll stay long."

"No?" He comes over to sit beside her. "'I'm in the mood for love,'" he hums.

"Oh, Christ, you are so corny."

"Come on, Renata. We can't always agree. It's not the end of the world."

But it is. Or something close to it. Just walk a few blocks and look across the river. Take the subway to Chambers Street, as she's done twice on the way home from work, and look through the chain-link fence at the mounds of rubble guarded by soldiers.

"I think I'll go home," she says. "We had a nice walk, anyway. We heard that music."

"If that's the way you want it. I'll walk you."

"You don't have to."

"I want to."

"In Hawaii," she says when they're back on the street, "people take in kids all the time, informally. Relatives' kids, friends' kids. Anyone who needs a home. It's an old custom. A good one, don't you think? They have a word for it. *Hanai.*"

"But only if the parents can't take care of them, I bet. You don't know if that's the case here."

"Okay, have the last word."

"The last word is, I'll call you tomorrow," he says, and kisses her lightly at her door.

"The last word is, is it okay if I use your car tomorrow? I'd like to go see my mom."

"Sure. You still have the keys, don't you? I haven't used it since you went last week. Nice not to have to keep moving it for a change."

Is he really one of those people who believes there's some good in everything, even tragedy? That out of the ashes will rise wisdom and compassion, even mere common sense? No, Jack doesn't deserve cynicism right now—he's so generous with his car, after all.

"Thanks."

Fifteen

The next morning, Sunday, as they sat over breakfast, Renata announced to Gianna, "We're going for a ride to the country. I was going to tell you last night but you were fast asleep when I got home." She paused as if for a reply. That was only polite, even though there was little chance of any reply. Odd how the usual rhythms of conversation persisted. Speak, pause, listen, respond, occasionally interrupt, though there was never any need to interrupt with Gianna. "We'll borrow Jack's car." Pause again, to see what his name evoked. Nothing. "You didn't like him, did you? Any special reason?" Gianna spread marmalade over a third piece of toast, helped herself to scrambled eggs from the pan on the table, poured coffee for both of them. "Well, anyhow, I've got to see my mom. It'll be a change, won't it, getting out of the city for a while. Do you like the country?" A faint shrug. "Maybe you're more of a beach person. Still, it's nice up there, right on the river."

She did her best to prepare Gianna for the atmosphere of the therapeutic residence, half-way house, group home—there were so many euphemisms. Jack had gone there with her once or twice and seemed quite at ease, but then Jack carried his ease with him. The uninitiated needed to be clued in, like orientation for a Reality Tour. So she told Gianna about the old, the infirm, the slightly mad but harmless housemates, the no-lives, as she'd come to think of them. The Miss Greffs. Refusers of *ahmintu.* "They might act a little strange but don't worry, it has nothing to do with you. And my mother's okay, more or less. You don't have to stay with us the whole time. You can walk around."

Gianna tilted her head ironically and offered the merest smile, as if to say that she, of all people, would be unfazed by odd behavior. She wasn't a baby, Renata reminded herself; now and then she caught herself talking to Gianna as if no time at all had elapsed since she was lost, as if she were still seven years old.

In the car, Gianna slipped a U2 CD into the player, glancing at Renata first as if to ask permission. "Sure, go ahead." Making herself right at home, wasn't she? She must have bought some CDs with the money she gave her before she flew to Houston. So, bouncy music accompanied them through the three boroughs and on to the suburbs.

The house sat serenely on the hillside, its windows glinting in the sun. It was unusually empty as they walked up the flagstone path, no one about except for Helene, the new young woman who had insulted Renata last time she came—"the white tramp with her black baby"—and now lay sunbathing in a beach chair on the lawn. On the porch, Dr. Schaeffer perused the travel section of the Sunday *Times.* Strains of music from his Walkman reached them as they approached the door. *"Don Giovanni,"* he announced. He looked more contented than ever before, perhaps because his daughter, who worked on the fortieth floor of the South Tower, got out safely. Perhaps this good fortune would keep him in high spirits for some time to come. Otherwise, no one was around, no noisy card games or gossiping voices or squabbles.

"Hi, Cecilia. Where is everyone?"

Cecilia, looking drowsy, flipped the pages of a magazine at the front desk. "Gone to the mall, mostly. Don took a group in the van. The President said to shop, so we're doing our duty. Actually we do it every other Sunday morning. Some go to church and some shop. Take your pick."

"Did my mom go too?"

"No, she never goes. She prefers the TV. I see you brought a friend. Hello."

"This is my niece Gianna. Gianna, meet Cecilia."

Gianna smiled politely. By now Renata was used to these silent introductions, yet she wished Gianna might muster a word or two. How hard could it be to say hello?

Cecilia was quick to catch on. "Hi, Gianna." Her faintly suspicious look was for Renata. "Your niece? I didn't know you had any more family."

"Yes."

"Well, I'm sure Grace will be glad to see you both. She's been in good shape lately. She's taken to watching the news."

"No kidding? What about your boyfriend's brother? Was he ever . . . found?"

"Nope."

"I'm so sorry."

"Yeah, it's a bummer. Go on up, you'll find her. There's fresh coffee if you want some."

The only occupant of the lounge was a youngish man in jeans and a black T-shirt playing computer solitaire at one of the card tables. He looked up with a start, as if abashed to be caught out in such idleness. It was Dr. Stevens, Renata realized, putting in his time on a quiet Sunday. She waved and smiled indulgently. Gianna followed her up the stairs and into the TV room, where Grace sat alone, very close to the set, so transfixed by CNN that she didn't hear them enter. From the back she appeared younger than her age, with her short hair, her sleeveless shirt, her slender arms. A group of self-styled sages was analyzing the President's speech to the Congress two days ago, with the inevitable replays: "Every nation now has a decision to make. Either you are with us, or you are with the terrorists. This is the world's fight. This is civilization's fight."

Would Grace see the resemblance right away? And faint from shock, maybe? "If the child don't look like you, if you feed him long enough he'll be starting looking like you." Renata's fed her long enough. Yet there were days when Grace didn't even recognize her own daughter.

"Hi, Mom," she said loudly. A kiss on the smooth, wan cheek. "How are you? I brought another visitor today."

With effort, Grace forced her eyes away from the screen. "Renata." So casual, as if she saw her every day. "You were just here, weren't you? Every time you visit, lately, you bring a kid. Hello, dear. What's your name?"

The usual sweet, shy smile from Gianna. Her eyes, too, were drawn by the screen's magnetic pull. "Whether we bring our enemies to justice or bring justice to our enemies, justice will be done."

"She's kind of quiet," Renata said.

"Oh, won't even say her name? Well, it takes all kinds. What happened to the baby you brought last time?"

"Julio. Jack took him back to his grandmother. I hated to see him go, but . . . "

"You hated to see him go? So marry this Jack and have a baby of your own. You're not getting any younger."

What Freud called the censor was apparently taking a day off. Idling on a slow Sunday, like Dr. Stevens.

Gianna sat down in front of the TV as if she were quite at home. Renata compared their profiles. She was seeing very clearly, none of that odd wavy-glass vision that had plagued her for several days. Yes, there was a resemblance. There had to be. Naturally Grace's face was far more worn, the lines no longer firm, the mouth curved downward, the chin slightly flaccid. Gianna's face was as finely drawn as a Botticelli. Still, there was something.

"You can watch this anytime, Mom. Let's walk a bit outside, okay? It's such a nice day."

While Gianna drifted off to inspect the flower beds and the tennis court, Renata said, "Do you recognize her?"

"Why, am I supposed to?"

"I thought you might. Can't you see how she looks just like Claudia did at that age? Like both of us? It's Gianna. Claudia's child."

When she held Julio in her arms a week ago, Grace had wept. Today she was as hardheaded as a bureaucrat, as impermeable as one of the grim faces from Washington. "What on earth are you talking about?"

"Last time I was here, when I said I didn't know where she was, you said to find her. Remember? Find her, you said. So . . . " She told Grace all about how Gianna turned up after the disaster, how she was found wandering among the Missing posters, herself a poster come to life. How she'd been staying in the apartment. How she liked to play with the farm. It all fit together. It was so obvious.

Grace narrowed her eyes and screwed up her face. "Are you serious? A child you found on the street ten years later? Who doesn't talk? Of all the millions of people?"

"I can see it on her face. I can feel it. She followed me home. She feels it too."

"You can feel it. And I'm supposed to be the crazy one."

Renata was afraid she'd be the one to weep this time. All her efforts, all her patience with Gianna's silence—for this? She'd been counting on Grace, but now even her own mother wouldn't believe her. She couldn't afford to weep, though; Gianna was coming across the lawn holding a bouquet of yellow dandelions. She handed them to Grace.

"Thank you, dear. That's very sweet of you. They're just weeds, you know, but we can put them in a glass of water anyway. Let's go back in. The sun's too bright. The last thing I need is skin cancer. We can do the Sunday puzzle. You want to help me? You don't have to say anything, just write in the words. Meanwhile you go for a walk, Renata. Clear your head. You've been under a lot of strain."

She was dismissed like a child. Obediently, she strolled around the well-tended grounds. She'd never seen anyone mowing the lawn or watering the flower beds, and yet it must get done, for everything was green and orderly, a little Eden of oblivion. A van turned into the driveway—ah, the shopping expedition—and pulled into the parking lot. The residents slowly climbed out onto the small stool the driver set up, Mrs. Hernandez first, bulky in a lime-green pants suit, taking the steps gingerly, then two middle-aged black women she didn't recognize, one scrawny and disheveled, the other robust, then four old men in plaid shirts and Bermuda shorts. The driver handed one man his walker, another his four-pronged cane. The other two moved on spindly, bowed legs. "Go on, folks," the driver called. "I'll bring up your shopping bags." They made their way across the lawn, the three women together, the four men behind them. The men's progress was cumbersome, what with the walker and cane, but their talk was brisk, and so loud that Renata could hear them from the garden.

"Why, you ask? Because they have nothing to lose, that's why. They have no self-respect because everybody's been shitting on them for years. First the British, then us, not to mention their own rulers. You keep shitting on people, no wonder they start shitting back. Just look at the history."

"I don't give a damn about their self-respect or their history. You start using history as an excuse, you have to excuse everyone. Everyone has problems. Everyone has history. The fact remains, it takes lunatics to do something like that. And they think there'll be whores waiting for them in heaven? What kind of religion is that?"

"Not whores. Virgins," the third man put in.

Quite right, Renata agreed. Seventy-two virgins, to be precise. It was made very plain in the publications she'd been studying. Seventy-two virgins, which seemed more than any man would need, but never mind. There were other rewards too. Eternal life in paradise. A sighting of the face of Allah. A chance at life in heaven for seventy relatives—wouldn't that be cozy? Although some people might regard it as a penance, depending on the relatives.

"Whatever," the second man retorted. "What do you want, a Marshall plan for them after what they did? A reward? Then you're the lunatic. We've given them plenty already and look what we get in return."

Renata followed at a discreet distance, marveling at how their words cut through the claptrap on TV, drew the lines so clearly. They reminded her of Shakranik, a language spoken by an almost extinct tribe in Mongolia, which she'd heard on tape two years ago at the library. Shakranik had very few abstract nouns or verbs and was notable for its absence of euphemism; facts were presented in brutal, often exaggerated terms, which the listener was accustomed to toning down automatically, just as in English we are accustomed to sharpening the intentions of our many euphemisms. Discretion was not a virtue in Shakranik; if something was considered unfit to be uttered, people kept silent. As a result, speech was concise and immediately comprehensible. This didn't preclude lying or error or misinformed or biased opinion; it simply lessened the opportunity for half-truths and the more subtle kinds of sophistries. Another unusual feature of Shakranik: reports of fact were trusted only if they were offered by eyewitnesses. Anything relayed second- or third-hand was discounted as unreliable. This, of course, made practical matters and material progress difficult, but on the other hand it eliminated the evils of rumor and subjective distortion.

"Come on, the whole religion isn't that way. Most of them are ordinary people like you and me. It's just a few fanatics causing all the trouble." That was the one with the walker, silent till then.

"A few fanatics is all you need. I still say we should blast them out of their caves. I don't know what we're waiting for."

"They're planning something in Washington, don't you worry. They're just biding their time." The man with the cane.

"While they bide their time they should figure out why so many people hate us. Because they do, you know. They don't see us as so generous. They see us as bullies."

"It's just jealousy. Is it our fault that we're smarter and richer and not lazy? For that we deserve to be destroyed? Don't give me such nonsense. We better not bide our time too long or it'll happen again."

"It won't happen again. At least not right away. Not with all the new security at the airports. My son told me it takes two hours to get through security."

"Security! You think they know what they're doing with that security? They've got illiterates checking the baggage. They can't protect us in the long run if anyone really wants to do us in. We should try a little humility."

"Humility! What—turn the other cheek? How naïve can you get? You don't turn the other cheek when you're dealing with murderers."

Why not put all four of them in dark suits and sit them in front of the cameras, she thought. They wouldn't be any worse than the talking heads, the pundits. Better, maybe.

At a table in the lounge, Grace and Gianna were bent over the *Times* crossword puzzle, almost one-third filled in. "We should be going," Renata told her mother. She'd had enough. She longed to go home and sleep for hours, or maybe leaf through her folders. Think about transformed lives rather than observe them.

While Gianna was in the bathroom, Grace whispered, "Listen, Renata, you need to get this child to a doctor. Something happened to her. I asked but she won't say. She can't keep hiding out with you. She needs some kind of treatment. Someone who can get her to speak."

"Oh, so you're an expert on treatment?"

"Well, in a way. Wouldn't you say so? And also, you've got to stop using these children."

"Using them?"

"Yes, using them. You know what I mean."

"I thought you'd be glad to see her. I thought you'd understand. . . . She's your own grandchild."

Grace touched her hand awkwardly, impatiently, as if she were close to the limits of what she could offer. "Don't you go crying now. Pull yourself together. It worries me, the way you're talking."

"You're worried about me?" This was the first time in years that Grace had expressed concern about anyone. It was what Jack would call a good sign, in fact it was practically a miracle, just what Renata had yearned for. What a far cry from the Grace who hadn't had the strength to lift a coffee cup. But this wasn't the form she'd wanted the miracle to take. "You think I'm crazy too? I did what you asked, and now you think I did wrong."

"Stop it, she'll be back in a second. It's no good getting her more upset."

"You're seeing things so rationally, all of a sudden. Did they change your medication or what?"

"Nothing has changed. I have good days and bad days, like always. Just stop it."

But she couldn't stop. She was drowning in bitterness and regret. Why couldn't Grace be the mother she was supposed to be, the mother she needed, a mother she could talk to about her visit to Peter, and together they could deconstruct the scene on the pier and lay it to rest? Grace could be if she tried; she knew the things she pretended not to know. Why did everyone she loved insist on lying, pretending, vanishing? Why couldn't they all be like Gianna, so good, so compliant? "You sound almost like your old self. Maybe you're nearly ready to move out." Maybe we should change places.

"I don't want to move anywhere. Why, is this getting too expensive? You haven't lost your job, have you?"

"No. I could talk to Dr. Stevens. He's right downstairs. You might try living on your own. I'd help you."

"I'm not ready to go out there. Don't push me. And listen, don't bring me any more children. I can't take it."

Gianna was back, and though her hair was freshly combed, her new bag slung jauntily over her shoulder, she wasn't ready to go out there either, Renata knew. She'd only go where Renata took her.

"Goodbye, dear." Grace patted Gianna's shoulder. "It was nice meeting you."

How could she look at her face and not see it?

"There's nothing for me out there," Grace murmured as they parted. "Nothing. You can't make things the way they were before. Don't bother trying."

"Why don't you put in another CD?" Renata said as she started the car. That was your grandmother—the sentence she couldn't speak. She was getting like Grace, using meaningless words to cover up all she knew. "There's a nice place not too far where we can stop for lunch."

At home, she couldn't wait to collapse on her bed. Surely she'd provided Gianna with enough diversion for one day—a drive to the country, a glimpse of the best in geriatric care, an excellent meal on a terrace overlooking the river. But the phone machine was blinking.

"Renata, hi. It's Cindy. Give me a call, would you? I have something important to tell you."

She kicked off her shoes, shut the bedroom door, and lay down, until curiosity won out and she reached for the phone.

"Cindy? What's up? I hope Hal is okay."

"Hal's good. Getting better every day. They may be able to re-open the deli soon, they're cleaning it up. So he might even have a job to go back to when he can walk better."

"I'm glad. So what did you have to tell me?"

"It's about Peter. . . . Renata, are you still there?"

"I'm here. What about him?"

"He's, uh, . . . gone. Like, you know, dead?"

"Dead." She didn't know why she was so stunned; he'd looked on the verge. He'd told her so himself. "When? How do you know?"

"It happened yesterday. He called me a couple of days ago to say you were there. You were, weren't you?"

"Yes."

"Okay, because with him, you never know. He sometimes makes things up. Anyhow, he said you gave him a hard time."

"A hard time? That's what he called it? That's almost funny. What does he call what he gave us?"

"I'm not blaming you, Renata. I'm just saying. So I called back this morning, just to see, you know, how he was. The nurse told me. Passed on, she said. I guess that's how they talk in hospitals."

"When my father died they said he didn't make it. That was the police, though."

"I guess there's a million ways to say it. Anyway, he's dead. So, what do you think of that?"

"Not much one way or the other," said Renata. "He was a shit. He got away with murder. It was the same as murder, standing by while she drowned. And then pretending he didn't know a thing about it."

Cindy didn't speak for several moments. "You're right, he was a shit. But I was married to him, he was a part of my life, I have certain memories, if you know what I'm saying."

"I suppose so. Okay, I'm sorry. I mean I'm sorry if you feel bad. I can't be sorry he's dead. He wanted to die, he told me. He wanted me to pull out the tubes, or put a pillow over his head, but that's not exactly my style. So he got what he wanted."

"He told me what you said to him. I have to say, you have guts. I don't think I could have looked him in the eye and said things like that."

"It doesn't take much guts to accuse someone in a hospital bed. It was a low moment for me. But what could he do to me? He'd done the worst already."

"He didn't do the kidnapping. He kept saying that. He didn't want you to think he did."

Renata laughed cruelly. "You mean he cares what I think? Cared, I mean. That's hard to believe. But all right, maybe he didn't do that. I'll never know. He did enough."

"Well, it is a kind of . . . What do the politicians keep saying these days? Closure."

"Closure, right. I don't know if there's ever any kind of closure. But thanks for letting me know."

"How's the kid doing, by the way? Jane? Still with you?"

"Yes. She's fine."

"Don't you think you should, like, try to find out where she comes from? Shouldn't she be in school or something? What're you going to do about her?"

"I don't know, Cindy. I really don't know."

The knowledge made Renata edgy; her legs twitched with the urge to move; her heart flopped around. What did it mean, that he was out of the world, out of her reach? Beyond torturing and beyond forgiving, though neither was a temptation. There was nothing to be done about him, dead or alive.

Back in the living room she found Gianna walking around, fingering objects on shelves, glancing at the twenty-dollar bill on the table, staring out the window. MTV was on but she wasn't interested. She was restless. Bored. What do you think about if you've forgotten who you are? If she'd forgotten. Your father, the shit, is dead, Renata thought as she looked at Gianna, but you'll never know. Just like you'll never know about your mother. Those are things you won't have to forget.

Sixteen

Monday morning, as Renata heads for the subway, the bookman beckons from behind his table. Either he's out early or she's late again. Since she went back to work last week, she hasn't been as punctual as usual. Why rush? The single pressing thing remains the morning news. The ordinary items don't interest her; she needs only to hear the announcers' voices. The startled, bewildered, and, as the hours passed, excited voices of that Tuesday two weeks ago linger in her ear. She'd recognize the tone right away, like a new kind of music you can't get out of your head, a background to everything else. So far, for thirteen mornings, nothing but a slight edge to the usual bland-ness, as if the announcers, too, are expectant, almost tired of waiting.

Once that's done, she takes her time, no more watching the clock or running down the stairs. This morning she paused to kiss the sleeping Gianna goodbye and smooth her spiky blonde hair, which popped right back up. Wrapped in a tangled sheet on the living-room couch, Gianna opened one eye and made some small sounds, then rolled over. Renata tucked the sheet around her.

The bookman keeps smiling and beckoning, so she stops at his table. Is there something special he thinks she might like? No, just a new batch of children's books in fairly good condition—*Goodnight, Moon*; *D'Aulaire's Greek Myths*; a few Ramona books; *Tales of the Round Table*. Someone's child has grown up, or died, or disappeared. Also a battered collection of travel books: *Let's Go Brazil*; *Exploring the Philippines*; *Wonders of the Holy Land*.

"Nice weekend?" he asks. Then, without waiting for an answer, "Come with me a minute. I have something to show you." He reaches out to take her arm in courtly fashion.

"Where? I'm on my way to work."

"It'll just take a minute. Around the corner. You'll see."

"What about the books? Can you leave them?"

"No one ever steals the books."

She goes along, past the café and the Thai restaurant and Blockbuster, until they reach the local market with its big neighborhood bulletin board out front. There he stops. For as long as she can remember, the bulletin board has displayed a changing array of notices, three-deep, angled helter-skelter like a cubist collage. Roommate Wanted Non-Smoking. T'ai Chi Class Forming. Computer Problems? Don't Fret, Call Yvette. Moving? Strong Sam Lugs Anything Anywhere. Now, of course, many of those commonplace notices have been plastered over by the Missing signs. Lars Paulsen, worked on 101st floor of the North Tower, tinted aviator glasses, mustache, stud in left ear, class ring. Judy Nguyen, walks with slight limp, six months pregnant, wearing black sleeveless dress and pearls, diamond engagement ring. The bookman stands silently by as if there's something Renata should be seeing, but what? She catches sight of a dark scrawl in Arabic on the brick wall beside the bulletin board. She can't decipher the first word, but anyone could figure out the meaning, since below is a crude drawing of a bull's-eye with an arrow in the middle. The next words she can read: "Bin Laden, bomb Tel Aviv next! Terrorism breeds terrorism." It's ugly, especially alongside the Missing signs, but surely the bookman couldn't have brought her here just for that.

She looks at him, baffled, until finally he points to an eight-and-a-half-by-eleven sheet at the lower left. The grainy photo is large, occupying the top half of the page, frontal view, pouting face. MISSING: Jenny Halloway, Stuyvesant High School student. Short blonde hair, it says, sleeveless print dress, red backpack, wearing silver bracelet (but she wore no bracelet when Renata first saw her), butterfly tattoo on right hip. Forget the backpack, long gone. Renata's never seen any butterfly tattoo, but then again she's never looked. Gianna tried on the new clothes alone in the Gap fitting room. At home, she's shy going in and out of the shower, always wears one of Renata's robes.

"Your girl," he says. "Your niece."

"How . . . ? No. It must be a mistake."

"These are the parents," and he points to the letters in large block type, carefully centered. Lionel and Celeste Halloway, a phone number, an address in Tribeca so close to the site that they must have had to show ID to get home that first week. "URGENT. PLEASE call right away. She was passing the WTC Tuesday morning and never arrived at school." Did she always take detours or did she have an errand? Or was she planning to cut classes that day?

"A schoolgirl," he says. "They must be so worried about her. They must be suffering."

This sounds better in Spanish than it would in English. Suffering, Renata thinks: they use that explicit word in the Romance languages so much more readily than we do. What would we say? Upset, frantic, devastated? Suffering is much better.

The bookman goes on talking but his voice, soft, kind, unjudging, comes from far away, because a black screen is moving in from all directions, above her head, rising from the ground, at the peripheries of her vision. She knows the feeling. She nearly passed out in the police car after they found Claudia's body, and again a year later when they lowered her father's body into his grave, even as the neighbors were whispering what a brave girl she was, organizing the whole funeral all by herself. She won't pass out now, though; she's older and stronger; she resists. She sits down on the pavement and lowers her head to her knees. The bookman crouches beside her. "Can you get me some water?" He disappears into the market and a moment later is back with a bottle, which he unscrews and holds to her lips. She forces her eyes wide open to catch the fading light.

"Thanks. It's okay. I'm okay now."

"Sit a few minutes. There's no hurry." A couple of people are hovering nearby. "Everything okay," he says in English and waves them away. "No problem."

After a while she gets up. At the bottom of the notice is a fringe of small strips, each with the Halloways' name, address and phone number, same as for the notices of computer wizards and house-cleaning services and language lessons. Accent Elimination, reads a notice partly hidden by MISSING Jenny Halloway. What will they think of next? But if you wear a turban or are brown-skinned, even accent elimination won't do you much good these days.

The bookman tears off a strip and holds it out. "Here. You'll need this."

"She's doing fine with me. I take good care of her. She was lost, you know. Something terrible happened and she was lost—"

"Yes, she was lost. And it's lucky that you found her. That she was found by a good person. Her family will be so relieved. Here. Take it." He presses the tiny scrap of paper into her hand, and then, as she refuses to close her fingers around it, he tucks it into her purse. "Come, I'll walk you to the subway."

"Thanks, but you don't have to. I'm fine. I want to stop for some coffee."

She slips into the café, and once she sees him moving on, returns to the bulletin board, waits for a moment when no one's passing, tears off the notice and crumples it. She'll toss it out in the subway station. Yes, hurl it in front of a moving train. It will be as if she never saw it. It's just a piece of paper. Nothing has to change. The bookman means well, sure. But it's not fair. She's lost too much. She will not think about those people, Lionel and Celeste Halloway, whoever they are and however they came to possess Gianna's photo. She will not allow them to be real. Let the train wheels grind down their suffering.

Children's books are an excellent way to learn the structure and syntax of a language. From the stack on her desk Renata chooses one about a desert boy named Abdullah from the Age of Ignorance—meaning the pre-Islamic age—who saves his camel from a band of marauders. Meanwhile, she's looking forward to lunch with Linda. Lunches with Linda are reliably entertaining, and today's will be especially so if Linda has been reunited with Roger. If her weekend has been uneventful, there's always her store of arcane knowledge, like the bit about the composer who might never have existed but for his one piece of music and one historical reference. Just this morning Renata found a tease of an e-mail from Linda. "Since you're deep into Arabic, you might like to know this, from Stendhal, *On Love:* 'I see in their convention for divorce a touching proof of the Arabs' respect for the weaker sex.' Things have sure changed, right? And not for the better. This must have been in the Age of Ignorance. 'During the absence of the husband from whom she wished to separate, a wife would strike the tent and then put it up again, taking care that the opening should be on the side opposite where it was kept before. This simple ceremony separated husband from wife forever.' Clever, no? See you at lunch."

Close to noontime, as she struggles through an editorial in the Beirut *Star*—so much less appealing than the adventures of Abdullah and his camel—there comes a knock on the door. "It's open," she calls absentmindedly.

When she looks up, leaving off at "America has been made to know the suffering that so many other countries understand all too well," instead of Linda she finds Jack, carrying his jacket, his white shirtsleeves rolled up as if he has a major task ahead.

"What are you doing here? Is something wrong?"

"No, I'm fine." He seems anxious, though, running his hands through his hair, biting his lips, all the conventional signs. He's so unoriginal, it strikes her.

"I've never been here before. Interesting." He gazes around at the shelves piled with papers and periodicals, the stacks of dictionaries, the children's books, the lists of words tacked to the wall, color-coded to the adjacent maps. "You weren't easy to find."

"I'm not supposed to be. You want to sit down?"

"Sure. What are you doing?"

She holds up the Beirut *Star.* "My lessons. 'This is the wrath of Allah. . . . When Allah catches hold of you, there is no escape.' Stuff like that. What are *you* doing? I mean, what brings you here? Is everything okay with Julio?"

"Fine, last I heard. There's something I must tell you. You're not going to like this, but I have to."

Pamela, it must be. She's caught hold of him and there's no escape. The misery she offers is better than the misery I offer. Qualitatively speaking. Suits him better. Okay, fuck it, then. Let him go.

She's so irked with him for invading her sanctuary and ruining her lunch plans that she's ready to ditch the whole thing. So she thinks. Although she won't be thinking that in the middle of the night, wanting his warm body, or when she sees him and Pamela in some local restaurant, holding hands or clinking glasses.

"You have to? Okay, let's hear it."

He reaches into his ancient briefcase, its leather worn shabby—a good girlfriend would have bought him a new one long ago—and pulls out a sheet of paper. "This came in the mail last week. I didn't get around to opening it till today. With Carmen gone and things so frantic I can't keep up." He reaches out to hand it over but she sees what it is and won't accept it. He lays it on the desk squarely in front of her, on top of the Beirut *Star.*

"Renata," he begins in his judicious tones. "This child has a family. They need to know where she is. They want her back."

"I've seen it."

"You have?"

"Just this morning. On Clinton Street."

"And?"

"And nothing." She rips the paper, halves, quarters, eighths.

"Oh, give it up. They must be all over town. Maybe they just didn't think of trying Brooklyn right away. Anyway, I wrote it all down."

"You did? You mean you would . . . "

"Yes, I would. It has to be done. If you were thinking straight you'd see that. What are you planning? To keep her around like a pet? To indulge some . . . " He catches himself. His voice softens, becomes the crooning Jack-voice he uses in intimate moments. "Look, Renata, I do sympathize. I can imagine what this means to you. The child you told me about, your sister's child. You lost touch somehow and you miss her, so—"

"Stop it. Will you stop it this minute!" She gets up and stands behind her desk, fierce, like a teacher reprimanding an insolent student. "You can't imagine anything. You have no idea what you're talking about, you know that? Stop interfering in things you know nothing about."

"Okay," he says calmly. "What don't I know? Tell me."

"I can't tell you here." Not in her haven, where she does the one thing she can do happily, where she can be . . . Well, she's not sure who, only not that person carved by the chisel of loss. She hardly ever thinks about all that melodrama while she's here, up to her neck in words. She doesn't even want the walls to hear. To absorb the knowledge and echo it back at her, spoiling her peace of mind.

"We'll go out, then," Jack says. "We'll go to the park."

She gathers up her things without speaking, and in the hall, pauses at Linda's door. "I have to cancel my lunch date. You might as well come in and meet Linda." Linda's been curious about him for a long time. Good, let her have a look. He's more than presentable; Renata even feels a kind of pride. See this choice specimen who could have anybody and wants me! Before they enter she assesses him through Linda's eyes, the thick shoulders, the very slight paunch, the sturdy thighs, the abundant coarse black hair flecked with gray, mussed because he keeps running his fingers through it, the ice-blue eyes, generous lips. . . . But why bother to catalog his assets when she's about to lose him?

"Linda, hi. Jack dropped by, so I thought we'd stop in and say hello."

Linda's been staring into the computer as if it were a crystal ball, her elbows on the desk, cheeks cupped in her hands. She looks up brightly, her face shiny with enthusiasm for whatever obscurities she's tracked down, her red curls a tangle, her huge earrings jiggling.

She's dressed in New York black, tight sleeveless Lycra, more like an East Village waitress than a research librarian.

"So this is the famous Jack. What a surprise!"

Immediately his body grows alert, the sexual voltage rises. He's wondering what Renata has said about him. Let him wonder. "Renata's kept you a secret," he says. "Good to meet you." They shake hands. "Are you a linguist too?"

"Not exactly. More of a fact-checker."

"She's modest," Renata says. "There's nothing she doesn't know. She has a photographic memory."

"We're all freakish in some way," says Linda. "You've got to be, to stay here. Aren't we lucky they've got these back rooms for people like us?"

"I'm really sorry," Renata says, "but I can't have lunch. Something's come up that we've got to talk about."

"Oh yeah, sure." From Linda's knowing laugh, Renata can tell what she's thinking: that they're taking a leaf from her book, going off to some closet or stairwell for an urgent fuck. Both women chuckle, while Jack keeps his all-purpose flirtatious smile, mildly confused.

"No, really. I'd ask you to join us but . . . it's kind of a family matter. Some other time."

"It's like in high school," Linda says. "Remember, some girls, they'd always cop out on a plan with their girlfriends if a boy asked them out? A subsequent engagement. Were you one of those?"

"I hardly had dates with anyone, girls or boys," Renata says.

"No kidding," says Jack. "And all this time I had you pegged for the popular type."

She shakes her head in mock amusement. They're carrying this little scene off well, she and Jack. No one would guess they're in the midst of betrayal, revelation, recrimination. "Well, now it can be told. I'm sorry, Linda. See you later. Thanks for the Stendhal."

"Oh, by the way," Linda says, "I had to consult a map of St. Louis this morning, don't ask why. Guess what I found for you? Broadway Street. Olive Street Road."

"Thanks."

"This must be serious business with you two. You're not even excited. Okay, so long. Have a nice, uh, lunch."

It's usually impossible to find chairs in Bryant Park on a fine day at lunchtime, but they're lucky: two pink-cheeked young executives, dark suit jackets slung over their shoulders, are just leaving. Jack darts over to take possession. The scene around them is urban bliss, the rainbow coalition out in force, in every age, shape, and variety of dress: plump ladies in saris, homeboys in baggy jeans, sleek girls with bare, bejeweled navels, homeless men in smudged sweatshirts, and dressed-for-success lawyers on cell phones, all eating out of plastic containers. There's even a trio of cops, their holsters and billy clubs dangling over the delicate green metal chairs. And the ubiquitous men in camouflage, pacing, observing.

"You hungry?" Jack asks.

"No."

"All right, I want to understand. You think I'm against you in this. I'm not. What's it all about?"

"I didn't lose touch in the way you mean. She was stolen. The couple who adopted her had to leave town in a hurry. They were dealing drugs, I think, and someone was after them, the cops or the robbers, I don't know. They gave her to me, just brought her over one day and took off. She was three years old. So I took care of her, I did everything. She was mine. She was all I had left. My mother, well, you've seen her. And then one day—"

"What?"

"I was so careful. I tried to do everything right. I was so proud of myself, that I learned to do it, because before she came I was, . . . well, not in the best of shape. The first two years I worked at a day-care center so I could be near her. When she went to school I started taking classes too, but I brought her and picked her up every day. I got work I could do at home, commercial translating. But in the end I was no good. In the end I failed her. She was entrusted to me and I failed."

"I don't get it. What did you do?"

"She got stolen, I told you. Right out from under me. Ten years ago. It was on the merry-go-round in the park, I let her go by herself, she wanted to, it was a special horse, the kind that goes up and down. . . . " It's no use trying not to cry; she doesn't care anymore. Let him see. It doesn't interfere with her story, it's not choking sobs, just tears rolling down her face. "I was standing there waving, but . . . I walked away for a couple of minutes . . . to get ice cream and then . . . she wasn't there."

Jack is holding both her hands tight. "The police?" he says finally.

"I did everything, believe me. I still do. I check with them every few weeks."

He tries to take her in his arms. It's awkward, with the metal chairs. "I'm so sorry. I'm terribly sorry. I had no idea."

"That's how I wanted it. I thought with you, you know, clean slate and all. I could be changed. Have a different life."

"So now, you want to try again?"

"Look, it sounds incredible, but . . . when I saw her there, near St. Vincent's, I had this funny feeling. Then when I got a good look at her, . . . I know what you'll think, but it's her. I can feel it. It's like a miracle. But people do turn up, the cops say. Can't you see the resemblance? If you'd ever seen me at seventeen, or Claudia, . . .

well, no, by then she, . . . I know it sounds crazy, but it's her. It's like I was punished all those years and then the punishment was over. I got her back."

"You can't mean—"

"I do mean it! The thing that torments me is . . . I can't . . . what she must have gone through all these years. You know what happens to lost children, kidnapped children. Why do you think she doesn't speak? It's unspeakable. I can only imagine. And she recognized me, too. She did. She followed me home. I didn't chase after her. Remember that day we went to Coney Island? I saw her near your building. She knows she's safe again. I don't care. . . . I don't care how long it takes before she can speak. At least she's back where she belongs."

"Renata—"

"No! I won't let anyone take her away again. Whoever those people are or how they got her. She's mine."

He keeps an arm around her and doesn't speak for a long time. Then, "I can see how it feels like she's yours."

"You're talking to me the way they talk to crazy people. That tone. I've heard it in the hospitals with my mother. You're humoring me."

"I'm sorry. I don't know how else to . . . Look, you have a very strong feeling. Okay. If you want to be absolutely sure, you could do a DNA test."

She shakes free of him. "How typical! I don't want to do a DNA test."

"Because you don't want to know for sure."

She weeps again, frantically. "You! You take care of everyone, all those people who come to you. I just want to save one person. One person! Five thousand people are gone, turned to ashes, and one is found. And you don't want to let me save that one. I let her down once, I can never make up for that, but at least . . . She's mine."

"You can't know for sure that she's yours."

"I've made her mine!" she cries, so loud that people nearby turn to look. She breathes and swallows and mutters under her breath, "I've fed her long enough." If the child don't look like you, if you feed him long enough he'll be starting looking like you, the quilt-maker said. But Jack doesn't know what she's muttering about. He thinks she's gone mad. Madder. "How does anyone know for sure? And she *does* look like me."

"All right, maybe there's a slight resemblance. But she may look more like those parents who put up the sign. They must feel the same as you did when you lost your niece."

"It's not my business how they feel. I know why you're doing this, too. Don't think I don't. You're guilty over Carmen. You want to do everything exactly right from now on. By the book. You made me give up Julio, but at least we knew who his family was. Now you want me to give up Gianna. Jenny, they call her," she says with contempt. "Maybe they picked her up off the street. Maybe they're the ones who kidnapped her ten years ago. Maybe . . . who knows what?"

"I am guilty over Carmen, you're right. I may feel guilty for the rest of my life. But that's not why."

"It's because basically you have the mind of a petty bureaucrat. You see a piece of paper and you're ready to sacrifice me. You're like those people in the child welfare agencies. They're so busy with pieces of paper that they don't keep track of real children who are meanwhile being tortured and starved to death. You see it in the papers all the time. Each time I read one of those stories I go through hell . . . " Suffer, she thinks. If I were speaking Spanish or

Italian I'd say "suffer," but it's hard to say "suffer" in English without sounding pretentious. "I suffer," she says, "thinking of what she must have suffered."

"Look, this . . . the attack, the tragedy, it affects people in different ways. With your family, with all that went on, it figures. . . . But try to be rational. Her parents are suffering too. At least call and talk to them. Or let me do it for you."

"That's the last thing I'd do. I don't want you anywhere near her. Didn't you see how she looked at you, how frightened she was that maybe you'd . . . God, I don't know."

"Shit, how can you even think—"

"I don't mean you would. But . . . It's been ten years. What's she done in all those years? What's been done to her? How can I just send her away, back to I don't know what?"

"Renata, that child, your child, we can't know what happened to her. And I swear I'll do anything to help you find her, if she can be found. But this other girl . . . You have to do the right thing. I mean, think of her future."

"What future? For all we know the future is more buildings coming down tomorrow, more attacks, more awfulness. You know there's going to be war any day now. They keep promising us. They can't wait to start killing someone, anyone. They're men. They have to do something. The only thing that can relieve them is revenge. It excites them—you can see it in their faces. Bombs away. And then? Who says we even have a future?"

"We have to live as if there's a future. Please, don't make me do this to you. It's better if you do it. You know you'll have to give her back in the end."

She can only weep; words are no use anymore. He'll win. He has reason on his side, and the ones with reason always win. They're so certain. Her kind of certainty disperses like smoke, in the face of theirs. But like smoke, its residue stays in the air for a very long time.

"I *don't* know that. You know it. At least give me a few days, will you?"

"I'll call you tomorrow." He moves his chair close and puts his arm around her again. First she lets him; it feels good. Then she pulls her chair back.

"This is disgusting, you know? That I have to beg you for my life? Who the fuck are you, to decide about my life? What are you to me anyway? Compared to her."

"I'm someone who loves you. And also wants to do the right thing."

"If you only knew how pompous you sound. All of you. You could go on TV with all the others who are so sure they're right. You're no different."

"I won't argue that. You're speaking out of rage. Look, how about a sandwich from the stand over there? I'm starved."

"No."

"I'm going to get something. I'll be right back."

"Don't come back. I don't want to look at you anymore."

"Can I walk you back to your office, then?"

"Are you deaf or what? Leave me alone."

"So, I'll call you."

"I know. You said that already."

Seventeen

But when he calls the next night, as threatened, she doesn't pick up, lets his sexy voice go to waste, curling idly as smoke through the dim bedroom. Wednesday night, just as his message is winding down— "Please, Renata, I don't want to have to do this . . . "—she picks up.

"All right. Don't do anything. I'll do it myself tomorrow. Just . . . don't," and she hangs up before he can say a word. Unplugs the phone. Goes into the living room to sit on the couch beside Gianna and watch *Sex and the City.* Gianna's made a batch of popcorn in the microwave. They share it, their hands reaching rhythmically, companionably into the bowl between them, while Sarah Jessica Parker dresses carefully for yet another date, only to undress in haste moments later. Renata isn't much interested in that brand of sex, but she does enjoy the spectacular clothes. Soon, after one or two more silly sitcoms, they'll have a little talk.

E-mail is not a medium Renata and Jack have made much use of in their love affair. Too cool for them, too remote, too snappy. They

like each other's voices too much. They like—he, especially, likes—
to murmur indiscreet sweet nothings into a cell phone at odd moments. So e-mail is the medium she'll choose, late the following
night, to report her news. "I brought her back," she'll write. "Don't
call me. And don't doubt me either. It's the truth."

Jack being Jack, however, he may feel obliged to check up. Ask
Nestor if you don't believe me, she might have added. Nestor is
the bookman. After their long acquaintance, particularly after he
agreed so readily to accompany her on her mission, they ought to
call each other by name, Renata decided. Anonymity is all right for
the street. Real friends know each other's names. Nestor. So fitting
that she had a twinge of startled delight when she heard him utter
it. "*Gracias,* Nestor. So shall we meet you here at the corner? And
. . . will you take her in if I can't?"

After *Sex and the City* and a much-aired *Law & Order* rerun—the
poor woman who wants to believe her autistic son is talking to
her through a computer is cruelly disillusioned by a courtroom
demonstration—Renata has her little talk with Gianna. "Your
parents," she begins. "They're looking for you." Gianna's eyes open
wider, not in alarm but in mild curiosity. As if to ask, Parents?
What are they? Renata says their names, their address.

"They love you and they want you back." She waits. "I love you
and I want you too. What do you say?"

What a ridiculous question. Gianna says nothing. She reaches
for the remote but Renata takes it gently from her hands. The girl
is like Grace, she thinks, in her most recalcitrant moments. She *is*
sick. Something happened in there. Something slammed down.
Jack is right. She needs help.

"Tell me, just try, try to answer me. Were they good to you? Was
there any . . . trouble at home? You can trust me. Please trust me."

After a few moments she lets her have the remote back. That night Renata hardly sleeps, worried that Gianna might pack up her few things and slip away, back to the streets she came from. All night she lies awake listening for footsteps. In the morning she hurries out briefly to ask Nestor's help, and when she returns Gianna is still wrapped in the sheet on the couch.

Renata touches her hair, her cheek. She has no idea, really, who or what is behind the silent face. She won't find out, either, not this way, not by sheltering her. She calls in sick to work, afraid to let Gianna out of her sight. They walk along the Promenade, stop for lunch, browse in the shops, and finally meet Nestor at his corner. It's odd to see him without the table set up, without the books, but now that they're friends she has no trouble recognizing him. He's ready.

"Would you call first? Please?" She hands him her cell and the crumpled slip of paper he stuffed in her purse three days ago. "Tell them we're coming?"

He calls. "Mrs. Halloway?" He introduces himself with a smile, as though he's meeting her face to face, then keeps nodding as he speaks, the bringer of glad tidings. "Yes, yes, she's good, she's fine, she's well." He has to say it over and over—the Halloways must have thought she was dead. "She's fine. Yes, for sure. One thing." He lowers his voice, although Gianna is a few feet off, gazing up and down the street as if none of this concerns her. "She doesn't talk. . . . No, no, not hurt. Just . . . confused in her head."

Struck dumb, Renata thinks. *Tabakkamat,* in Arabic.

"Yes, now, right away," he says.

Renata doesn't ask any questions. All the way there on the subway, she's as mute as Gianna.

"I brought her back," she wrote Jack. She might have said lots more. A renovated warehouse building converted to loft apartments, she might have said. Typical of its kind: nicely done, elegant would be overstating, but done with taste. A sturdy, shabby old building spiffed up for a certain class of people—a bit of money, a bit of style—the lofts bought cheaply twenty years ago, today worth close to a million if not more. Not the kind of place kidnappers or lowlifes or porn moguls would choose, but then you never know. She might have said all this, but didn't.

Nestor rings and they wait to be buzzed in. At the elevator Renata says, "I'll wait down here, okay?" She turns to hug Gianna goodbye and studies her face instead. Are the surroundings familiar? She hasn't resisted coming, nor does she show relief, or recognition, or fear. What is the maddeningly blank child thinking? Feeling? When the elevator comes Renata follows them in. She can't let go yet. She'll wait in the hall, outside the door. But of course the door is already open and a fiftyish couple, weary, plump, and benign, are already rushing out to seize Gianna and embrace her. A huge gray sheepdog comes bounding out, too, to leap all over her.

Nice place, she might have told Jack. Books, plants, comfy furniture, river view. All the dust cleaned up. You'd never know, from the shiny surfaces, that two weeks ago it must have been strewn with ash. Fancy kitchen. Patches of glass brick, thick and wavy, translucent. An island counter with copper-bottomed pots and pans hanging over it, how about that?

"Jenny, my God, it's you! What happened? Are you all right?" Lots of that. A typical reunion scene, just what you'd imagine, she might have told him. She almost felt she was watching it on TV, without the commercial interruptions. Tears, exclamations. After all, once you've expected the worst. . . . Nothing from Gianna, though. She's the same as ever, looking around as if she's never seen the place before, or maybe as if she knows it so well, what's the big deal? It's hard to tell.

"Your room, let me show you your room. Don't you remember it? Don't you know us? Jenny! Sweetheart!" They can't let go of her, especially Celeste, whose lipstick is all smeared now from kisses, her curly gray hair flying about. Renata doesn't follow them into Gianna's room. She looks out at the river, the empty rectangles in the sky, the lowering sun. Nestor studies the bookshelves with professional interest. They exchange glances once in a while, amid the drama.

It was the dog, she might have said to Jack. That clinched it. Without the dog I might not have let her stay. I might have, I don't know, put up a fight. Said it was all a mistake. Tried to make them prove it. Birth certificate, maybe? For after a while the Halloways let go of her—Lionel sits down on the nubby couch, rests his elbows on his chinos, takes off his glasses and puts his head in his hands, while Celeste steps back and pats her hair, smoothes down her sweater—and the dog takes his turn. The dog leaps and licks at Gianna and, yes, she plays with him. She smiles. She knows the dog. She kneels down to stroke him. She ruffles his fur. She recognizes the dog. She looks up at Celeste and Lionel and smiles. She knows the dog.

"Remember his name, Jenny darling?" Celeste says. "Bounder. You named him yourself, when we first got him."

Gianna goes off with the dog to a big pillow under the window, where they sit and nuzzle one another.

"Are you hungry, Jenny? Do you want anything? Do you remember where your things are? Where did you get those clothes?"

At last Celeste invites Renata and Nestor to sit down. She looks them over: they make an odd couple. Renata has dressed for the occasion to look ultra-respectable, in buff-colored slacks and a silk shirt; her hair is up, pulled away from her face. Nestor is a head shorter and several decades older; his checked shirt is crisp and his eyes, magnified to larger than life size, gleam behind the thick glasses. He's removed his ancient fedora to reveal thinning black hair, slick with pomade. Celeste offers coffee, which they decline. She's more collected than Lionel, who sits apart, weeping discreetly. First come the profuse thanks, then come the questions. No need to tell these to Jack, even if Renata were feeling expansive—he'd know what they are. How long have you had her? How did you find her? The questions get a bit sharper, possibly because Renata's answers are vague and inept. There's even a whiff of anger. Two weeks? But what's she been doing all that time? Why did you wait so long to call? As Celeste speaks, she keeps turning to gaze at Jenny to be sure she's still there. That she hasn't been mistreated. That she's still Jenny.

All Renata can do is shake her head, so Nestor takes over. He explains that they didn't see the notice until . . . A pause, while Renata wonders what he'll say. Until yesterday. Bless you, Nestor. We didn't know, he goes on, because she wasn't speaking. He tells them how Renata took such good care of her. Of Jenny.

"But . . . " Celeste begins, and gives up. There are so many questions to ask, she doesn't know how to continue. Renata can read her mind: What does it matter, so long as Jenny's safe. These two may be an odd pair but they seem all right, and they brought her back safe and sound. Given all that's happened, given what might have happened, what does it matter? We'll take her to a doctor, she'll speak, she'll remember. As long as she's in one piece. That's all that matters.

So Celeste switches into another mode. The "isn't it terrible, what happened?" mode. Where we were, what we were doing that morning. Where were you, what were you doing? And almost as an afterthought, "You didn't lose anyone, I hope?"

"No," Nestor answers for both of them. And he shifts about, as if ready to leave. But Celeste isn't finished. She lowers her voice, even though Gianna is way across the large room, occupied with Bounder. Tossing a rubber bone around for Bounder.

"After we checked the hospitals and all," Celeste whispers, "we were so terrified at the thought of her roaming the streets, I can't tell you. Because that's where she was before. Before we adopted her, I mean. She was found on the streets and put in foster care and—" She starts to cry.

"You adopted her?" Renata says. Suddenly she's alert. "When?"

"Almost three years ago. We . . . we had a child who died, a long time ago. She was sick. We—"

"We don't have to go into all that," Lionel says. "Not in front of strangers. Do we?" His face is gray and tear-streaked. He takes off his sneakers and goes to sit on the floor under the window, where he watches Gianna and the dog.

"No. All right. But you're not exactly strangers. I mean . . . we just wanted someone to love," Celeste says. "Most people don't want to adopt older children with problems, but we didn't mind."

Renata looks at Nestor. They wanted someone to love, so they took Gianna. Well, they can feed her as much as they like, she'll never look like them. She should have known. The Halloways are thickset, pink-faced, insipid really. Gianna is dark and lean and fe-line in movement. She will be beautiful very soon. Their kind of looks, Renata knows, her own, that is, Claudia's, Gianna's, improve with age; darker skin (thank her Italian grandparents) has the ad-vantage, and bones last. *Buscaban a alguien que querer,* she translates for Nestor, though it's quite unnecessary, his English is more than ad-equate. She just wants to hear the words aloud again. They disgust her. She's disgusted by the whole scene, the smug, well-off couple, reunited with the child they selected to receive their love, the cozy furniture, the copper pots, the plants, the L.L. Bean clothes, the coffee, which had they accepted it would have been designer coffee. . . . They picked out someone to love. They picked Gianna the same way they picked Bounder. She looks at Nestor, but he's delighted at the sentiment. He beams. He nods his approval.

"What was her name? I mean, when you adopted her?" she asks.

"Her name? Jenny. Jenny Wright. But once we signed the papers . . . Now her name is Halloway. Why?"

She can't answer. Her mind is too muddled, nor can Nestor help with this. Wouldn't Gianna have known her own name? She was seven when she vanished. Children of seven know their names and more. They know their addresses and phone numbers. Can you forget that kind of information? Can you forget your own name, your aunt's name? Can you forget to tell the people who pick you up off the street that you have an aunt in this very city who'll take care of you, who's longing to have you back? Maybe. Maybe, if what happened to you in the intervening years is enough to make you forget.

Jack. He would know how to proceed, but Jack has become a pain in her chest. Anyway, there's nothing to be done right now. She can't demand to see the adoption papers, not that they would help. Jenny Wright.

Enough. It's time to go. We brought her and then we left. End of story. I brought her back, she wrote Jack. My *hanai*, off the street. I did what you said I must.

"Let's go," she says to Nestor, and they both stand up. Everyone stands up except Gianna. Lionel comes over and shakes their hands. More tears, more thanks. Effusive thanks. All the while, Celeste is busy thinking. Renata reads her like a book. She wants to offer a reward, but she's not sure how to do so without offending. After all, Renata and Nestor don't appear needy; they're not bounty-hunters.

"Is there anything at all I can do to show our appreciation?"

"Nothing. It's not necessary."

"You took care of her for two weeks. The clothes, at least. Let me reimburse you for the clothes."

Renata shakes her head. It occurs to her to ask to see Gianna's room. That could be her reward. On second thought, no. She doesn't want to picture Gianna later in some girly room with movie-star posters and hip-hop CDs, schoolbooks and clothes strewn around. . . . No.

She and Nestor walk to the window, where Gianna is curled up on the floor with the dog in her lap. Nestor kneels down and offers his hand. "God bless you." Renata hugs her. "Goodbye, Gianna."

"What did you call her?" Lionel asks.

"Nothing. Jenny. In Spanish." It pains her to give mistaken information about a language, but there's so much pain already that the aesthetic variety hardly figures.

"Do you have a card or something," says Celeste, "in case we want to write you, or call? To thank you again?"

"You've thanked us enough. It's okay." And I know how to find you, she thinks but doesn't say—it might frighten them.

"God bless you," Nestor says in farewell. In the elevator, he remarks, "Good people."

"They're okay, I guess. Thanks for coming with me. I couldn't have done it alone."

So I'll never know, she might have told Jack. Like the people who sustain themselves with the word "missing," implying that their loved ones are wandering the streets stunned or lying anonymous in a hospital bed, so as not to say, in the nonexistent English term, "lost-beyond-recovery," meaning dispersed among the rubble, transformed to dust. The people waiting for a scrap of fingernail or a hair to be found. No, not quite the same, Jack would reply, and explain the distinctions. Plus there's DNA testing, he'd add. Those people may eventually be relieved by DNA testing. You could do that too. But Renata doesn't dare, and so she's not the same as those bereft people. Don't flatter yourself, Jack would say. Don't appropriate their tragedy. Well, no, he wouldn't be so unkind as to say that. He'd think it.

After she gets home and sends him her terse e-mail, leaving out so much of consequence, she reaches for the remote. That might bear traces of Gianna's DNA—she was so often holding it. Alone in the apartment, Renata almost misses the inanities of MTV. She turns on the news, which is full of speculations on how and when the war will begin. Continue, rather, for according to the President, the war began the moment the first fire blossom exploded in the sky. On impulse, she pops in a videotape Denise's brother made the morning of the attack. He had his TV on when it happened; he got it all, Denise boasted, from the first instant. Copies proliferated and were passed around their section of the library. The appetite for reliving that morning is insatiable, Renata's included, even though she witnessed it from across the river.

The terrible scenes can never cease to shock, even though she's seen them so many times that she knows what's coming. What's newly startling about the tape is the bewilderment of the TV commentators. They begin with shock, the Bliondan fifth degree, *dra-doskis,* and struggle through the stages of knowing, trying all the while to frame impromptu sentences, for unlike most of the news they report, this news has not had time to be minced into small, digestible phrases. Even so, it's hard to grasp that they actually don't know what's happening. It's hard, a mere two weeks later, to believe there was ever a time when we didn't know what is now known indelibly. That small sliver of time, that not-knowing, seems eons away, lost in pre-history. Yet here it is, resuscitated, with all the freshness of a brand new story. A man with a microphone stands on a terrace somewhere in midtown, doing his best to describe what he sees in the distance: an enormous pillar of smoke where formerly there was a pillar of concrete and steel. It's like a Greek tragedy, where we all know what will happen and must watch in pain as the chorus gradually arrives at the same knowledge. "I don't know what we'll see when the smoke clears," the newscaster says, his tone almost childlike in its innocence, "but I fear it may be nothing."

Eighteen

It felt, for so long, as if it had happened yesterday. The blue sky, the burst of fire so high up, the pillar of cloud, the rain of paper, the macabre dancers drifting down hand in hand. It refused to assume its proper location in the artifice of linear time—three weeks ago, six weeks ago, eight—demonstrating just how artificial is the notion of linear time. Every morning was the morning after.

That only-yesterday vividness lasted for a good while, and yet bit by bit, distance has begun edging its way in. What makes for distance is weather. It's cooler now, some days even cold, even gray. It's early November. Wisps of smoke still rise from the site; the fires will burn into the winter. The heavy machinery keeps clawing through the mounds; the newspapers chronicle the lives forever lost, whose numbers change every day—ashes are infernally difficult to count. But the sky and the air—their changes are undeniable. They prove time's passage. And that makes it worse. It's definite now. It really happened. Each day that the city wakes to the fact, the fact is firmer. Written in shattered stone.

If tragedy has improved the national character, the change is not yet evident. We are more somber, yes, and more angry, but those are not virtues. Like millions of others, Renata sits on her couch waiting to hear the President's speech to the United Nations. He'll talk about the war, naturally, about hunting down the evildoers in their caves, maybe the very caves where Bodo and Zuna once raised their family, and about liberating the people of Afghanistan and dropping parcels of food to show our goodwill. He'll mention bioterrorism, since for several weeks now anthrax has been turning up in the mail and killing people at random. At the library there's been talk of inspecting packages, particularly those from overseas. Denise even suggested rubber gloves, but Renata and Linda and the others didn't go for that idea.

While she waits, she rereads a new clipping in her Transformed Lives folder. It doesn't quite fit with the others, with Franco or Letitia or Mrs. Stiller, since it doesn't describe a change in profession or way of life; it properly belongs in a different folder, one that might be called Lives Restored, but Renata's filing has grown lax. The article is about Carmela Ortega of La Paz, Bolivia, who believed that four of her children, undocumented immigrants living in New York City, were killed in the attacks on September 11. She had good reason to think so: they all worked in or near the World Trade Center. "If you could only see the twin towers like we do," her daughters would say when they called, and Señora Ortega would think, "How beautiful they must be." Her children hadn't telephoned that week as promised, and the money they sent regularly to support the grandchildren stopped coming. Then, in October, her fears were confirmed. She received word from her government that two of her children were dead. Señora Ortega managed to get a visa so she could attend an October 28 memorial ceremony in New York for the families of the victims. Once she arrived, she called a friend of her son's and learned that he was alive. He came to her hotel in Queens and told her the other three were alive too. "We're suffering, we're bitter, but we're alive." Señora Ortega visited each of her sons and daughters in turn, "was tearfully reunited with them for the first time since they had left home years ago." Four happy, tearful reunions: Renata can easily picture them. But why hadn't they called their mother? "All four were in shock," the article says. One son is quoted: "I didn't want to do anything. I didn't want to speak with anybody. I was left with nothing. I was in very bad shape."

Here he comes. The speech is about to begin. First there's applause, then a hush in the august chamber. He's learned to control his face much better now; he doesn't look perpetually on the verge of a grin. He speaks about the war. "We choose the dignity of life over a culture of death. We choose lawful change and civil disagreement over coercion, subversion and chaos." As usual, he pauses an extremely long time between sentences. So long that it seems maybe his mind is roaming off somewhere else, somewhere more pleasant, as Grace's used to do at her worst moments. Linda, who knows everything, once gave Renata an explanation for those long pauses. He's got a little thing in his ear, she said. It's telling him what to say. He finishes one sentence and they feed him the next. Just a few words at a time, you know how it is. The pauses give Renata time to think about Señora Ortega and her children. Her story is a transformation tale after all, she decides, a before-and-after tale. And just as Renata has seen herself as Franco Donati becoming one of his homeless subjects, or Mrs. Stiller traversing the broad deck of the QE2, she can see herself in this story too. She and Celeste Halloway both. Celeste is like Señora Ortega after, tearfully united with her lost child. Birthing Renaissance. And Renata is Señora

Ortega before, not knowing for sure, but fearing that her child is dead.

"Peace will only come when all have sworn off forever incitement, violence and terror," the President finishes. She could really turn it off, there's nothing much to be learned from the fawning analyses to come, but he induces such paralysis that her finger won't move. In the midst of the applause and the standing ovation, the phone rings.

"Renata? Did you see him?"

"Jack?"

"Well, did you?"

"Yes."

"I knew it was coming, but somehow seeing, hearing him . . . At least if he understood what he's getting us into."

"You called me up to discuss politics? Whether we should go to war?"

"Well, not only that, but, . . . I just had to talk to someone about it."

Jack offers a geopolitical analysis, apparently forgetting that they haven't spoken for over six weeks. How difficult it is to root out terrorists with conventional military apparatus. . . . How volatile is the situation. . . . She might as well have listened to the commentators, and says so. What she doesn't say is that she likes hearing his voice again, never mind the words. She feels suddenly warmer, more alert; the hairs on her arm actually tingle, as in a Harlequin romance.

"I'm sorry. Maybe you're not as bothered by what he said. You're more into revenge than I am. You were probably concentrating more on his grammar, right?"

"His grammar was pretty good, as a matter of fact. Not a bad speech, as far as grammar goes."

"How're you doing, Renata? Are you okay?"

"Fantastic."

"Okay, I see you're not thrilled to hear from me. I wanted to ask you something, though. I'm going to see Julio this Sunday. I just arranged it with his grandmother. Teresa, remember? I kind of miss him. I want to see how he's doing. For Carmen's sake, too. Do you want to come?"

Julio. The name conjures up the seventeen-pound weight in her arms, the nub of terry cloth, the dark eyes under long lashes, the softness of his cheek under her knuckles. It seems so long ago, that brief idyll with Julio, a prelude to Gianna and her silence. Sure she'd like to see him.

"Why should I go anywhere with you, Jack?"

"That's not the question. The question is, is it better this way? Apart? Tell the truth."

"No, it's not better. But you made me give her up. How can I ever forget that?"

"You don't have to forget it. You can get past it."

"You mean like a roadblock? It's kind of large. I can't see the edges."

"You would have taken her back yourself after a while. You know that. You just saved her parents a few days of anguish."

"What about my anguish? You cared more about theirs than mine. You could have waited."

"How did it go? You never told me. Except for that e-mail. That was a punishment. You're very punishing, you know that?"

"She was adopted."

That keeps him silent for a moment. Good. Just as she's beginning to doubt her willed conviction, he's starting to doubt his rational certainty. Very good.

"When?"

"Three years ago. From foster care. Before that, the streets. So you see—"

"Do you still think—"

"I don't know. I try not to think too much."

"I'll help you if you want to look into it."

"Oh, thanks. Thanks a lot. Now you'll help me. You'll bring the full weight of your wealth and bureaucratic savvy to bear on this ambiguous case—"

"Would you cut it out, please? Will you please remember we spent almost a year together? We slept together. We loved each other. Is this a way for us to talk?"

"Of course." She may not know much about love, but she knows this much. "Only people who loved each other talk like this. I would have thought you knew that. You're the one who was married. Speaking of marriage, how's Pamela? You still seeing her?"

"Not any more. I saw her a few times. It was something to do. A diversion."

"Oh, was time hanging heavy? With all your other rescue work to be done?"

"You're jealous." He has the gall to chuckle. "That's a good sign."

"You used her as a diversion?"

"We used each other. When we had enough, we stopped. Desperate times, desperate measures."

"I see. Did you give back the dress?" Or did you cut it in strips and piece it together and cover up under it for love?

"The dress? Oh, the wedding dress. No. I forgot all about it. Maybe she did too. She never mentioned it. So, what about Sunday?"

"I'll come."

"Great. I'll pick you up around two."

"I'd rather meet you there. What's the address?"

The twenty-dollar bill Renata picked up from a mound of paper on September 11 has been under the vase on the dining-room table for two months and she's tired of seeing it. If it meant anything at all—an inscrutable message? an assertion that the past is never over?—that meaning has drained away. The chance of its being the same bill her sister stole from her when they were eleven was always statistically nil, less, even, than the chance of Gianna being the real Gianna. It's time to get rid of that bill. Throw it away. Donate it to the survivors. Spend it. Sunday afternoon, just before setting out to meet Jack, she tucks it into her purse.

On the stairs she runs into Philip, the man from upstairs whose wife is somewhere in the rubble. He's sweaty, been out jogging again, and still can't manage more than a meager nod. She holds the door open for Mrs. Stavrakos, who's lugging a full shopping cart and has reverted to her usual surliness. Her mumbled thank you sounds resentful. Well, something's back to normal. Outside, it's brisk and bright, the streets bustling with people. The trauma they've suffered is not evident except for a suspicious, vulnerable cast in their eyes, a tautness in their downturned mouths. Strangers might not notice, but the locals do.

As Renata heads for the subway she knows all at once how she'll use the money burning a hole in her pocket.

Nestor is busy with a customer, so she waves and looks over his wares. They have the casualness of intimacy now, of family, after what they witnessed together. There's nothing too intriguing on the table, but she'll buy something, anything, to get rid of the bill. It's weighing her down, heavier every minute. Books about Islam and the Arab world are everywhere, all of a sudden, rushed into print or retrieved from the past. She picks one that might be useful for her translations. She takes one of last year's best-selling novels. She finds a tattered copy of *The Guinness Book of World Records*, twelve years old; that will make a nice surprise for Linda, right up her alley. At Nestor's rates these will add up to only three dollars, far short of twenty, but more books would be too cumbersome to haul around all day. For who knows, maybe she'll be spending the day with Jack. The night. Maybe she'll have a change of heart. He's persuasive. Why not use him as he used Pamela?

"I'm off to visit Julio," she tells Nestor when he's free. "Remember, the baby I had for a week back in September?"

"Oh, the one whose mother—"

"Yes. He's with his grandmother. I haven't seen him in so long. I'd get him a book but he's much too young." Together they laugh at the very idea.

It's a relief to hand over the twenty and watch it disappear into his pocket. As he counts out her change she says, "You really should keep the change, Nestor. I've bought so many books at these ridiculous prices. You've practically given them to me for nothing."

"No. A dollar apiece is all. You take the change." He puts the bills firmly, soberly, into her palm.

Perhaps she's offended him. Does he think she meant to pay him for his help, for the trip to the Halloways? If only she could explain how much she needs to get rid of the money, to spend it where it would become innocuous. And how much she would like to spend it all in one swoop.

"It just doesn't seem right."

"No," he says, smiling. He's not offended. *Mas valen amigos en plaza que dineros en casa.* "Buy Julio a present for me. God bless you."

Of course. Why didn't she think of that? Julio must have a present, and there's a toy store right around the corner. What was it the Vice President said—not to let what happened "throw off the normal level of economic activity"? And yet Renata, despite her taste for nice clothes, has barely shopped at all. Aside from the few things she bought for Gianna, nothing. It's high time to start contributing to the war effort. But no slyly symbolic toys, nothing that would burden Julio with her history or assign him a role he shouldn't have to play. Nothing reminiscent of the toys she used to buy for Gianna, and definitely no Fisher-Price farm.

It's familiar, being back in a toy store after a decade. She and Gianna used to stroll through toy stores looking at dolls and stuffed animals and jigsaw puzzles. After the first year of her absence, Renata put all the toys into a closet. After three years she gave them away, for even if she were found, by then Gianna would have outgrown those toys; she'd be ready for . . . what? Renata didn't know what a big girl might want. Her expertise ended with age seven. A computer, most likely. CD player? For Julio, she selects a large stuffed giraffe, elegant and comical in the manner of giraffes. Gianna never had a giraffe.

Toys have gotten expensive. She has to spend more than what Nestor gave her back in change. Meaning she has to mix those seventeen dollars—three fives and two ones—with the ordinary bills in her purse. Oh, never mind. That seventeen dollars is simply money, like any other. She hands it over happily to the clerk.

"Could you gift wrap it, please? Make it look really nice?"

"You're late." Jack's greeting. "I thought maybe you changed your mind."

"Sorry, I had a few stops."

"What's that?"

"A giraffe."

"Oh, you got him something. Good idea. I should have thought of that."

They're standing in front of an eight-story beige brick build-ing, functional, nondescript, and severely respectable for this fray-ing, maverick neighborhood. Across the street is Tompkins Square Park, the scene of countercultural escapades years ago, before Renata's time. Now it's merely shoddy, yet lively. Skateboarders skitter along the paths, dodging a few homeless stragglers, and adolescents with blue and purple hair cluster here and there like forlorn relics of a more colorful era. The trees appear in a state of partial dress, having shed half their leaves, which lie in unruly drifts of orange and yellow.

It's easier to gaze at an unfamiliar neighborhood than at Jack, so familiar. But she must. He takes both her hands so that they're face to face. The feel of his warm hands evokes the feel of his whole body: synecdoche, she thinks, the part for the whole. And despite herself, she flushes with pleasure. He looks the same, blunt, heavy-featured and powerful, and he's wearing a suede jacket she's never seen before. Been shopping, Jack has. Always the useful citizen.

"It's good to see you." He makes the banal words sound like something more intimate, like something he'd say in bed. He runs his hands up her arms, to her shoulders, to her face. "Your face is warm," he says. "I miss you."

"Let's go in. Teresa, right? And Pilar?"

"Pilar won't be there. She's a nurse. She works weekends. Teresa works at Met Life, she told me. Administering some department or other."

"Shh, he's sleeping," Teresa says as she opens the door, finger to her lips. "I'll wake him in a little while. Come on in."

Teresa is a surprise. Renata hasn't thought much about her—her thoughts were all of Julio—but she must have been expecting someone different, someone stout, grandmotherly, like Mrs. Stiller, or a female version of Nestor, old, lined, and mysteriously wise. Wise Teresa may be, but hardly old, fifty at the most. And already she's lost a daughter. Nonetheless she's quite chic, coiffed and made up and perfumed. Renata can't help wondering where she got the velvet burgundy jeans and the slate gray pullover. And could those silvery streaks in her black hair be natural?

Her apartment, compact, neat, and blandly furnished, is more comforting than the Halloways' verdant, book-lined loft. On this visit, Renata accepts the coffee that's offered, and as soon as it's poured out, Teresa goes into another room to fetch Julio.

Renata gets teary when she sees him. "Why, you've grown up," she says as she takes him in her arms. "You're a lot heavier. You're a big boy." He settles cozily into her embrace, but she can't be sure he recognizes her. Jack leans over them both, making silly noises. "Do you think he knows us?" she murmurs to him. "What do you think? I think he might."

"Sure he does," says Teresa. "Sure he does."

She's just being kind, Renata can tell. How good she seems. What a good grandmother she'll be for Julio. She lost her daughter—one of her daughters—but at least she has the grandchild. Grace wasn't so lucky. She lost more. All Grace has left is Renata, and that doesn't seem to comfort her much.

Thoughts of mothers and children are inevitable, the thousands lost and those remaining.

"Carmen . . . " Jack begins, and clears his throat. Her name must be spoken, and he takes on the task. "Carmen would have loved to see how he's growing. He's even starting to look like her. Around the mouth and chin."

So then they're all three weeping, Teresa with restraint because her grief is farthest from the surface. The only one who's not crying is Julio. He's supremely contented, passed between Jack and Renata, and when she gives him the gift he's ecstatic, swiping at the noisy wrapping paper.

"Oh, and he can crawl now," says Teresa. She sets him on the floor for a demonstration; he scoots across the living room, then tries to pull himself up using the legs of a chair. "See, he'll be walking soon. Any day now, right, Julio?"

It's a good visit, good as could be, even if Renata isn't absolutely sure Julio remembers them. The coffee is good too, and the cinnamon cookies. What she feels for Julio is good: she loves him, but has no trouble saying goodbye and leaving him. She loves him because of the days they spent together, not because he represents an opportunity for redemption. It's not fair to lay any such burden on a child. Briefly, again, she recalls the Halloways, who chose Gianna to shoulder the gift of their wounded love.

It's been so long since she's found anything unreservedly good—like sleeping with Jack, also unreservedly good—that she nearly weeps again at the door.

"Come back soon." Teresa holds Julio and makes his hand wave goodbye. "Come any time. Then he'll start remembering you."

"I'm so sorry," Jack says. "I can't tell you how sorry—"

"No more of that," says Teresa. "No more. How could you know? You were good to work for. She always said so."

Walking to the car, Jack takes her hand and she lets him. Not for the future. For the past. That way she can justify holding his hand. For what we lived through together, Julio, and Carmen, and now Teresa. For what we saw and felt that day, for what it was like to discover we were each alive and unhurt.

They sit in the front seat of the car but Jack doesn't make a move to start the engine. "So?"

"So what?"

"So there's only one issue here," he says. "Is it better together or apart?"

"That's it? So simple?"

"Uh-huh."

"It's not better apart. That's not hard to answer. The hard part is . . . I'm not sure I can do it. I'm not sure I want to."

Since she's resumed her usual tasks at the library, she's gotten to know Etinoi, her favorite language, pretty well. It has a word that perfectly mirrors her condition. *Tsubari,* a noun for an emotional and intellectual state (the language does not strictly separate the two), means harboring feelings so conflicted as to produce an impasse, a paralysis of the will. People gripped by *tsubari* want two mutually exclusive things equally, and they can find equally compelling reasons for either choice. It's a word with a humorous cast, although the situations in which it applies are not always humorous. Those who tend often to be in such a state are called *tsubarendi,* unable to distinguish between the essential and the extraneous. Jack would never find himself in a state of *tsubari*; he would always cut through the extraneous and make the sensible choice. Therefore people like Jack, earnest, well-meaning, and so pragmatic as to be oblivious to the finer points, are judged to be good administrators but poor at diplomacy, on the large and small scales. People like Renata, prone to *tsubari,* who think far too much and too tortuously, are judged to be useless in the public or practical sphere, yet are respected for their subtlety and may be consulted on matters requiring close analysis. Often these are matters concerning *ahmintu,* the principle of engaging thoroughly with one's fate. Everyone wants to honor *ahmintu,* but how to do so, which choices to make and which to refuse, is not always clear.

Such as now: If she cedes herself to the future and gives up clinging to the past, would it be a betrayal? What about her dead father and sister, the lost Gianna, her anger, her remorse?

We have to live as if we have a future, Jack said, the last time they really spoke. Even if the future is an endless war, as the government promises? She could ask Jack, but she knows exactly what he'd say. Sure, war is terrible, but it has nothing to do with whether you'll have dinner with me and then come home and sleep with me.

There is a connection between the public and private life, but Renata knows that that connection, just now, is merely a distraction. It's not what's causing confusion and making her a *tsubarenda*. Something else is working its way through her, a creeping vibration in her cells, an uneasy humming, but one that may lead her out of paralysis. It concerns what is finished and what is not. For all her anger against Jack, his obtuseness and simplicity, for all her hesitation, the vibration now undeniable as a pain or a hunger tells her she's not finished with him yet. Simple: they haven't come to the end of each other. There's more they have to find out, more common life to partake of, more to relish or suffer at each other's hands. As for the rest, the past, there's nothing more there.

"Well, do you want to go somewhere and have a drink? Maybe even dinner later? It's not a lifetime commitment."

"Let's start with a drink."

They get out of the car and walk, no longer holding hands. "Are you still reading the Arabic newspapers? Do you sound like a native speaker yet?"

"Nowhere near. I sometimes talk to the waiters in the restaurants on Atlantic Avenue. They think my pronunciation is pretty funny, but they're very helpful."

"So you're going to restaurants without me," he says wistfully.

"Well, I have to eat. Did you expect me to waste away?"

"Okay, say something in Arabic, then. Let me hear if you sound any better."

"Nothing can ever be the way it was," she says in flawed Arabic, echoing what her mother told her weeks ago.

"And that means?"

She tells him.

"You mean the world can never be the same? Is that what they're saying in the papers over there? That's what they say here, too. But, really, we have no perspective yet."

He can be so dense, it makes her laugh. "I wasn't thinking on a global scale."

"Oh. I see. Okay, say something else. See if I do better this time."

"Make me love you again," she says.

"Wait, don't tell me. Let me guess. That sounds like, 'I can't forgive you but I still love you.'"

He's close, very close. Remarkable, to be so known. She hasn't felt so known since Claudia was alive. "Not quite. It means, okay, let's have dinner."

The light starts fading earlier now, in November. There's a chill in the air. She puts her arm through his, for the warmth.

Acknowledgments

The quotations and information about Chinese calligraphy come from *The Embodied Image: Chinese Calligraphy from the John B. Elliott Collection,* by Robert E. Harrist, Jr., and Wen C. Fong, The Art Museum, Princeton University, 1999.

The characters in the Transformed Lives folder are based on articles from the *New York Times.* The names and some other data have been changed.

The information about the Gibbons twins is from *The Silent Twins,* by Marjorie Wallace, Ballantine Books, 1986.

The experiments testing children's testimony in abuse cases were reported on National Public Radio's *Morning Edition,* June 26, 1997.